FIGHTING TO SURVIVE

TOR BOOKS BY RHIANNON FRATER

The First Days
Fighting to Survive
Siege (forthcoming)

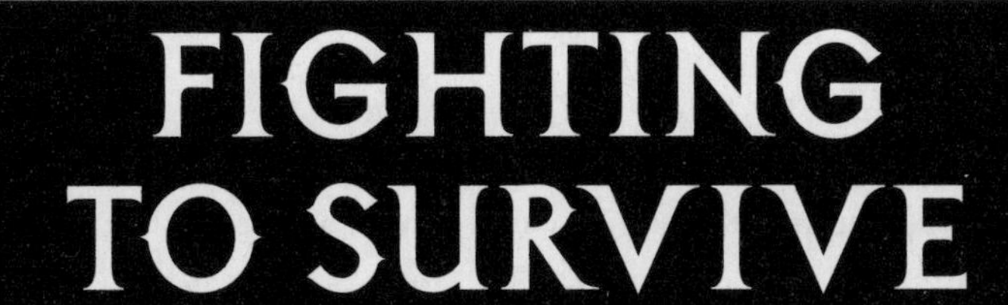

·AS THE WORLD DIES·

BOOK TWO

Rhiannon Frater

A TOM DOHERTY ASSOCIATES BOOK · NEW YORK

This is a work of fiction. All of the characters, organizations, and events portrayed in this novel are either products of the author's imagination or are used fictitiously.

FIGHTING TO SURVIVE: AS THE WORLD DIES

A Tor Book
Published by Tom Doherty Associates, LLC
175 Fifth Avenue
New York, NY 10010

www.tor-forge.com

Tor® is a registered trademark of Tom Doherty Associates, LLC.

Library of Congress Cataloging-in-Publication Data

Frater, Rhiannon.
Fighting to survive / Rhiannon Frater.—1st ed.
p. cm.—(As the world dies ; bk. 2)
"A Tom Doherty Associates book."
ISBN 978-0-7653-3127-4
1. Zombies—Fiction. 2. Texas—Fiction. I. Title.
PS3606.R4255F54 2011
813'.6—dc22

2011021609

First Tor Edition: November 2011

Printed in the United States of America

10 9 8 7 6 5 4 3 2 1

Dedicated to my cousin Claudia

ACKNOWLEDGMENTS

Thanks to George A. Romero, for your movies and all the wonderful nightmares you've inspired.

Those nightmares ended up in this trilogy.

Also, thanks to Kelly, Julie, and Kody, for helping me shape the original draft into a coherent story. Y'all are awesome.

Special thanks to Mom, for your constant support of my writing and your dedication to helping me achieve my dreams. You are the greatest!

Very special thanks to my husband, for your encouragement and your patience when I spend long hours writing.

And, as always, thank you to my fans, for your support! You keep me writing!

Somewhere in Texas

The Fort

· CHAPTER ONE ·

1.
Terror in the Darkness

The hallway was barely lit by the blue glow shimmering up the stairs from the TV in the living room. The light flickered along the walls and ceiling, providing just enough brightness to make out her path. Groggily, Jenni walked toward her youngest son's bedroom, near the top of the stairs. She shoved her long dark hair out of her face and glanced down the staircase. Through the railing, she could see her husband, Lloyd, in his usual seat in the living room, staring at the plasma-screen TV. She could clearly discern the black silhouette of his head against the brightly lit screen.

Warily, wanting to avoid alerting him to her presence, she hurried into Benji's room.

The Mickey Mouse night-light illuminated the room, revealing the form of her sleeping three-year-old in his racing car–shaped bed. His little hand was thrown over his dark blond curls, his lips parted as he softly snored. Smiling, Jenni knelt down and tucked his Winnie-the-Pooh blankets closer around his body. He was just recovering from a cold and she wanted to make sure he didn't get chilled. Her fingers gently caressed his soft, full cheek, then smoothed his curls back from his face. He looked like Lloyd, and every day, Jenni prayed that Benji did not have his father's violent temper or cruel streak. She wanted him to grow up to be a good, strong man who would love his family and protect them, not brutalize them and make them fear him.

A noise from downstairs startled her. She tensed, listening intently for the sounds of Lloyd's footsteps on the stairs, but heard only the distant hum of the TV.

Lloyd hated it when she "coddled" the boys. He grew annoyed when she checked on them at night and accused her of using that as an excuse to spy on his late-night habits. Frankly, she preferred it when he stayed downstairs, watching porn, calling his girlfriends, and leaving her to sleep alone in their bed.

"I want you not to be like him," she whispered to Benji as he slept. "Don't be like him."

She kissed Benji's forehead and breathed in his sweet baby smell. She loved him so.

Standing up, she looked at the remains of Benji's bedtime snack on the side table. There was one oatmeal cookie on the plate, but the milk glass was empty. Both the boys enjoyed a nighttime snack before bed. She didn't see the harm in it, even though Lloyd said she was spoiling them. To pacify her health-freak husband, she used all-natural ingredients in the cookies, and they were delicious. Feeling a little hungry, she grabbed up the cookie and started to nibble on it.

Don't grow up to be like him, she wished again.

He won't grow up, a voice echoed in her mind.

She frowned as she chewed. What a horrible thought. Where had it come from?

He doesn't live past tonight. You know that.

"No," Jenni whispered, pressing her hand to her forehead. "No."

Images flashed in her mind: bloody, chaotic, and terrible.

"No," she moaned. She closed her eyes, stuffed the rest of the cookie into her mouth, and chewed vigorously, hoping to banish the thoughts.

"What the hell are you doing?" Lloyd's sharp voice startled her.

Jenni looked at him, trying to swallow before he could see that she was eating outside the strictly regimented diet he had created for her, claiming that it would keep her thin and beautiful.

"What the hell are you eating?" Lloyd's dark form in the doorway terrified her.

"Nothing . . . I—"

"What did you do to Benji? Oh, God, Jenni, what the hell is wrong with you?"

Jenni stared at her son. His tender belly was torn, and his intestines were strung across the bed. One of her hands clutched the glistening flesh tightly. Slowly, she raised her other hand to her mouth and felt that her lips were slick with blood.

"Jenni, what did you do?"

She began to scream. . . .

She woke and sat up sharply, her heart thundering in her chest. In the dim light leaking in around the edges of the makeshift tent, she could see the sleeping form of Juan, her tall, sexy Mexican-American boyfriend. Laying her forehead against her drawn-up knees, she took deep breaths and tried to calm her wildly beating heart.

Juan's hand gently touched her back, then withdrew. Jenni was glad that he understood she didn't want to be touched or soothed when she woke from a nightmare. It often took her several minutes to gain full control of her senses and convince herself she was truly safe and far away from her dead family.

The blue tarp that made up their tent rippled gently in the night breeze. She held up her hands, inspecting them in the narrow beam of light that came into the tent through a tear in the tarp. Her hands were clean. There was no blood on them. Outside the tent, she could hear people softly talking, snoring, coughing, and sneezing, as they, too, dealt with the night terrors that came with sleeping and dreaming. The familiar noises were an anchor that she used to pull her mind free of her nightmares.

Pushing her damp hair out of her eyes, she took calming breath. She was slowly accepting that this was reality. Why did her mind keep trying to convince her that she had not escaped the morning the dead took over?

That morning, it was Lloyd who had eaten Benji's tender flesh, Lloyd who had become one of the undead, who had destroyed their family and home forever. She barely escaped the house. Had it not been for Katie, Jenni probably would have joined the ranks of the zombie hordes. Katie had heard her screaming and driven up in that battered white truck to save her. Together they escaped into the Texas Hill Country, rescued Jenni's stepson from a state park, and found safety with a group of survivors holed up in a construction site in the town of Ashley Oaks. To her surprise, she had found love with one of the construction workers, and now, free from her dead husband's reign, she was strong and living her own life.

Taking a last deep breath that did not feel forced or ragged, she slowly relaxed. After letting herself fall back onto the cot, Jenni curled up on her side, facing away from Juan. Sleeping on twin cots that were bound together with bungee cords was uncomfortable, but she liked feeling him near her. In the gloom, he slid his arm around her waist and she smiled.

In silence, they lay side by side and waited for sleep to come again . . . sleep that would hopefully be free of the past.

2.
A Moment of Peace

Juan listened to Jenni's breathing become deeper and deeper until he knew she was asleep once more. He didn't move, even though his arm had grown numb. She was holding on to his wrist tightly. He didn't draw it away. He wanted her to feel his presence even in her slumber. She was his passionate little Irish-Mexican firecracker and it was hard to see her struggling with nightmares. It was especially hard knowing that he could not give her any real comfort.

Jenni kept her dreams to herself, mourning in ways he could not understand. He was convinced that her evolution into a woman who could dispatch zombies with eerie efficiency was her way of coping with her children dying. As far as he knew, she didn't even talk to Katie, her very best friend, about the death of her children. In Jenni's waking moments, she was loving, outgoing, and funny. But in her dreams, she was afraid and emotionally shattered. It broke his heart.

His long body pressed up alongside hers, he could feel the softness of her black hair against his chest. He was sore and tired from all the work he was doing on the fort. The survivors had to get into the old-fashioned hotel that loomed over the construction site. Unfortunately, neither of the hotel's entrances were accessible from the construction site without the risk of being out in the open. The construction crew would have to break through the wall of the hotel. Also, Travis and Juan had no idea if the hotel was zombie infested. Travis kept postponing breaching the hotel, for fear of compromising the security of the fort.

Juan's first major task had been to construct a secure passage into the fort for the vehicles they were sending out to salvage supplies and find survivors. He had created the "Panama Canal," two gated enclosures leading into a walled-off area where they parked the vehicles in the garage of an old newspaper building. The rest of the building was completely uninhabitable and would take months to clean out and repair. The construction site was quickly becoming crowded as more survivors found their way to Ashley Oaks. There was only one shower and one bathroom—both in city hall—for everyone in the fort, and it was increasingly more difficult to keep things safe and sanitary.

Jenni's grip on his arm lessened as sleep caught her completely. He kissed her shoulder, hoping and praying that her dreams would be pleasant. Closing his eyes, he tried to block out his body's aches and capture what little sleep he could before the next day's hard work.

He was so tired in both body and mind. Jenni brought him

happiness, but he wanted a respite from the daily terror they had all experienced since the beginning of the zombie apocalypse. He wanted to sleep in a real bed with Jenni and not to feel afraid. Was it wrong to hope for a little peace for both of them? He hoped not, because that was what he prayed for every night.

Beyond the walls of their little fort, the world was still dying and the dead were walking, but all Juan wanted was a moment when he and those he loved could feel alive and good. Maybe that was too much to hope for. Perhaps this moment, listening to Jenni breathing as she slept peacefully, was all he could truly wish for.

With a long sigh, he tightened his deadened arm around her waist and closed his eyes.

3.
The Lurking Past

On the roof of city hall, Katie sat in a plastic chair with her arms folded over her breasts and her head tilted back to stare at the stars. A cigarette dangled from the fingers of one hand. Katie was done with sleep for the night. One more nightmare about her dead wife, and she would start screaming and never stop.

She raised the cigarette to her lips, took a long drag, then exhaled, watching the smoke unfurl against the backdrop of a stunning black sky shot through with the pinpricks of stars. She quit smoking when she met Lydia, though she'd never even considered doing so before. Lydia had hated smoking with a passion, and after one look into Lydia's amazing eyes, Katie would have done anything for her.

A tear slipped free and traced down her temple. Sniffling loudly, she took another drag on the cigarette, desperately seeking some sort of satisfaction in the ritual.

Katie had barely survived her morning commute. Thankfully, she was rescued by a minister in a white pickup, but her savior had been dragged down by the zombies. Katie raced home in his battered old truck and found her beautiful wife gorging on the body of a fallen postman.

Her life with Lydia had ended in that terrible, brutal moment. She would never hold Lydia's soft, delicate hand, kiss her sweet lips, or feel her gentle caress ever again. The greatest joy she had ever felt had ended. The reality that Lydia was still out there, one of the many undead hordes, tormented Katie.

Another tear slipped free and she blinked hard.

How could she still love Lydia so much and yet feel drawn to Travis? How could she betray Lydia's memory like that, with a man she had met only a few weeks before?

Nearby, the guard on the roof coughed and stretched. It was Bill, the deputy sheriff from a little town where she and Jenni had taken refuge during their initial flight from the city. Like the majority of the survivors in the fort, Bill was a local of German-Czech stock. Bill was a good-natured guy with sandy hair, a big ruddy friendly face, and a beer belly that was always fighting with his belt. He was watching the street for any sign of the zombies. Recent operations had cleared the majority of zombies from the town, but many still lurked in the streets and the nearby countryside. Caught in bushes, trapped in buildings, wandering through the hills . . .

Who could ever have imagined that the dead would walk the earth outside of a George A. Romero film? Not Katie. She had functioned in the real world. She had worked hard as a prosecutor, doing her best to achieve justice while living a simple life with Lydia. And then it had all ended.

This new world confused her. It was full of the walking, hungry dead. Surviving from one day to the next was everyone's top priority. But worse, there was little time to mourn before you were forced, by that drive for survival, to make new connections, new friends, and even new loves. She saw it all around her. Families torn apart by the zombie rising were forever gone, but new families were being born all around her. Strangers were becoming brothers, sisters, aunts, and uncles to one another. The elderly in the fort were now everyone's grandparents. The thought of Old Man Watson brought a smile to her face. Although he could barely hear, he was everyone's great-grandpa now, who always smiled, who hugged and kissed them all, happy to be one of them, a survivor.

Jenni was her new sister. Jenni's stepson, Jason, felt like a nephew; Juan was her annoying new brother-in-law; and Travis . . .

Katie rubbed her nose with irritation.

Travis was the man everyone loved. Everyone listened to him. Everyone believed in him. He was calm strength in the midst of chaos. He was humble and kind. Despite herself, she smiled at the thought of him.

From the moment she met him, she had known he was important to her life. She had believed in him instantly. And as they got to know each other, it became more than apparent that he had fallen in love with her.

Travis believed his affection for her was a lost cause. As far as he knew, Katie was a lesbian and therefore unattainable. Katie had encouraged that belief, since she was afraid if he realized she was actually bisexual, he would immediately pursue her, and she knew in her heart that she could not resist him for long. Her strong will—which her father had once dubbed her "Nordic ice"—was all that was keeping her from giving into her emotions.

Katie hated this new world where everyone seemed to be living at an accelerated pace. Life was so precious and short, and there was no time to mourn the world they had lost. They had to seize whatever small moments of happiness they could find, or else the life they had fought so hard to preserve would be meaningless. But she wanted to mourn Lydia. She was not ready to move on.

"Oh, God, Lydia," she whispered, wiping tears away.

"Huh?" Bill looked toward her.

"Nothing, Bill. Just talking to myself," Katie answered with a forced smile, and sat up. She put out her cigarette on the roof and sat with her elbows resting on her knees.

"Gotcha. I find myself doing that, too." Bill's big, round face beamed at her before he returned his gaze to the street.

Katie stared down at the lace-up boots she wore. They had been given to her by Ralph Toombs, the sweet old man who had run the hunting shop where she and Jenni took refuge that first terrible night. Clad in jeans and a tank top, Katie felt completely unlike the tailored and perfectly coifed prosecutor persona she had cultivated for years. She had to admit that her attire fit who she really was: a no-fuss woman who liked to wear comfortable shoes and casual T-shirts.

Standing up, she ran her hands through her blond hair and walked toward the edge of the roof. The hotel loomed over the construction site, which was full of makeshift tents. The elderly and the few surviving women with children were asleep in the city hall, but most of the younger people were tucked into the blue tarp tents. The nights were growing warmer as summer unfurled.

"Got one down in the far corner, but I can't get a bead on it," Bill stated sorrowfully. "Poor old bugger."

She eyeballed the location he pointed to and caught sight of a figure swaying near an empty building on the far side of the fort walls. A lamppost and tree partially blocked it from view.

"I think it got its foot caught in the sidewalk cracks. It's really uneven there," Bill said.

Katie didn't say anything. There wasn't much to say. A lone zombie was a pretty sad thing, at least from a distance. The mutilated form always spoke of a terrible ending to a person's life. But she knew the second it saw a human, it would become the most horrible thing anyone had ever seen. Its eyes would flash wide and its mouth would open to reveal broken teeth; it would reach toward its prey and let out a horrible shriek.

"Hey," Travis said from behind them, and Katie turned to see him exiting the stairway onto the roof. At the sight of him in a dark T-shirt and jeans, Katie felt a pang of desire. She tried to ignore it, but his broad shoulders, tanned skin and brown curly hair made her want to touch him. Setting her lips tightly together, she looked away from Travis, still unwilling to betray Lydia's memory.

"Hey, Travis. What's up?" Bill stood up and tugged his shirt down over his beer belly.

"I think we're going to try to take the next street tomorrow," Travis answered. "Time to take the territory closest to us."

"Taking the Dollar Store over?" Bill waved toward the buildings lining the side street that they had yet to claim into the fort.

"Yeah. Can't put it off anymore."

"Why didn't y'all take it over right away, anyway?" Bill asked.

"We figured it was better to get supplies from the outskirts of town and beyond first and stockpile before going into the buildings around us. It's kinda like going to the store and buying new food instead of using what's stored in the pantry." Travis shrugged. "Seemed like a good idea when this all started."

"Guess that makes sense," Bill conceded.

"There's no telling how long canned and dry goods will be available out in the deadlands," Katie agreed. "I'm sure there are other survivors out there looking for food and supplies."

"Like those damn rednecks that killed Ralph," Bill muttered angrily.

Katie inhaled sharply, the sting of Ralph's violent death adding to the ache of her heart. "We haven't seen them around. Maybe they moved on."

Travis furrowed his brow as he shook his head. "I would bet they are still out there. Who knows what the hell they are up to. We gotta think about ourselves. Time to expand the fort and make more room."

Katie could feel Travis studying her expression. She folded her arms over her breasts to try to steady herself. She was feeling so lonely; she wanted him to hold her, but she feared what that might lead to. She had given in to temptation before. The feel of his lips against hers was a memory that brought her both pleasure and guilt.

"I figure you'll want to be part of that, so if you want to go get some sleep, I can take over," Travis said to Bill.

Bill mulled over the suggestion before asking, "Did you sleep, Travis?"

"Yeah. I'm good for tonight." Travis paused, then added, "We'll head in around nine or ten in the morning."

Bill glanced at his watch. "Gives me about four hours to sleep." He handed his rifle to Travis, who took it awkwardly. He wasn't very comfortable with guns, but he was trying to learn.

"Catch you later, Katie," Bill said, patting her arm as he headed off.

"Sleep well, Bill!" she called after him.

Then she was alone with Travis.

"Did you sleep?" he asked, scrutinizing her.

Finally, reluctantly, she looked at him and nodded. "Did you? Or did you lie?"

"I slept enough," he answered, shrugging. Moving closer to Katie, he looked at the spot Bill had been studying and immediately spotted the tangled-up zombie. Realizing he didn't have a clear shot, he frowned. "Is everything okay with you?"

"I'm fine. Really." Katie stepped away from Travis. She knew it was time to go, because she wanted to cry again and she wanted him to comfort her.

"Katie," he said softly, reaching toward her.

"I'll catch you later," she said, and briskly walked away.

When she reached the stairs, she hurried down the steps and quickly put as much distance between her and Travis as she could. Down in the hallway, she leaned against the wall and gave in to her pain. Tears streamed down her face as she wept.

4.
The Lonely Guard

Travis wanted to follow Katie, but knew he couldn't. Guard duty was a serious commitment. Glancing over the construction site, he could see the other five guards at their posts along the wall. In the last few days, they hadn't seen many zombies, but he knew that was a temporary condition. Sooner or later—and probably sooner—more of the walking dead would come wandering out of the landscape to screech and moan outside the walls.

Rubbing his face with one hand, Travis yawned. He had seen the torment on Katie's face and had wanted to comfort her, but knew she wouldn't let him. That kiss a few weeks ago had changed things between them, much to his regret. Before the kiss, they had been friends, and maybe a little more. After, she had withdrawn from him. Now there was nothing he could do but wait and let her work things out for herself.

If he couldn't fix his relationship with Katie, he could make sure that the small haven they were carving out in the world of the dead stayed safe. Tomorrow they would secure the road next to the fort and take over the Dollar Store. The shops on either side of the discount store were empty, so the fort's residents might be able to use them as well, if they weren't in bad shape.

He glanced over his shoulder at the hotel. Soon, the fort survivors would have to occupy the structure. But Travis and Juan were extremely nervous about risking the security of the fort to take the hotel. The fort was as safe as it got in the new, dead world, and the thought of breaking through the hotel wall made his chest tight with anxiety. The hotel could be empty of all life: undead or otherwise. But what if there was a door open somewhere and zombies had wandered inside? Juan's crew had built a special enclosure flush up against the back wall of the hotel to provide secure entry into the building. It seemed like a good idea in theory, but Travis had his doubts.

Hell, he had his doubts about everything. He couldn't help but second-guess himself when so many lives were on the line, including his own. The mere thought of being mauled to death by one of the undead kept him sufficiently paranoid.

Travis narrowed his eyes as the zombie staggered free from whatever had temporarily trapped it. Raising the rifle, he fumbled with the safety, then aimed for the zombie's head using the sight. He felt uncomfortable using the weapon, but they needed to keep the area as zombie free as possible.

The zombie stopped walking, and he could see a skirt flowing in the breeze around its crooked legs. It slowly raised its hand. Before it could issue its horrifying screech, he pulled the trigger. It collapsed onto the sidewalk as the echoes of the shot faded away.

With a sigh, Travis lowered the rifle.

Tomorrow was a new day.

A new beginning.

And that was all any of them could hope for anymore.

· CHAPTER TWO ·

1.
Taking Risks

Beads of sweat slid down Juan's spine as he stood on the wall. The side street that ran alongside the fort had been left open until today, in case it was needed as an escape route. Now, because they wanted to expand the fort, Juan and his crew were using the huge crane to block the ends of the street with long storage containers. Once that was done, they would send a team in to clear the buildings of any zombies.

By tomorrow, new walls would be in place to hold off the zombie hordes, and the fort would gain the use of four more buildings. Luckily, the downtown area was so old that the buildings were flush up against one another. The fort's inhabitants only had to worry about the two ends of the street and securing the back entrances of the newly accessible buildings.

The breeze was still cool despite the sun's rays. Juan wiped his forehead beneath the brim of his cowboy hat. Looking over his shoulder, he could see the survivors watching from the safety of the old construction site. Excitement was already building. It was going to be an intense day, and they all knew it. If their luck held out, it would be a good one, too.

Travis joined him on the wall, and they both looked down at the front windows of the Dollar Store, which were covered in huge advertising posters. The featured items were mostly Easter baskets and Easter treats. Juan frowned as he realized the holiday had passed without anyone even noticing.

Because of the ads, it was hard to see into the building. No one had seen any movement inside the store, but that did not mean there wasn't anything undead waiting for them..

"Think someone is in there?"

Juan shrugged. "If there is, they ain't alive."

Travis yawned, rubbing his face.

"No sleep?"

"Not a lot. You?"

"Once we're in the hotel, I think I'll sleep a lot better," Juan replied.

"Yeah. I can't argue there."

"When are we going in?" Juan jerked his head toward the hotel.

Travis shrugged. "When it feels like we can handle the risk."

Juan studied the towering building. The empty windows gave him the creeps. He knew they needed to go in soon, but he was just as worried as Travis. All sorts of things could go wrong.

"Hey, guys," a voice called out. Eric, an engineer from Austin, was climbing up the ladder to the wall. Eric and his girlfriend, Stacey, had been rescued a week before from a water tower on the outskirts of Ashley Oaks, where zombies had trapped them for almost a month. They had nearly starved to death. Eric was still far too thin for his height, but he looked better than he had when they'd found him. He hesitated at the top of the ladder and looked up at them worriedly. His pale skin was more burned than tanned and his glasses and mussed brown hair made him look like a grown-up Harry Potter.

"Whazzup?" Juan cocked his head curiously.

"I really feel like I need to inspect the store and the other shops once they are clear. I heard a rumor that you are thinking about moving some of us over the wall. All these buildings are really old, and we can't be too sure they are structurally sound."

Juan almost laughed. He was pretty sure most of the old buildings were better built than the newer ones, but Eric looked very sincere. So he just said, "Yeah, man, that's cool."

Eric climbed onto the wall and cautiously stood up. He gained his balance and folded his arms over his chest. "What you guys did with the construction site to make it into a fort is outstanding, but—"

"Eh, I understand." Juan shrugged. "We're taking risks all the time."

"But we can't risk too much, or we might lose everything." Eric pushed his glasses up on his nose.

Juan couldn't blame him for looking nervous. He had heard Eric's story and knew that he and his girlfriend had barely survived.

"I don't see that as an issue—after we're sure it's clear, you can inspect the buildings," Travis agreed. "Besides, we're not sure how we're going to use the space yet. We need to take a look around before making any solid plans."

"We're all just—" Eric motioned to the people watching them from below. "—scared to be on the other side of this wall."

Juan and Travis looked back at the line of stores. Juan knew they were both thinking the same thing.

They had no choice.

Travis sighed faintly, then spoke in a firm voice. "I know that they sent you up here for reassurance. I can promise you, and everyone down there, that we will not move anyone into the new area until we're absolutely sure it's clear of zombies. We'll also make sure the zombies won't be able to breach the stores."

"I guess the way things are set up right now just feels so safe. Risking anything is just scary. I'm not dissing what you guys are saying or insinuating that you don't know what you're doing, just some of us. . . ." Eric faltered as he gestured down into the construction site.

Juan looked down as well. A good-sized group of people huddled together. Eric's still-emaciated girlfriend was holding their

Jack Russell terrier, Pepe, and looking up at Eric with a worried expression. Juan thought she was a pretty little thing. She had long tanned limbs and pale blond hair, but her cheeks were hollow and her shoulders bony. He could understand Eric's desire to protect her. The dozen or so people gathered around her also wore expressions of concern. Juan realized Eric was a spokesman for more than his own fears.

"Man, we got loved ones, too. We're not going to risk them. Okay?" Juan tried to give the man a reassuring look.

Travis reached out to grip Eric's shoulder lightly with one hand, looked him in the eye, and said in his most earnest tone, "Trust us. We have this under control."

Eric shifted his gaze from Travis to the Dollar Store. He seemed to reach some sort of peace with the situation. "I'll let them know," he said finally, and climbed down the ladder.

"You can't blame them," Juan said once Eric was down below and talking to the group. "They weren't here when we made this construction site into a fort. They don't know what it was like before."

Travis looked calm, but Juan could tell he was upset by the set of his jaw. "We're doing our best to keep them all safe and keep things as sanitary as possible. We're damn lucky the power is still on."

"It's that new hydroelectric power station they built a few years back; I betcha anything."

"But for how long will it stay operational?" Travis lifted his sunglasses for a few seconds so he could rub his eyes. "So much can go wrong if we're not careful."

"Just another day in zombie land," Juan said with a wide grin. "Gotta love it."

Travis chuckled. "Yeah, ain't life grand?"

Juan flicked the brim of his cowboy hat up. "Never a dull moment."

"I miss dull moments," Travis mused.

Slinging his arm around his pal's shoulders, Juan wondered if life would ever be dull again. "It looks so peaceful out there."

"But it's not," Travis reminded him.

"Got those guys out there that killed Ralph . . ."

"And the walking dead," Travis added.

"And who knows what else," Juan finished.

"You really know how to cheer a guy up," Travis joked.

"I do my best. I do my best."

Both men stared down at the Dollar Store with trepidation.

2.
Waiting

After leaving Travis on the roof, Katie had managed to sleep a few hours in the small room she shared with Nerit. When she awakened, Nerit was gone. Yawning, she pulled on her shoes and headed to the community dining room.

Katie poured milk onto her cereal, staring at the watery white liquid filling in around the flakes. She was slowly getting used to reconstituted powdered milk. It didn't taste bad; it just looked off. Picking up her spoon, she dug into the cornflakes, wishing for a banana to add. The salvage team that had looted the grocery store brought back tons of food, in boxes, cans, and bags. But by the time they'd been secure enough to send people out for supplies, the fresh fruit had all gone bad.

Rosie, Juan's mother, had salvaged seeds from some of the rotten fruit and was planning a garden with Peggy, the city secretary. The two women just needed a good spot within the walls to plant. Katie hoped their efforts were successful; she missed fruit desperately. With a sigh, she reached out and picked up the small Dixie cup of vitamins that everyone was required to take in the morning. She downed it with orange juice made from a powdered mix.

Jenni crashed into the chair across from her. "We're heading in!"

"Huh?" Katie tried to get her brain up to Jenni speed as she stared at her friend. "We're what?"

Jenni gulped down her vitamins, dry. "Dollar Store. We're heading in." The dark-haired woman poured Froot Loops into a bowl and reached for the pitcher of milk. "Travis says I can go with Ed, Bill, and Felix."

Katie tried not to frown, but knew it slid over her features before she could stop it.

"Oh, c'mon. You volunteered to go into the hotel. You and I have more experience with zombies than most of these guys, from when we were out on the road. You so cannot get in my face for volunteering for this. The place is probably empty!"

"I just worry," Katie admitted.

Jenni snorted. "You're such a mom."

"I had a bad night last night. I worry about the ones I love."

"You love someone other than me?" Jenni widened her eyes playfully. "Oh, wow, I have competition? I'll cut 'em!"

Despite herself, Katie laughed. "Yeah, I'm so sure you can take down Nerit. Or Jason. Or Old Man Watson. Or . . ." She faltered at Travis.

Jenni crunched her cereal. "You're such a dork."

"Thanks, I needed that." Katie shoveled more food into her mouth.

"I had a rough night, too. Fuckin' nightmares." Katie waited for Jenni to go on, but as usual, she changed the subject. "I'm going to take this ax that Ed got from the grocery store. I've been practicing using it, and I like it so much better than the spears. It has this really great energy when you swing it." Jenni added more cereal to her bowl. "I'm going to have such a great sugar high from this stuff."

"Pure carbs, Jenni. We seriously need more protein in our diets." The salvaged meat from the grocery store freezer wouldn't last much longer. It was already held for dinner only. Lunch was usually stuff from cans.

Jenni wrinkled her nose. "Whatever. So, my new ax . . ."

Amused, Katie listened to Jenni prattle on about her new weapon. Her friend always avoided talking about the past or the life she had lost. Katie marveled at Jenni's ability to move on, but at the same time wondered if all the things she was ignoring would one day catch up with her.

Jason, Jenni's stepson, and Jack, his ever-faithful German shepherd companion, joined them. Before the teenager managed to sit down, Katie and Jenni had both hugged him. The women showered the dog with attention before making him settle down under the table. Jason's bangs were long enough that he tended to stare at the world through brown, straggly clumps of hair, but he was a good, smart kid. Katie was glad they had been able to rescue him from the camp he was attending during the first days of the outbreak.

"I was talking to Roger, that science teacher, and he says my plans for a catapult are really good. Think if I talk to Juan, he could get me the stuff to make it?" Jason picked out Grape-Nuts from the boxes on the table, which impressed Katie until he drowned the healthful little nuggets in sugar and milk.

"Yeah. He would totally do that. But probably not until we get the hotel under our control. He's obsessed with getting us in." Jenni slurped down the sugary milk in her bowl.

Jason scowled, then shrugged. "I'm just trying to help out."

"Don't take it personal. The guys are all fixated with getting into the hotel. The city hall's air conditioner is not that great, and some of the older people will suffer if the heat gets any worse." Katie rubbed the boy's back to reassure him.

"Yeah, but we're not building enough defenses. What if a bunch of them show up? Or the guys that killed Ralph? Juan calls them the banditos. Or . . ." He shrugged. "Whatever. I'm just a kid."

"And a moody one," Jenni teased.

"Mom!"

Jenni leaned over the table to hug and kiss him relentlessly. Jason tried to fight her off at first, then started laughing. Satisfied, Jenni slid back into her chair.

"Gawd, Mom," Jason said, his cheeks flushed.

Katie grinned and tucked back into her breakfast. Suddenly, she didn't feel so down or so alone. It was a good feeling.

3.
Going In

"Go in, secure the front. Jenni and Bill, you take right. Me and Felix, we'll take left. Do not fire your weapon unless you have to, and only if you're sure everyone else is clear. We don't need friendly fire in there," Ed said firmly. He was a scrawny, grizzled white guy in his late fifties, a tough Texan who had run a small farm on the outskirts of town. His peach groves were the only fresh fruit they had any hope of bringing into the fort, but the salvage team had yet to get out that far.

Felix, a good-looking young black man from the Houston area, balanced his makeshift spear in one hand. He had modified it to have two deadly ends, and he often practiced with it. Jenni thought his skin was beautiful; the color reminded her of grackle feathers. He was so black, his skin gleamed purple in the sunlight. He dressed like a thug, but when he spoke, you quickly realized he was much more than he appeared to be. African-born, he had been adopted by white parents and raised in an affluent part of Houston. He'd been a student at the University of Texas when things all went to hell, and he'd barely made it out of Austin alive. Felix didn't talk about it, but Jenni got the impression he was torn between many different worlds. He was one of the few people of color among the white majority of the fort and had at first kept to himself. Like Jenni, he had eventually found his place in the family of survivors.

Bill looked toward the store from their perch on the wall. "I can't see there being anyone in that store if they haven't shown up at the front door." He hitched his belt a little higher and looked somber.

Ed shrugged. "In this world, can't be too sure about nothing."

"Amen," Jenni agreed, and lifted her ax. "I'm ready to choppy, choppy."

"You're one crazy bitch," Felix chided with a grin.

"Uh-huh. Your point is?"

Felix held up one hand and twirled a finger to indicate she was loopy.

Jenni smirked.

The road was blocked off on both ends by huge storage containers and cement bags. Snipers, including Nerit, stood on the fort's wall, ready to shoot any approaching zombies. The small entry team had to worry only about what was inside the Dollar Store and the neighboring abandoned shops.

"We all know Jenni is batshit crazy, but that's okay. She's good at killing the goddamn zombies," Ed said with a wry grin. "So let's go in and see how things are cooking in there."

Jenni scanned all the people staring up at them from the fort. She spotted her loved ones and waved to Katie and Jason. Juan was up on the far wall, and she blew him a kiss. He caught it in one hand and pretended to smack it onto his ass. She laughed.

Ed headed down the ladder first, followed by Felix, then Bill, and finally Jenni. She jumped down the last few rungs, landing on the hot road. The entire downtown area was paved in red bricks, and the roadways were in good condition, though a few blades of grass stuck up here and there.

Despite the heat, they all wore jeans, boots, gloves, and jackets to protect them from zombie bites. Jenni's long hair was braided and pinned up on her head so the zombies wouldn't have anything to grab on to. Her work gloves were lightweight, but would be a bitch for any zombie to bite through. She was overheated already, but knew she had to stay safe.

The four warriors slowly approached the Dollar Store. The interior was hard to see, given the advertisements taped to the windows and the fact that the lights were off. Everything seemed gloomy and unwelcoming. Bill went down on his knees before the door and started to pick the lock. Busting the door open would be the last resort.

"Ha. I bet everyone thought the black man would be doing that," Felix observed with a sly grin.

"You learn things on the job, being a cop," Bill replied somberly.

"Don't care if you're black or white or brown or whatever," Ed gruffly said, "just as long as you don't turn green and bite me."

Jenni laughed and Felix smiled.

Bill's brow furrowed as he concentrated. With a twist of his wrist, the lock spun, and the door opened slightly.

They all gagged at once. The smell coming out of the store was putrid.

"Fucking shit," Felix gasped.

"We got a dead one in there, all right," Ed uttered grimly.

Bill crawled away from the door, eyes watering, trying to get a clean breath of air.

Jenni pulled her bandanna up over her nose. "God, that is awful."

"Enclosed space and rotting dead stuff: not a good combo. Let's do this, people," Ed urged, pushing the door all the way open with one foot. He stared into the gloom, holding his rifle. Hey!"

As his voice echoed through the store, a low growl answered.

"It's dead and talking," Ed said somberly, and walked in.

Felix moved in right behind him. Bill climbed to his feet and joined Jenni. He wiped his eyes and cheeks with a bandanna, then nodded to her. His eyes were still smarting, but he appeared eager to get inside. Jenni slid into the darkened interior slowly, with Bill at her heels.

4.
The Store

The first thing Jenni saw was a line of small shopping carts. Beyond them, both checkout stands stood empty. Jenni walked cautiously toward the first aisle to the right as Ed and Felix moved to check out the left side of the store. Holding his machete, Bill peered behind the checkout stands just to make sure they were truly unoccupied. A swift motion of his head showed that nothing lingered there.

Jenni lifted her ax a little higher as she headed down the aisle, which was for makeup and skin and hair care. A lone bottle of shampoo lay on the floor. She scooted it out of her way with the tip of her boot. Bill moved up alongside her, close enough for Jenni to hear his steady breathing. It was comforting. At the back of the store, she slowly edged around the corner, looking into the long aisle that ran along the rear wall. It was empty.

Ed and Felix were obviously not finding anything as well, from the silence on their end, but the stench and moans indicated that clearly something was dead in the store and still moving. The aisle Jenni and Bill entered next, packed with baby supplies, made Jenni's head swim for a moment; then she shoved all thoughts of Benji out of her mind and set her jaw determinedly.

The baby aisle was clear.

They reached the front of the store and turned to enter the next aisle.

Groans reverberated through the space.

"Is anyone alive in here?" Felix's voice called out.

Another low moan was the only reply.

"If you're human and hurt, say something," Felix continued.

The moan grew into a hungry growl.

"Zombie," Ed's voice declared.

"For sure," Felix agreed.

Bill froze for a second as he and Jenni reached an aisle full of photo books and frames. The floor was littered with broken and smashed merchandise. Scanning the area, Jenni spotted an arm dangling off a shelf above a display of cute, cheap frames. The arm was savagely bitten in several places. A low wail came from the shelf. The arm was attached to a zombie.

"Found one," Bill called out.

The zombie arm twitched.

"I bet he crawled up there to get away," Jenni whispered.

The zombie, wedged tightly between two metal shelves, wiggled excitedly, knowing human flesh was nearby.

"How do we do this?" Bill looked perplexed.

Jenni motioned to the zombie's foot. "Drag it down and deal with it?"

Bill frowned. "Could go wrong on the way down. Could twist around and land on us or something."

The zombie thrashed, unable to free itself.

"Let's go to the other side," Jenni suggested.

Household supplies were next. The zombie's other leg and arm were hanging out in that aisle. Jenni observed that the zombie was a young man, probably in his late teens. If he hadn't such a slim build, he may never have wedged himself between the two metal shelves. He saw them and thrashed even more, growling. Jenni spotted a small stepladder that had probably been used to stock the higher shelves. It was toppled over on one side, not far from the zombie's feet. Probably the kid had used it to try to climb up out of the way of a zombie and gotten stuck and bit. Grabbing the ladder, she dragged it over to the front of the zombie. Out of the corner of her eye, she could see its decaying hand reaching for her, but she was out of reach.

"Hold me," Jenni ordered Bill, then climbed onto the top step.

As Bill's big hands held her hips, Jenni faced the zombie. Its hand waved in front of her eyes, straining desperately to reach her. The kid's face was stained with tears and blood. Jenni felt sorry for him—he didn't look much older than her stepson. But his time was done on this earth. She was ready to send him on.

With a grunt, she swung her ax as hard as she could into the face of the zombie. He grabbed her wrist just as the ax head buried itself into his skull. Almost as soon as his fingers seized her, they went slack. Jenni wrenched the ax out of the zombie's head. Bill tightened his grip on her hips.

"One more whack to be sure," she said.

She swung the ax again and cleaved the zombie's skull in half. Now she was sure it was done. Black goo slid out over the edge of the shelf.

"It's done!"

Her voice echoed.

A growl from the back of the store responded.

"Sounds like we got another one," Ed called out.

"I figured that. This one climbed up on a shelf to escape something," Bill replied.

A more desperate moan answered.

Jenni dropped off the stepladder and held her dripping ax tightly in her hands. She felt a little sick about the death of the kid. His first death, not the one she had given him. The world was just fucked and awful.

The next area was full of hanging clothes and bedding supplies. Jenni and Bill made sure to study any shelving above eye level. The moaning continued from the back of the store. The assault team moved on cautiously. It was far too dangerous to let down their guard.

"Found her," Felix called out. "She's on your side. And you won't believe this."

Bill and Jenni finally reached the back of the store and turned the corner.

A female zombie was reaching toward Felix and Ed, who were approaching from the opposite side of the store.

"You have to be fucking kidding me," Jenni said in disbelief.

The ground was covered in overturned trash bins of all sizes, plastic clothes baskets, and storage containers. Some were broken and many were splashed with blood, clear evidence that a struggle had happened here. At some point, the female zombie stepped into a bucket and her foot had become stuck. When she tried to pass between the metal shelving and a support column, the bucket had become wedged. She'd been left standing on one foot and trapped. Jenni couldn't see her face, but her body looked slim and young. She wondered if this was the one who had bitten the boy.

"Kinda dumb, ain't they?" Ed smirked.

Jenni hefted her ax and brought it down hard onto the zombie's head. The blade lodged halfway into the thing's skull. The zombie slowly collapsed to the floor, and Jenni yanked the ax out of the dead girl.

Bill leaned down and examined the zombie carefully. "I see one bite on her hand. Only mark other than her head being split apart."

"So, she gets bit, dies, attacks the boy here, he gets bit up, she gets caught, he goes and climbs onto a shelf." Felix shrugged. "And he dies. Makes sense."

Jenni frowned down at the body. "But who bit her?"

"They're both wearing vests and name tags. Boxes are open in the aisles. They were early-morning stockers. Do you think she came in bit?" Bill looked thoughtful.

Slowly, they all turned to look at the swinging metal doors to the stockroom.

"Great," Felix moaned.

"We do this right and careful," Ed said firmly, indicating the back of the store. The battered metal doors swung open to reveal a long, narrow room. Boxes were piled along one wall almost to the ceiling. At the far end, a narrow bathroom could be seen through an open door.

"Hello?" Jenni called out cautiously.

She jumped when the metal doors that opened to the loading dock started to shake as something on the other side beat on them.

Snarls and growls that set her hair on end emanated from beyond the closed doors.

"Okay. We got at least one outside, but those doors are holding for now. Let's check the storage room," Ed ordered.

It took ten long minutes to scour the narrow room. They moved slowly and purposefully. They checked the shelves, the boxes, the bathroom, and the manager's office. They made as much noise as possible to try to lure something out.

"Nothing," Jenni sighed with relief.

"One more sweep through the store," Ed said.

Twenty minutes later, they left the Dollar Store and stood in the street, breathing in clean air.

"Got the empty stores now," Ed said.

Jenni nodded and brandished her ax. "Let's do it."

· CHAPTER THREE ·

1.
Army of One

An hour later, Nerit climbed down the ladder slowly to the street below. Her long, yellowish white hair was braided to keep it out of her gray green eyes, and she wore jeans, a plain T-shirt, and a denim jacket. Her joints ached as she descended, and she cursed her sixty-two years. Her mind was sharp, but her body sometimes failed her. Lately, one hip was giving her more trouble than usual and she winced as it sent a jolt of pain down her leg. Juan watched with concern as she gingerly climbed to the blocked-off street.

"Be careful, Nerit."

"I'm not that old." Though her voice was stern, she winked at him. She ignored Bill's attempt to help her off the ladder, but he still took hold of her arm as she lowered her booted feet to the redbrick road.

"Stores are all clear, but we got one or two dead guys trying to bust through a back door. Making an awful fuss now that they know we're here," Ed said.

Nerit nodded. That was why she was here. Bill had called for her when no one could get a clear shot at the zombie or zombies. Bill had previously seen her in action and knew she was a deadly shot. She knew that the survivors were fascinated by her past as an Israeli army sniper and there were rumors about her being a Mossad agent. That amused Nerit. But it felt good to have a purpose in her new home and to be appreciated.

When she left the home she'd shared with Ralph above the hunting store, Nerit had taken only a few personal possessions. Perhaps the most important was her old Galil sniper rifle. Over the years, it had developed a few issues, but Ralph had carefully restored it. Nerit had to conserve her ammunition because she didn't have much, but she wasn't ready to change to a new weapon. The sniper rifle was a good, reliable weapon, but also it was a reminder of her deceased husband's thoughtfulness and appreciation for her skills.

"I can get him," Nerit assured Ed.

"You ain't seen him yet." Ed raised a bushy eyebrow.

"Doesn't matter," she said firmly.

Ed studied her for a long moment, a thoughtful expression on his grizzled face, then shrugged. "We'll get you up on the roof."

Nerit smiled warmly at Jenni as she passed the much younger woman. The brunette, who was holding an ax smeared in foul, congealed zombie blood, watched the older woman apprehensively. Nerit knew Jenni had confidence in her abilities. Most likely the look of concern was because Nerit had lost her husband recently. Jenni perhaps expected Nerit to be grieving, but what Jenni didn't comprehend was that Nerit had accepted her loss. It was not easy to let Ralph go, but he was gone. She was part of a new family, and she was determined to help them survive.

"Good luck, Nerit," Jenni said.

"Thank you, Jenni."

Bill followed Nerit into the darkened store as Ed led the way to a staircase near the back. The store smelled of mold and mildew; the wood floor creaked as they walked. Motes of dust swirled around in the few shafts of sunlight that managed to penetrate the grime that covered the large plate glass windows in the front. There were a few shelves along one wall and an old cash register listing on an old counter, but there was no real indication what wares the store had once sold. Nerit was not one for sentiment, but it was a bit sad to see the remains of what had probably once been a thriving business.

The stairs moaned as she and Ed climbed. She was careful with her footing, as it was obvious that the store had stood empty for nearly a decade. Rat droppings and dead insects littered the wooden flooring of the second story.

"Got windows here, but the view of the loading dock is blocked by the Dollar Store," Ed explained.

Nerit glanced at a broken window as she passed. A spider had taken great pains to fill in the gap between the glass and the wood frame with an intricate web. Stepping closer, Nerit could see into the back alley behind the Dollar Store. She could hear the zombie or zombies howling and slamming against the doors, but she could not see the undead.

"Roof is this way," Ed said, guiding her up another set of very rickety steps.

Nerit was worried about Bill's weight on the unstable stairs, but he followed them, treading very carefully. Ed pushed open a wobbly door and they stepped out into the sunshine. The roof was not in the best condition. Long swaths of tar paper were torn off or peeling, revealing the rotting wood beneath. Cautiously, Nerit stepped out onto the roof.

Ashley Oaks spread out around them in a panorama. The red-brick buildings of downtown looked lovely against the scenic green hills surrounding the town. It was beautiful, despite the cement brick walls closing off the construction site, the long-abandoned storefronts, and the few zombies wandering around in the distance.

Nerit gingerly walked to the edge of the building. A warm breeze buffeted her yellowed silver bangs back from her face. Most of the zombie on the Dollar Store loading dock was hidden from view by the side of the building; only one leg was slightly visible.

"See? Can't get 'em," Ed pointed out.

"I can," Nerit assured him, and unslung her sniper rifle from her shoulder. As usual, the rifle felt good and comforting in her arms. It was like an extension of her. She closed one eye and focused through the sight. Her senses narrowed down to just her vision, and she removed herself from the world around her.

She pulled the trigger. A gout of black blood erupted from the zombie's newly shattered ankle. The thing lost its balance and tumbled. When its body fell into view, Nerit quickly adjusted her aim and fired. A plume of blood and gore erupted from its head; then it lay still.

Lowering her gun, she listened.

The pounding and growling had ceased.

"You got him," Bill said in an awed voice.

"Yes." Nerit shrugged. She watched the shadows dwelling behind the Dollar Store. "Looks like that was it."

Ed gazed down at the body, then at a bike lying on its side in the alley. "Looks like the Ramirez boy. I heard he was in trouble for dating some girl in town. His dad worked on my farm."

Bill sighed. "Betcha he is the one who bit the girl and they managed to lock him out."

"And then it went to hell from there," Ed agreed.

Nerit looked back toward the fort and the people gathered to watch what they could of the proceedings. "Let's get some sentries up here to watch for any more approaching this way."

"Yeah. Gotta inspect the buildings, too." Ed headed back toward the stairs.

Bill looked down at the remains of the young man. "I bet he only wanted to see her and he ended up killing her instead."

Nerit could hear the sorrow in Bill's voice and knew it had nothing to do with the boy, but everything to do with his own loss.

It was an emotion they were too well acquainted with in this new world. She reached out and laid her hand gently against his round cheek, the stubble tickling her palm. "We all do foolish things. It's best to learn and move on."

Bill's fixed gaze was broken by her words and he glanced toward her. "Yeah, you're right, Nerit. I just think of all those poor, dead souls out there. How many of them did stupid things that ended up killing the ones they loved?"

"We can't worry about them anymore. We need to concentrate on the living."

Bill nodded soberly. "Yeah."

In somber silence, Nerit followed Bill out of the building. There was more work to be done.

2.
Claustrophobia

Travis had almost reached city hall when Eric caught up and matched his stride. Tired and a little cranky, Travis was not in the mood for yet another discussion about the efforts to expand the fort.

"How's it going, Eric?" he asked neutrally.

"I checked all the buildings. They're sounder than I anticipated." Eric pushed his glasses up on his nose as he tried to keep pace with Travis.

"They built stuff to last, back in the day." Travis circumvented a few of the makeshift tents and headed for the back entrance of city hall. The sun was high in the sky and it was brutally warm despite the clouds in the west.

"I have to ask about the hotel. There's been talk about whether or not we're going to ever move into it." Eric pointed toward the building that was the bane of Travis's existence. Not too long ago, a zombified maid had taken a header out of one of the windows.

Travis stopped walking and Eric nearly plowed into him. "We're trying to make sure that when we go in, we keep all of you safe."

"Some people are saying that taking the side street is a way to avoid going into the hotel, and they're not happy about that."

The city hall door, behind them, creaked open, a welcome interruption as far as Travis was concerned. Mike and Peggy emerged; muscles rippled under Mike's T-shirt as the former army sergeant trotted down the stairs. He was formidable in appearance, but gentle at heart—traits that served Mike well as he trained people to become zombie killers.

Peggy, the city secretary, looked harried as she pulled her brown hair into a short ponytail, securing it with a plain rubber band. Travis suddenly had the feeling he was not going to enjoy whatever she was about to say.

"Hey, Travis. I got that ETA on the new walls you asked for." Mike took a long drink from the bottle of water he held in one hand. "After Eric checked the buildings, Juan and I worked out a timeline. To get the walls up and secure the backs of the buildings, it'll take close to twenty-four hours using round-the-clock crews."

"That's faster than I thought." Travis raised his eyebrows, impressed.

Peggy snorted. "Why can't y'all just construct some new buildings inside the walls?"

"We don't have enough supplies for that," Mike answered. "Building a wall is a lot different from building new structures."

Peggy glowered at Mike, then flicked her gaze toward the high wall that enclosed the construction site. "I just don't like the idea of going over that wall. I know what's out there. I don't feel like tempting fate."

"I know exactly how you feel," Eric concurred.

Feeling surrounded, Travis took a few steps toward the door. "No one will head over to the new area until the new walls are up."

Mike vigorously bobbed his head in agreement. "Yep. And those will be sturdy walls. No zombies are going to get in. Trust my crew. We know what we're doing."

"Oh, I don't doubt that," Peggy reluctantly admitted. "It's just . . ."

"We're afraid of something going wrong," Eric finished.

"Exactly." Peggy nodded her head. "What he said."

"Then you both worry way too much. Trust us. We got it covered!" Mike waved at the group as he headed off across the construction site.

Realizing the conversation was over, Eric turned away. Peggy and Travis went into city hall.

"I hate to be the bearer of bad news, but Steven Mann and his bitch of a wife are talking with Mayor Reyes about the hotel." Peggy folded her arms over her chest. "The mayor asked me to come find you."

The Manns were newly rescued. They had been holed up at their estate outside the town since the zombie uprising. Shane and Philip had found them during a scavenging run. Travis had met the Manns before, on social occasions in Houston, and it had been Steven Mann who hired him to work on the renovation of downtown Ashley Oaks. Mann's intent had been to reinvigorate the town and bring in tourism. His model had been Fredericksburg, Texas, which had used its history as the birthplace of Admiral Nimitz to create a tourist mecca in the Hill Country. Mann had hoped that Ashley Oaks' ties to old Hollywood would be as big a draw.

Travis sighed. "This isn't going to be pleasant, is it?"

Peggy shrugged. "What is nowadays?"

Walking down the hall, Travis ran his hands over his hair, tucked in his shirt, and adjusted his belt. He was sure he looked grimy and tired. Technically, Steven Mann wasn't his employer anymore, but the man had once had a lot of clout in town. As Travis neared the office of Mayor Manny Reyes, he could clearly hear Steven Mann's wife, Blanche, saying, in her thick East Texas accent, "You just have to make them understand, Manny."

Slipping through the doorway, Travis gave the three people in the room a slight smile. "I heard I was needed?"

"Travis! Good to see you," Steven declared, smiling broadly. A descendant of the first German settlers in the area, he was tall and blond. His gaze was always a little unsettling because of the vivid robin's egg blue of his eyes. His jeans, crisp white shirt, cowboy hat, and deep suntan gave him the look of an ordinary local rancher, but most local ranchers weren't billionaires.

"Nice to see you, Mr. Mann. Nice to see you, Mrs. Mann," Travis said.

Blanche sat back in her chair, crossed her long, lean legs, flicked a lock of her blond hair away from her immaculately made-up face, and said, "Why the fuck aren't you doing something about the hotel?"

"Blanche, let's give the man a moment to catch up with our conversation," Steven said quickly as the mayor cleared his throat, looking uncomfortable behind his big desk.

Travis took a seat near the mayor's desk as Blanche rolled her eyes. A former beauty queen who still looked the part in her early thirties, Blanche was dressed in a tight denim skirt, high-heeled, strappy sandals, and a red tank top covered in sparkling stones.

"We were just discussing why we have not yet entered the hotel. I was explaining to the Manns that you, Juan, and Mike have been very careful with the security of our . . . fort and that we are not going to make any rash moves." Manny's fingers played with the pen on his desk as he spoke, his gaze locked on the writing instrument.

Travis was about to speak when Blanche cut in.

"That's utterly ridiculous! There are hardly any zombies out there right now. Maybe this whole plague or whatever it is, is almost over. How many of those things have y'all seen in the last week? Maybe a dozen? Less? Hell, Steven, we should go back home."

After clearing his throat, Travis said, "The supply and rescue crews have actually seen quite a few zombies during their runs. Some of the people we have rescued have reported seeing mobs of fifty or more zombies not too far away. It's not safe out there. We'll get into the hotel—but we want to do it right."

"I got the front door key right here." Steven fumbled with his keychain.

"We considered that, but we need to secure the front of the

building so the zombies can't get in. It would take too much time to transport building materials around front, and the construction crew would be in the open for too long. It's better to go in through the back. Trust me, we have a plan. Hell, that map you gave us of the interior of the hotel has been a great help. The teams we are training know exactly where to go and what to do once they're inside."

"I'm glad I could help, but we're still suffering in this damn construction site when we could be safe and comfortable in there," Steven insisted. "My wife and I are sharing one very small room here in city hall. It is not acceptable."

"We're sleeping on an air mattress!" Blanche shook her head with disgust. "Manny, you have to do something."

Mayor Reyes sank back in his chair and sighed as he finally raised his gaze. "I defer to Travis and Juan when it comes to construction. They know what they're doing. That's why y'all hired them. As for security, Mike was in the military, and so far, he's done a great job training our folks and keeping us safe."

"That he has," Travis heartily agreed.

Blanche stared at Manny for a tense moment, then poked her husband's arm with one long nail. "They work for you. Tell them what to do, Steven."

"Look here, Travis, Manny, I know y'all got your concerns, but we have our own. Lots of people around here aren't sure y'all are up to the job." Steven's tone was low, firm, and full of the power he was used to wielding.

"If we don't do it, who will?" Travis snapped. The four hours of sleep he had managed the night before were beginning to show. "You? You want to take over construction? Security? Supply-gathering? Rescues? Inventory control?"

Blanche frowned, her brow puckering. "Steven is the man at the top."

Manny unexpectedly chuckled. He had seemed so cowed before that this surprised Travis. "The man at the top of what? I'm sorry, Blanche, but we're all a bunch of tired old sods just trying to live another day in a world gone completely mad. Y'all want into the hotel, well, so do I. But I don't want to push this good man here to do anything he doesn't feel we're ready to handle."

Steven gazed at Manny with a startled expression. "Manny, you know I'm just thinking about all of us."

"No, no. You're thinking about *Blanche*. I don't blame you. She's lovely, and I'm sure you love her very much and want her to be comfortable and safe. But safe is more important than comfortable right now," Manny continued. "So, I say we sit back and let the men and women with the know-how handle all of this."

Travis folded his arms over his chest. Manny's confidence in him made him feel uncomfortable. Every day, Travis just tried to do his best. Lately, he was second-guessing himself just a little. Maybe he was putting off going into the hotel out of fear—but these days, fear kept everyone alive.

Standing up, Blanche nudged her husband again. "Let's go, Steven. Obviously, these two need to get some sense drilled into those thick heads of theirs. Maybe when enough folks complain about them sitting on their asses, they'll finally do something."

Unfolding his tall body from his chair, Steven's expression was grim. "I wish you both would reconsider. I'd really hate to have your leadership qualities become an issue with the fine folks out there."

Raising an eyebrow, Travis wondered if it was the Manns Eric had been referring to earlier. Maybe the couple was already trying to spread discontent and push the fort leadership into action.

Manny spread out his hands. "Do whatever you like, Steven. Just remember that you are both alive and safe because of him." He pointed toward Travis. "You should thank Travis, not tear him down."

Steven didn't answer. Instead he offered his arm to his wife and they left. As the door closed behind them, Travis let out a long, loud yawn.

Manny grinned. "Yeah. I couldn't agree more."

"I've never seen her quite like that. She's usually all peaches and sugar."

"Well, you haven't been on her bad side before. Steven and Blanche have very little patience. I've known them a very long time. Right when they first arrived, I knew they would be trouble after a while. This is a little sooner than I expected, but . . ." Manny rolled his shoulders.

"About the hotel, Manny," Travis started.

"We all want in there, Travis. I won't lie to you. But we're all scared shitless that you'll open up that wall and zombies will come pouring out. I have nightmares about it."

"So do I. That's why I've been so damn cautious about going in."

"I respect you for that," Manny assured Travis. "I do. But at some point, you're going to have to take the risk."

Leaning back in his chair, Travis whistled softly. "Damn."

"Leadership is a bitch, huh?" Manny looked a little cocky, but Travis couldn't blame him. After all, nowadays Manny mostly helped Peggy organize the community's inventory and made small decisions about some of the daily aspects of fort life. The big issues weren't his concern anymore.

"I can't help but think about the people who have volunteered to go into the hotel. If they die, it's on my head," Travis said with a sigh.

"They all volunteered freely, Travis. They made their choice."

"I volunteered," Travis said. "I didn't want them doing anything I wasn't willing to do myself."

"That doesn't surprise me. Now, go get some sleep. Your eyes are so damn red, they make me tired."

Travis slid to his feet and started for the door.

"Hey, Travis," Manny called. Swiveling about on his boot heel, Travis paused in the doorway. "If you need any advice, I'm here for you," Manny assured him.

For the first time since he entered the office, Travis smiled.

"That's good to hear. Now, if I can make it back to my room without being stopped by every single person in the fort . . ."

"Have Peggy run interference for you. She's a killer at it," the mayor advised.

Chuckling, Travis headed out to find Peggy.

3.
No More Time to Wait

Near sunset, Katie pulled laundry from one of the lines strung up in the corner of the construction site. Folding the few pieces of her wardrobe, she tucked them into a banker's box she had snagged from Peggy. It was a far cry from the walk-in closet she'd had in her old home, but it was big enough to hold her meager possessions.

The sky was a lush purple with great swaths of bright pink illuminating the horizon. It was a beautiful evening. The still air was cool against her skin, a relief after the heat of the day.

Balancing the box on her hip, Katie walked up the steps into city hall. She heard voices upstairs and could tell from the snatches of conversation she could make out that people were sitting down to a dinner of fried Spam sandwiches, barbecue beans, and chips. She had never eaten Spam before coming to the fort and still wasn't sure what her final verdict on it was, but at least it kept her from feeling hungry. Edging past a few people tromping down the stairs, she returned their smiles of greeting.

She was almost to her room when she saw Travis leaning against the wall, scarfing down a sandwich.

"There are tables in the dining room, you know," she said.

"Yeah, but they're all full," Travis answered around a mouthful of Spam.

"It's amazing what Rosie can do with the canned goods they bring in, huh?" Katie said, bravely trying to make small talk.

"The best damn sandwich I've had since the last sandwich I

had," Travis answered. He mopped up the beans with the bread and shoveled it into his mouth. "Hey, you volunteered to clean the store. Thanks for that. Lots of people are afraid to head over the wall."

Shrugging, Katie adjusted her hold on her box. "Well, I know that once you give the all clear, it will be safe. I trust you."

"I appreciate that. I don't think everyone shares that sentiment right now."

Katie sighed. "Well, if you mean the Manns, they have been doing a lot of smack talking today. Blanche was really on a roll. She usually doesn't talk to anyone, but today she was sweet as pie to just about everybody."

"Let me guess. I'm not a suitable leader." Travis shook his head and continued to eat.

"Something like that." Katie wasn't about to tell Travis about the war of words she'd gotten into with Blanche Mann. He didn't need to know how passionately she had defended him. It had even shocked her a little.

"I can't let it bother me," Travis decided. "Just have to do what is right. Whatever that is."

"You're sounding more and more like a leader."

"I don't want to be, Katie. I really don't. Once we're into the hotel, I am more than happy to turn over the reins."

"To Steven Mann?"

Travis winced. "Well, maybe not him, but—"

"Hey, Travis, there you are." Curtis's voice came up the stairs, followed by the young police officer himself. "Sorry to bug ya, but something's happened." His expression was sobering, and Katie felt her stomach knot with fear.

"What is it?" Travis asked warily.

"You know that group of survivors all the way out by San Angelo we've been talking to on the ham radio?"

"Yeah," Travis answered, "Reverend Morton's group."

"They're gone," Curtis said plainly. "Wiped out."

"What?" Peggy gasped from behind him. She scrambled up

the last few steps to join the others on the landing. "What are you talking about, Curtis?"

"They're wiped out. Gone."

"Zombies?" Travis asked, his brows drawing together.

"Nope. Tornado," said Curtis. "Got a call in around ten minutes ago saying there was a massive storm slamming them and that one of the guards saw a tornado on the ground near their compound. I heard what sounded like a freight train over the CB, then nothing. Dead air."

Katie winced at his words. It was too horrible to consider.

"Shit," said Peggy. "Shit! There were twenty people there!"

"Where's that storm front heading?" Travis asked worriedly.

"Away from us." Curtis shook his head. "They had a good setup, too. This is sad. Real sad."

"Good ol' bad Texas weather," Peggy grumbled.

"San Angelo is too far away for us to check out, isn't it?" Katie asked.

"Two-and-a-half-hour drive on a normal day," Curtis said. "With the zombies out there, it would take a lot longer."

"Have to bypass a lot of towns. Very risky," Peggy agreed.

Travis let out a sigh. "What was their compound like?"

"Warehouse with a high fence around it. Used to hold farming equipment before the zombocalypse, but they got it fixed up pretty good," Curtis said.

"If the fence came down, where did they plan to go?"

Studying Travis's expression, Katie could see that he was processing everything that was being said. The furrows in his brow were deepening. She wanted to reach out and comfort him. Instead, she held on to her box with an even tighter grip.

"I don't rightly know, Travis. I never discussed it with them," Curtis said. "They were settled in for the long haul. But the tornado did them in."

"Can we be sure?" Peggy asked. "Can we be sure they're gone?"

"They're not answering the radio, and from the sounds I heard, I'm sure it hit them. If they don't get back on the air, I think that pretty much confirms it, right?" Curtis looked to Travis for support.

"I think you're right, Curtis." Travis rubbed his tense brow. "Peggy, I need to talk to Mike and Juan right away. Can you find them?"

"Sure, but why?"

"We're going into the hotel." Travis said, "It's time to take the risk."

"You got it," Peggy said, then pounded down the stairs.

"I better get back," Curtis headed toward the door. "Maybe they got lucky and I'll hear from them."

"Keep me updated," Travis said.

With a nod, Curtis hurried away.

"Are you sure about this?" Katie asked.

Travis nodded sadly. "Yeah, I'm sure."

"Why now? Because of the tornado?"

"Yep," Travis answered honestly.

"I don't get it."

"I just realized that no matter how well you plan, how hard you try to make sure every condition is perfect, in the end, you can't predict everything. We can't possibly know when a tornado is going to set down and wipe out all our hard work. I keep waiting for it all to be perfect, but that just won't happen. Will it?" Travis raised his eyes to stare directly into hers.

Katie averted her gaze and avoided his question. It suddenly felt far too personal.

"That's what I thought," Travis breathed, and walked down the stairs.

Katie turned to watch him leave, wishing she could follow. Once more, she resolved to stay away from him. She wasn't ready to move on. Not yet.

Letting out a sigh, she continued to her room.

· CHAPTER FOUR ·

1.
Plans

Travis admired the new wall as Mike and Juan beamed with pride. "It looks really solid."

"No zombies are coming through this wall. Everything is just like I told you it would be," Mike assured him.

"And we're done a little early," Juan pointed out.

Grinning, Travis said, "Yeah. Great timing. Now we can get the crews in here to clean up the store and get it ready."

"So we're definitely going into the hotel?" Mike lifted his eyebrows.

"Yeah. I've made up my mind. We can't keep second-guessing ourselves. Besides, with the hot weather coming and the storms picking up, we need to get people inside. The Dollar Store is not going to house everyone, and the rest of the stores need too much work to make them livable. So . . . yeah . . . the hotel." Travis folded his arms across his chest and felt his resolve deepen.

Somewhere beyond the walls, out of view, zombies keened and moaned. The sounds sent a shiver down his spine.

Juan pushed his cowboy hat up on his forehead and lit a cigarette. "Okay, so how is this going down?"

"Just like we planned. Evacuate everyone not participating in the hotel operation to the store. Set up guards along the perimeter and then do our magic."

Mike chuckled. "Oh, we're going to need magic if our zombie estimates are off."

"Leave it to zombies not to cooperate," Juan groused.

"Travis, you're not doing this because of the Manns, are you?" Mike jerked his head back toward the construction site. "They're talking a lot of shit, but people know what's what around here."

Shaking his head, Travis answered, "No. No. It was the tornado wiping out the group near San Angelo."

"Curtis told me about that. Damn, that really sucks." Juan took another drag on his cigarette. "Mother Nature is a real whore."

"Well, it made me realize that I was waiting for the perfect moment, and that that's not going to happen." Travis rubbed the back of his neck, trying to work out the big knot that never seemed to quite go away. He felt it tightening as he spoke. "So, it's time."

"My teams are as ready as they'll ever be," Mike said.

Travis cast a look over his shoulder, scrutinizing the new section of the fort. The street was empty and the doors to the Dollar General were propped open. The cleanup crew was hard at work, and soon others would start boxing up the merchandise.

"Back on that first day, I never dreamed that we would end up building a fort," Travis mused.

"So much for revitalizing Ashley Oaks, huh?" Juan smirked.

"Oh, we revitalized it, all right—zombie-survival-style," Mike corrected, high-fiving Juan.

Travis chuckled, shaking his head.

Juan took a long drag on his cigarette, then said, "I know it's hard to believe, but things are looking a lot better than they were back then. My cousin Monica made it here, all the way from El Paso."

Travis felt a little embarrassed that he hadn't known that. "That's great!" He clapped Juan on the back.

"Yeah, one of our teams found her at a fuel station. She escaped El Paso and crossed the freakin' desert to get here. She's a tough *chica*," Juan said proudly.

"Too bad her cousin is a pussy," Mike joked, elbowing Juan.

"Dude, she could kick your ass," Juan declared.

A call of "Hey, guys!" broke up the good-natured tussle. The men looked over to see Belinda climbing down a ladder. Mike's girlfriend had a tote bag slung over one shoulder. Her long hair billowed around her face as Mike rushed over to lift her down the last few rungs. Laughing as her boyfriend carried her over to Travis and Juan, Belinda waved.

"Rosie sent you guys some lunch," Belinda said, holding out the tote bag.

"Tacos!" Juan gasped with delight. "I love her tacos! Mom makes the best!"

Travis snagged a couple of the foil-wrapped tacos before Mike and Belinda walked off to eat together in the shade of the new wall. "Oh, the tacos are still hot."

Shoving half a taco in his mouth, Juan savored the flavor. "I love my mom."

Unwrapping one, Travis took a big bite. "Delicious. And I am glad to hear about your cousin, Juan."

"After losing Sergio 'cause of that asshole Ritchie, it's good to know his sister is okay. We lived right next door to each other growing up. They were like my brother and sister. It makes me feel good to have more family here." As he chewed, Juan glanced at Belinda, his unrequited love since grade school. "She looks happy."

"I think she is," Travis agreed. "But so are you."

"I wouldn't trade my *loca* for the world," Juan said swiftly. "I'm over Belinda for good." He looked sharply at Travis. "How are things with Katie?"

Travis shrugged.

Juan shook his head. "You and the unobtainable woman. It's your disease, man."

"I'm not that bad," Travis declared. "Besides, I'm okay with just being friends."

"Right. I don't believe that for a second." Juan shoved more taco in his mouth. "Tomorrow is going to be a bitch."

"Let's just get through today," Travis requested. "We'll worry about tomorrow when it gets here."

"I couldn't agree more," Juan said. "But tomorrow is still going to be a bitch."

On the other side of the wall, the zombies continued to moan.

2.
Facing Reality

Peggy swore for the third time in as many minutes as she double-checked her inventory lists.

"My brain has gone to shit," she muttered. The stack of requests on her desk was getting thicker. Some people needed very specific medications; others were hoping for a small indulgence. Peggy kept two lists for the salvage teams: one was necessities; the other, luxuries, to be acquired only if circumstances permitted. She had forgotten to add feminine napkins to the list of necessities for the second time in a week. Hopefully the Dollar Store would be a good source of necessities and luxuries, even if she wasn't looking forward to inventorying all that merchandise.

Beside her, Cody played quietly with his toys. He was a sensitive child, and it had taken weeks for him to start playing with the other children in the fort. Peggy considered that a tremendous breakthrough, but since he'd overheard some chatter about the hotel and the zombie threat, he'd become fearful again and was refusing to leave her side.

"Peggy, do you mind if we talk?"

Forcing her gaze from her work, Peggy was surprised to see Yolanda Roccaforte, the widow of the former city manager, standing beside her. After Tobias Roccaforte's death, Yolanda hadn't risen from her bed except to eat. The days of weeping showed on her face. The fine skin around her brown eyes was swollen. Her dark skin looked unusually sallow, making the light smattering of freckles over her nose and cheeks more pronounced. Though she was nearing fifty, Yolanda still had a girlish way about her, from her slim figure to her tousled, chin-length hair.

"Sure. How can I help you?" Peggy tried not to sound gruff, but there was a little bit of bad blood between them.

Yolanda sank down into the chair across from Peggy. "I know I haven't been much help around here since Tobias died, and I would like to change that."

Peggy raised her eyebrows. "Oh?"

"I know that when we came to town, there was some tension between you and my husband."

Peggy snorted despite herself. "That's putting it lightly."

Yolanda bristled. "I know Tobias wasn't too nice to you at times, but he was worried about losing his job. We lost everything in Hurricane Rita, and moving from Beaumont to Ashley Oaks was rough on both of us. We were blessed that our children followed us here, but it wasn't easy at first, being among strangers."

Peggy settled back in her chair and shrugged lightly. "It wasn't easy for anyone."

"Well, Ashley Oaks going from a town with hardly any African-Americans to us nearly taking up twenty-five percent must have thrown y'all quite a bit." Yolanda's gaze was steady.

"We ain't racist in this town," Peggy answered defensively. "We weren't used to y'all's ways. And I don't mean because you're black, but because you're a bunch of East Texans."

Yolanda laughed briefly. "I know how much the rest of Texas looks down on us for being Southern hicks."

"Well, you are almost the same as Louisianans," Peggy said, smiling for real. "Anyway, most of the people in this town don't really give a rat's ass about skin color as long as you're not a dumbass. It's a 'live and let live' kinda thing. Tobias and I didn't get along, because when the city council hired him, we both know they were catering to the evacuees to make y'all feel at home—but it still meant that my job was on the line. I was sure that the city council would ask why they had both a city secretary and a city manager. So, no, I didn't look too kindly at Tobias at that time, but it wasn't 'cause his skin was darker than mine."

"Plainly spoken and the truth," Yolanda said. "But Tobias just wanted to fit in here. Same as me. We just wanted a new start. We missed Beaumont something fierce, but Rita took away more than our home. It killed our jobs and left us with barely any choices. Tobias getting the job here was our new beginning, and it was good until . . ." Tears sprang to the other woman's eyes and she dabbed at them with a well-used tissue.

Peggy felt all her belligerence slide away as the other woman tried not to weep. Grabbing a fresh tissue from her desk drawer, she thrust it at Yolanda. "I'm so sorry. I was mad as hell at him, but I didn't want him to die."

Gratefully, Yolanda took Peggy's offering and wiped away her tears. "I miss him so much. He just couldn't believe our whole family was dead and gone. I struggle with their loss, too. I miss them, too. Sometimes I even think I see Tobias out of the corner of my eye. . . ." She sighed. "But I have to move on." She sat up and faced Peggy squarely. "I know Rosie is handling food distribution and you do just about everything else. I want to help. I was an office manager back home, and I know a thing or two about organization."

The thought of someone helping her was thrilling, but at the same time, Peggy felt a little panicked. She had her systems and was set in her ways. Her fingers played with the edges of the legal pad in front of her as she pondered Yolanda's words. Slowly, she realized she couldn't say no. Exhaustion and overwork were making her careless—and the survivors in the fort couldn't afford for her to make any more mistakes.

"I think we can work something out," she answered. "You could start with this. It's the supply list. I'm having trouble keeping track of all the requests."

Yolanda grinned, relief sweeping the tension from her features. "Oh, that sounds good. I'd like that."

"We're also going to have to inventory the merchandise coming out of the Dollar Store. I'll need help with that."

"Sounds good." Yolanda suddenly reached across the desk and grabbed Peggy's hand. Her palm was damp and her fingers a little cold, but Peggy didn't draw away. "Thank you, Peggy. You've done good work here, and I just want to help. I have to start doing something or I'm going to lose my mind."

Squeezing Yolanda's hand, Peggy felt tears spring to her eyes. "Then I'll keep you so busy, you're gonna wish you hadn't volunteered."

"Can we be friends, Ms. Peggy?"

"Yes, we can, Ms. Yolanda," Peggy answered, and meant it.

3.
Packing Up and Moving On

"It still smells like zombie in here," Stacey muttered under her breath. The too-slim younger woman made a face and rubbed her pert nose.

"Zombie and bleach," Katie amended with a wry grin.

"Sounds like a drink almost." Stacey laughed and puffed air up at her flyaway bangs. She was packing the contents of a shelf: boxed dinners and cans of soup. The store bustled with activity as the shelves were emptied into boxes.

"Yeah, in some freaky bar down on Sixth Street in good ol' Austin, Texas." Katie grinned at the thought and continued clearing the shelf. Sweat was trickling down her back and beaded on her forehead. Katie had no idea when the Dollar Store's air-conditioning had failed, but it had been long enough ago that the store was stifling. A couple of the men on the recovery team had discovered that the breaker had been tripped. They'd flipped it back, and now the air conditioner was humming loudly, but it would take some time to cool the store down to a comfortable temperature.

Stacey sighed ruefully. "The good ol' days."

Katie's smile faded. "Yeah. The days of yore."

"In the B.Z."

"Before Zombie?" Katie arched an eyebrow.

"Yeah," Stacey answered. She taped the box shut and scrounged around for the black marker they were using to mark the contents of the boxes on the outside flap.

"I can't wait for the A.Z., then," Katie said.

It was nearly two in the afternoon and they had been working for hours. Katie's legs were aching and her arms felt bruised.

"Sometimes it doesn't feel real. Sometimes it feels like just yesterday I was a coach at an elementary school, refereeing dodgeball and hoping the bullies didn't kill the nerds," Stacey said in a sentimental tone.

"I know the feeling," Katie replied as she taped her box closed. "It just . . . changed so fast. One second the world was normal, and the next it was all wrong."

"One second people you loved were alive, and the next . . ." Stacey shook her head, as if to shake the bad thoughts from her mind. "At least here we're safe, or as safe as it gets."

Katie shoved her box onto the pallet behind her, stretching her back. Stacey glanced toward Eric and Travis as they walked by. The men were talking earnestly and gesturing around them. Stacey shot Katie a bemused look and Katie quirked her eyebrow upward.

"When they talk engineering and architecture, I have no idea what they are saying," Stacey confessed.

"You and me both." Katie wiped more sweat from her face. She was wearing gloves to prevent cutting her hands. They felt obscenely warm.

"Don't get me wrong. I'm glad Eric is involved with fort business, but sometimes I just wish—" She let out long sigh. "—you know, sometimes I wish we could just relax. But it's always about scrambling to be safer, scrambling to survive, scrambling to anticipate every little thing that could go wrong."

"I've been thinking about that lately," Katie confessed, "that maybe we'll never know real peace ever again. You know, that feeling that the world is safe and sane, that there will be food on the table, a job to go to, a loved one to curl up with at night." Lydia and their beautiful home once again filled her mind.

"I guess if that's true, then we should hold tight to any little bit of happiness we find," Stacey said, glancing at Eric once more. Katie knew from what Stacey had told her that they had fallen slowly in love with each other as they struggled to survive. "I guess, maybe, just being here with him is enough."

Katie found herself watching Travis. "Maybe," she said at last. "Maybe." She quickly filled the next box, stacking cans neatly inside.

Stacey lifted her now-sealed box onto the pallet behind them and reached for a new empty box from a stack nearby.

"Hey," Travis said as he joined them. "You two have been in here long enough. Why don't you finish up those boxes and take a break?"

"Thanks, Travis." Stacey swept the remaining casserole boxes into the box with one stroke of her arm. "Done!"

Travis laughed and helped her tape up the box and heave it onto the pallet.

"See you on the next shift. I'm going to go sunbathe," Stacey said to Katie, then jogged out of the store into the bright sunlight.

Hurrying to stack cans, Katie expected Travis to move on, but instead he squatted down next to her and helped her pack the box. She didn't know what to say, but it felt awkward not to talk to him. She searched for words, but the ones that filled her mind were not ones she was ready to say.

"It looks like we'll be able to get this area secure by tonight," he said, "so we can go into the hotel tomorrow or the following day."

"I'm looking forward to having my own room. I adore Nerit, but I need my own space," Katie confessed.

"It is hard to find actual alone time around here, isn't it? But it's kinda lonely at the same time."

She finally looked up at him and saw his hazel eyes were staring at her flushed face. "I'm sorry." It was all she could think to say.

Travis started to say one thing, then visibly changed his mind. He closed his mouth, thought for a second, then said, "I just want to be your friend."

"No, you don't," Katie corrected him in a soft voice. She was painfully aware of all the people in the store, packing boxes, breaking down shelves, and cleaning up. This was not a conversation she wanted overheard and repeated around the fort.

He winced. "But I can settle for being your friend." He closed the carton and reached for the tape.

Katie rested her hands on the box and leaned toward him. "I need time to think."

"Being friends with me is not a threat to your memory of your wife," Travis countered.

She couldn't reply without giving herself away, so she busied herself by grabbing the marker and labeling the box in bold letters. She could feel Travis searching her expression, seeking to understand. It made her nervous. She wanted him to walk away before he figured it out.

"Or is it?" he speculated.

Her green eyes flicked upward, and she saw that he was suspicious of her silence. Maybe something in her gaze gave her away, because he took her gloved hand in his. She yanked away, but only managed to pull her hand out of the glove. Travis caught her fingers gently and held her hand, apparently not caring that it was covered in sweat.

"Katie, I'm not a threat to the memory of your wife, am I?" Travis asked in a whisper.

The tears in her eyes and lump in her throat made it hard to speak. At last she was able to say, "Please . . ."

The word could mean many different things, but, surprisingly, Travis seemed to understand. "Okay."

There was a spark of hope in his gaze now, and she averted

her eyes quickly. She knew that in that moment, she had opened the door to her heart. Just a crack, but she was terrified.

"I better go check on how things are going," Travis said after a beat. He let go of her, then pulled a bag of M&M's from his shirt pocket and handed it to her. "Sorry it's a bit mushy. I have a feeling there will be a run on the chocolate soon, so I thought you might like this."

Katie couldn't help but smile despite herself. "Giving me chocolates now, huh?"

"I'm just a romantic." He winked.

Her gaze followed him as he walked away. She looked down at the bag of candy and happily tore it open.

4.
Safety in Twos

Juan handed Jenni a big bag of tortilla chips. Seated on the wall, side by side, they could see the final shift mopping the floor of the Dollar Store. Night had come and the air was cool as it ruffled their hair and dried the sweat on their tanned limbs.

"Are we really done?" Jenni yanked open the top of the bag and pulled out a chip. The smell was amazing and she breathed it in deeply.

"Yep. Eric gave the okay on the bricked-up windows and the reinforced doors. And it doesn't smell so much like zombie in there anymore," Juan said with a grin.

"Yum. The smell of Doritos is so much better." Jenni munched a chip with relish.

Juan laughed and shook his head. "Ah, the simple things in life."

"Are we going in tomorrow morning?" Jenni looked over her shoulder at the dark countenance of the hotel.

"Travis is going to make the call after he inspects the new area one more time. He's really nervous about all this. He hates the idea of putting anyone at risk. He even put himself on one of the teams to go into the hotel."

"Travis hates guns," Jenni said in disbelief.

"Yeah, but he's doing that whole thing where the leader won't ask his people to do what he won't do." Juan shrugged. "Since I've known him, he's been like that. He's annoyingly good at times."

"Not a bad boy like you, huh?" Jenni elbowed her boyfriend and stuffed another Dorito into her mouth.

Juan pulled off his cowboy hat and smoothed his hair with one hand. "Yeah, he can't stand up to my cool factor."

Jenni smirked as she leaned her head on his shoulder. A red-headed newcomer named Katarina was standing sentry nearby. Jenni didn't know her well, but knew she was a good shot. As more people came into the fort, the dynamic was changing, from primarily locals from Ashley Oaks to a mix of people from all the towns in the area. So far, each new arrival contributed in some way that benefited everyone. Jenni thought it was good to have diversity. Jenni's contribution was as the crazy zombie killer, and she was fine with that. She crunched another chip.

It felt good to be on the brink of something new and big. The fort was about to grow in a dynamic way. Taking the hotel would change everything. Unless they failed. But then again, that would change everything.

"You be careful in there," Juan said softly, staring at her face. His finger lightly slid down the bridge of her nose. "Nothing wild, okay. I know you're *loca,* but try to curb your natural *loca* tendencies."

Jenni grinned at him. "I know I'll come back alive. I've got too much to live for. Like giving you hell and eating Doritos." She tossed a chip into her mouth. He laughed and slid an arm around her waist.

Jenni savored the flavor of the tortilla chip and the feel of Juan's arm around her. She had no intention of dying. There was no way in hell she was going to let a zombie get her. Not now, when she had a new family, when she wanted to be with Juan forever. That was worth fighting for. Looking toward the swarthy man with the dark green eyes, she grinned.

"Let's go have sex," she said, and shoved the bag into his hand. Before the startled man could react, Jenni climbed down the ladder into the construction site.

"Uh, what? Okay!" Juan scrambled after her, abandoning the chips.

At the bottom of the ladder, he caught her up in his arms and threw her over his shoulders. Both of them laughed as he carried her to their makeshift tent.

• CHAPTER FIVE •

1.
The New Season

The sun was barely peeking over the edge of the fort's walls at six thirty in the morning, when Katie set out on her daily jog. Her hair was up in a ponytail and she wore a T-shirt, jogging shorts, and brand-new jogging shoes. Peggy and the mayor inventoried everything brought into the fort during the scavenging expeditions, then meticulously laid out everything in boxes and bins and opened a store of sorts in the basement of city hall. No currency was exchanged; instead you had to sign for anything you took. Katie had been surprised to find a box of jogging shoes and even more surprised to find a pair that fit.

Katie started on her trek around the fort, enjoying the brisk morning air as it nipped at her cheeks. Before long, summer would be in full swing and the mornings would be balmy. She was on her second lap around the fort when Jenni joined her, dressed in jeans, a red tank top, and her boots. Glancing at her friend, Katie saw that the younger woman was glowing with something other than the cool morning air. Jenni grinned.

"God, I think I hate you, Jenni! Every freakin' night?"

Jenni laughed as she easily matched her pace. "Yeah, so?"

"I almost feel bad for Juan," Katie said.

"Yeah, I'm pretty brutal. I don't know how he puts up with me."

"You're *loca,* and he loves *loca,*" Katie reminded her.

Jenni's expression said it all. She was wonderfully in love, and

Katie was happy for her. "I hope you find someone soon, Katie. It makes this life easier."

Katie just shrugged and kept running.

"I know there aren't any lesbians in the fort, but you know, you have options," Jenni offered cautiously.

Katie shrugged again. She debated opening up to Jenni. Her best friend could be terribly blunt and loud at times. If Katie confided in her, there was a good chance that everyone in the fort would know her business fairly quickly.

Jenni frowned as they took another corner. "Look, I know nothing about lesbians. I never even watched *The L Word*. But haven't you ever kissed a boy?"

That made Katie laugh out loud. "Lots, actually." There, it was out. She had said it.

"So you tried guys out? Before you realized you were a lesbian?" Jenni raised her eyebrow.

"I'm not a lesbian," Katie said, deciding to fess up.

Jenni's eyebrows arched even higher. "Huh?"

"I'm bi," Katie answered.

"Huh?" Jenni looked confused. She almost ran into a pile of concrete bricks, but Katie yanked her out of the way. "What does that mean?"

"I find both men and women attractive. I just happened to end up with a really fabulous lesbian woman instead of a really fabulous straight man. The odds usually work against that. There are more straight men than lesbians, so a lot of bisexual women end up getting married to men. But Lydia was the right one for me."

Jenni's eyes widened, her mouth dropped open, and she made an *oh* sound that lasted for a few seconds. She smacked Katie on the arm. "Then you do have options, you bitch! Travis!"

Katie smacked her back. "Shut up!"

"No, seriously! If you like both guys and girls, you have options! Real options!" Jenni had the mad gleam of a matchmaker in her eyes.

"I don't want him to know that I'm bi or that I have some feelings for him," Katie said decisively. She almost regretted telling Jenni, but it had felt good to tell the truth. "At least, not now."

"You have feelings for him?" Jenni grabbed Katie's arm and dragged her to a stop. "Oh, my gawd! You have feelings for Travis!"

"But he can't know, so keep it down!"

Jenni twisted up her face, confused. "Why not? I mean, I'm relieved. I was afraid you'd be alone for the rest of your life unless some hot lesbian came along."

Katie sighed. "Just because you put two lesbians in a room, that does not mean they'll hook up. Well, unless you go with the second-date U-Haul theory . . ."

"What's that?"

"What does a lesbian bring to a second date?"

"Oh . . . a U-Haul. That's funny!" Jenni giggled. "So lesbians move fast."

"That's not what we're talking about!"

"Okay, but I mean, well, you have options! You can have Travis!" Jenni was almost jumping up and down with excitement. "Katie, I'm so happy!"

Katie felt her stomach tighten nervously. "I don't want options right now. I just . . ." She trailed off.

"She's gone, Katie," Jenni said sorrowfully. "You're still here."

"I know. But I just can't forget her and move on. Even if I do—" Katie wiped a tear from her eye. "—even if I do have feelings for Travis. I don't want to talk about this."

Jenni sighed. She reached out and touched Katie's shoulder gently. "I just want you happy. Is it wrong for you to be happy?"

Katie shook her head. "I don't know if I can be, without her. I loved her so much, Jenni. When I met her, I just knew she was the one. When I met Travis—" She closed her eyes and shook her head. "It felt . . . similar. Not the same, but like he was important to me and to my future. Maybe I'm just admitting it to myself now, but I think I sorta fell for him. I sorta knew somewhere in the back of my mind that he was going to be my new love. . . ." She couldn't continue; her emotions swirled and her throat closed.

Jenni threw her arms around Katie, nearly crashing them both into the ground. "It's okay, it's okay," Jenni assured her. "At least you know that you're not alone and that people love you. And he'll wait until you're ready. You know that."

"I'm so grateful to have you," Katie whispered. She kissed Jenni's cheek. "You're a good friend."

Jenni whispered back, "I love you."

2.
Shelter from the Storm

Stacey held the squirming Jack Russell terrier firmly in her arms as Bill and Ed helped her over the wall. Eric climbed up behind her and she could feel him reaching out to steady her with one hand. Pepe was not happy and she didn't blame him. Though the new area was well fortressed, she felt vulnerable outside the construction site.

A big black girl, Lenore, reached up to help her with Pepe as she climbed down the second ladder into the new area. Lenore's best friend and constant companion, Ken, stood nearby, clutching the cat carrier that held his ticked-off cat, Cher. The sun glinted off the gold highlights in his dark hair and sweat beaded his tanned skin. The two friends were complete opposites of each other: Lenore homely, chubby, a bit sloppy, and always grumpy while Ken was cute, fit, immaculately dressed and always in a good mood. Lenore often told people she was Eeyore and Ken was Tigger. Stacey had to agree with that analogy.

Most of the survivors from the fort were climbing into the new area. The elderly and disabled were being lifted over the wall on a pallet being hefted by the construction site's big crane. Old Man Watson looked a little befuddled, but he gave Stacey a thumbs-up when he saw her looking his way. Stacey reached the street and turned to watch people settling into the Dollar Store. She hoped the smell—a terrible combination of zombie and bleach—was gone.

Peggy, the city secretary, and her little boy, Cody, reached the street just as Stacey did. Cody was crying softly and the sound of his whimpering made Stacey feel even more nervous. His mother looked tense and worried as she tried in vain to comfort her child.

"The zombies are going to eat us," Cody sobbed.

"No, honey. They can't reach us here. We're okay. I promise," Peggy assured him, but she appeared just as unnerved as her child to be outside the construction site.

"I wanna go back! I wanna go back!"

Peggy wrestled her child into her arms, casting a nervous look toward Stacey before hurrying across the street to the store.

"It's going to be fine, honey," Eric said as he reached the ground. He pressed a soft kiss onto her cheek. Pushing his glasses up on his nose, he looked around warily. "We made damn sure this area is secure. We'll be fine."

"You can't blame me for being nervous," Stacey answered. She slid her arms around his waist and leaned against him. The love she felt for him pulsed hard inside her, and she felt a lump in her throat.

His laid his arm over her shoulders, his fingers stroking her skin. "No, I can't. But we'll be okay. I promise."

"I cannot wait until this is over," Ken said, and pouted slightly. His cat yowled as if in agreement.

Lenore set Pepe down, holding firmly to his leash. Pepe zigzagged back and forth in front of her. "It'll be done soon enough, and we'll have nice beds to sleep in tonight. I need some good sleep. So sick of that damn cot."

"We can be roommates!" Ken clapped his hands excitedly.

Lenore narrowed her eyes, mouth pursing in disapproval. "Oh, no! I am so not putting up with listening to you talk in your sleep about how hot Daniel Craig is. Besides, aren't you supposed to be inside the fort, helping Juan? Gimme Cher and get back to work, slacker."

Ken handed over the cat carrier, giving Lenore a mock-disdainful look. "You're so mean."

"Move it," Lenore ordered gruffly. "Go do something productive with your white ass."

"Good luck, Ken!" Eric called out as the younger man made his way back up over the wall.

Ken posed cutely on the ladder. "I will stun and amaze all with my mad skills!"

"You're a gopher," Lenore said. "Like that's hard."

"Bitch," Ken sniffed, and hurried away.

"He better not screw this up," Lenore groused.

Stacey couldn't shake the knot in her stomach.

"We'll be okay," Eric repeated, but she could see the fear in his eyes.

"Zombies don't got a chance against this crew. We're tough," Lenore said. "We're mean. We're nasty. Plus, Ken could talk them to death."

Stacey laughed and took Pepe's leash from Lenore. The terrier danced around her feet, looking up at her anxiously. Together, Stacey, Eric, and the dog walked toward the Dollar Store.

Overhead, the skies opened and it started rain.

3.
The Waiting Room

Peggy found an open spot in a corner of the Dollar Store and sank down on a cot resting against the wall. Holding her trembling son against her chest, she tried to calm her wildly beating heart. She couldn't believe she was outside the fort. She didn't care what Mike said about the walls—she was terribly afraid.

The murmurs of conversation around her were slightly comforting as other groups found places to hunker down and wait. A few people were already trying to sleep, while others were playing card games or chatting.

Rocking Cody, Peggy drew in a deep breath and slowly let it slip out between her lips, trying to settle her nerves. Nearby, Lenore and Stacey played with the little Jack Russell terrier as Eric conversed with a few of the older men not involved in the day's activities.

"It smells like bleach in here," a familiar voice bitched. "Have someone do something about that, Steven."

Blanche Mann carefully maneuvered through the gathering, her high-heeled boots clicking loudly against the floor. At least she was wearing jeans and not her usual short skirt.

"I'll see what I can do, sugar," Steven assured her. "At least we'll be in the hotel soon."

"It's about time Travis listened to you," Blanche said loudly, smiling with satisfaction.

Peggy was about to say something nasty when Yolanda sat next to her on the cot.

"Mind if I sit here with you?"

Peggy shook her head, trying not to let the sound of Blanche's voice rub her last nerve raw. "I could use the company."

"So could I." Yolanda tilted her head to study Cody. She frowned slightly at the sight of the six-year-old sucking his thumb, but Peggy was grateful when she didn't comment. If it made Cody feel better to revert to babyish ways, Peggy would allow it. Yolanda smiled at Cody and gently brushed his hair with her fingers. "It's a little frightening being on this side of the wall, isn't it? But there are new walls to keep out the monsters, so we'll be fine." Yolanda lightly touched Cody's cheek, smiling at him. "I saw men and women with big guns ready to kill them."

"I want to go back," Cody whispered.

"We will. When it's safe. Then we'll have a nice new home in the hotel," Yolanda assured him.

"That's what Mama says," Cody admitted with a sigh.

"And she's right."

"Can I have your attention, please?" Mayor Reyes called out as he stepped up on a chair in the center of the store.

The din quieted down as people twisted around in their seats to view the mayor. Peggy smiled, knowing Manny was quite good at this sort of thing.

"As you all know, Juan and the construction crews worked long hours to secure this area for us, so we can wait in comfort and safety while the hotel operation is under way. Steven Mann provided valuable information about the hotel that helped us plan. Mike did a fine job training the people who have stepped up to put their lives on the line for all of us—the volunteers who are going into the hotel at eight this morning." Manny smiled and waited for the smattering of applause to die down before continuing.

"Another brave group of volunteers will enter the hotel and fortify the bottom floor. And I know that a large number of you have offered to clean up the hotel once it's been cleared of the zombie threat, while others have asked me what they can do to help out since they don't have a direct role in today's events."

Peggy would have called the people too scared to volunteer a bunch of chickenshits, but the mayor was much more diplomatic than she was. Of course, the very old, the infirm, and small children were not able to contribute. Peggy gave them a free pass.

Mayor Reyes continued: "I know it's hard to stand by and wait while people you love and care about do the hard jobs. Let's all join in a prayer to our Creator, asking him to protect our volunteers and their souls. We're a God-fearing town, and I think it only right that we take this moment to bow our heads and pray together as one."

Around Peggy, people were nodding. Yolanda muttered, "Amen."

"So, please join me for a minute of silence and pray in whatever way you wish." Manny lowered his chin, closed his eyes, and clasped his hands together.

Peggy didn't feel much like praying, but she closed her eyes, too. Her eyes felt hot and tearful and she stifled a small sob. Yolanda's hand settled over hers. Peggy couldn't focus her thoughts into a coherent prayer. She just kept thinking, *Please, God, please,* over and over until Manny said, "Amen."

"Amen," echoed the survivors.

"Thank you, Jesus," Yolanda said under her breath.

"And now to wait," Peggy muttered.

"It will all be okay. One way or the other," Yolanda said.

Peggy could only hope she was right.

4.
Check-in Time

Nerit strode up onto the platform overlooking the designated point of entry to the hotel. Clad in her old jeans, a button-down shirt, and Ralph's hunting jacket, she was warm, despite the cool, damp wind gusting through the small fort. Her yellowish white hair was tied back from her face. Her senses felt sharp and her vision keen.

She felt like killing.

"Almost eight, Nerit," Mike called out from below. "You ready to go?"

"That I am," Nerit replied.

In Israel, things had been rough when the nation was first created after the Second World War. Then, she had fought bravely and with pride in her fledgling country. Not only was she a brilliant marksman, but she also had the cool detachment needed to be a sniper. Her almost eerie ability to nail any target from a great distance had given her an illustrious reputation.

Some had called her one of the most calculating and aloof women they had ever met. In reality, she was just good at her job. There were moments when she was haunted by the people she had killed and by the people she had seen killed, and sometimes there were nightmares, but she had always tried to stay focused on the greater good. Defending Israel had been her priority, and she had done her job well.

Nerit still killed with skill and cold detachment, but she no longer had nightmares about those she shot. After all, she was living in a nightmare. Now she destroyed not terrorists, or the enemies of her homeland, but the undead citizens of her adopted country. America had fallen. This fort was Nerit's new home, and the zombies were the enemy.

She lit a cigarette, taking a drag, and exhaled the smoke in a long plume. She was already in a dispassionate mode where the world was gray and devoid of anything other than her pulse and breath.

She was elevated above the construction site so she could see easily into the brick pen they had built around the old entrance to the hotel. The walls were high enough to keep any zombies from getting into the fort. An old wrought iron gate was the doorway into the small courtyard. The pen was as safe as it could be.

The construction crew that had volunteered to brick up the doors and windows in the front of the hotel huddled together under the makeshift tarp tents erected over the equipment. Wheelbarrows were set aside for fresh cement, while the bricks that would be used to secure the bottom floor were piled up on pallets that were already hitched to pallet jacks. The men and women who had volunteered to act as sentries sipped steaming coffee under another tarp as they watched the morning activities.

Dark gray clouds slid through the blue sky, briefly obscuring the bright sun as drops of rain fell on the fort. In the distance, almost-black clouds spoke of a violent storm, but Nerit ignored the weather. Slipping into position, she relished the feel of the cold metal of her sniper rifle in her hands. Closing one eye, she became one with the gun; the sight became their mutual eye, harsh and unblinking. She could easily see everyone gathering to go in. She could see the bricked-up entrance.

She was ready.

Travis was not ready. His stomach was in knots and his hands wouldn't stop sweating. Looking around at the people gathered in small tight groups around him, he felt panicked.

What if hundreds of those things had somehow gotten into

the hotel? What hope would they have of holding them off? The small walled-in enclosure abruptly seemed so inadequate.

Travis glanced up at Nerit. She looked calm, deadly, and ready. His gaze flicked to Juan, who was talking intently to Jenni. Travis knew Juan was very worried about Jenni helping clear out the hotel, and he understood why. Jenni was excellent at zombie killing, but the situation was fraught with danger.

Katie was standing nearby, also preparing to enter the hotel. Travis knew she was a good shot and had more experience dealing with zombies up close than just about anyone, but that didn't keep him from being worried sick. He had confidence in her abilities, but still he felt a sense of dread. He had come close to losing her too many times before.

After their surprising kiss a few weeks ago, Katie had drawn far away from him. That stung him, though he tried to understand. Then, yesterday, she had given him hope. When she had whispered *please* to him, he took it as a sign that she wanted time to deal with the feelings she had for him. He had seen something surprising and encouraging in her eyes. He was willing to give her time, but now that they were going into a dangerous situation, he craved one last significant moment with her.

Mike, the man in charge, moved to the center of his groups. He had taken the people who had volunteered and made them into effective fighting units. If he was worried, he wasn't showing it. His dark skin was beaded with sweat and rain, but he looked strong and unafraid.

"Remember to stay with your group. Stick to your predetermined route. If you meet with a large amount of zombies, call for reinforcements. You are not to return to the fort until the hotel is clear. If you feel you're going to be overrun, start climbing and go to a higher floor.

"We know that the power is off and has been off since an energy surge on the second day after the zombies rose. We expect to eventually restore power to the hotel, but for now, it is still dark, and with the storm coming in, it's going to be very gloomy in there. The good news is that this is Texas, so that storm will be in and out of here fairly quick. Just don't let it distract you.

"Keep your eyes open and remember to sweep each area carefully with your flashlight. Remember how we practiced clearing the rooms? Take up your positions and don't let your guard down. We've got twelve hours of daylight. Let's not waste any of it."

His voice was firm, intent, and commanding. Travis could see people responding to Mike with deep respect despite their fear. Maybe, once they were settled in the hotel, Travis could find a way to fade into the background and let Mike take over. The other man definitely had the leadership abilities Travis felt he lacked.

Once Mike finished rallying his troops, everyone stepped back to let the first two volunteers, Jimmy and Roger, step up and unlock the wrought iron gate of the small courtyard. Travis watched anxiously, feeling sweat starting to trickle from his brow down his cheeks. This was the moment he had been dreading for weeks now.

The workers gave the thumbs-up to Mike, entered the small area, and locked the gate behind them. Taking turns with sledgehammers, the two men chipped away the bricks, creating a small hole about shoulder high in the wall. The sound of the hammers filled the hushed silence of the fort. With one last blow, Jimmy punched through the bricks and cement. As the hard little bits of the wall crumbled away and the dust cleared, the hole—around two feet wide and two feet high—stood stark and black against the red wall.

"We're through," Jimmy said with a smile.

Travis wiped the sweat from his brow and cast a glance in Katie's direction. She was biting her bottom lip as she watched the events unfolding.

"What's inside?" Juan called out.

Roger cautiously leaned forward to peer in through the gap in the wall. A hand lashed out of the hole. Roger yelled and jumped back. A torn, gray, black mottled face came into view, teeth gnashing.

"Get back!" Mike ordered.

Bill unlocked the gate and pulled it open. Jimmy and Roger dashed out. Once they were clear, Bill slammed the gate, locked it, and backed away.

The creature snarling behind the broken wall was Travis's nightmare. What if there were more inside? The zombie's head jerked back as a nice round hole appeared in the center of its forehead, oozing black blood over its suddenly limp features.

Travis was shocked, then realized what had happened. He glanced over to where Nerit was poised for another shot.

The zombie hung awkwardly in the hole, caught on the bricks by its chin; then a skinless hand appeared from behind it, desperately reaching toward the humans. Struggling to get past the other zombie, the new one grunted and growled until the truly dead zombie was dislodged and fell away into the darkness. Triumphant, the new zombie thrust its head through the gap. A bullet hole was punched through its forehead and it dropped out of sight.

A third zombie appeared, this one feminine. Blond hair clung to the dried blood on its face. Someone screamed in horror, "Natalie!" then the zombie's head snapped back and she, too, was gone.

They all waited and watched. Travis could feel rain trickling down the sides of his face.

The broken opening remained empty.

Bill unlocked the gate and entered the courtyard, rifle in hand. He flicked on a flashlight, shone it into the room, and gingerly peered in.

"Check the floor!" someone shouted.

"Clear! Inside door appears to be locked." Stepping back, Bill motioned for Roger and Jimmy to finish the job.

As the sledgehammers busted through the wall, creating a more sizable entrance, Travis started walking toward Katie. As he neared, he could tell that she was tightening her grip on her gun.

"I wanted to talk to you before we go in," he started.

She didn't answer, just nodded slightly.

He regarded her intently. "If anything happens to me . . . if I'm bitten—"

"I will," Katie promised. "You'll do the same for me?"

"Yes," he swore with a hitch in his voice.

Katie stood on her toes and kissed his rough cheek. Her lips lingered near his ear. "We'll be okay."

He breathed in the scent of her hair and skin and looked into her eyes as she drew away. "We will?"

"Yeah," she answered.

He almost kissed her, but the moment was shattered when Nerit strode past them, smoking a cigarette.

"Let's go clear it out, children. Daylight's burning."

5.
Breakfast Is Served

"Let's go zombie killing," Jenni said with a wild grin of delight. Throwing one arm about Juan's neck, she drew him down for a long, smoldering kiss. When she let go of him, she hugged a very surly Jason.

"Loca, be careful," Juan said urgently. His fingers trailed along the nape of her neck lovingly. "Please, don't be too *loca*."

"No worries. Seriously, I'll be fine." She gave him a reassuring smile without letting go of her son.

"Mom," Jason said, his voice cracking.

"It's okay," Jenni assured him with a kiss on his forehead.

"Mom, just don't be *loca*. You know, like Juan said."

"Have a little faith here, Jason. I'm good at this."

"Maybe a little too good," Juan teased her.

She rolled her eyes. Leaning over, she kissed Jack on the top of his head. "Be a good dog. Take care of the boy."

Jack whined a little and pawed at her knee.

Jenni's smiled grew wider as she felt their love pouring over her. She felt needed, wanted, desired, and important. All the things she had never been before the zombies came, when she had been Lloyd's child bride . . . and punching bag. She wouldn't let her family down.

"Be careful in there. Don't do anything crazy. I can't come rushing in to save your ass if something goes wrong," Juan said, his voice slightly catching.

"I know that," Jenni answered. "You have a job to do. So do I."

Juan forced a smile and kissed her lips. "Just be careful."

"See you later," she said with a parting wink.

She joined her two partners in crime, Ashley and Ned. A former waitress, Ashley was a frail little thing with a determined expression on her face. Ned had been a school bus driver. Jenni wondered how he'd fit behind the wheel; he was tall and gangly and moved a little awkwardly.

Each team consisted of three people, all armed with a gun and a short spear or bowie knife. Though Jason had desperately wanted to volunteer, only people above the age of eighteen were allowed on the assault teams. Jenni had been relieved to know her stepson would not be entering the hotel with them.

Jenni's long hair was tied up on top of her head and under a cap. No one was allowed to leave their hair down. It would be too easy for a zombie to snag it. The cap felt itchy and heavy on her head, and she scratched at it awkwardly. Clad in jeans, boots, a denim jacket, and work gloves, she felt overheated and slightly claustrophobic. She understood the importance of shielding themselves from zombie bites, but that didn't make her attire any more comfortable. It was little solace that all the other volunteers were dressed the same way.

Jenni was in charge of her team. She was the best shot and had the most experience with the zombies. It was hard to know how good Ashley and Ned would be at shooting zombies, since they'd all used ammunition very sparingly during training, but she was hoping the sessions with Mike would pay off. Her life depended on it.

Ed and Bill took their places at the entrance to the enclosure. Ed unlocked the gate as Mike gave the signal to enter the hotel. Mike, Felix, and the former Walmart driver, Chuck, were the first into the room beyond the jagged, door-sized hole in the wall. Nerit followed, along with the two construction workers who made up the rest of her team, Jimmy and Shane. Jenni hated Shane with a passion. He had attacked Katie after she killed his brother during a battle with the zombies. Shane's brother had been bitten, so what Katie did was a mercy, but Shane just went wild.

Ed shut and locked the gate behind the first teams.

Jenni moved to the entrance and smiled at Ed, who nodded in response. She pushed up on her tiptoes to see over his shoulder and watch the teams enter the hotel. Mike's group went first, then Nerit's. Once in the room, the groups moved cautiously toward the door that would let them into the hotel's hallway. Mike swung the door open as Nerit covered him. Checking the corridor with his flashlight, Mike gave the all clear, and the first two sets of volunteers disappeared into the gloom.

Ed unlocked the gate and pulled it open.

"Here we go," Jenni muttered, and led her fighters into the enclosure. The stench from the small room assailed her senses, and her eyes watered. Drawing up all the bravery she could muster, she stepped past the broken bricks and into the hotel. Gore, desiccated and black, was splashed on the walls.

"Shit," Ned whispered, looking at the remains of the zombie feeding frenzy. The zombies Nerit had killed had been shoved out of the way against the walls.

"Don't let it get to you," Jenni ordered. It was easier to say than to put into practice.

"What do you think happened?" Ashley asked.

"I betcha they all hid in here and one of them or all of them were bitten by a zombie. They turned and—" Jenni shrugged. "—it got messy."

Ned stared at the carnage smeared on the wall. "Obviously."

She moved across the room, her eyes still adjusting to the lack of light. The gloom was stifling and the reek overwhelming.

The storm was drawing closer and loud booms of thunder filled the room. What a perfect background for the day—lightning, thunder, hard wind, and rain. It was like a horror movie. Jenni shivered at the thought.

Behind her, Ashley used a high-powered flashlight to illuminate their path.

Stepping into the hallway, Jenni walked slowly, her feet silent on the plush carpet. With a carpet this thick, would they hear anything creeping up on them? She didn't want to think about that too much. She had a job to do and she didn't need to freak herself out. It was bad enough just knowing that zombies were in the building. Following the route she had memorized during the many briefings, she headed down the hall that would lead into main dining room.

Glancing over her shoulder, she caught sight of Katie, Travis, and Roger entering the corridor. She liked Roger. That morning, he had put on a red T-shirt and playfully dubbed himself "the red shirt on the away team" in homage to *Star Trek*. It had cracked up everyone at breakfast, but now Jenni was worried. Maybe you shouldn't joke about death.

"It is a good day to die," she heard Roger mutter in his best Worf imitation.

"Did you close the door?" Travis's voice questioned.

There was a brief hesitation, the click of a door, and then Roger said, "Of course I did."

Jenni suppressed a smile. She cautiously approached the arched doorway that led to the lobby. This was where Katie's group was headed. Katarina's group would travel down the hallway in the other direction, then enter the lobby through the matching archway on the far side of the hotel. Nerit's and Mike's groups were supposed to start with the conference rooms that opened up off the main corridor.

Jenni's destination was the hotel dining room, but first, there was more hallway to get through. Luckily, there were no doors in this part of the hall, which was decorated with pretty gilded mirrors, fancy artwork, and the occasional table or chair resting against the wall. It was a tasteful way to decorate a very boring stretch of hall.

Unlike more modern hotels, with their separate restaurants, here, meals would have been served in an elegant dining room, their price built in to the cost of a guest's stay. Since the hotel had not yet reopened, Jenni hoped that it would be an easy room to clear. Reaching the dining room, she stepped in and swung her rifle from side to side as she scanned the round tables covered in white linen and decorated with wilted floral centerpieces. The china and silverware were laid out meticulously, with napkins twisted into the shapes of swans resting on top of each large plate. Jenni felt overwhelmed by the old-fashioned opulence of the room. The hotel had obviously been carefully restored with the hope of luring in high-end clientele. There was no sign of any of the violence.

Moving determinedly toward the kitchen, Jenni caught a faint whiff of decay.

"Shit!" Jenni screamed "They're here!"

Abruptly, the door to the kitchen was flung open and the waitstaff flooded into the room, ready for their breakfast.

· CHAPTER SIX ·

1.
The Away Team

Katie took point with her group since she was more experienced with weapons. She could see Jenni's group moving toward the dining room, but her own team's destination was the first-floor lobby.

The irony did not escape her that she was finally what her father had always wanted—a good soldier. She had considered following his footsteps into the marines, but had opted for college and law school instead. Now she was wondering if she shouldn't have gone into the marines after all. If she had, maybe she wouldn't be scared shitless now. Her team fanned out behind her as she kept a keen eye on the shadows.

Travis tripped and fell over a chair in the hallway, obviously missing it in the gloom. They all froze.

Katie shot him a reproachful glare and whispered, "Shhhh."

"Sorry," Travis muttered.

Katie moved forward, her steps measured. Nearing the archway, she steadied her nerves. They were hoping for a limited number of zombies, but if more had somehow entered the hotel in search of a human meal, it might be very difficult to clear out the building. Pale sunlight shimmered on the far wall, illuminating their way. Something was open. Katie hoped it wasn't the front door.

Travis and Roger trailed her as she stepped cautiously down

the short hall and out onto the tiled floor of the lobby, her boots making soft tapping sounds. A huge oak staircase cut the lobby in half, and the three fighters slipped along its side. One of the large front windows slowly came into view, then the front doors. Muted light filtered through the glass as a light rain tapped on the window. To Katie's relief, the doors were closed and chained. Walking over, she pulled on the chains, making sure they were secure.

"This is good," Travis said with relief, his voice echoing.

A low moan answered him.

Katie whirled around.

On the stairs, a female zombie in a blood-splattered maid's uniform was staring at her. The dead woman's head was hanging at an impossible angle, held on merely by a few sinews. From behind, she would have appeared to be headless. In the beam from Roger's flashlight, Katie could clearly see the zombie's rictus grin and crazed eyes. It seemed confused and scuttled from one side of the staircase to the other, uncoordinated.

"Damn," Roger whispered.

Katie drew her bowie knife from her belt and stepped warily up the stairs. The creature blinked at her, its mouth open, trying to scream, and started snapping its jaws. With a grunt, Katie shoved the zombie over with her foot. It landed hard on the steps, its head flopping to one side, its teeth still gnashing. Lifting the knife, Katie narrowed her eyes, aimed, and struck the zombie through the eye as hard as she could. The knife hit bone and she twisted, pushing the blade farther in. The jaws stilled. Katie braced her foot on the head and drew out her weapon. Cleaning it on the dead maid's dress, she looked up to see Roger and Travis watching her with stunned expressions.

"What?"

"Damn," Roger said. "You were like Alice in *Resident Evil*. That was hot."

Travis gulped. "Never seen you take one out like that before. That was pretty impressive."

Katie rolled her eyes, then spotted the team lead by Katarina entering the far side of the lobby.

The walkie-talkie sputtered. "Dining room! Now! Fuck! Fuck! Fuck!" Jenni's voice was frantic.

The next instant, they heard gunfire.

2.
Nothing Ever Goes as Planned

In some ways, it was just like a video game. Jenni fired until her gun clicked empty, reloaded, fired again, reloaded. . . .

If an annoying male voice had kept telling her when to reload, it would be perfect. But there wasn't. Instead she heard Juan's voice shouting over the walkie-talkie for someone to help her, and, unlike in a video game, the zombies rushing at them didn't vanish when hit by gunfire. The dead were all dressed in waiters' uniforms. The quick zombies went down first and fast, since they were at the front of the pack, but their speed was startling. Luckily, Ashley and Ned did exactly what they were supposed to do. Mike had taught them to divide any group attack into "pie slices," with each person concentrating on one slice. Jenni fired right down the center, Ashley fired to the left, and Ned took care of the right.

The three humans backed up slowly, trying not to panic and to keep their nerves steady. The gush of zombies faded to a trickle, then stopped. As the last shot echoed through the room, Jenni and her companions sighed in relief.

"We did it!" Ashley beamed happily.

Jenni was about to agree, but when a noise caught her attention, she said, "Listen."

From the distance came the sound of running feet, grunts, and growls.

"Shit, there's more coming," Ned stammered.

The three living people ran across the dining room, jumping over the dead bodies. Jenni shoved over the heavy tables near the bar to make a barrier. Ashley and Ned did the same. Mike, Nerit, and their teams ran into the room. Seeing the upturned tables and the dead bodies, they quickly understood what was happening.

"Check the kitchen," Mike ordered, pointing behind Jenni. As Felix dashed through the kitchen door, Nerit motioned to Shane to heave her up onto the bar behind the upturned tables. She took a position that gave her a good view of the main doors.

The grunting, moaning, screaming zombies were drawing closer.

"Kitchen is clear. The loading dock to the side street is closed," Felix said, returning.

"If we have to, that's the way we'll fall back," Mike answered.

The dining room doors sprang open as Travis, Katie, and Roger ran in. They sprinted across the room, evading the tables and bodies. Roger, slowed by his size, still managed to reach the overturned tables just as Katarina's team raced through the doors, shrieking. The reason for their desperation quickly became clear—the mangled, mutilated dead were right behind them.

Katarina fell in her haste to get around a table. The first zombie in the mob reached down to grab her, and Nerit blasted a hole through his head. The people huddled behind the tables were reluctant to fire, afraid of hitting their living companions, but Nerit did not hesitate. Her sniper rifle began to crack as she fired. Jenni aimed for the zombies farthest from the running humans and fired.

Katarina managed to get up, but four zombies grabbed hold of her denim jacket. She twisted, yanked, and squirmed her way out of the jacket and ran for shelter.

Jenni heard a scream and, out of the corner of her eye, saw one of the men, whose name she did not remember, go down. Gunshots rang out steadily, but the man kept screaming.

"Nerit!" Mike's voice was an order.

Another shot, then the man stopped screaming.

Katarina reached the tables and squirmed behind them. "I need a gun! I dropped mine!"

Travis immediately handed his over. "I'll reload for everyone!"

There was no sign of the other man from Katarina's group. He had gone down so silently, no one had noticed. The room was now clogged with the undead. They were tripping over their dead comrades and falling over chairs and tables. The most agile had pursued Katarina, but as they had drawn near the barricade, they went down in a hail of bullets.

Jenni kept firing, aiming as much as she could, but she was more terrified than she had been since she'd reached the fort. Fear threatened to overwhelm her; some of her shots went wide.

Her gun clicked empty, and Mike shouted at her, "Reload!"

She almost burst out laughing.

3.
The Madness of War

Katie found herself wedged behind a table with her back against the wall. Travis was crouched beside her and Nerit stood above them on the bar. Katie hated feeling stuck in the corner.

Her gun kept jerking in her hands. Her fingers ached. She tried to aim true and take the heads off as many zombies as possible. When they'd been planning this assault, they had estimated that there were no more than twenty people in the hotel. Obviously that guess had been seriously low. The invaders from the fort had killed at least a dozen already; maybe thirty more were still trying to get to their living flesh.

A zombie charged the barricade. He hit the table sheltering Katie, and it started to tip onto her. Pressing her back against the wall and bracing the table with one foot, she aimed at the creature's head as he snarled, reaching for her. She flinched as she pulled the trigger, anticipating being doused with blood and gore.

"Gross," she muttered as she wiped the dead thing's brains off her face and aimed at a fresh target. Next to her, Travis was busy reloading someone's gun. Jenni was screaming as she fired.

In contrast, Nerit was absolutely silent as she systematically eliminated the quickest of the undead.

"Gawddammit! Why are there so many?" Felix shouted. Beside him, Shane shoved the end of his rifle into a snarling zombie mouth and fired.

Four zombies hit the barricades at the same time. Jimmy, Roger, Katarina, and Mike had to stop firing to brace the tables against the onslaught. Nerit was reloading as quickly as she could, but Travis had to deal with a snarling female zombie reaching for him over the tables.

"Shoot it!" Felix yelled at Travis.

"I gave my gun to Katarina," Travis grunted as he picked up a heavy candlestick lying on the floor near him. He bashed out the zombie's brains before she could get her teeth into him.

Katie screamed when something grabbed her leg. She looked down—a zombie was gripping her ankle through the gap between the table and wall. Its growling face was barely visible. With surprising strength, it tugged on her leg and sent her tumbling back into the bar.

Travis brought the candlestick down hard on the head of another zombie as more slammed into the barricade. Now only a few people were firing as the rest tried to keep the tables from toppling over. The room was filled with the screams of the humans and the growls of the zombies.

Everyone was shouting at once: Mike ordering people to hold the tables in place, Katarina screaming that her table was slipping, Nerit telling everyone to be calm, Felix and Shane yelling wordlessly as several zombies tried to topple their table, Katie shrieking as the zombie tried to drag her leg into the open. It was chaos.

Travis continued to slam the candlestick down on the heads of the zombies, blood and gore flying everywhere. One of the zombies seized his arm. Nerit fired a bullet through the creature's head, but more were already grabbing at Travis.

"Jacket off!" Katarina yelled.

Travis yanked his arm through the sleeve as fast as he could;

an instant later, his jacket was dragged into the mouths of the hungry zombies. Jenni grabbed Travis's arm and saw that he had escaped without a bite.

"Shit! That was close!" she said, and went back to firing at the very frustrated-looking zombies.

On the floor, Katie tried to pull her leg free. She was having trouble getting leverage. "Some help here!" She tried to aim at the zombie's head, but it was blocked by her captured foot.

"Keep the tables in place!" Shane roared.

Beside him, Chuck and Ned struggled with a table. Mike's voice was fierce. "Hold the line! Don't let them through!"

Nerit kicked Mike in the shoulder. "Katie's in trouble!"

Mike quickly assessed Katie's situation. "Shit! Travis! A zombie has Katie!"

His face draining of color, Travis grabbed the first thing he saw on the bar. Falling to his knees, he stabbed the only visible part of the zombie—its hand—as hard as he could with a corkscrew.

"Fuck!" Roger cried out.

Four zombies were pulling down the table Roger was desperate to hold up. They growled and reached for him. He lost his grip as he tried to evade their grasp and the table toppled over.

"Shit!" he screamed.

Katarina hurled a chair at a zombie trying to climb over the table. The snarling creature was hit square in the face and rolled onto the floor, where it immediately tried to crawl under the table. Roger shoved the table over, pinning the zombie to the floor.

"Someone shoot it!" he cried out.

Jenni fired point-blank into its head.

"Someone shoot this sonofabitch!" Travis kept stabbing the grayish dead hand as Katie struggled to get free. The zombie's bones and tendons snapped and broke as it struggled with its meal. It felt no pain and kept pulling. Soon her tender calf would be exposed.

"I can't get a clear shot!" Nerit yelled above the gunfire, the screaming, and the growling.

Katie grabbed hold of Travis, trying to pull herself free. The zombie's grasp was unrelenting.

Abruptly, the room fell silent. "That's it!" Katarina shouted.

"Gawddamn, fuckin' zombies!" Shane cursed, and upended his table onto the dead creatures.

"Help!" Travis shouted as the last zombie's other hand grabbed Katie's ankle and yanked her whole leg into the open with one swift pull.

"Fuck!" Katie yelled, kicking frantically.

Travis heaved the table over onto the zombie, trapping it. Mike and Roger grabbed Katie and yanked her free.

Jenni jumped on top of the table and began hopping up and down on it, grabbing one of the legs to keep her balance. Roger, laughing manically, joined her as the table seesawed dangerously. Katarina climbed up, too, braced herself on the wall, and jumped up and down as hard as she could. Mike added his weight as well.

"Crush that fucker!" Felix ordered.

There was no more room on the table, but the others joined in by leaning on the legs or onto their teammates. There were almost hysterical smiles on their faces as the adrenaline rush in their veins spurred them on. As they slowly crushed the zombie into mush, its bones cracking under their weight, they did a jovial little dance of death.

Nerit let herself down from the bar slowly, cursing in Hebrew, while Travis helped Katie to her feet. Looking around the room, Katie was overcome by the stench of death and by the sight of the gore that was splattered everywhere.

There was a loud, sickening popping noise from under the table, and the zombie's growls ended. It was all too much.

Katie ran into the kitchen and threw up in the sink. She was shaking, her hands trembling.

"Well," she heard Jenni say from the other room, "I'm glad I'm not cleaning up this mess."

4.
Words Are Dangerous

Juan stood helplessly outside the hotel along with everyone else who was not part of the original volunteer teams. He felt horror and desperation as he heard the gunfire, the screaming, and the unholy sounds of the walking dead. It took all his willpower not to run in to try to save Jenni. It would be an idiotic move, and he knew it. She could take care of herself and he believed in her, but waiting outside was agonizing.

Like the others, he could not take his eyes off the closed door into the janitor's closet. The bluish gray door, splashed with dried blood, seemed ominous. What if it cracked open and those things poured into the small enclosure? Suddenly, the wrought iron gate seemed inconsequential.

His grip tightened on his gun as he lifted his walkie-talkie to his mouth. Then he hesitated, realizing that in the midst of battle, the last thing they needed was him yelling at them to report in.

After several excruciating minutes, silence fell.

He immediately pressed the button on the walkie-talkie. "What the fuck happened?"

There was a long pause, static, laughter, and then, finally, Mike's voice. "We got swarmed, but we're okay now. I have a feeling that every zombie not locked in somewhere is headed our way."

Juan was about to ask after Jenni when he heard her laughing in the background. He felt the tight knots in his back release. "Did we lose anyone?"

"Yeah, Mark and Wallace."

"Damn."

"Send in the backup team and have them meet me in the dining room. Use caution, there could be stragglers," Mike said through the static.

Juan heard Jenni yell, "Love you, babe!" and relief washed over him.

"Okay, sending them in. Take care of yourselves."

Turning, he motioned to Bill and Curtis to head in. As he watched Bill and Curtis's team disappear into the building, he felt the knots in his back tighten.

Ashley stood quietly to one side as some of the others flipped the tables upright and began making sure the zombies were truly dead. Caution was the keyword, and everyone was being very careful. But their aim had been true and the many dead were finally at peace. During most of the fracas, Ashley and Ned had been busy reloading guns for the others. Toward the end, she had helped brace a table. Now she stood looking at her fingers and the long scrape that ran across them.

Nearby, Jenni used a broken chair leg to bash in one zombie's head as a precaution.

Ashley stared at her hand.

It was just a scrape. That's all it was. Just a scrape.

Katie rinsed her mouth with water from the hotel kitchen's faucet. Watching the water swirl down the drain, she ran her wet fingers over her brow. She took a deep, steadying breath . . . and sucked in the overwhelming reek of decay.

She threw up again.

Finally, she was done. She wiped her mouth again and looked around. On a nearby counter, a row of buffet bins were filled with decayed food. Above them, a large menu was tacked up on a board. Given the chaos of the dining room, the kitchen seemed serene.

Beside the counter stood an easel holding a large placard that read THE DAUGHTERS OF TEXAS PRESENT THE RESTORATION OF HISTORICAL ASHLEY OAKS BREAKFAST at the top. Guest speakers were listed below.

Katie staggered out into the main room and looked at the piled-up dead. The top layers of the heaps were mostly made up of women's bodies. They wore neat little matching outfits and shoes. Below them were the waiters and kitchen staff. Walking around, studying the bodies, she identified the front desk receptionist and a doorman. That meant there might be maids and janitors elsewhere in the building.

"Shouldn't be too many left," Mike said as he reverently laid a tablecloth over the two men who had fallen during the battle.

"Actually, these are mostly guests. There was a breakfast meeting here that first day," Katie said. "I also see staff from the lobby and the kitchen."

Mike studied the zombies. "Yeah, I see." He paused, thinking. "We killed two janitors and a maid in the janitor's storage closet when we came in."

"I killed a maid in the lobby, and there was the one that took a dive out of the hotel window a few weeks back. But how many were on shift?"

Ashley spoke up. "I worked in a hotel. There should be a work schedule up at the front desk!"

Jenni headed out the door with her teammates close behind. Ashley looked a little pale and unsteady while Ned swaggered with more confidence than he should have had, considering the situation.

Katie sighed as she regarded her surroundings. "I'm thinking that the maids may have barricaded themselves into bedrooms."

Travis stood nearby, looking at his slimed-up jacket, and then he tossed it away with disgust. "Which means every room we enter could be full of really hungry zombies."

Katarina handed him his weapon before picking up her own dropped weapon. "Really, really hungry zombies," she said.

"Nothing about this is easy," Roger groused, and kicked a pink Ferragamo high heel across the room.

"Just gotta find them and shoot them in the head," Shane said from where he was straddling a chair and appearing bored.

"Unless they eat your ass first," Felix grumbled.

Mike patted Felix on the back. "The trick is to shoot them in the head before they get the chance."

Bill and Curtis entered the room, followed by a guy named Davey. They all looked impressed at the carnage.

"Been busy, I see," Bill said.

"Nothing we can't handle," Shane retorted. "Despite the lesbos, fatsos, and old people."

Everyone ignored him.

Jenni ran back in, waving a clipboard. "I got the roster. And I found a bunch of master keys!"

She handed the roster automatically to Katie even though Mike had been reaching for it. Realizing what she had done, she sheepishly handed Mike the jumble of keys instead. He just smiled slightly and started to pass them out.

"Okay, gimme a second. . . ." Katie counted the kitchen staff and waitstaff, then studied the list. "It looks like all the dining room and kitchen people are accounted for. Both front desk people are here, as is the doorman. We're missing four maids—" She flipped a page. "—and two plumbers. They were called in to look at the showers on the sixth floor."

"So the sixth floor is a potential hot spot," Mike said thoughtfully.

"And the maids could be anywhere," Travis said with a sigh.

"Six zombies," Katie said. "Plus the manager of the hotel."

"Not so many compared to this," Bill pointed out.

"Yeah, but they could be anywhere—upstairs, in closets, under the beds—anywhere," Travis replied.

"And we may have straggler guests from this luncheon that no one told us about," Mike said, sounding peeved.

Ashley seemed pale and a little unsteady on her feet. Putting her head down, she tried to settle her queasy stomach. Katie still felt a little nauseated, but there was so much to do. Travis gave her a weak smile and she reached out. He took her hand and squeezed it.

"We stand here any longer, and we're going to freak ourselves out," Mike said after a beat. "We survived this. We survived all the shit that went down the first days. We have to keep going."

Katie nodded, as did most of the others. Mike was right.

"So, let's get this done. What more can go wrong?" Mike said with a laugh.

Ashley looked up, growled, and bit into Mike's throat.

5.
What Should Have Been

He's not supposed to die, was Jenni's first thought. *Mike's the black hero of this tale. He's supposed to survive, isn't he?* At least until the end, just like George Romero's films. But Mike was struggling, his throat caught in the angry bite of the petite blond woman. Her bony arms were around him, crushing him as she tore at him. Everyone was frozen in disbelief.

It wasn't real. It couldn't be.

But it was.

"Get her off! Get her off," Mike gasped.

Travis grabbed Ashley's braid and yanked her back. Blood sprayed everywhere, hot and red with life.

Katie acted fast, bowie knife in hand. The others were responding sluggishly, the shock of the attack dulling their reactions.

The thing that had been Ashley turned toward Travis, chewing the flesh she had torn from Mike's neck. Hissing, she was about to strike again. Travis tried to duck away.

Holding the knife over her head with both hands, Katie brought it down hard. With a disgusting sound, the knife plunged through the zombie's cheek, shattering her teeth and wedging into her jaw. The two women fell to the ground, the zombie beneath, Katie on top.

Jenni ran forward, flipping the safety off her gun.

Katie pinned the small zombie to the ground and kept slamming its head on the floor until its skull cracked and the thing that had been Ashley shuddered and went still and silent.

Mike lay on the ground nearby, shivering violently, his hands pressed to his throat. Blood was bubbling up between his fingers and spreading on the floor around his head like a red halo. Jenni fell to her knees beside him. Feeling impotent, she laid her gloved hand on his cheek. He looked at her, his expression regretful and sad.

"I didn't . . . see . . . her . . . ," he gasped.

"I didn't either," Jenni answered.

"Keep . . . going . . . ," Mike whispered, and was gone.

Jenni drew her hand back. Tears streamed down her face.

Travis pulled out his gun and aimed at Mike's head.

"Do it," Katie said softly as she got to her feet and wiped her knife blade on her jeans.

Travis narrowed his eyes. His hand trembled.

"Do it before he comes back," Nerit said sternly.

Travis struggled to pull the trigger. Jenni could see the agony in his eyes. "Can't," Travis sighed, beginning to lower the gun. "Someone else—"

Mike's eyes flashed open, and he growled.

Blood exploded between his eyes, and he was truly gone. A delicate little pit bubbled with blood as Nerit stepped over Mike's body.

"If you hesitate again, I will shoot you. I will not lose anyone else because you could not pull the trigger," she said briskly and brushed past Travis to stand guard at the door.

"This isn't right, man. This isn't right," Felix whispered, falling to his knees beside Mike.

"What do we do now?" Katarina asked softly, shock clear on her face.

Jenni stared down at Mike, so peaceful in his final death.

Bill leaned down and grabbed Mike's walkie-talkie. "We finish this. Easy as that."

Curtis shook his head and grabbed a tablecloth.

Jenni sighed.

You were supposed to make it to the end. Mike, does this mean this is the end?

Even Shane was solemn as Curtis laid the white tablecloth over Mike's still features.

· CHAPTER SEVEN ·

1.
Pieces of Hell

"How could she turn so fast?" Katarina asked.

Katie had knelt beside Ashley, inspecting the dead woman's body. Now she looked up at the others and showed them the scrape on the blonde's hand. "She was bitten. Looks like one of them got her here. It's more like a scrape than a bite, but it was enough."

"Ashley's been anorexic for years and has all sorts of health issues. That's probably why it took her down so quick," Curtis said softly. "Poor thing."

"You have to kill whoever is bit immediately or we'll lose more people," Nerit said coldly. "We don't know how long it will take before someone turns."

Katie shivered at her tone and observed Travis. His head was down and he was staring at the gun in his hand in a strange, almost angry way.

"That's bullshit. What if the person don't change? What if the bite don't take? We can't just shoot everyone like that lesbo bitch shot Patrick!" Shane's voice was fierce as he glowered at Katie.

"And what if we let someone with a bite live long enough to begin spreading it through the fort? That's the end of us all. Do you want to be one of those things? Do you? Do you want to be the reason everyone else dies? Tell me. Do you want that on your hands?" Nerit gave Shane a fierce look.

Shane didn't answer, just looked away.

Travis hesitated, then said to Nerit, "With Mike gone, you're the only former military officer we have in the fort."

With a slight nod, Nerit turned her gaze on Travis. "I know. I'll do my best to continue his work."

Bill patted Nerit's shoulder lightly. "You'll do a good job, Nerit."

Assuming control, Nerit began reorganizing the teams, trying to balance the groups by skill level. Everyone was emotionally and physically exhausted, but they had to go on. This was what Mike had trained them for, and even though he was no longer with them, they had a job to do.

Katie looked around again. Jenni was standing nearby, her expression a little distant and disturbing. Katie reached out to take her hand, and Jenni raised her eyes. They had a glazed look Katie hadn't seen since the first day of the zombie rising.

"Jenni?"

Jenni frowned a little and said softly, "He wasn't supposed to die."

Katie hugged her. "None of us are. Not like this."

Jenni drew away, clutching her gun tightly. "I just don't want it to be the end."

"It's not," Katie said confidently. "We just have to keep going. Fighting. For everyone's sake, Jenni, we gotta get this done."

Jenni appeared a little more focused as she absorbed Katie's words. "Yeah, for everyone still alive."

Nerit had moved over to the doorway and was watching the hall. Bill asked her, "Nerit, we clear?"

"No movement," Nerit answered.

"But be cautious anyway," Bill reminded everyone.

There were nods, and people visibly drew on their inner strength as they prepared to leave the dining room.

Bill raised the walkie-talkie to his mouth and pressed the button. "Juan, we're moving out. Send in the sentries for the first floor."

"We heard more gunshots," Juan's voice crackled through the receiver.

"Yeah, we lost some people. Mike and Ashley."

"Shit," Juan answered.

"We'll be in touch." Bill motioned to Nerit.

The older woman started down the hall, followed by her new team of Katarina, Shane, and Jimmy. The other teams followed as Bill pointed to them. They were back on schedule and heading to their assignments.

Katie walked over to Roger and Travis, who were talking in low tones. Roger looked ill at ease.

As she drew closer, Travis sighed. "I'm sorry, Katie. I won't fuck up again," he vowed.

"No one thinks it's easy killing what used to be your friend, Travis." She could see the pained expression in his eyes.

Travis answered in a tortured tone, "Just a living nightmare, isn't it?"

Katie blinked, abruptly comprehending what Travis had just been through. Weeks ago, Travis had confided that he had been struggling with bizarre visions since the first day. He told her that he often saw his friends briefly transformed into zombies. Now he was seeing those nightmares become reality. No wonder he had been reluctant to shoot Mike.

She reached out and touched his cheek. He nuzzled her fingers, comforting himself, then straightened. With a grim expression, he said, "Let's do this."

Room after room was empty. Offices, closets, bathrooms, empty . . .

Each time a door swung open, Nerit's gut clenched and her finger prepared to squeeze the trigger. Nerit rarely flinched in the face of danger. In fact, she rarely felt afraid. She prided herself on her calmness, but now she felt fear struggling to get hold of her.

Each large piece of furniture could have a zombie lurking behind it; every partially opened door held the potential for death. . . .

As they walked through the hotel, Nerit saw numerous signs

of violence. The storage room near the loading dock was where the kitchen crew and waitstaff had apparently met their ends. One of the conference rooms was a slaughterhouse. It was evident the poor women from the breakfast had tried to barricade the doors, but the barriers had given way and the breakfast guests had perished. Behind the front desk, she spotted a pool of dried blood that was littered with pieces of intestines and other organs. In the manager's office, all the furniture was knocked over and the heavy desk had been shoved aside, but there was no blood visible. Maybe the man had escaped.

Walking quietly down the narrow hall, opening closed doors, Nerit and her team moved with silent efficiency. The remains of the life that had existed before the zombies danced before their eyes, tombstones of days gone by. TVs and computers sat silently, screens blank. In one bathroom, a newspaper lay on the floor. The front page read, THE DEAD WALK.

One supply closet held the neatly folded banners for the hotel's grand opening. Nerit shook her head, knowing that grand opening would never take place.

The last door opened onto a small office. Inside were three bodies: a woman and two children. None moved.

The woman had strangled the children with her stockings, which were still knotted around their throats. They were carefully arranged on the floor, their arms around each other. It looked like the woman had then clutched an ice pick in one hand and fallen sideways onto it. She was lying next to the children, her eyes wide and staring. They were all most definitely dead.

Making sure the room was clear, Nerit approached the door and studied it. There were scratches and smears of blood on the frame and door. Nerit thought she knew what had happened. The woman—probably the mother of the children—had hidden back here, terrified, until she had made a desperate choice as zombies had attacked the door, trying to get in. Something about the family looked familiar. Leaving Shane and Katarina on guard, Nerit took Jimmy back to the manager's office, where she picked up the framed photo on his desk. It showed a young man, the dead woman, and three young children. Nerit took the photo with her when she and Jimmy rejoined their teammates.

"She's the manager's wife," Nerit said.

"What do you think happened?" Katarina asked.

"I think he told her to hide with the kids. Maybe he tried to go for help," Nerit answered.

"And never came back," Jimmy finished. "And she stayed here."

"She may have been too terrified to try to go for help or try to escape," Shane said.

"The construction site was so close, safety was so close," Katarina whispered.

"I don't think she had a choice. Zombies were outside the door at some point. She did what she had to do." Nerit lifted her walkie-talkie to her mouth. "Juan, the first floor is clear. We're joining the teams on the second. The manager's family was visiting, and one of his kids is not accounted for."

"Shit," Juan's voice rasped through the speaker.

"Zombie kids. I hate them," Shane muttered.

Nerit and the others moved down the hallway in silence, leaving the mother and her two children to rest in peace a little longer.

Jenni was leading Ned, Felix, and Chuck along the second-floor hallway, guns drawn. Ned illuminated their way with a large flashlight. The interior of the hotel was dark, musty, and terrifying. They could see the other teams moving in and out of rooms farther down the hall.

Whoever had designed the renovations had been determined to maintain the hotel's old-world charm. The doors were unlocked not by card keys, but with regular keys. Chuck carried their set in his meaty hand. He looked very nervous as sweat poured down his face.

The team rigidly followed Mike's strategy for clearing a room. Jenni and Felix would keep watch up and down the hall while Ned aimed the flashlight at the room's door so Chuck could unlock it. Then Chuck would fling open the door while Jenni and Felix aimed straight into the room, ready to fire at anything that stirred. If nothing immediately popped out, they would move slowly into the room. They would check the bathroom and the closets and look under the beds. Felix would rip away the bedding and Jenni would squat down to make sure there was nothing lurking under the old-fashioned four-poster beds.

They'd worked through four rooms, and Jenni could feel her teammates growing tense. She herself felt an increasing sense of dread. Maybe it was the darkness that filled the hallway, the cloying stench of death that seemed to hang in the musty air, or the way the world outside seemed so far away as the storm boomed overhead.

The fifth door loomed before them. Chuck wiped his brow with his hand and said to Jenni, "Anyone else just wanna quit and go back?"

Jenni laughed. "Ever since we came in."

Chuck bent over and unlocked the door.

Felix made a little noise in his throat.

"What is it?" Chuck looked at him nervously.

"It smells worse here," Felix answered.

Jenni sniffed the air and flinched. "Shit. It does. Get ready, everyone."

Chuck flung open the door.

Nothing stirred inside.

Cautiously, they moved into the room. The space under the bed was clear. The wardrobe was empty. The closed bathroom door loomed before them, taunting and terrifying.

The stench was so bad, their eyes were watering.

"I hope I don't get this room," Chuck muttered, and flung the bathroom door open.

The room was empty. Nothing confronted them except a toilet, with a tidy little white strip of paper across it, and an empty clawed tub.

"Where the fuck is that smell coming from?" Ned wondered.

Jenni looked toward the open hallway door, then back into the bathroom. "We're missing something."

The zombie stepped out from behind the door and bit into Ned's cheek before anyone could react. Ned screamed in horror and pain and staggered under the dead woman's grip. Jenni raised her gun immediately and shot both of them in quick succession.

"No," Chuck gasped.

"That was fucked up," Felix said, and wiped his brow. "Shit!"

Jenni was breathing hard, staring at the bodies. Lifting her walkie-talkie, she said, "Make sure to check behind the fucking doors. One was hiding there and got Ned."

There was silence; then Nerit's voice said, "Understood."

Jenni waved at Chuck and Felix. "Let's go."

As they moved out, she picked up the flashlight that had fallen from Ned's slack fingers.

Katie stood near the stairwell, shivering. They had been in view of the other teams on occasion throughout the inspection of the second floor, but it had been nerve racking. She and her team found nothing in the rooms they had cleared. There had been one loss on the second floor—and it had been on Jenni's team. That terrified Katie. She did not even want to consider the possibility of losing her best friend.

Jenni, Chuck, and Felix now drew near, with Nerit and her group close behind. Jenni looked very pale, and there was a dark expression on her face.

"You okay?" Katie asked.

"No," Jenni answered. "This isn't fun."

To a stranger, that might have seemed like a bizarre answer, but Katie knew that Jenni usually enjoyed killing zombies. The losses had been high today, a terrible reminder of the insanity and fear of the first days of the zombie plague. Katie was sure that Jenni was thinking of her lost children. She knew she was thinking of Lydia.

"Let's go," Nerit said, and led the way.

The other teams would be going up the staircase on the other side of the hotel. Nerit moved easily up the stairs, showing no sign of her age. Katie felt immense affection and respect for the Israeli woman. She seemed so in control of herself, much more than Katie was.

The stairwell was painted a boring white. The banisters and steps were made of a dark wood; vases of dead flowers adorned metal small tables on the landings. The survivors' footsteps echoed as they climbed. Katie cringed inwardly at the sound.

"This is scary as shit," Chuck muttered. He had fallen behind everyone else, his bland features looking doughy and pale.

Jenni glared at him with an annoyed expression on her face. "Don't be such a wimp," she said sharply.

"Look, we have no fucking clue what's going to happen next," Chuck said "Who is going to die next?"

"Bad thing to say," Roger snapped. "In horror movies, bad shit always happens after someone says something like that."

"Like what?" Chuck shot back.

The zombie dropped down from above. It ricocheted off the banister, but managed to grab Chuck's shirt as he let out a startled gasp. The zombie rebounded off the banister sideways; its momentum dragging Chuck over the rail. Both figures plummeted nearly three stories to the bottom of the stairwell. Everything happened so fast, no one had a chance to grab Chuck.

"Fuck!" Jenni screamed.

Katie and Jenni raced down the stairs with the others close behind. On the bottom floor, they found the zombie and Chuck. The zombie, a male, had landed headfirst; its skull split open, spilling curdled brains. Chuck lay nearby, his head twisted about in an unnatural angle. Both were completely stone cold dead.

"I told him," Roger grumbled.

"Fucking stupid way to go out," Shane said with a shrug.

"I think we found one of the plumbers," Travis said, pointing to the name of the plumbing company on the zombie's tattered shirt.

Jenni stared down at Chuck's body. "I hate today."

They kept going. They had to. Too much time and energy had been invested and too many lives lost to give up on taking the hotel. They were now more cautious, more terrified, and more determined, but they were still in hell.

"I feel like I'm next," Jenni muttered as she joined Curtis's group. Seeing three of her teammates go down so quickly had made her feel very vulnerable. Felix had joined Katie's group, and Jenni missed him.

Rooms were searched diligently, then the doors were closed and locked. Large blue checkmarks on the doors indicated which rooms had been cleared. Room by room, floor by floor, the hotel was scoured. Jenni moved with graceful ease behind Curtis and his team, watching every shadow. They were now on the fifth floor, and there had been no sign of zombies since the one that had killed Chuck.

Jenni was feeling claustrophobic and hemmed in by both the building and by the cap on her head, which was hot and heavy. She wished it were over, wished she could abandon this mission. It was eating at her, making her feel weak and helpless. Their little world had felt so safe until now. The walls around the construction site and city hall had given them a sense of security. Their fort barely took up a one-block radius, and it was cramped but at least livable. She knew they needed the hotel, but right now, she hated it.

Anger was building up within her. She had actually felt safe and happy for the last few weeks. Her relationship with Juan was still evolving, but it was good. He was not quite the knight in shining armor she imagined, but he was sweet and made her laugh. She wanted to bask in his love and forget the past. Forget Lloyd, forget the dead children she had failed, forget the beatings, forget the pain . . . She just wanted peace in this little fortified construction site in this small town. She was beginning to hate this opulent hotel and its apparent false dreams.

"Fifth floor clear," Bill's voice said over the walkie-talkie. He was on the other side of the hotel.

Jenni and Curtis eyed each other, and then peered down the hallway with all its blue checkmarks on the doors.

"It would be nice if it kept going this way," Curtis said.

Jenni smacked him. "Don't say shit like that!"

"Jinx," said Jimmy, rubbing his bald head. "Don't jinx us."

"Shit, sorry," Curtis mumbled.

Katie, Travis, Felix, and Roger came around the corner. All four looked just as harried as Jenni felt. Katie gave Jenni a little smile and squeezed her arm affectionately and Jenni smiled. It was good to at least have friends in this world.

"Sixth floor may be a hot spot," Bill's voice said over the static. "Remember that from the roster."

"Roger that," Curtis answered as the two teams started upward.

The last person in Curtis's group, the short, skinny man named Davey, took off his hat and ran a hand over his blond hair. "Anyone else thinking this was a bad idea?"

Jenni, aware of the origins of the plans to take the hotel, glanced back at Travis. "Nah, we need this building. Right, Travis?"

"We're expanding our little world," Travis agreed.

Katie scrutinized the stairwell. "Doing what we gotta."

Davey frowned. "Well, damnit, this new world is a pain in my ass."

And with that, they continued upward.

The clatter of their heels against the stairs seemed incredibly loud, and they all pressed close to the wall as they climbed. Chuck's death had taught them a lesson.

On the sixth floor, the teams split up again, heading in different directions. Moving toward the first door, Jenni felt her stomach tightening. Just four more floors and it would be over.

Jenni hesitated at a window, staring over the rooftops toward the hills, which were soaked by the torrential rain. The storm was moving quickly, sunlight flashing out from gaps in the gray cloud cover to wash over the green landscape like spotlights. The sight was so beautiful that her breath caught in her throat. Looking down, she could see into the construction site. From above, it looked small and vulnerable. With a sigh, she hurried to catch up with the rest of her crew.

"Same routine as before," Curtis said.

Jenni unlocked the door. "Ready?"

When everyone gave the thumbs-up, she flung open the door and was rewarded with a sharp thud as the door hit the wall with a resounding smack. No zombie hiding there.

Most of the rooms they'd entered had been dark, curtains closed. In this one, the curtains were open, and pale sunlight streamed in, illuminating the room. This room was much bigger and more opulent than those below. It even had a balcony that Jenni spotted through the closed French doors. Cautiously, she stepped in. Davey followed directly behind her.

Jenni advanced slowly toward the bed, squatted down and pulled the comforter sharply off it.

Nothing below the bed.

Behind them, Curtis and Jimmy entered the room.

Jenni moved very cautiously toward the open door to the bathroom and peered in. Everything gleamed and sparkled inside the bathroom, but there was no sign of anything dead.

"Clear?" Curtis looked nervously around the room.

"Wardrobe," Jenni answered.

Davey approached the large piece of furniture. His slender frame crouched slightly as he reached out and took hold of its handle. Jenni moved closer, her gun aimed at the wardrobe.

"I don't think you should—," Jimmy said.

"What?" Davey paused, but his hand put enough pressure on the lever to release the latch. There was a click.

The doors exploded outward, knocking Davey to the floor and tossing Jenni onto the bed. Her gun flew out of her hand, hit the floor, and skittered under a chair in the corner. The largest zombie Jenni had ever seen rushed out, stepped on Davey, and rushed toward Jimmy and Curtis.

Jenni rolled off the bed as fast as she could, heading for her gun as another form, mostly eaten, slithered out of the wardrobe.

"Davey!" she screamed.

He climbed to his knees only to be confronted by the grisly creature. Enough strips of flesh hung off its bones for Jenni to identify the thing as female. It lunged forward and bit deep into Davey's cheek.

Curtis shot the other zombie in the head, but the giant male just kept barreling forward.

"It's Bubba Wilkins! He has a metal plate in his head!" Jimmy shouted.

"Shit!" Curtis yelled.

Jimmy turned and shoved Curtis out of the hotel room. The door slammed shut behind them.

Jenni stood in shock, breathing heavily. Only the bed stood between her and the two zombies.

• CHAPTER EIGHT •

1.
Waiting Is Hell

Jason sat on the floor of the Dollar Store with his arms around his German shepherd's neck. Jack woofed lightly as another peal of thunder broke overhead and the lights flickered briefly.

"It's coming down hard out there now," someone nearby said.

Jason tried to fight back his fear. He wanted to rush into the hotel after his stepmom and make sure she was okay. The hours were ticking away, and the storm was gnawing on his nerves. He knew that it would take some time to make sure the hotel was zombie free, but Jason couldn't stand how the minutes were creeping by.

Across the room, the girl he had a crush on gave him a slight smile. Michelle was sitting with her younger brother and her father, who had a secure hold on both his kids. His eyes were closed, but Jason could see his lips moving. Jason knew Michelle's father lived in terror of losing the remnants of his family and was pretty sure the man was praying.

"Here you go, Jason," Rosie, Juan's mother, said as she handed him a sandwich and small bag of chips from a basket she had slung over one arm.

"Thanks, Rosie. Have you heard anything?"

Shaking her head, Rosie handed Jason a plastic bag full of kibble. "Nothing yet. I'm sure it's going to be okay," she lied.

Jason could tell by her eyes and expression that something bad had happened inside the hotel. "Rosie, tell me, is it my mom? Is she okay?"

Hesitating, Rosie leaned over and ruffled his hair. "When I saw my son, he said your mom is fine."

"But someone else isn't?" Jason persisted in his questioning, ignoring Jack as the dog helped himself to the kibble.

Biting her bottom lip, Rosie shook her head before moving on to pass out more sandwiches.

Frowning, Jason took a bite out of his Velveeta cheese sandwich. Turning his gaze toward the front of the store, he saw Peggy talking animatedly to the mayor. Looking over his shoulder, he saw Yolanda holding Cody, rocking him as he slept.

"Do you know what's going on?"

Yolanda shook her head. "Not yet. Peggy is trying to find out."

Steven Mann joined the mayor and Peggy. Blanche Mann stood behind him, peeling the bread crust off her sandwich. Around Jason, people were beginning to notice the gathering at the front of the store. The mayor raised the walkie-talkie to his mouth and started to speak, turning his back to the room. Jason picked up the bottle of lukewarm water he had been nursing all morning and took a long sip. He could feel his stomach coiling into a tight knot, and he pulled Jack closer to him.

"What's going on?" an older man called out. Others echoed him.

Jason saw Steven Mann realize he had an audience. Steven spoke again, this time loudly enough to be heard by everyone in the store. "I didn't keep track of little details like that! The manager must have approved it! How the hell was I supposed to know?"

"Besides, Peggy should have known about it," Blanche added angrily. "It's not Steven's fault."

"Oh, hell no! Tobias would have handled that as city manager and he didn't tell me jack shit!" Peggy said defensively.

"What is happening? I want to know!" Old Man Watson shouted over the growing din.

The mayor looked somber as he turned around to face the store full of frightened people. "They are making good time through the hotel and have cleared most of it. But there have been some deaths. There was a breakfast meeting of some sort taking place that first day, so there were a lot more zombies than we anticipated in the building."

"Who is it? Who died?" a woman cried out. "Tell me it wasn't Davey!"

"As soon as I know the names of those who gave their lives, I will come talk to the loved ones. I promise," the mayor declared.

Swallowing hard, Jason buried his face against Jack's neck. "It won't be Mom. It won't be," he whispered. "It can't be."

The survivors of the fort fell silent as the mayor slowly walked over to where Belinda sat with her friend Gretchen. Mike's girlfriend shook her head adamantly, tears already flowing down her face. The mayor tenderly reached out to comfort her, and Belinda screamed as the storm sounded again overhead.

2.
Dance with Death

"This is how you die," she heard Lloyd say. "I may not have gotten you, but *he* will."

Jenni stood very still. The large zombie was banging on the door. It hadn't noticed her yet; it was still trying to get to Jimmy and Curtis.

Davey sobbed in pain as the female zombie ate his face. The munching and slurping noises were horrible. Jenni wanted to scream at Davey, to tell him to shoot the creature, but she couldn't speak, didn't dare speak.

Moving as slowly and silently as she could, she squatted down so she could reach under the chair for her gun. Her breath was so loud and harsh in her ears that she was sure the male zombie would hear her, but he just kept pounding on the door. Her heart thudded in time with the meaty fists banging against the door. Her skin felt slick and cold.

She groped blindly under the chair, trying to find her weapon, not daring to take her eyes off the zombie in the plumber's outfit. Her knees protested as she fought to keep her balance and not move too quickly. The last thing she wanted to do was attract the huge zombie's attention.

Davey wasn't making any more sounds, and she knew what that meant. Soon there would be three of the things to deal with.

Her mind began playing tricks on her; memories overlapped with reality. For a moment, it was Lloyd at the door and Benji on the other side of the bed. She forced those images away.

"You don't understand, Jenni. You're a stupid, crazy bitch. And it's time for you to die. To turn into what we are and eat the face off your spic boyfriend," Lloyd's voice taunted her. "You always were such a stupid little Mexican. Can't do a damn thing right. Guess your mother's blood fucked you up more than I thought. I never should have married a half-breed."

Her fingertips touched the gun just as the enormous zombie turned around. The flesh from its forehead had torn free, and a metal plate was visible under his lank black hair. His glazed gaze rested on her. He howled and surged forward.

"Shit!"

In her panic, her hand jerked and she knocked the gun farther away. She had to give up on retrieving the weapon and just get out of the room. Rising to her feet, she saw the zombie stumble on the far side of the bed. Probably over the other zombie and Davey.

Jenni backed up and felt something hard hit her hip. Looking behind her, she realized she was up against a door to the balcony.

Ripping it open, she stepped out into the rain, then slammed it shut before backing away. The zombie growled in fury as it smacked into the edge of the bed. It adjusted course and kept coming.

Jenni spun around, trying to figure out what the hell to do next. The white metal patio furniture—two small chairs and a table—were possible weapons, but he was so big. . . . He smashed into the door with a resounding thud and pounded on the glass.

Jenni backed up against the stone railing. Her heart was beating so fast, it literally hurt. Gulping down air, she tried to steady her nerves. She looked around frantically. To her left, about six or eight feet away, was another balcony.

The zombie's fist burst through one of the panes and reached for her.

Jenni ran to the far end of the slick balcony and climbed carefully onto the wide railing. Looking across the gap, she saw that she had no room for error. She would have to fling herself across to the other balcony and hope she could catch onto the railing. The wind buffeted her, and the rain stung her face. She tried hard not to look down and see how far she was from the ground.

"Mexicans can't fly. Just swim across the river," Lloyd laughed in her head.

"Lloyd, shut the fuck up," Jenni said through gritted teeth.

Another loud crash. Glass shattered behind her.

Near tears, she lowered her feet until her heels were resting on the floor of the balcony between the ornate stone slats that held up the railing. Her butt rested on the edge of the wet rail and her hands held tightly to the slippery stone.

This was not how she had planned to die. Falling to her death trying to escape a zombie was just not acceptable to her. Hell, dying period was not acceptable to her. Things were finally changing for her. Yes, the world was dead, but she was alive.

The zombie was breaking apart the door behind her.

Jenni whispered a prayer and threw herself toward the other balcony. Her chest smashed into the stone railing and she flung her arms around it. The pain of the impact ripped through her as she knocked most of the air out of her lungs. Struggling to breathe, she slowly pulled herself up and over the railing. Falling into a metal chair, she gasped in pain, staring back at where she had come from.

The zombie stood on the balcony, looking confused. It gazed straight ahead, as if searching for her in the clouds as a peal of thunder ripped overhead. Finally, it turned and saw her. With a raging growl, it ran straight toward her, leaping onto the rail and launching itself into the air. Jenni watched in horror as the zombie sailed toward her.

Like Jenni, he did not quite make it. His chest hit the rail and he fell back, his torn hands gripping the rain-slick stone.

"Gawdammit!" Jenni yelled at him as he managed to hold on. Picking up one of the heavy metal chairs, she bashed at the zombie's hands as hard as she could. She screamed as loud as he growled. As he struggled to pull himself up, she hit his huge hands with the metal chair. It was heavy and hard to wield, but she used it the best she could to batter the damn thing.

"I'm gonna fucking bash your gawddamn skull in," she hissed at him.

Lloyd's voice was quiet now.

"I choose when to die!" she screamed at the top of her lungs. "And it's not now!"

The zombie kept trying to pull himself up, but she kept smashing him as hard as she could.

Davey appeared on the neighboring balcony. His face was completely stripped away, and his bloodied, fleshless skull stared toward her. Only his eyes remained and, comically, his ears and a flap of his skull. With a desperate hiss, he ran toward the battle between the living and the dead.

"Bring it on, fucker!" Jenni shouted without pausing her attack on the big zombie.

Davey hurled himself over the rail. He managed to grab on to the first zombie and they both hung suspended over the street far below. Davey ripped at the large male's arms, trying to pull himself upward. The assault from above and below was too much. With a hungry growl of rage, the massive zombie lost his grip and they slipped out of sight.

Holding the chair tight in her hands, Jenni stood with her chest heaving, listening intently, and didn't relax until she heard the impact of their fall. Looking over the edge, she saw them far below. Davey was on the pavement, trying to crawl away with only one good arm. The other zombie was impaled on an old-fashioned streetlight, its arms and legs pumping as it tried in vain to escape.

As Jenni watched the zombie writhing below, she became aware of the number of zombies gathering before the hotel. They shambled around, as if sensing that there was living flesh nearby. Suddenly one of them looked up, saw Jenni, and reached toward her, growling. Following the first one's gaze, about ten more screeched at her. Backing away, Jenni looked at the doors behind her. The curtains for that room were drawn over the window and doors. She had no gun and no idea if anything lay beyond the glass. Soaked from the rain and gasping for breath, she knew she had to risk it.

She reached out to open the door when the doors began to shake under the hammering of fists on the other side.

Jenni regarded the other balcony she had come from. Her gun lay that way . . . as did the female zombie.

Looking once more at the door quivering before her, she made a choice.

3.
Nightmares Realized

Katie ran down the hall with Travis and Felix close behind. They had heard the screams and reacted immediately. Roger huffed and puffed behind them as they rounded the corner. Curtis and

Jimmy were shouting at each other as screams came from beyond the closed hotel room door.

"Where's Jenni?" Katie shouted.

"Jimmy flipped out and shoved me out of the room and shut the damn door. Jenni is in there. I'm pretty sure Davey is a goner," Curtis responded, his face red with anger. "Now he can't find the damn keys!"

Jimmy was desperately checking his pockets when Katie whirled on him. "Jenni is in there? What the fuck were you thinking leaving her alone?"

"I got it." Roger unlocked the door with their set of keys.

Next to Roger, Travis steadied himself, ready to fire.

"The zombie was Bubba! He has a metal plate in his head!" Jimmy screamed at Katie. "Our shots didn't even faze him!"

"You don't leave people behind!" Katie shouted angrily. For a moment, Lydia flickered in her mind. She fought back the image. "We don't leave people behind."

"Ready?" Roger asked.

Katie collected herself and nodded. Roger shoved the door open. Something that had once been human was on the floor, crawling toward the balcony. When the door banged open, it slid around, opened its mouth, and hissed. Katie felt her stomach flip-flop but managed not to vomit as she raised her gun and shot the thing in the head.

"Jenni," she called out anxiously. That thing on the floor could not be Jenni. Jenni had to still be in here, somewhere, alive. But if she wasn't . . .

Entering the room, Katie held her gun out before her. If Jenni were turned, she would have to kill her. Jenni was her friend and she loved her. It would be only right for her to be the one.

Jenni couldn't be gone. . . .

A shape loomed in the doorway to the balcony.

It took a second for her to take in the long black hair. The person limped into the room and raised its head. Blood poured out of its mouth.

It was Jenni.

Katie felt like screaming. Behind her, Travis raised his gun. "I'll do it."

"Fuck no," Jenni choked out.

Katie hit Travis's arm as the gun went off; the bullet hit the chandelier over the bed and sent it swinging.

"Goddamn." Jenni spit blood.

Katie moved slowly toward her.

"I thought—," Travis started, obviously shaken.

"Are you bit?" Tears were burning in Katie's eyes. Jenni looked bad. Katie could feel chills sliding up and down her spine and her stomach clenching.

"No." Jenni spit again. "I busted my lip jumping to the balcony. Twisted my ankle climbing over." She tucked her hair back behind her ears and licked her lips with a bloodied tongue. "Bit my tongue, too. Juan is so not going to like that."

Katie couldn't help but laugh. She lowered her gun.

"Shit, girl. We thought you were dead!" Felix said from the doorway.

"I'm not that easy to kill." Jenni grinned, then got down on the floor and reached under a chair to retrieve her gun.

"You're fucking lucky she's still alive," Curtis hissed at Jimmy.

"Look, my bullet bounced off Bubba's metal plate," Jimmy protested.

Katie walked onto the balcony and studied the area. She pieced together what Jenni had done to escape the zombies. Peering down, she saw a zombie impaled on a streetlamp and another crawling slowly up the stairs to the front doors of the hotel.

"Travis," she called out.

He walked out and peered over the rail. "Shit." Lifting his walkie-talkie, he pressed the button. "Juan, get a crew inside the hotel and secure the front door and windows. We can't wait. We've got a crowd gathering."

"Gotcha," Juan said. There was a pause, then, "How is it going?"

"We lost Davey. Almost lost Jenni. She's fine now. We're moving on."

Jenni appeared in the shattered doorway. "There are some in the room next to us, too."

"How do you know?" Katie asked.

"I was over there," Jenni answered, pointing to the other balcony, "and they started banging on the door." Jenni pushed her hair back from her face again. "Damn, when did I lose my hat?"

Katie reached out to touch Jenni's bruised cheek lightly. "I'm glad you're okay."

Jenni sighed. "Well, I just don't think I'd make a good zombie. I'd try to hump Juan, not eat him."

Katie smirked and Travis chortled.

"You are crazy," Travis said to her.

Jenni shrugged. "Yeah. But it's probably what keeps me alive."

"I wouldn't doubt that one bit," Travis answered.

Curtis came onto the balcony. "I say we move on together as a group. Might be slower, but probably safer now that my group is down to two."

Roger and Felix stood in the room, looking down at the skeletal creature on the floor.

"You know, I really don't want to be wearing a red shirt anymore."

"I told you it was a bad idea," Felix reminded him.

Jimmy stood near the doorway, looking pissed and sheepish at the same time. "He had a plate in his head. Bullets didn't work!"

Katie could feel her anger against him building. He had left Jenni to die, and she couldn't forgive that. "Just shut up, Jimmy."

Jenni limped across the room and stared at Jimmy in the eye. "Yeah, shut up."

Katie followed Jenni out into the hallway. She pulled pink chalk from her pocket and marked the door with an X, indicating a body inside.

"Glad that's not for me," Jenni decided.

Katie glanced warily at the next door. "So there are some in this room, huh?"

"Yeah." Jenni pulled her hair up out of her face and wound it into a bun. "Banging on the window. I didn't see how many."

Katie tilted her head. "You know, for a moment, I thought you were gone."

Jenni winced. "Yeah, me, too. But I was very determined not to go out like that. If I go, I'm going down for something big. Very heroic. Not just . . . not like that. I've really made up my mind on this."

"Yeah, I can tell."

Travis and Curtis joined them as Roger and Felix finally looked away from the dead female zombie. Jimmy sulked behind them, silent at last.

"Let's get this done," Curtis said bleakly, and moved ahead of them.

Katie felt her stomach tense as she readied herself once more.

Jenni unlocked the door.

Curtis flung it open.

Katie shot the zombie maid banging on the balcony door.

It was that easy.

Katie entered the room first and the warriors systematically checked it. Katie paused to look at the dead maid. The woman had been untouched except for what looked like a bite on her forearm. Katie marked the door with an X.

"Why did you tell Davey not to open the wardrobe?" Jenni asked of Jimmy abruptly.

"I saw dried blood under the doors," he grumbled.

"You got him killed," she said. "You distracted him."

Katie could feel the tension building. "Let's keep moving. There'll be time for this later."

They pushed on.

Door by door, room by room. Chalk mark after chalk mark. With the second plumber dead and another maid dead, they were feeling a bit better as they checked off the list of possible zombies from the hotel roster. Of course, there could be others they did not know about in the hotel, but the number of possible zombies was falling steadily.

"Sixth floor clear," Bill finally declared.

Jenni was walking with a limp, so Katie stayed near her. She could see that Travis was stressing over Jenni's injury, but was keeping his anger at Jimmy in check. Curtis was so red with anger, Katie was afraid he was going to have a heart attack. But they kept going, and Roger trudged along, mumbling to Felix about his red shirt.

4.
Friends in High Places

Juan waited impatiently while the gate into the hotel was unlocked. Word from Travis and the sentries inside was that there was a growing number of zombies outside the front of the hotel. They could no longer delay walling up the windows and front door.

As soon as the gate opened, he hurried through, followed by several construction workers with their tools and equipment and a small force of armed people. Stepping into the janitor's room, he grimaced. The stench was pretty intense and his eyes watered. He kicked the dead zombie bodies out of the way so the equipment could get through, and grimaced as bits of gore clung to his boots.

Stepping up to the door, Juan felt his palms sweating. They were going to have to trust that the teams had done their job and that no more zombies were roaming around on the first floor.

"Let's get it done," he said.

Swinging the door open, he stepped into the darkened hallway and flicked on a flashlight. He flashed the beam up and down the hallway. Nothing stirred.

"Scary, huh?" Ken said from behind him.

"When is it ever not scary?" Juan called out. "We're coming in!"

"We have you covered," a sentry answered, stepping out from an archway farther down the hall.

As they drew nearer, they heard the zombies banging on the doors and windows. Juan and his crew broke into a brisk run. The sound of their pounding feet against the tile, the tools jangling on their belts, and the humming of the wheelbarrow wheels echoed through the lobby, mixing with the moans and screeches of the zombies. The heavy oak doors were shuddering under the impacts of many fists; the dim outlines of the zombies' upper bodies could be seen through the heavy, frosted glass windows in the doors and on either side of the entry.

"Let's make this fast," Juan ordered.

The wheelbarrows of fresh cement were wheeled into position while the pallet jacks, loaded with bricks, were pulled into the room. Layers of wet cement and brick were laid as men and women worked in the humid heat of the hotel lobby.

While the bricklayers worked, Juan turned to survey the lobby. Spotting the nearly decapitated zombie body on the steps, he walked over, looked down at it, and grimaced. "Damn." Taking out his walkie-talkie, he pressed the button. "How is your progress up there, Nerit?"

"Moving along. We're on the seventh floor," she answered.

"Curtis? How about you?"

"Also on the seventh floor. Making some progress. Jenni's hurt, so we're moving slower," Curtis answered, then added quickly, "Nothing major, just knocked up a bit."

Juan felt his chest tighten. His Latin temper got the best of him, and he said, a little shortly, "I thought you said she was okay?"

"She's limping," Curtis said blandly.

Juan heard Jenni's voice through the background static, saying, "Tell him not to worry."

Curtis said, "She says not—"

"I heard her," Juan interrupted. He took off his hat and ran his fingers through his curls. "Take care up there. We're busy down here blocking these fuckers off."

There was a loud crash against one of the windows, and Juan whirled around to see the dim outline of a zombie with something quite large in its hand banging against the leaded glass.

"Shit!"

The front doors were set down at street level. Stairs inlaid with marble rose up to the lobby floor from the entrance. The only windows Juan had any concerns about were the ones framing the doorway. The rest of the windows on the first floor were at least eight feet above the street. More zombies were picking up items to smash into the windows and doors. It was as if they understood that living flesh would be within their reach if only they could break through.

The construction crew worked faster. Four people were spreading cement, laying brick, and then spreading more cement. Other workers kept refreshing the bins of cement while yet more handed down the bricks.

"Juan, we have cracks in this window," one of the men said.

Juan motioned to those standing nearby with guns to take up new positions. "Keep them covered."

"Faster, faster," people were saying to one another as they worked.

Juan wiped the sweat off his brow and looked at the right window. He could see long cracks in the glass. The shady figures behind the frosted window were banging on it with large, heavy objects.

"Concentrate on that window," Juan said.

Overlapping each other in their haste, the four bricklayers struggled to seal off the window. The new wall was almost five feet high when the first chunk of glass fell out of the windowframe. The workers hesitated, then kept going.

The guards looked nervous. "We can't get good shots with people in the way," one of them said.

Juan realized it would take some keen shooting to deal with the increasingly dangerous situation. "Nerit, I need you down here," Juan said into the walkie-talkie. "We're going to have trouble hitting the zombies."

"On my way," she answered.

Over the sound of the workers placing bricks, Juan heard another chunk of glass fall out of the window. "They're pushing on the wall," said his cousin Monica as she set another brick into the cement. "I can feel it."

"Shit!" Juan ran down the stairs and put his hands on the wall. He could feel it shifting under the force from the other side. "Shit, they are."

Motioning to Ken, he said, "Brace the walls."

"I'm on it!" Ken waved to a few construction workers that were helping pass along the bricks.

Another chunk of glass crashed down, and a hand pushed through the gap between the broken window and the new wall.

"Watch out!" Monica yelled.

Juan ducked but the zombie grabbed his hat and yanked it out of sight.

"That was my lucky hat!"

Monica slammed two more bricks into place. She was protected by a pair of heavy gloves and by the fact that in their desperation to get into the hotel, the zombies were struggling with one another to reach through the opening in the window.

Ken and his crew braced the walls with sheet metal and lumber.

The window continued to shatter under the zombies' relentless assault. Decaying hands appeared above the heads of those working on the wall. No one dared lay more bricks now, though Monica used her trowel to stab at one hand as it dislodged a brick.

"Keep going," Juan said.

"What?" Ken yelped. "They're coming in!"

"Not yet," Juan answered, and picked up a trowel. "They can't bite us that high. They'll just try to grab our hands. We're wearing gloves. Keep going."

The workers hesitated and then nodded, acknowledging that he was right. They went back to work, and the wall grew again. The bricks were laid as quickly as possible, given that the dead on the other side kept trying to grab the trowels and gloved hands of the workers.

The window on the other side of the door, where no one was working, cracked.

"Hurry it up!" Juan lifted the walkie-talkie. "Nerit, where are you?"

"Eliminating your problem," Nerit answered after a beat.

"What?" Juan said, feeling confused.

Monica was laying a brick when a zombie hand grabbed her wrist firmly. Yanking at her, it pinned her against the freshly made wall. Screaming, she struggled to get free.

"Taking care of your problem," Nerit repeated.

Suddenly, Monica fell away from the entrance, the zombie hand still attached to her arm, but now severed right above the wrist.

"Now leave me alone. I have a dozen more to take out," Nerit said.

Juan laughed and ran a hand over his curly hair. He imagined Nerit standing in a window high above, systematically killing the zombies gathered at the front of the hotel.

The moans dissipated and, finally, ceased. The dark shadows disappeared from the windows and suddenly the room was eerily silent.

"All done," Nerit's voice crackled over the static.

Juan looked down at the walkie-talkie, then looked at Ken. "She's a tough old lady."

Ken nodded. "She scares me."

"Good thing she's on our side. Now, let's get these walls done!"

5.
Upward

Nerit leaned over the balcony railing and made sure that there were no more zombies moving below. Bodies littered the street and were bunched up around the front door. It had taken some time to eliminate all of them, but she felt a sense of satisfaction at their demise. There was only one "living" zombie left, the gigantic one impaled on a lamppost. She was leaving him alive for a reason.

Her task complete, she moved back into the hotel room. Much to her surprise, she saw an old woman gazing at her with an intense expression on her face. Abruptly Nerit realized she was looking into a mirror. Her hand flew up to her face as she stared at her worn countenance. She had slipped so thoroughly into her role as sniper that she had felt young again. It was like a slap not to see the powerful blonde she had been when she was in the Israeli army, but instead, the older, stern woman she had become. Her eyes still glinted fiercely, but they were now surrounded by fine wrinkles.

Well, enough of vanity. Ralph had found her quite lovely in her old age, and that was all that had mattered.

She dismissed the old woman in the mirror and walked out into the hallway. This floor had been cleared, and blue checkmarks adorned all the doors. Moving at a quick pace, she felt at ease; her gun was a cold, comforting presence in her arms.

As a young child growing up in Israel, she had been acutely aware that the world was not always kind. Her mother was a survivor of the concentration camp where most of that side of the family had died. Her father often said that he felt Nerit had inherited her mother's finely tuned senses and fighting spirit. He had taught her and her brothers to shoot when they were all very young and had been thrilled when his young daughter immediately showed an uncanny ability to hit the bull's-eye every time. Soon he had her enrolled in competitions, and many of the photos of her childhood were of her and her father standing proudly beside a shooting trophy.

Ah, her father . . . how she missed him. He had raised her to be strong and confident. Not once did he try to dissuade her from pursuing her dreams. Her marksmanship had thrilled him. When she had been awarded a medal for her valor in the Six-Day War, he crafted a fine little display case for it.

His only disappointment had been her decision to marry instead of pursuing riflery and attempting to make the Israeli Olympic team. She wondered how he would feel about her role in this bizarre afterlife of a once-thriving planet. Her medals now were the shattered heads of the walking dead. Her accolades, the thanks of those she saved. There was no real victory now, just the heavy burden of doing what must be done.

Thoughtfully, she turned and headed up the stairs. How vividly her father's face came to mind. She knew he would be proud of her and how she was handling her bitter responsibility. Had he not raised her to defend her people and do what was right?

And the people in this fort were her people now. Nerit and her first husband had moved to America in the mid-eighties. When he died, leaving her a single mother, she had remained in the country to build a life for her children. She married a second time; her husband relocated the family from New York to Texas, where they had settled in Fort Worth. Some years later, he divorced her for a much younger woman, and to clear her head, she had gone on a hunting trip with some good friends. During that vacation, she met the love of her life, Ralph Toombs. He had brought her to that wonderful hunting store in the hills of Texas. Grown, her children said amicable good-byes and returned to Israel.

Nerit had firmly believed she would live with Ralph until they both left this world, but instead, Ralph had gone on without her. Now she was fighting for her life and the lives of others in a makeshift fort in the middle of nowhere.

Sometimes, she thought wryly, it was as if they were playing some terrible game of cowboys and Indians, hiding in their fort made of odds and ends. Of course, in this case, if the Indians breached the walls, they would eat the cowboys alive.

Entering the ninth floor, she began following the blue checkmarks on the doors. The teams were moving more swiftly now that the end was in sight. She hoped her fellow survivors were not being rash.

Going around a corner, she saw all the teams at the end of the hall. Some were clearing another room; Katie and Travis were hanging back slightly, covering the ominous-looking double doors that led upward to the last floor and its opulent ballroom. One of the doors was slightly ajar, but Nerit could see only darkness beyond it.

"How are we doing?" she called out.

Katie turned toward her and smiled slightly. "Okay. We haven't found anything up here. I don't think anyone got this far."

Nerit strode down the hallway, ignoring the pain in her hip and the numbness in her toes. She hated getting old. "We still need to be careful."

"Room's clear," Jenni said as she stepped into the corridor. She was hobbling, but trying not to look like she was. The poor girl was really beat up, but Nerit knew she was a scrappy fighter. When they'd first met, Jenni had seemed to be on the edge of a breakdown, but somehow she'd pulled away from it. Yes, she was still a bit crazy at times, but Nerit had a feeling that it was what kept her going. But then again, weren't they all a little crazy now?

"We're heading upstairs," Curtis said as he drew the checkmark on the door. "We're almost done. Juan took a team into the basement so he can get the power on. I sent Katarina, Felix, and Shane down to help."

Katie headed toward the double doors, her pistol held firmly in one hand. "I just want to get this over with."

Travis said, "I hear you there."

When Jenni moved, she favored her injured leg. Curtis took her arm to help her. Nerit raised her rifle as Katie neared the double doors. The pricking on the back of her neck had triggered her reflexes, and she trusted her instincts.

Before Katie could open the door all the way, a maid pitched through the gap, right into Katie. Flinging up her arm to protect herself, Katie fell back. From the moment the maid appeared, time seemed to slow for Nerit. Each movement was distinct and vivid to her. She could see the female zombie shaking her head, trying to rend flesh from Katie's arm as Katie screamed and Travis lurched forward to pull the zombie off.

Nerit became one with her rifle as she had so many times before and through its eagle eye, saw the top of the zombie's head. She fired and watched a blossom of blood explode into view, then dissipate.

Travis kicked the dead zombie away as Katie stumbled back, staring at her arm.

"She bit her! She bit her!" Jimmy yelled, near hysteria.

"No!" Jenni rushed forward.

Nerit swung the barrel of the rifle toward Katie, and her friend's beautiful eyes danced before her like jewels, lovely and sparkling with life. Then Travis's back blocked her scope. He had stepped between her and Katie.

"Travis, move away," Nerit ordered.

Travis paid her no heed and shouted, "You can't! You can't!"

Nerit took a step to one side to get a clear line of fire. Katie was such a lovely girl and Nerit adored her, but she had a job to do. Katie would not want to become one of the undead. It would be a great injustice to such a strong woman.

"Nerit, no!" Travis once again blocked Katie from view.

Jenni sobbed uncontrollably, one hand pressed over her mouth.

Nerit could hear Katie whispering Travis's name softly, a sob in her voice.

"Travis," Nerit said firmly. "Step aside and let me do what is right."

"It didn't go through!" Travis whirled around. "The bite! It didn't go through." He had stripped off Katie's denim jacket and now held her bare arm out for everyone to see. Bruises were already forming from the pressure of the zombie's mouth and hands, but there was no sign of the skin being broken. The heavy fabric of the jacket Katie had been wearing was intact and had protected her.

"Thank God!" Jenni cried out, and flung her arms around Katie. Katie, looking dazed, held tightly to the dark-haired woman.

Nerit lowered her rifle and walked deliberately toward them. She felt hope rising within her, but could not yet give in to it. At times, she hated the cold splinter that sliced through her soul, the place she could go when she needed not to feel and not to care. It had always been there, even when she was a child, even when she was with her beloved father. She was the woman who did what must be done.

Taking Katie's arm lightly in her hand, she turned it this way and that. Her keen eyes examined the brutal purple and green bruising. No puncture. No broken skin. No wound.

Stepping back, she nodded.

For a second, she let herself feel the pure joy that came from knowing that she would not have to release Katie from this nightmare world; then she shoved it away.

There was work to be done. . . .

"Let's move on," Nerit ordered, turned on her heel, and started up the stairs to the ballroom.

6.
The Top of the World

Travis wasn't sure he knew how to breathe anymore. Seeing the zombie lurch out of the darkness and fasten on Katie had been one of the worst moments of his entire life. In fact, he was pretty sure this day was responsible for all the worst moments of his life.

From the dining room massacre to Jenni's appearance on the balcony, he had felt his hold on his emotions slipping. He had not experienced the sheer horror of the first days, and to him, the zombies had mostly seemed far away and impersonal. But today, there was no denying their absolute power to terrify and destroy.

Moving slowly up the stairs after Nerit, he struggled not to hate her. He resented her hyperawareness of all that was around her and didn't understand how she could coldly deal with situations that made him feel ready to shit his pants. He hated how easily she killed people who had been her friends when the worst happened.

Yes, he offered to kill Jenni when she had appeared to be a zombie, but that was to spare Katie. Even now, he wasn't sure he would have pulled the trigger. No, if she had tried to kill Katie, he probably would have been able to take Jenni out. But all this shooting and killing were far removed from how he had been raised. It did not come naturally to him as it did to Nerit or the others.

He looked over his shoulder at Katie and Jenni. Both of them were bruised and favoring injured limbs. Guilt ate at him. Though the leadership of the fort had agreed to take over the hotel, it had been his call to enter today. It was his decision that had brought about all the death and pain of the day. Now he desperately wanted it to be over. The worst part was that because of his feelings for Katie, he lived in terror not only for his own life, but also for hers. Every moment was nerve racking. He was madly in love with her and if he lost her, it would be devastating.

Stepping into a vast foyer, he was startled by the sunlight pouring through high windows. The storm was receding over the hills to the west. The marble floors of the entryway shone beneath a fine layer of dust, and an ornate gold-gilded metal ceiling gleamed overhead. An enormous, sparkling crystal chandelier threw diamonds of light all around.

"It's beautiful," Jenni sighed.

Roman goddesses were tucked into alcoves, and plush red velvet couches adorned a few walls. Bouquets of dead flowers rested on small tables. Ahead of them were sets of French doors that opened out onto a patio that encircled the entire top floor. To their right were the restrooms, which they swept quickly and efficiently. Gleaming and empty.

"When we are done, I'm so using the ladies' room," Jenni said firmly.

Nerit motioned to the ballroom. "We're almost done."

The doors to the ballroom were wide open, revealing a room with an ornate fireplace and high vaulted ceilings. Chandeliers sparkled overhead. Heavy red curtains were drawn back from the windows to let the sun pour through gauzy white organza sheer curtains. Now that the storm had passed, the room was awash in sunlight. On the far end of the room, there were French doors that opened to the patio. Old-fashioned, short-legged chairs with plush velvet seats were neatly stacked against one wall.

Nerit led them into the room. They were careful to look along the walls beside the doors as they stepped onto the thick carpeting.

"Perfect for a wedding." Jenni sighed again.

"That's what it was used for in the old days," Curtis said.

Travis felt slightly overwhelmed by the opulence of the room. Its elegance was almost too much of a contrast to what his life had become down in the construction site. He looked at Katie, who was turning slowly, surveying the ballroom. Even bruised and exhausted looking, she was beautiful. He wondered what it would feel like to take her in his arms and dance with her in a room like this.

The group thoroughly scoured every corner of the room for zombies. Travis was tired and desperately wanted to be done with their mission, but he was careful to check behind the potted plants, stacked chairs, curtains, and tables.

"Nothing," Jenni called out from across the room.

The others echoed her declaration as they finished checking their areas.

Travis pulled back one last curtain and sighed with relief. "Nothing here either."

"Let's check the patio," Nerit said. She opened the doors to the patio and stepped out slowly.

On the patio, a beautiful Roman gazebo stood beside a pool of dank water. A waist-high stone railing surrounded the entire roof of the hotel. Travis walked over to the rail and looked down. He spotted a maintenance walkway a few feet below, tucked down out of view with a safety net extending outward around five feet.

To stop suicides, he thought.

Katie leaned over the rail to peer down, then toward the diminishing storm. "It's really beautiful up here."

Travis smiled. "I was thinking the same thing." He loved the way the sun was glinting off her curls. He wanted to touch them, but refrained.

"Keep alert," Nerit barked.

He frowned. Katie poked him. "She's just good at her job."

"Yeah," he said, almost resentfully.

They spread out and looked around, but there really were no hiding places on the patio, not even in the gazebo.

"How about up there?" Travis asked, pointing at the roof of the ballroom.

Nerit lifted her gaze. "Good point."

They all started to search for a way up. Travis walked around the patio, alongside the ballroom. He was more in the shadows on this side. The wind was quite fierce. Katie and Jenni followed him.

"That smell . . ."

A terrible stench was carried on the gusts. Travis immediately looked around for zombie. He saw nothing and felt panic rising within him.

Katie glanced up and uttered, "Oh, shit."

Travis followed her gaze and saw a zombie struggling to her

feet at the very edge of the roof. Travis recognized her as Brenda, a waitress from the diner near the construction site. She had always smiled at him when he came in for breakfast. She must have taken a second job at the hotel. Heartbreakingly, she seemed almost intact except for two bites on her hand. Her face was stained with dry tears.

"Oh, God!" Katie said. "She must have crawled up there and died."

The zombie snarled in frustration and finally managed to stand. She lurched forward and made a desperate leap at the living below her. Travis and the two women ducked, and the zombie sailed over their heads and the railing. Looking down, Travis saw her struggling on the safety net.

Katie started to aim, but Travis pushed her arm down. "I need to do this."

Seeing his expression, Katie lowered her weapon. "Okay."

Travis felt the sting of possible tears, but fought them back. He raised his weapon and forced himself not to flinch. He had to do this. He had to be able to kill zombies to protect those he loved, even if they were people he had once loved. "Sorry, Brenda," he said, aiming for the back of her head. For a moment, he saw her in his mind as she had been, a pretty blond girl with a big smile and rosy cheeks. Then he fired, and the thing she had become fell silent and still.

Katie touched his arm but didn't say a word.

"That sucked," Jenni said.

Travis felt shame and pride struggling inside him for dominance. He finally pushed both away and fully accepted that what he had just done was now part of his reality.

"Did you know her?" Katie asked.

"Yeah. I thought about asking her out when I first moved here. An opportunity lost," he sadly answered. Turning his gaze toward Katie, he knew he could not let another chance slip away.

"It's all clear up here," Nerit said from above. She was standing on the roof. "There is a ladder on the far side," she said in answer to his unspoken question.

Curtis appeared beside Nerit. "Damn pretty up here. Almost looks like nothing bad is happening."

Travis wondered if Curtis even saw the girl lying dead on the net.

Jenni hobbled past Travis, heading for an entrance. "Almost done."

"The basement is left," Curtis said.

"I hate basements," Jimmy grumbled.

"Monsters are always in the basement," Roger added. He had been quiet for a while now. Travis had a feeling that the seriousness of the situation had finally sunk home for Roger somewhere around the sixth floor.

"We'll hold position here. It's up to the crew downstairs to take care of the rest," Nerit said.

Travis gazed at the beauty of the hills. "It almost looks normal."

"Almost," Katie agreed, staring at Brenda's dead body.

The others drifted away, looking for places to sit down and relax, now that they had completed their primary objective.

Travis and Katie stayed where they were, staring out over the hills. Katie rubbed her wounded arm, looking very tired, but to him, she was beautiful, inside and out. She was strong and smart. He adored her. He made a decision.

He leaned over toward her, and she tilted her head questioningly. "Tonight," he said.

He knew she would understand what he meant, and from the look in her eyes, she did. She raised one hand to touch his cheek, then nodded.

Turning his head, he kissed her palm, then held her hand against his face. Exhausted, they walked back to the ballroom to join the others.

7.
All Clear

"I fucking hate basements," Juan said for the fifth time. He had insisted on coming downstairs with Katarina's group as they cleared the basement. He wanted to get the power on and had no patience anymore.

The flashlight beams slit the darkness and illuminated the monstrous machinery that was the internal organs of the hotel. Huge industrial laundry machines stood silent along one wall, and Juan looked at them warily. In horror movies, washing machines always had bad things in them.

Eight armed people systematically worked their way through the basement, while Juan headed for the fuse box. Katarina walked with him, her weapon in her hand.

"I hate basements," he said again.

Standing before the biggest fuse box he had ever seen in his life, he set to work. With a flashlight in one hand, he checked all the fuses.

There was the sharp bark of a gun. Someone said, "Clear."

"I hate zombies," Katarina sighed.

Juan looked around nervously, then nodded. "Yes, me, too. Basements with zombies . . . much worse."

Flashing the light around, he spotted a door labeled SUPPLY ROOM and pointed. "I need fuses."

Katarina frowned a little. "Great. Another closed door."

Juan walked over and knocked on the door.

"What are you doing?" Katarina asked with a little fear in her voice.

"If there is one in there, it should flip out and start banging back, right?"

Katarina raised an eyebrow. "You got a point."

Juan knocked again and waited. There was no response.

"I guess it's clear," he said, and opened the door. Immediately, a zombie lying on the floor inside leaned forward and bit the pointed toe of one of his shitkickers.

Juan jerked back with a startled yelp and Katarina shot the woman in the head. She pointed at the zombie's lack of arms. "Couldn't knock back.

"Well, there goes that theory," Juan said with a frown. "And she scuffed my boot. Damnit."

"Good thing it's not like in the zombie movies where they can bite through anything," Katarina smirked. "In the movies, she would have bitten your toes off."

Juan rolled his eyes. "It would take a zombie a damn long time to chew through a leather boot." He shone the light all around the small supply room. It was clear. He stepped in, shoving the zombie to one side with the same foot she'd tried to eat, and located the fuses.

Returning to the fuse box, he began replacing the burnt-out fuses, working quickly, safely, and efficiently. "That power surge the first day really fucked things up. I wonder what caused it."

Katarina continued to watch the darkness, her flashlight making long sweeps and occasionally revealing the other people in the basement. People kept calling out their status as they moved methodically through the basement.

"I got it!" Juan said triumphantly.

Suddenly, the basement filled with fluorescent light. Machinery growled to life. Everyone let out a gasp.

"Clear," someone called out. "All clear."

In the lobby, Monica started as the lights came to life, brightening the rich dark wood and fancy furniture.

"Wow," she said in awe.

The elevator on the right side of the lobby chimed and the doors opened. A little girl staggered out, looked around, and rushed toward the nearest person, growling.

"Freaky zombie kid!" Ken shouted.

Panic swept the room as people realized all the armed guards were in the basement. Monica picked up a brick and hurled it at the girl, hitting her in the chin. The zombie child staggered backwards. Monica smiled as her softball years paid off.

Another brick went careening toward the zombie and spun her around.

There was a flurry of excitement as people continued to pelt the girl with bricks until she fell to the floor. Monica ran over and stared down at the growling face of what had once been a living child, then slammed the brick in her hands down on the creature's head, shattering it into bloody chunks.

Travis, Nerit, and the others had assembled in the foyer to the ballroom when the electricity came back on. Nerit had pushed the buttons to summon the elevators. The first one had been empty. Now they were waiting for the last one. Travis stood ready, his gun aimed at the elevator's doors. Nerit stood beside him, her rifle steady.

A bell chimed and the doors opened. Inside the car was a body, a truly dead body.

Nerit looked closely at the emaciated form and said, "It's the hotel manager." It was evident from the state of the body and the condition of the elevator that he had died of either dehydration or starvation. He was curled into a ball, clutching his wallet. Pictures of his family spilled from between his fingers.

Travis said, "I guess we're done."

Nerit nodded.

And just like that, the day from hell was over.

Jason wished the crying would stop. As the mayor learned the identities of those who had died, he spoke with their loved ones as promised. People were consoling the bereaved throughout the store, and all the grief was nerve racking. Jason just wanted to see his mom and to know everything was okay.

Jack panted beside him, occasionally licking his hand. The

teenager was certain his dog understood that Jason needed to be comforted. The warmth of the animal's furry body and the smell of his kibble breath were strangely soothing. Jason rubbed Jack's back and was rewarded with a slurp across his face.

"They're done! They're done!" someone shouted.

Looking up, Jason saw his mother and Katie through the glass windows at the front of the Dollar Store. Jason scrambled to his feet and pushed through the crowd of people gathering near the front. The bell over the door rang as it opened. There was light applause from a few folks, but it died down as people shouted out questions.

Travis appeared above the crowd as he stepped onto a chair. He signaled for silence.

"Jason!"

He barely caught sight of his mom before she was gathering him up in her arms. She held him close, kissing his cheek. She reeked of blood, body odor, and something truly rank, but she was alive and he hugged her tight. Jack leaped up excitedly, trying to lick both of them.

From above, Travis said, "I want to thank you for your patience and prayers. It's been a long, long morning." He looked at his watch. "I can't believe it's only one fifteen." He shook his head. "But the hotel is clear—"

The cheers were raucous and the applause deafening.

Raising his hands, Travis again called for silence. "But we lost people. Good people who volunteered to lay their lives on the line. Let's all remember Mark, Wallace, Mike, Ashley, Ned, Chuck, and Davey. They will be missed."

"Mom, all those people died! You could have been killed." Her bruised face terrified him.

Jenni smiled and kissed his forehead. "I'm alive and so are you. That's what matters right now, honey."

Travis stepped down and Ed appeared, apparently standing on the same chair Travis had used. "Okay, cleanup crews, front and center. It's our turn now. Let's get it done!"

"That's us," Eric said beside Jason, grabbing his girlfriend's hand.

Jenni smoothed Jason's bangs back from his forehead. "I'm starving. Think you could hook your mom up with some lunch?"

Jason grinned. "I have connections." Wrapping his arm around her waist, he pulled her toward Rosie and her stash of sandwiches.

· CHAPTER NINE ·

1.
Beginnings . . .

There seemed to be very little time to rest and enjoy their victory. Almost immediately, cleanup crews came in and began the messy job of preparing their new home for occupancy. Wearing kerchiefs over their noses and mouths as masks, the hardiest of the volunteers set about wrapping the dead bodies in thick plastic sheets taken from the construction supplies. The corpses were then piled onto a pallet jack and removed through the hotel loading dock into a waiting truck.

Nerit and a few others who had proved to be deadly shots covered the disposal of the bodies from windows and balconies above. They took out any zombie trying to get too close. So far, there hadn't been any major incidents. A few zombies made runs at the truck, only to be taken down by the snipers.

Teams cut the carpeting in the dining room into long swaths that were then rolled up, put into plastic trash bags, then dumped in the same truck that would haul away the bodies of the dead. Some of the volunteers, who were not as physically fit, were given gloves and large buckets of water mixed with bleach and asked to clean up the blood splatter. Anything that had been contaminated by the blood or innards of the zombies was removed or scrubbed ferociously.

A sense of relief permeated the atmosphere. With so many people working, things were taken care of rather quickly. All the entrances to the hotel were double-checked to make sure they were secure. Several groups would be working deep into the night to brick them all up. The loading dock would be left operational, but only because the doors were thick metal and could be securely locked.

As the sun set, the hotel came alive with lights. The smell of bleach had wiped out the reek of death, and the upstairs windows were letting in cool, fresh evening air.

It was time to check in.

Peggy flipped through her list one more time. Standing behind the reservation desk, she shifted on her feet, feeling slightly uncomfortable. Despite being told repeatedly that the hotel was clear of zombies, she was still nervous. Cody was under the desk, playing with his toys. Every time she took a slight step away from him, he'd grab the hem of her jeans and her heart would break.

On Peggy's left, the mayor studied a copy of the map they were giving out to all the fort occupants along with their room assignments.

"So I just mark on the map where their room is and hand it to them with the key, right?" Manny asked.

"Yep," Peggy answered, trying not to sound irritated. "That's how it works." Though she was grateful he had volunteered to help her, she was annoyed at the same time. Like most city secretaries in rural Texas, it was Peggy who had truly run the town. Of course, the mayor always got the credit. He was a political creature, and she suspected he had offered to help now so that he would look good in the eyes of his constituents.

"This shouldn't be too hard," Manny said.

Yolanda and Rosie slid behind the desk and took up their positions. Peggy was glad she had accepted Yolanda's offer of help. Peggy was already feeling a lot less pressured.

"We got all the older folks settled in on the first floor," Rosie informed Peggy.

"It went easy as pie," Yolanda added.

"Juan is putting out the word for everyone to grab their stuff and head over for room assignments, so we're about to get swamped," Rosie said, pushing her silver-streaked dark hair back from her face. "It feels so good to be in here at last."

"You can say that again," Yolanda said with a grin.

Peggy wished she could agree. Her stomach was a mess of knots and she kept jumping at small sounds. Even footsteps made her shiver, and she clutched her pen tightly before looking up to see not zombies but her fellow fort inhabitants approaching the desk. People were smiling and laughing as they got into line at the desk.

"Checking in," Felix said, stepping up and setting his duffel bag on the counter.

"I need a credit card and your driver's license," Peggy drawled.

"Huh?"

His confused expression made Peggy laugh and loosened the ugly knots in her soul. "Gotcha," she teased, then gave him his room assignment as he shook his head with amusement. Beside her, Yolanda and Rosie were similarly quick and efficient, while Manny took his time.

"Hi, Katie," Peggy said with a smile, handing over her key and a map.

The blond woman was pretty banged up and looked exhausted, but she returned the smile. "Thanks, Peggy. You have no idea how desperately I want a bath."

"You better hurry up, then. I have a feeling everyone is going to be rushing for the bathtubs. Who knows if the hot water will last?"

"Good point," Katie said, then picked up her box of possessions and disappeared into the crowd.

Rosie handed her son a set of keys. "You have a suite, *hijo*, since you have Jenni and Jason with you."

"Don't forget the dog," Juan said with a wink. He took the keys, then threaded his way through the gathering to where his new family was waiting for him near the elevators.

"I think I'm going to cry," Rosie confessed, sniffling. "I never thought I would see the day my boy would finally find the right girl."

"If only I could find the right guy," Peggy grumbled playfully. It was good to see everyone looking relaxed and happy. The good moods were infectious and her fear was lessening. Peering down at Cody, she said, "Honey, don't be afraid. I promise you. The zombies don't live in the hotel no more. We do. And it's all good."

Slowly, her son smiled.

Taking the elevator—it still reeked of bleach—Katie was relieved not to have to climb the stairs again today. Her legs ached horribly.

Her new room was nice, spacious, and welcoming. The four-poster bed and heavy Victorian furniture were not her cup of tea, but there was something very homey about it. She pushed back the heavy dark pink curtains covering the tall, narrow windows and observed the street outside the fort. A few figures staggered below, zombies too mutilated to run or to pose much of a threat. Closing the curtains, she started to put away her things.

It was sad how quickly everything was tucked away into its proper place. In this new world, she barely owned anything. Maybe that was good, less to be attached to.

She turned down the bed and, out of curiosity, flipped on the TV. To her surprise, the hotel's closed-circuit broadcast was working and it seemed that someone was running *Terminator 2*. Katie briefly compared her arms to Linda Hamilton's. All this hard work had her looking pretty buff.

With a sigh, she headed into the bathroom for a long bath. She undressed, her body protesting every movement. Looking into the mirror, she saw why. There were bruises all over her body. The marks on her arm were the most terrifying, but they were a lesson learned. Time was short. Too short to worry about what had been and what could be.

Using the hotel's rose soap, shampoo, and conditioner, Katie washed herself thoroughly and was relieved to finally not smell of death. Feeling refreshed, she sat in the hot water as her muscles slowly relaxed.

After her bath, dressed in a tank top and pajama bottoms she had claimed from the Walmart stock in the city hall basement, she felt restless and started rearranging the furniture. The bed was far too heavy to shift, but she moved the chairs, desk, and vanity into a more comfortable arrangement. There were a few little decorative knickknacks on the tables; these Katie mostly set aside to be returned to the hotel's storage space. She switched the paintings around and fussed with a mirror until it was set at a good height on the wall. Partway through her redecorating, Katie found herself glancing at the clock and realized she was waiting for Travis. His earlier comment had been full of promise.

Finally feeling that the room was hers, she sank into a chair and read a book she had borrowed from Peggy's makeshift library.

When the knock came, she tried not to panic. Laying the book aside, she slid to her bare feet and walked to the door. Another knock, quieter now. She knew Travis was giving her time to change her mind, to pretend to be asleep.

Opening the door, she gazed out at Travis. His hands were resting on either side of the doorway. He was scrubbed clean and his hair was still damp. He looked tired and anxious. She realized he was waiting for her to send him away.

Reaching out, she tangled one hand in his hair and kissed him deeply. With her other arm, she tugged him into her embrace and into her room. He almost stumbled, he was so startled. Then he came easily and willingly into her arms.

Together, they shut the door behind them.

2.
Letting Go and Moving Forward

Travis has been a nervous wreck when he knocked on Katie's door. His stomach had been twisted into knots and his throat was so dry, he couldn't speak. He had been pretty sure she was going to turn him away. He had begun to second-guess their short conversation up on the patio of the ballroom. He slowly concluded that he had not been clear in his intentions and she had not understood what he meant.

From the moment he realized he had feelings for Katie, he was sure he was doomed to heartbreak. But he couldn't stop himself from hoping. Their kiss—well, two kisses—had been enough to stoke the fires of hope within him.

When she opened the door, his heart skipped a beat. She looked so beautiful, so ethereal, with the light behind her glinting off her blond locks. Her sparkling green eyes regarded him beneath the fringe of her eyelashes and he braced himself, sure she was about to reject him again. Hell, there was a bottle of Jack Daniel's back in his room to keep him company after she said no.

Instead, she reached out and kissed him in a way that made his knees weak and the butterflies in his stomach turn into a tornado. He almost fell into the room in surprise.

The next kiss was everything he had hoped for: sweet yet passionate, loving yet lustful, soothing yet exciting. He wrapped his arms tightly around her and dragged her closer and—

"Ouch!" Katie grunted.

Not the reaction he was expecting.

"Sorry," he said, quickly letting go of her.

"Bruises," she explained with a wince.

He nodded.

Again they kissed deeply, her hands trailed down his back, and—

"Shit," Travis muttered against her lips.

"Oh, sorry," she said.

"I kinda have a bruise there."

Katie laughed and pulled away from him, holding out her discolored arms. She turned around, displaying her back, a patchwork of purple, green, and black.

Travis grinned and returned the favor, showing Katie his arms and the welt on his side.

"Well, we match," she laughed.

Travis looped his hand around her neck, drew her close, and pressed his lips to hers. He lost himself in a kiss that felt like no other. He was completely enraptured with her. To his great surprise and delight, she seemed just as enamored with him.

"I love you," Travis whispered, stroking her curls, gazing into her eyes.

"Yeah, I kinda figured that out."

"I know it's not the same for you, since you're gay—"

"Actually, I'm not," Katie said, to his amazement. Drawing back, she took his hand and guided him to sit beside her on the edge of the bed.

"You had a wife," he pointed out.

"And I love her with all my heart. I would have gladly and happily spent the rest of my life with her. But I've dated men and women; I'm bisexual."

"So you've been with men before?" Travis asked cautiously.

Katie nodded.

"Oh, thank God," Travis proclaimed. "I was worried sick about not knowing how to please you."

Katie grinned and wrapped her arms around him. "You're really silly sometimes."

Travis laughed with relief. "You have no idea of the performance anxiety I was having. Hell, I was afraid you'd take one look at—" He looked down at his lap. "—you know . . . and run screaming."

Her eyes widened and then she really started to laugh. "No,

no, I promise you I won't. It's been a while, but I am pretty sure I remember how it all works. Not that you're getting any—"

Travis blinked, realizing how presumptuous he had been. "No, I mean, of course not, I didn't mean—"

"I'm just giving you a hard time, Travis," Katie said with a soft kiss to his cheek. "But honestly, this is not easy for me. I'm. . . ." She sighed, apparently at a loss for words.

Travis gently stroked her hair and kissed her cheek. "You don't have to say or do anything you don't want to, Katie."

"I'm just dealing with a lot of guilt," Katie said after a long pause. "I lived in the gay community for almost a decade. Lydia and I made sure we were both covered legally should either one of us die. We worked hard for gay rights after we decided to live openly as a lesbian couple. We were well known in our community and I dealt with a lot of flack from my superiors at work. Even my own mother and father had trouble with the choices I made. When I broke up with the guy I was engaged to before I met Lydia, my mother told me that I had crushed her hopes and dreams." Katie paused, pain filling her eyes. "She told me never to speak to her again. Thank God my dad was always there for me even when he didn't fully understand what I was all about."

Travis listened quietly, trying to understand. He knew it wasn't a good parallel, but a number of years earlier, he had dated a black woman for a short time. Her family had been staunchly opposed to their relationship, and though Travis had worked hard to keep them together, she opted to end it when the pressure on her became too great. When he told his parents that they had broken up, he was surprised to find that his very liberal parents sighed with relief. He hoped that maybe because of that, he had an inkling of what Katie was talking about.

"So, the point of all this is, I became very used to living in the LGBT community and sometimes it was very difficult. If I identified myself as bisexual, I was sometimes told I just hadn't fully accepted that I was lesbian. Lydia always defended me, but I eventually stopped telling anyone that I was bi." Katie laughed bitterly. "After that, this one woman we knew congratulated me on finally accepting myself as a lesbian and not being in denial anymore." She gazed into Travis's eyes. "Lydia understood that I had made a choice to be with her because of who she was, not because her gender. I need you to understand that, too."

"I do, Katie. I do. And I don't expect you not to love Lydia anymore or to think badly of your old lifestyle. All I ask is that you let what we have grow and be what it wants to be. Give me a chance to love you."

Katie took a deep breath. "For a long time, I wasn't sure I wanted to do that, but now I am. I can't let my nightmares or my guilt keep me from enjoying what life I have left. I realized that today. After all the death and violence, I realized that in the end, I just wanted you to hold me."

Travis felt the heaviness that had been on his heart dissipate as she spoke. He took her face gently between his hands and kissed her very tenderly. "I want to hold you."

Smiling, she kissed him back, and then slid away from him.

In silence, he slipped off his boots and his jacket and lay back on the pile of pillows on the bed. She came into his arms and laid her head on his chest. With infinite gentleness, he stroked her bruised flesh and kissed the top of her head.

He felt deliciously good.

Eric emerged from the sparkling tub in the bathroom of the new, comfortable hotel room that he now shared with Stacey and Pepe. It was a relief not to have to stand in line to use the restroom or sign in to take a shower. He grinned as he wrapped a fresh towel around his hips.

With another towel, he vigorously dried his hair as he wandered into his new bedroom. His attention was caught by Pepe, who was lying in the new doggie bed they had snatched from the Dollar Store, wagging his tail despite his sleepy expression.

"Hey, isn't Pepe going to sleep with us?" Eric asked. He was used to the little guy snuggling with them.

"Absolutely, not," Stacey answered.

Eric finally looked at his girlfriend. Stacey was lying across the bed, naked and beautiful. She had insisted on showering first and now he understood why. She was smiling the sweetest, most sultry smile he had ever seen on her lovely face.

"Sorry, Pepe, you're out of luck," Eric said with a laugh. He dropped his towels and strode, transfixed, to the bed.

Stacey laughed with delight and held out her arms to him. "At last, we can make this official!"

"And no one will hear us!"

She plucked off his glasses and tossed them onto a chair nearby. "Tell me you love me."

"I love you," Eric whispered.

Lenore opened the door to her hotel room and stared out at Ken with her most grumpy expression. He was dressed in new pajamas and held Cher's cat carrier in one hand and a bottle of champagne in the other.

"Slumber party!" he said with a grin.

"No," Lenore answered gruffly, and slammed the door.

She knew it wouldn't deter him. She waited for the knock she knew was coming.

"Lenore, let me in. I'm your best girlfriend."

Lenore harrumphed.

"You love me. Please, Lenore, let me in. I'm afraid of zombies and I can't sleep alone. Please! I know you have two queens in there."

Lenore looked over her shoulder at the two beds.

"Another one won't hurt," Ken pleaded through the door.

Finally, she opened it and stared out at him. "One word about Daniel Craig, Clive Owen, or Hugh Jackman, and I'm throwing you out!"

Ken grinned and hurried past her. "Yay!"

Lenore shut the door, grumbling, but a slight smile crept onto her lips. At least she had her best friend in this stupid world, even if he was tremendously annoying sometimes.

"Shit," Juan said as Jenni almost slipped and fell headfirst into the tub. She had been trying to grab the bottle of champagne off the counter when her injured leg gave way.

Juan took hold of her naked hips with his sudsy hands and held her steady as she finally managed to get into the tub without killing them both. Lowering herself into the mountains of white bubbles until she was straddling his lap, she grinned.

"See, nothing to it!" She took a long swallow of champagne and handed him the bottle.

Juan gulped down some of the warm champagne. "Shit, that's nasty."

Jenni giggled and pressed her bare breasts against his chest. "Almost as nasty as me?"

"Shit, girl," Juan said with a grin, "no one is as nasty as you."

Laughing, she kissed him and they both nearly went underwater before Juan managed to grab the edge of the tub.

"You're trying to drown us!"

"Oh, shut up and kiss me."

Juan obliged. The champagne bottle fell off the edge of the tub and onto the floor, splashing the last of the bubbly all over the bathroom rug.

Neither one of them noticed.

Katie awoke a few hours later to gentle snoring. She felt a little disoriented by the sound and by the shape of the body she felt in her arms. Lydia snored, but the body pressed against hers was not one bit female.

She came more awake and smiled to herself.

It was Travis.

He was sound asleep. His arms were around her as he spooned up against her. The lamp next to the bed was still on. When she turned her head to see his face, she had to suppress a giggle. He was so deeply asleep that his mouth was hanging open.

Stretching a little, she managed to turn in his arms and get into a more comfortable position despite her aches and pains. Observing Travis's arm, draped over her waist, she could see where the zombies had grabbed him. Their handprints were distinctly pressed into his flesh.

They had both been immensely lucky.

Stirring, Travis turned onto his back, one arm slung over his forehead. He looked more serene than she had ever seen before. She had really grown to love his face. It was so strong and kind. Propping herself up, Katie ran her hand under his T-shirt along the length of his chest. He was so manly and muscular that she almost felt intimidated. Enjoying the feel of his skin under her hand, she felt a surprising pulse of desire.

"Travis," she whispered.

One eye slowly opened. "Um?"

She slid up his chest and kissed him deeply. She knew when he came fully awake and was very aware of her body against his. Through her pajamas and his jeans, she could feel him stirring.

"I promise I won't run screaming," she said very softly.

"I thought we were just going to sleep," he replied.

"Well, if you want to," she answered, feeling a slight pang of disappointment.

Travis instantly flipped her onto her back and grinned down at her from above, where he was supporting himself on his arms. "Sleep can wait." He lowered his head.

Responding hungrily to his kisses, Katie felt her reservations fading. Travis was gentle and tender. His kisses passionate but loving. Any awkwardness she felt faded away as her desire grew.

Simple things like the width of his shoulders and the narrowness of his waist and hips enthralled her. His cheek was scraggly against her skin and she enjoyed the sensation. Travis soon had her gasping and moaning and her bruises were forgotten. She buried her face in his neck and wrapped her legs tightly around him as her body shuddered beneath him. He kissed and nuzzled her neck, stroking her hair as she trembled with pleasure.

"Love you," he whispered.

"Love you," she answered, and to her joy, she meant it.

In the drowsy aftermath of lovemaking, he stroked her skin with infinite gentleness. She ran one hand down his side and rested it on his hip. They shared little kisses and whispers of endearment. It felt good and wonderful. Katie fell asleep smiling.

When Lydia's zombified ghost appeared in a dream, Katie was not surprised. Angry and fierce, the specter rose over her and Travis where they lay together in bed.

"How could you do this to me?" zombie Lydia demanded.

"If you were really Lydia, you would be happy for me," Katie answered bluntly.

The zombified Lydia hesitated. "You left me."

"You were already gone. All that is left now is the shell of who you were," Katie said as firmly as she could, though her voice quavered. "You're not Lydia. You're my guilt that I didn't save her. I'll always love her, but I need to move on. I need to be happy. And if you were truly my Lydia, you would understand that. You would understand that, because you would love me from beyond the grave. You're not her, and I'm not giving you power over me anymore."

The zombie staggered back, lost its form, and disappeared. The true Lydia stepped out of the darkness. She looked whole and beautiful, her smile as wonderful as always. This spirit was full of Lydia's wonderful essence. Katie could feel love radiating out of her.

"You finally let go of your guilt," Lydia whispered.

"I wish I could have saved you," Katie said in a voice that was ragged with emotion.

Lydia swept Katie's curls back from her face with a delicate hand. "It was not meant to be. I died minutes after you left."

Katie whimpered and clutched Lydia's hand tightly. Drawing it to her lips, she kissed it. "I'm so sorry, babe."

"My thoughts were of you, Katie. I prayed you would escape. I prayed you would live," Lydia said soothingly.

"I love you, I never wanted to be without you," Katie said, tears in her eyes.

"And I love you," Lydia answered with the gentlest of smiles. "I wouldn't want you to be alone. We were so happy together. No one can ever take that from us. Be happy again, Katie. Be happy and live your life."

"Lydia," Katie sobbed, desperately missing her.

Lydia kissed her on the lips, then drew away and vanished.

Katie awoke with a start, her hand flying to her mouth. She could almost feel the softness of Lydia's lips on her own. The sun was higher in the sky. Light was pouring through the slit in the curtains.

Beside her, Travis was on his elbow, looking down at her. He looked worried and he slid his hand over her hair tenderly. "Are you okay?"

"I dreamed of Lydia," Katie answered truthfully.

Travis nodded, his brow furrowed. "I know. You said her name."

"It was like she was really here. Not like in my other dreams. I really felt her here, with me. It's so odd."

Travis stroked her arm. "She's a part of you, Katie. Of course she's going to haunt you in some way."

She could see the tension in him, his fear that she would push him away. "You don't have to compete with her ghost," Katie assured him.

"I don't?" Travis's voice was strained. "Are you sure?"

Katie smiled and took his face between her hands. "I'm sure. I'm very, very sure."

• CHAPTER TEN •

1.
Shuffling the Deck

Nerit's morning started as simply as her night had ended. After sliding off the bed, she opened the curtains to take in the first rays of dawn and check the street for zombies. She noted a few wandering around and mentally made a note to deal with them later. Then she took a long, hot shower that helped loosen up her stiff joints and spent five minutes combing and braiding her long hair and applying the only makeup she ever wore, a bit of mascara and some lip gloss.

Dressed in olive green jeans, hunting boots, and a green T-shirt under Ralph's jacket, she made her way down to the dining room for an early breakfast. The room looked nothing like the scene of bloody chaos of the day before. Under the ornate rug had been a very pretty but faded tile floor that a few volunteers had spent all night mopping and polishing until it gleamed under the chandelier lights.

Old Man Watson and several other elderly people were gathered at one table, eating oatmeal and toast by the look of it. He smiled warmly at Nerit as she passed and gave her a little wave. As Tucker, Nerit's old dog, wandered along behind her, the old man reached out to pat his head and call him a good dog.

The early-morning breakfast crew had laid out breakfast on a buffet table. Oatmeal, toast, reconstituted powdered eggs, and dry cereal with large chilled mugs of powdered milk greeted her. Nerit served herself some oatmeal and eggs and sighed as she poured out the thin, bluish milk. She missed whole milk and fresh eggs. A glass of orange juice completed her breakfast. While she was doing that, her dog wandered over to one of several food bowls set on the floor for pets and started to eat, looking as weary in his bones as she sometimes felt.

Nerit took a seat at an empty table, but before she could begin to eat, a voice said, "Can I sit here?"

She looked up to see Jason holding a tray of food; she smiled warmly and said, "Of course!" The boy sat, surrounded by a cloud of sullen teenage angst, and stabbed his spoon at a bowl of cold cereal.

Jack strolled over to join Nerit's dog.

Jason sighed. "Juan lives with us now," he said.

"Yes, I know. I heard," Nerit answered, starting in on her eggs.

Jason sighed a little more dramatically. "I don't understand why."

"Well, your mother is doing what many people are doing right now, living in a kind of desperate rush. Death could come at any time. When you know that, you want to grab life and enjoy it before it ends," Nerit explained. "I think you will see many people doing that, especially now that we have what feels like a safe and comfortable home."

Jason frowned a bit as he chewed his cereal. "I guess. It just feels weird. They talk in Spanish to each other a lot and I feel left out."

"Ah," Nerit said. "Well, why don't you ask them to teach you Spanish or at least translate so you don't feel left out?"

Jason shrugged again, then said, "It just feels so different now. I don't like how everything keeps changing."

"Neither do I, but we have to do our best."

Jason hoisted a large backpack onto the table and pulled out some notebooks. "I've been working on weapon ideas to keep my mind off of . . . you know . . . stuff. . . ."

"Really? Like what?"

The boy opened a notebook to show her his notes and illustrations. "We really can't use fire in the fort. It's way too dangerous. We could end up setting our own stuff on fire, and burning down the hotel would not be good. But outside the fort, we could make some sort of firetrap. I was looking into making concussion grenades to rip the zombies apart and maybe doing some stuff with shrapnel to rip up their bodies. I noticed the more fucked . . . um . . . messed-up ones are slower and easier to kill."

"Yes, they are," Nerit agreed.

"Michelle's little brother came up with a lawn mower, wood chipper–type machine to chew them up." Jason showed Nerit the youngster's crayon illustration of zombies getting ripped apart by a large lawn mower. "It got me thinking. We could take apart some lawn mowers and use the engines and blades. Not sure how yet, but working on it."

Nerit looked at several pages of the notebook. "These are very good ideas."

"Yeah, but I'm not sure how to do some of it."

"Maybe Juan could help you, or Travis."

Jason peered at her from under his bangs. "I guess so. I just don't think they'll listen to me."

Nerit laughed a little. With her own children long grown, she had forgotten how moody teenage boys could be. "Oh, I think they will. We need all the clever ideas we can get to survive this."

"Maybe." He frowned.

"Jason, I really do believe they will listen to you. You're a smart boy with clever ideas. You should talk to Juan and Travis. I think they will be able to help you figure it all out."

Jason fidgeted with his notes, then finally agreed. "Yeah, I guess. I'm just used to older guys not listening to me. My dad never gave a rat's ass what I thought or said."

Nerit took a long sip of her orange juice, pondering her response. "Well, Jason, I think you need to do what your mother is doing. Make a new life. Get a fresh start."

Jason stared at her, then ducked his head down. "Yeah. I guess."

Shoveling more cereal into his mouth, he looked up at her through his bangs again. She could tell he was considering her words.

Finished with breakfast, Nerit stood, stretched stiffly, and picked up her rifle. "I will see you later, Jason. I need to get to work."

"Thanks, Nerit," Jason answered. "You know, for listening."

She nodded and walked out of the dining room, her dog falling into step behind her. Today she felt particularly stiff and clumsy. It was hard for her to accept her age, and most of the time she did not feel her years at all, but today she did. She had deliberately chosen not to sit with the other seniors. This was not a time for her to give in to age, but to fight it. With Mike gone, she had a role to play.

Approaching the front desk, she found Peggy typing away on a computer. Amazingly the Internet still existed where there was power. Nerit remembered the mayor saying that several server farms were up and running because the workers had barricaded themselves into their office buildings. They were trying hard to keep the Net functioning so that information could be exchanged among surviving scientists and also so that the living could reach out to others who were still alive. Peggy often logged on to monitor other groups of survivors. From time to time, a group would vanish and with each disappearance, Nerit felt that part of civilization was lost. Real news, national or international, was hard to come by. No one had any idea if there was any semblance of the government left. The Internet was rife with rumors.

"Do you have the duty roster?"

Peggy started, then laughed. "God, you gave me a fright. Yeah, right there. I updated it like you asked."

Nerit scanned the list. If he had reported for duty on time, Jimmy was already on watch, right where Nerit had assigned him. "Excellent. I'll make sure to get you a new schedule for the next few days as soon as possible." With Mike and several others dead, the roster would have to look very different.

"I can take you off kitchen duty, since you've taken over for Mike," Peggy offered.

Nerit shook her head. "No, no. Cooking is relaxing. Keep me on it."

Peggy shrugged, then cocked her head. "Nerit, I was wondering. . . . Could you teach me how to shoot?"

With a grin, Nerit answered, "Of course. I'm thinking about making lessons mandatory, not voluntary."

"I just don't want to feel so useless, so helpless."

"That seems to be the theme of the day," Nerit replied, and strolled away. She was halfway across the lobby when she saw Curtis. "Curtis, there's something I need to attend to. Mind joining me?"

Curtis hesitated, then said, "Sure. What are we dealing with?"

"Jimmy."

Curtis frowned. "Yeah. I talked to Travis and Juan about what he pulled yesterday. Juan wants him banned from any more dangerous missions."

"I think he just needs to learn a lesson," Nerit answered evenly.

She entered the elevator and Curtis followed.

"I don't know, Nerit. He's always been twitchy."

"We're all twitchy."

This brought guffaws from Curtis.

She raised an eyebrow at him.

"You're the coldest of us, Nerit, a true killing machine. You're never twitchy."

Nerit shook her head. "I'm just well trained."

"We don't need cowards," Curtis said heatedly. "We don't need people who will sacrifice others to protect themselves."

"No, we need well-trained people," Nerit spoke sharply, and Curtis fell silent.

They found Jimmy on duty in a room on the second floor that had been designated as a sentry outpost. He was sitting on a windowsill above the front door with his feet propped up on a chair, looking bored.

"Jimmy," Nerit said.

Startled, Jimmy jumped up. "Hey, Nerit." He looked decidedly nervous; his gaze darted between Nerit and Curtis.

"Curtis, can I have the gun you used yesterday to shoot the zombie with the metal plate in his head?" Nerit held out her hand.

"Sure," Curtis said, sounding confused. He pulled a small .22 from his side holster. "It's my backup weapon."

Nerit stepped up to the open window, and fired at the zombie still languishing on the streetlamp. It took four shots, but at last the zombie collapsed into final death. Silently, she handed the weapon back to Curtis.

"Sometimes, with a small-caliber weapon, the bullets glance off hard surfaces. Not just metal plates, but bone. You have to keep firing. If you shoot a zombie through the eye, the bullet will bounce around in its brain and churn it into mush. The lesson here, Jimmy, is keep firing." Nerit's gaze grew steely. "Never leave anyone behind. If they are bitten, shoot them, but if they are alive, cover them. Understood?"

Jimmy stared at her sullenly. "Yeah, I got it."

"Good." Nerit walked out of the room, her job done.

Curtis shuffled after her. "That's it?"

Nerit turned to face him. "That's it. For now."

Curtis gaped at her, then stepped back. "Okay, but Juan and Travis will not like this!"

"Then they can talk to me," Nerit answered. She stepped into the elevator and hit the button. The doors closed on Curtis's frustrated features. Nerit sagged against the side of the elevator and sighed.

2.
Drawing the Tower

Juan and Jenni stepped out of the elevator on the seventh floor, arguing loudly in Spanish. Jenni was limping, her face well decorated with purple and green bruises. Waving her hand in frustration, she insulted Juan thoroughly before knocking on Katie's door.

Jenni was annoyed beyond words. Juan had ruined a perfectly nice morning by ranting on and on about how he was going to kick Jimmy's ass. Jenni had planned on stripping him naked and having lots of sex once Jason went down to breakfast and Juan had returned from his early rounds, but Juan only wanted to devise ways of making Jimmy miserable.

Katie opened the bedroom door, clad in a tank top and pajama bottoms. She was obviously freshly showered and behind her, Jenni could see Travis, in jeans, toweling off his chest.

"Damn," Juan said.

Jenni took a moment to admire Travis's very impressive chest, then looked at Juan. Lifting her eyebrows, she said in English, "See? They started off the morning right."

Katie rolled her eyes. "What's up?"

"Juan is having a hissy fit," Jenni answered.

"I am not," Juan protested.

Travis pulled on his shirt and started to button it. "A hissy fit about what?"

"Jimmy," Juan answered.

Travis made a face and sat on the bed. "I thought we talked about this last night?"

"We came to no conclusion." Juan flopped onto the couch.

Jenni slid into the room and Katie closed the door behind her, giving Jenni a demure smile that she didn't buy for one moment.

"Didn't we agree that Nerit needed to deal with it?" Travis asked.

"No, we didn't. Curtis was all for finding a way to discipline him."

"I don't know if we have to go that far." Travis tugged on his socks one by one. "We all had moments yesterday. I faltered in shooting Mike."

"Yeah, Travis, but you did better later. Nerit even told me so. You found your balls when you killed Brenda. And you did not almost get someone killed by locking them in a room with three zombies," Juan retorted.

"I'm not saying what he did was right, Juan," Travis snapped, his expression grim.

"He almost got Jenni killed!" Juan's anger was about to get the best of him again; his face had gotten red and his body was visibly tense. Jenni put her hand on his shoulder, but she knew his Latin temper was building up to an explosion.

Travis shook his head. "Juan, we need to let Nerit handle it."

"What if it had been Katie locked in a room with three zombies? Huh?"

Travis's expression when he glanced at Katie said it all.

"Exactly," Juan said, and stood up. "You know what? I'm going to deal with this man to man. Fuck diplomacy."

"Juan," Travis said softly.

"No, fuck it." Juan walked out and slammed the door behind him.

"He's having anger issues," Jenni said.

"Obviously." Travis stood and grabbed his new denim jacket. "I better go after him and calm him down."

After a soft kiss for Katie, Travis was gone.

"Juan is really pissed," Katie said.

"He'll get over it after he yells at Jimmy for a few minutes. But enough about Juan being a dumb-ass. Let's talk about you!" Jenni lifted her eyebrows. "Spill it!"

"What?" Katie asked, then broke into a huge grin. Jenni tackled her.

Like schoolgirls, they hugged each other and jumped around, laughing, until they collapsed into a heap on the bed.

"You have FFG!"

"Do not!"

"Uh-huh! Freshly fucked glow!" Jenni howled with laugher, pointing at Katie's flushed countenance.

Katie looked at herself in the mirror, then covered her face. "Oh, God . . . I do!"

For the first time since they'd met, the two friends laughed together and shared a long moment free of fear.

Missing Juan at the elevator, Travis looked for him in the lobby with no success. Confused and concerned, he walked up to Peggy at the front desk.

"Have you seen Juan in the last few minutes? Did he come by to take a look at the duty roster?"

"Uhmm . . . no."

Travis sighed with relief. Maybe Juan wasn't trying to track down Jimmy. Maybe he had just been blowing off steam.

"Something wrong?" Peggy regarded him curiously. "I saw him stalking around earlier this morning, before everyone got up, bitchin' about Jimmy. He looked at the roster then." She offered Travis the clipboard.

"Shit!" Travis quickly found where Jimmy was supposed to be.

"What's wrong?"

"Nothing," Travis lied, heading back to the elevators. Couldn't they have just a little time with no major drama? Couldn't they just fucking relax in the hotel without all of this? Hell, he hadn't even really had a chance to enjoy being with Katie this morning.

The doors slid open on the second floor and he strode out swiftly, heading for the room where Jimmy was supposed to be keeping watch. Juan stepped out into the hall, looking angry.

"Juan, you didn't do anything—"

"He's not at his post," Juan answered sharply. "I told you he was a pussy."

Travis lifted an eyebrow. "What do you mean?"

"Jimmy's not there. We have no coverage of the front of the hotel because that fucker is off somewhere picking his ass!"

Travis walked into the room and scrutinized the layout. There was a chair near the window, which was open, and the curtains were pulled back. A nearby table held a full ashtray and several soda cans. Travis looked out the window, spotting a few shambling zombies wandering around below.

"I told you—he's a fucking pussy who doesn't give a shit about anyone or anything," Juan ranted behind him.

Travis looked directly down and froze. "Shit, Juan. What did you do?" Below him, in a bush, what remained of Jimmy was struggling to get up.

"What?" Juan leaned out next to him. "Oh, man."

"Juan," Travis said again, very softly, "what did you do?"

"Nothing! I swear. When I got here, he was not at his post!"

Travis rubbed his brow.

"I did not throw him out the goddamn window, Travis!"

"Then who did?" Travis asked. "Who did?"

3.
Judgment Is Drawn

They gathered in the hotel manager's office. Travis stood in one corner with his arms folded across his chest. His face was solemn and his gaze intense. The mayor was using the manager's desk. Peggy, Curtis, and Juan took the chairs and Jenni and Katie stood near the door, both of them looking very pensive. No one said a word until Nerit strode in, her rifle over one shoulder, looked at Travis, and said, "It's taken care of."

Bill followed her in, holding a notepad. "Okay, we hooked the body after Nerit put him down and dragged it up to a balcony. I examined it and even though there was extreme damage to the corpse, I was able to conclude that there was no trauma other than some abrasions on his knees and hands. I think he was pushed out the window fully conscious. There was no sign of head injury, though his eyes and parts of his face were missing."

Manny fidgeted, then said, "Could he have fallen?"

"I might have considered that a possibility if not for the fact that we've already had one murder," Bill answered, referring to the drug dealer who had been tossed out of the fort a few weeks back.

"I didn't do it," Juan said gruffly.

"I hate to say it, but you are the most likely suspect, Juan. Both Ritchie and Jimmy were people you had a beef with," Bill said.

"We all had issues with Ritchie, and Jimmy did piss off a lot of people yesterday," Travis pointed out.

"True. We could have two different murderers on our hands, but the fact remains that two people were forced into the hands of the zombies," Bill said in a very serious tone.

"I can deal with this if you want, Manny," Curtis said to the mayor.

"No offense, Curtis, but I think Bill should deal with this. He has a lot more experience than you and he's an outsider, so he isn't biased," Manny replied.

"No one is an outsider anymore," Katie spoke up. "We're all intertwined in each other's lives. We can't just go after the first convenient suspect. For all we know, lots of people had reasons to want Ritchie or Jimmy out of the way. You need a solid case before any action is taken; we can't just go on a witch hunt."

"Spoken like a true prosecutor," Bill said with amusement.

"I don't want this getting out," the mayor said. "A party is planned for tonight and we need it for morale."

"People are already talking about Jimmy," Nerit cut in. "It is hard to keep things like that quiet in such a small community."

"She's got a legitimate point. Besides, hiding something this important from the general population will only end up blowing up in our faces," Katie remarked.

"I'll handle the investigation and keep it on the low down or as low as I can," Bill said. "And I'll start by questioning Juan."

Juan let out an explosive sigh and threw up his hands. "Fine. It's not like I have anything to do to keep us all safe."

Jenni sat down next to him and took his hand. "I'm staying with him." She looked pointedly at Bill. "I'm as strong a suspect as Juan is, after all. I'm the one Jimmy nearly got killed."

Bill nodded. "That's fine, but the rest of you should go."

Manny said, "Okay, but let me know what you find out." As he and the others filed out, the mayor drew Curtis aside, whispering, "We need damage control, Curtis. We can't let this get out."

Travis sighed and walked on, hands in his pockets. Some things never changed, he supposed; once a politician, always a politician. He caught up to Katie in the hall. The fact she was now with him still made him grin and feel a little overwhelmed. He laid his hand on her cheek and gave her a kiss. Her lips were soft and sweet against his. She slid her arms around his waist and rested against him and they kissed quietly for a moment. Then, "I need to get to work," Travis said, reluctantly.

"So do I. I have lunch duty," Katie murmured against his chest. "I'll see you tonight at the party."

"Are we going?"

Katie pressed against him and gave him a look he found hard to resist. "I figured we could make an appearance, then sneak away."

"How about just sneaking away?" Travis asked with a grin.

"Par-tee," Katie said firmly, but with a wicked gleam in her eye.

"Okay, okay," Travis conceded. "Anything you want."

"Good," she answered, and pressed her lips against his.

Travis slid regretfully out of her grasp and headed for the construction site. With the "civilians" now tucked into the hotel, the construction site was being reorganized. They would set up a third "lock" in the new vehicle entry to add more protection against the undead, then clean and repair the upper floors of the newspaper building and begin to use it for projects.

Jason was hanging out near Travis's office in the trailer, Jack at his heels and a big backpack at his feet. The teenager looked nervous and unsure, his bangs hanging heavily in his face.

"Hey, Jason, what's up?"

"I was wondering if I could talk to you about some ideas," Jason answered.

"What kind of ideas?"

Travis opened the door to his office, relieved that no one was living in the trailer anymore. The former residents had cleared out their personal effects the day before. He was glad to have his office back. Jason and the dog followed him in.

"Ways to kill zombies other than with guns or bows and arrows. No one is really good at archery anyway," Jason answered, "except for Lenore."

Travis raised an eyebrow. "True. What do you have for me?"

Jason heaved his backpack onto a chair and unloaded it onto a cleared desk. He looked nervous and hesitated a few times before laying down what looked like carefully organized notes. The piles seemed to consist of pages torn out of books, computer printouts, and crayon drawings, all topped with sheets of yellow notepad paper and fastened with paper clips.

Travis sat down and picked up the first stack.

"That's for a concussion grenade. It would rip off the zombies' legs, maybe their arms. If we get lucky, their heads. No fire, since fire would maybe end up burning us down," Jason said in a rush. "I have the main ingredients written out, but I'd need help finding the stuff to put them together."

Travis reviewed the list and rubbed his chin thoughtfully. "I think these are doable. We may not have everything on-site, but maybe we can figure it out."

Jason pointed to another stack. "This is for a catapult that would toss really heavy shit. I got that from *The Lord of the Rings*. We could flatten them. We'd have to make sure it was long range so they couldn't crawl up on the stuff we throw and try to get over the wall."

Again, Travis had to admit that was a decent idea, though he wasn't sure what they'd use for ammunition.

Soon Jason was talking in a torrent of words, pointing things out to Travis, getting more and more articulate as he went on. Travis found himself smiling at the boy's enthusiasm and impressed with his ideas. In many ways, the adults had been obsessed with survival and basic needs. But this kid obviously had killing on his mind.

"Jason, I think I'm going to hook you up with Roger. He used to teach science in junior high before the zombies took over."

"Okay, cool. Some of the other kids have ideas, too. They could definitely help out."

"Sounds like a plan." Travis gave the boy an approving nod.

"Cool!" Jason gathered up his material and started stuffing it back into the backpack. He hesitated, then looked at Travis. "Katie's not gay. She's bi. You should go for it."

Travis was surprised and a little taken aback. "What?"

"She told me not to tell anyone. I think 'cause she thought you'd hook up with my mom. But Mom's with Juan and life is short and stuff, so you should go for it."

Travis rubbed his brow, bemused. "Okay. I will."

Jason heaved his backpack over his shoulder and headed out the door. "So you'll let Roger know?"

"Definitely. And once we clean out the rest of the newspaper building, I'll let you kids have some space for your projects, as long as Roger is with you whenever you are working with chemicals or anything dangerous."

"Cool. We can deal." Jason opened the door and stepped out, with Jack beside him.

Travis leaned forward, resting his hands on his head. Why had he been foolish enough to think that once they were in the hotel, everything would be fine?

4.
Enter the Empress

Katie added more boiling water to the instant mashed potatoes she was making and stirred as vigorously as she could. The kitchen was a bustle of activity with the lunch crew working diligently to make a decent meal from their supplies of boxed and canned food.

After a rigorous run on the treadmill in the very modern hotel gym on the second floor, Katie had enjoyed a long shower before reporting to the kitchen. Rosie, Juan's mother, ran the kitchen with the efficiency of a woman who had supervised the high school cafeteria staff for the last few years. Today's lunch menu was chipped beef with mashed potatoes and green beans. Since Katie could barely make a sandwich without a recipe, she had been handed the box of potato flakes and put to work.

Rosie's great joy had been the discovery that the grocery store's cold storage had remained at freezing temperatures and that some of the frozen meat could be salvaged. The delicious smell of beef cooking in rich gravy blended with the scent of the big, flaky buttermilk biscuits that were being drawn out of the ovens to cool on the counters.

Gretchen, the librarian, had volunteered to make dessert. Big pans of peach cobbler were making Katie's stomach growl. Frowning into her bowl, Katie felt pretty sure the potatoes weren't supposed to look so stiff and hard. She added more hot water and really put her muscles into stirring.

"Well, Jimmy was a klutz, but I just can't see him falling out of the window," Gretchen said to Stacey.

"But why would anyone push him?" Rosie asked as she slid the hot biscuits into a large basket that would be set on the buffet in the dining room. "I can understand that *puto* Ritchie being killed after what he did to all those kids, but Jimmy? He was just a little grumpy man."

Roger carefully poured a large pan of green beans into one of the buffet tins. "He fucked up yesterday. He almost got Jenni killed."

Katie flinched. She had been really hoping that he would keep his mouth shut.

"Really?" Rosie's eyes grew stormy. "My Juan's Jenni?"

"Yeah. He freaked and left her in a hotel room with three zombies. That's why she's all banged up today. I heard she had to jump from one balcony to another to escape," Roger said with all the fervor of a well-practiced gossip.

Rosie's explosion of Spanish cuss words impressed Katie even though she understood only about one word in four. Juan's mother slammed a skillet lid down and waved her gravy-covered spoon about like a sword. "Then he deserved to fall out the window!"

"Maybe Juan pushed him," Stacey said softly.

"Oh, he wouldn't do that, would he?" Gretchen looked up from where she was spooning cobbler into little bowls. Gretchen loved to gossip and was obviously baiting Rosie.

"He might punch his lights out, but I'd be the one to throw him out the damned window." Rosie's expression was so intense that Katie felt certain that the older woman would indeed have shoved Jimmy out the window if she had known that his cowardice had almost killed Jenni.

Then the prosecutor side of her whispered, *Well, how do you know she didn't know? This could be an act.*

"Well, maybe someone took care of Jimmy," Gretchen said in a soft, conspiratorial voice, "like Ritchie was."

"A vigilante," Roger said.

"Yeah. A vigilante." Gretchen shook her head. "I don't think I like that."

Stacey leaned across the counter, snagged a biscuit, and pulled it apart. Rich, fragrant steam rose up from its center, making Katie even hungrier. "So we have to find the vigilante now and do what?"

"Thank him," Rosie said irritably, "or her."

"Or . . . um . . . put them on trial?" Gretchen asked.

Roger looked at Katie. "What do you think?"

"I think we need to finish lunch and not worry about all of this. Bill's going to find out what happened, and then we'll go from there," Katie answered as neutrally as possible.

"But aren't you worried?" Gretchen asked. "What if whoever took out Ritchie and Jimmy goes after Jenni next, or after you?"

Katie lifted the spoon and let a huge dollop of mashed potato fall back into the bowl. "Yes. But speculation isn't going to help Bill solve this any faster."

"My son didn't do it," Rosie said firmly. "He may look guilty, but he's just a very fiery Latino who loves his woman."

"Oh, aren't they cute? Juan and Jenni," Gretchen gushed. "They're so cute together."

Stacey continued to eat the biscuit, listening intently.

Roger dumped more green beans into another pan. "Well, Juan has the biggest reason to do something about Jimmy being a dumb-ass."

"I'm her best friend. Maybe I did it," Katie said pointedly.

"Crazed lesbian kills ex-girlfriend's almost killer," a man's voice said very sarcastically from behind her. "Oh, yeah. I see that."

Katie turned to glare at Shane, who had come in through the side door, carrying a box. He was part of crew sent to bring in more supplies from the grocery store freezer since the hotel's freezer was now cold.

Rosie waved her hands at him. "Don't go near the food. You're all sweaty and gross."

Shane just grinned at her. "Yeah, and we smell real funky. Had to kill more of those deadfucks." Shane turned his gaze back to Katie, cold, furious hatred in his eyes. "What's up, lesbo?"

"Nothing, dickwad." She moved to dump the potatoes into a serving bin.

"Fuckin' lesbo bitch," Shane hissed, stepping closer.

"Out! Don't mess up my kitchen," Rosie ordered, waving a towel at him.

Happy to get away from Shane, Katie busied herself carrying the big metal bins out to the buffet setup. Already the water that would keep the food warm was bubbling deep inside the buffet table, steam rising up to greet her.

It was five till noon and the old folks, as usual, were already lining up. Two walked with canes, one with a walker. Old Man Watson saw Katie, smiled, and waved. She smiled and waved back.

Stacey brought out the big basket of biscuits, which brought a lot of *ooohh*s and *aaaaaah*s from the line. Roger arriving with the big bin of chipped beef made them even more excited. Katie's somewhat pathetic mashed potatoes and the green beans had them positively beaming.

"They're gonna flip over the cobbler," Stacey whispered to Katie with a grin.

Katie laughed. When the cobbler was rolled out, it sent little waves of excitement through the growing line.

It was very rewarding to watch people happily digging into the food they had prepared. The construction workers came in to eat and Stacey was dispatched with lunch boxes for the guards. Mealtime was not the sheer chaos it once was, now that they had a decent facility. There was plenty of room to spread out and really enjoy the meal.

Katie was kept busy going back and forth from the kitchen. She kept the food bins full and made sure there were enough clean plates and utensils. Jenni and Juan came in, hand in hand. They both looked solemn as they sat in a corner, eating alone at a small table. On her way to clear a bin of dirty dishes, cups, and silverware, Katie stopped to check in on her friends.

"How did it go with Bill?" she asked.

"I'm his prime suspect," Juan responded grimly. "But he's got no proof."

"I could have killed Jimmy. Easily," Jenni said with a frown. "By the way, the food is great."

"Thanks. I did the potatoes," Katie answered, then said, "Juan, I'm sure Bill realizes that it wasn't you."

Juan shrugged. "Yeah, but who else would do it? Loca? Travis? You?"

Katie sighed and heaved the heavy tub up onto her hip. "I'm sure other people had motives."

Juan shook his head. "It doesn't fucking matter, Katie."

Rosie came up to the table and Katie hurried off under her stern eye. She glanced back to see Rosie hugging her son tightly and talking to him in a low voice. Katie hated to admit it, but

Juan was the most likely suspect. It killed her to think of him doing anything like that. But then again, she had been furious when she heard about Jenni being left in that room. If she had been there when it happened, who knew what she would have done to Jimmy.

Back in the kitchen, she helped rinse off plates and load them into the industrial dishwasher. Between loads, she managed to eat lunch. She was famished and loved every bite. Finally, the crowd thinned out and they were able to finish clearing the tables and wash the rest of the dishes.

"Did anyone see Travis?" Katie asked as she began storing the leftovers in Tupperware containers.

"No, can't say I did," Rosie answered.

Stacey glopped some mashed potatoes into a plastic container and shook her head. "Eric said Travis was working on something and said he'd eat later."

"Well, since we're pretty much done here, I'm going to take some food out to him," Katie said.

With a nod, Rosie handed her a clean plate. "Go take care of that boy. If it wasn't for him, none of us would be here right now."

Smiling slightly, Katie quickly assembled what she hoped was a man-sized meal for Travis.

Stacey, who was eating cobbler, asked, "What do you mean, Rosie?"

"Travis had the trucks made into a wall to protect us. That is why the zombies never got in," Rosie answered.

"Thank God for that, or we wouldn't have had anywhere to go," Stacey said thoughtfully. "Weird how things work out." She took another piece of cobbler. She had filled out since she'd been rescued, nearly starved to death, but still ate more than might be expected for someone so small framed.

"Plus, he is very good looking. If only I were younger," Rosie said with a wink.

Katie smiled quickly to herself as she covered the plate with foil.

"Oh, yes!" Gretchen affirmed. "Isn't he handsome? I remember when he moved to town and all the girls would just stare at him. I always thought he had a thing for Brenda." Gretchen's voice grew soft as she said, "Poor Brenda. Did they ever figure out how to get her body down?"

"I think they're gonna use a hook to drag her off the net," Roger answered. "No one is going to want to see her up there during the party."

"She was always so sweet," Gretchen sighed. "Always checking out romance novels from the library and waiting for Prince Charming to come."

"That's really sad," Stacey said in a small voice.

"Yeah, when Travis came to town, she thought he was the one. She told me all about him when she was checking out her books. It's sad how he found her body." Gretchen shook her head.

Listening to the conversation, Katie felt sorrow for the young woman who had been so enamored with Travis. So many dreams and hopes had died during those first days.

She slipped out of the kitchen and into the construction site. It was strange to see it so empty, without all the people milling around. It barely looked like a refugee camp now. The tarp tents had all been taken down and personal possessions no longer littered the grounds. Work crews were already reorganizing the site. She hurried over to the portable building that housed Travis's office and knocked on the door.

She smiled broadly as she realized how much she was anticipating seeing Travis. Now that she had allowed herself to embrace her feelings for him, she was actually getting butterflies in her stomach. She felt girlish and silly, but was enjoying it all the same. She hadn't felt this way since she first met Lydia. Then, she had been so hyper, she had danced around her apartment for an hour. And when Lydia called to ask her out, she had jumped on her bed with excitement.

Now she felt that way all over again about Travis. He was as amazing a man as Lydia had been an amazing woman.

When Travis opened the door, he looked very serious, but as soon as he rested his eyes on her, a smile spread across his lips.

"Lunch?" She lifted the plate.

"Thanks," he said, stepping back to let her enter. "I was just working on some plans to make the new entry more secure."

"How's it going?"

"Okay. I just get real paranoid that those things are going to get in and I start second-guessing what we're doing," Travis said.

Setting the plate on a desk, she turned to look at him. "I think we're all a little paranoid about that."

"Yeah, but after yesterday, I admit my paranoia is a little worse," Travis said with a grimace. "I just . . ." He sat on the edge of the desk, his hands in his jeans pockets. "I just feel like I need to work harder at keeping us all safe." He looked toward her. "Keeping you safe."

Katie moved into his arms and laid her hands on the sides of his neck. His fingers were warm against her skin as he slid them under her top to rest on her waist. "Well, you're doing a great job so far. I know a lot of us are very, very grateful to you."

Travis looked almost sheepish. "Yeah, well . . ."

She stroked the curls at the nape of his neck. The stress lines around his eyes and brow faded as he smiled at her.

"I look at you and I want to save the world. I can't help it"

"Are you sweet-talking me again?" she lightly kidded.

He chuckled. "No, no, I mean it. I've always had grandiose dreams." His gaze grew more intense. "Sometimes I get lucky and they come true."

Katie smiled tenderly and kissed him. He immediately responded and their kiss deepened as passion rose quickly between them. Katie relished the feel of his lips and tongue against hers. As his hands slid up to unfasten her bra, she drew back long enough to whisper, "What about lunch?"

"Later," Travis whispered huskily, and kissed her again.

It was hard to resist his touch and harder to resist her own desire. She felt intoxicated with him. As their kisses grew more fevered, they struggled to free each other from their clothes. The hunger for each other was so intense, they never made it to Travis's sofa bed or fully managed to undress.

· CHAPTER ELEVEN ·

1.
Past, Present, Future

Jenni was annoyed. Up three stories from street level on the fire escape of the hotel, she was on sentry duty overlooking where Main Street intersected Morris Avenue. It was way too hot and windy and the chair she had dragged out to sit on wasn't very comfortable. Slouching down in her chair, holding her rifle across her lap, and hooking her foot up on the railing, she surveyed the street as the wind blew her dark hair around her face. She wished a fucking zombie would show up so she could blow its head off. It would make her feel so much better.

When the window opened and Katie slipped out, Jenni was surprised and relieved. "Hey girlfriend!"

"Hey," Katie answered. She kissed Jenni's forehead, then sat down on the windowsill and studied the street. "Quiet, huh?"

"I find myself craving zombies. Isn't that twisted?"

"It's been a weird day," Katie agreed.

"But lunch was good."

"Yeah, it was, wasn't it?" Katie grinned, but her expression was odd.

Jenni reached out and tapped her knee. "What's up?"

"Well," Katie started slowly, as if measuring her thoughts before making them into words. "Travis and I just had some really intense, throw-you-up-against-the-wall, earth-shattering sex."

"All right!" Jenni held out her hand for a high five.

Katie looked at her hand and added, "Without any protection."

"Oh, shit." Jenni dropped her hand.

"Yeah. We both really spaced it. Completely. I'm not sure he even realizes what happened." Katie sighed softly.

"Um . . . shit?"

"Yeah. Shit." Katie ran her hands over her face. "Lesbian sex is not this complicated!"

Jenni giggled. "Nope, it's not. I mean your girlfriend can't knock you up. It's not like dildos come loaded with baby-making stuff."

Katie burst out laughing and covered her face with one hand. "Oh, gawd."

Jenni smiled; then her expression grew as serious as her thoughts. "You okay?"

"Yeah. I am. Weirdly. I don't really feel panicked at all. When I stopped to think, I realized that it's not the right time of the month, but honestly, I hadn't given pregnancy a thought. But now I guess I have to. Travis . . ." She smiled at the sound of his name on her lips. "Travis is like Lydia. The one you keep until death parts you. He's in my heart now and I guess I need to think like . . . uh . . ."

"A straight woman," Jenni offered.

"A woman who can probably have babies biologically with her mate and doesn't have to worry about assisted reproduction and finding the proper donor." Katie smiled, remembering her and Lydia's discussions about making a family. They had opted not to in the end.

"You know, I have a feeling that Travis would love to have a baby with you," Jenni said.

"Me, too. But what about you? You and Juan. Being careful? About babies and . . . other stuff."

"Tubes tied," Jenni said sadly. "Stupid Lloyd didn't want any more kids. Of course, I had to be the one to face the knife, the bastard."

"Oh, Jenni, I'm so sorry."

"It's okay. I told Juan. He was real quiet for a bit, then shrugged it off. Said it was kinda cool not to have to worry about condoms since we're both disease free. Later on, he said something about how when people do start having kids, Hillary Clinton will get her wish because it will be a village, literally, raising them. I guess he figures that somehow he'll get in on the kid thing. I mean, if you have a kid, I'm so gonna be Auntie Jenni."

"Oh, yeah, you will be," Katie said with a wide grin. Her smile faded and she looked very thoughtful. "I'm madly in love with him. His body, his . . . smell . . . the way he touches me . . . all so different from Lydia, but I love him. I kept wanting not to love him, but I do."

Jenni reached out and hugged her as Katie started to cry. She smoothed her blond curls back, kissed her brow, and held her close. Katie clung to her, sobbing, both happy and sad, and Jenni knew she just needed to hold her.

"Hey, lesbos," Shane's voice said from below. "Can you watch the fucking street instead of groping each other? We're heading out again."

Jenni looked down to see Shane and three other men getting into a delivery truck. They had been shuttling back and forth between the grocery store and the hotel all day, since it appeared to be a slow day in zombieville.

"Fuck off, Shane!" Jenni yelled at him.

"Save your pussy-eating for later, bitch," Shane responded.

"Bite me, asshole!" Jenni shouted back.

"I have no trouble smacking up a dyke. Trying to be all manly up there like you have a big cock," Shane snapped back.

"Somebody's gotta, since you're hung like a light switch," Jenni retorted.

"Fuck you, bitch."

Katie leaned over the rail next to Jenni. "You're just jealous 'cause the girls like me, not you."

Jenni saw such intense rage overwhelm Shane's features that, for the first time, she felt afraid of him.

He merely pointed at them and got into the driver's seat of the truck. It roared down the street.

"He's one a scary fucktard," Jenni said.

"Why doesn't someone throw him over the wall?" Katie muttered.

They were both quiet for a while, sitting back down and staring over the streets. The wind was hot and the sky was growing overcast in the distance. Another summer thunderstorm was coming. "I wonder if the heat will make them rot faster," Katie said after a while.

"Yeah, I wish they were like Romero's zombies. They'd be so much easier to deal with." Jenni wistfully sighed. "What the hell?"

A man was coming down the street on a motor scooter. Its engine was coughing and sputtering, and the exhaust was a cloud of dark smoke. He was dressed in very old jeans, a leather jacket, and a beat-up, greasy straw cowboy hat that was so badly warped, it looked like a banana sitting on his head. Even from a distance, he looked dirty and smelly.

"Who the hell is that?" Jenni stood up and tried to get a better view.

Seeing her, the man waved and steered toward them. Behind him in the distance were some shambling shapes.

Katie stood up beside Jenni and drew her pistol. "What does he think he's doing?"

The man cruised up to just under the fire escape. "Now, I am a taxpaying citizen of not only this country, but this city and county as well, and when the mayor decides to steal my property by sending rabid CIA clones to try to tear down my fence, I have a God-given, constitutional right to defend myself. And if you think I'm going to just sit back and not complain, you have another think coming. I fully intend to speak with the police, even if they are a bunch of coke-snorting, Mafia thugs, about what Mayor Reyes has been doing, and I will have justice. I killed the clones, but I figure since they are clones, they really don't count as a life-form, so it don't count as murder. Besides, the mixture was bad on that batch and they had all sorts of things wrong with them. . . ."

The man spoke earnestly, as if he were being interviewed by a reporter on TV, his hands moving eloquently.

"Is he for real?" Jenni asked.

"I think so," Katie answered.

". . . so even if they sit outside my house and snort up on coke so they don't feel a damn thing, I will defend myself. A good knock to the head seems to do the trick. Now the aliens, well, they don't die so easily. . . ."

Jenni was so fascinated by what the man was saying that she almost didn't see the zombie run around the corner. But her reflexes were fast and sure and she shot a nice hole through its head and sent it sprawling.

". . . and that's what I'm talking about. Now the damn clones are everywhere! I am going to write to the President of the United States, even if he is in league with the aliens, to let him know of the blatant abuse of taxes to fund this cloning program. . . ."

"You need to get the hell off the street right now!" Jenni yelled at him.

"The slow ones are closing in," Katie pointed out. She took aim and waited for them to be in range.

". . . I have my video recorder and I will record any meeting that is associated with my complaint because I know that Peggy alters the minutes to suit her Amazonian agenda . . ."

"Drive around to the gate!" Jenni yelled.

". . . and even if you are in cahoots with her, I want you to know that girl's feet stink. Once in church she came in and took off her shoes and it was the worst smell. . . ."

"Go around the block to the entrance!"

Beside her, Katie fired. "Get off the fucking street!"

A zombie came around the corner and Jenni lifted her weapon and fired.

"I am a citizen of this great nation and this town and you

cannot bar me from a public area during regular visiting hours. . . ."
The man whipped away down Main Street just in time, as four more zombies appeared from Morris Avenue, in pursuit of their prey. Jenni and Katie fired steadily, determined to take them out as quickly as possible.

"Just when you thought it couldn't get weirder," Jenni giggled.

"Well, at least you got your zombies," Katie answered, and pulled the trigger.

2.
Open the Gate and Let the Insanity In

"Open the gate," came the order over the walkie-talkie. "We got a survivor coming in!"

Juan rushed up the stairs and looked down from the sentry tower. Sure enough, stinky old Otis Calhoun was speeding along the street on his scooter. Right behind him, and gaining, were at least six zombies. As Juan watched, two more came running from a side street, running fast and screeching.

"Get ready! Get ready! We have zombies coming! " Juan shouted to the men on the wall. "And they ain't the slow ones!"

The sentry beside him took aim and fired. One of the zombies, who looked like he was about to grab Calhoun, went down in a spray of blood.

Ahead of Calhoun, the gate opened easily, its mechanism running smoothly since the last round of repairs. Guards stationed above the lock were already aiming at the widening gap. Juan lifted his hand, preparing to signal the man controlling the gate.

The scooter made hacking noises; plumes of dark smoke erupted from its tailpipe. A spout of blood and brains erupted from the back of another zombie's head and it went down soundlessly. There were at least three more zombies gaining on the old man.

". . . and now I'm being chased by clones and I hold Mayor

Reyes directly responsible . . . ," Crazy Calhoun shouted as he cruised toward the gates.

Juan wasn't surprised the old guy was still alive. If anyone was paranoid enough to survive the zombie apocalypse, it was Otis Calhoun. His property had a huge fence around it with razor wire at the top. It was well known that Calhoun only ate MREs and lived in an underground bunker. Juan couldn't imagine why Calhoun was coming into town.

The scooter coughed and sputtered into the lock and Juan signaled for the gate to be closed. The sentry fired again and more zombies went tumbling to the ground. Just as the gate was about to shut, a female zombie slipped in. She screamed and went charging after Calhoun. Her head exploded in a gush of gore.

Calhoun turned around and looked at her sprawled body with contempt. "Obviously not cloned from quality people. They're just insane. And where did all this come from? I do not remember hearing an agenda at city council to build a fort in the middle of town. I do not approve of my taxes going for this facility when we need to deal with the epidemic of evil clones . . . ," Calhoun rattled away.

Juan crossed his arms over his chest and chuckled. Life was about to get much more interesting in the fort. Calhoun hated the city government with a passion. He came to every council meeting and sat in the back, talking away nonstop as his video camera recorded every moment of the session. He hated Peggy, because he was convinced she was hiding the city government's deep dark secrets. There were rumors Otis Calhoun had spent a few years in a mental ward and that he was schizophrenic, but no one really knew for sure. Most of the townspeople had just regarded him as the town's crazy old man and ignored his wild rants.

". . . and I don't know who is going to pay for my scooter, but since it was damaged by my having to come all the way into town to file a complaint, I firmly believe it should be paid for by the mayor out of his personal funds. And I will know if it is out of his personal funds because I can attune my brain to the Internet. . . ."

Juan looked toward the road and saw more zombies en route. His smile faded as he realized Calhoun had led more zombies to the fort. With a sigh, he lifted the walkie-talkie.

"Peggy, Calhoun is here."

"Yeah, I know. Feels like old times, huh?" Her voice sounded amused and weary.

Juan laughed a little. "Yeah. Strangely, yeah."

". . . certain I did not vote on this fort being built . . ."

3.
Purple Dresses

Nerit walked into the large room used as the "store" of the fort. Everything salvaged from the Dollar Store and the Walmart truck was arranged in boxes and plastic bins. Every box was labeled. One long table held a row small boxes of personal hygiene products. She noticed the box with the condoms was much emptier than it had been the last time Nerit visited the storeroom. She supposed that people were finding comfort in each other. She could not blame them.

Snagging a box of Marlboro Lights, she tucked it into the plastic bag she was using as a shopping cart and headed to the far side of the room where gloves, hats, and scarves were grouped. She needed a new pair of gloves, preferably leather.

Coming around the corner of the aisle, she found Katie on the floor, going through boxes labeled WOMEN'S DRESSES. She looked frustrated as she dug down to the bottom of one of the big bins.

"Looking for a new dress?" Nerit asked as she sorted through the box of gloves.

"I got it into my head that I need one for the party tonight,"

Katie confessed. Next to her was a very sexy pair of high heels. "I found the shoes, but no dress."

Nerit found a pair of soft leather gloves and pulled one on. "Nice shoes." She flexed her hand in the glove, pretending to fire a gun. The leather was a little stiff, but it would soften up and mold to fit. "So, what brought on this need for a new dress?"

Katie looked up at her, her expression a little embarrassed. A glow seeming to emanate from her face. She looked happy.

Nerit grinned. "Oh, Travis."

Katie laughed. "That obvious, huh?"

With a slight nod, Nerit said, "Well, yes, if someone was paying attention. You've played it very low-key. He has been far more obvious."

Yanking out another dress, Katie sighed.

"This town wasn't the hub of fashion," Nerit said.

"Yeah, I noticed." Katie turned her attention to the next box.

Nerit slid the gloves into her bag and looked around. A carton filled with Halloween costumes caught her eye. It had been part of the overstock in the grocery store that was taken in soon after this had all started.

"What color do you like to wear?" she asked Katie, her mind swirling with ideas.

"Purple. Lydia always liked me in purple or blue," Katie said as she pulled out a plain navy dress several sizes too large for her.

Drawing a purple sorceress outfit from the box of costumes, Nerit looked at Katie. "Like this?"

"I am not wearing a Halloween costume."

"If we can locate a sewing kit, I can modify it," Nerit assured her.

"Really?"

"Oh, yes. It won't be as fancy as anything from Versace, but I can make it work."

"I'm desperate. If you think you can do it, I'm all for it," Katie said with excitement and quickly looked for sewing supplies.

Nerit laid the dress down on the floor and turned it this way and that, trying to figure out what she could do. "I am glad that you are moving on," she said thoughtfully. "Letting go is always hard."

"I wasn't sure I could," Katie confessed as she found some small sewing kits in a basket. "Honestly, I still feel guilty about it."

"I had three husbands. I understand very well," Nerit assured her. She was happy for Katie and confident that Travis and Katie being together was a good thing, but she also knew that Lydia would always be a part of Katie and never truly fade away.

"I'm doing better than I was," Katie admitted. "Accepting it more."

"It's a journey," Nerit agreed. "Just take one step at a time.

Katie offered Nerit the sewing kits. Nerit saw an unspoken question in the younger woman's eyes. "Yes?"

"Can you make it sexy?"

Nerit smirked. "Oh, yes. I can."

4.
The Stage Is Set

Travis stood up and stretched. He could no longer concentrate on his plans for walling in Main Street. He needed to take a break and not think about it for a while. He stretched again and felt the pleasant burn of the scratches Katie's nails had left on his back. It felt good.

He decided to walk around outside. Pushing the office door open, he moved down the hall, running his hand over his hair. It wasn't until Katie left that morning that he realized they had made a major mistake. It had been months since he was last with a woman and that had been a monogamous relationship where she had been on the pill. And Katie had spent years with a woman, so she probably didn't even think about contraception. . . .

Of course, that wasn't really an excuse. Their first time together, they had both had condoms ready to go.

Stepping into the hot afternoon air, he wondered if maybe they hadn't forgotten to use condoms "accidentally on purpose." He knew that he was done looking. Katie was it. Now and forever. Maybe in some sort of Darwinian, subconscious way, he was trying to secure their relationship with a child.

"Peggy, I am here to protest my treatment as a citizen of this city and the shoddy way that I have been treated since I arrived here in this fort that I did not vote on building. I was kept in that garage for over an hour being checked for bites. I do not allow anyone to bite me. I told this vampire once . . ."

Travis turned to see Crazy Otis Calhoun being escorted to city hall by Monica, Juan's cousin. Peggy was waiting for the town freak on the steps. She looked weary already. The old coot was carrying a video camera at his side and looked ready for an argument.

"Life just keeps getting more interesting," Travis muttered.

Shane stepped out of the enclosure as Travis walked toward it. "Hey, Travis, keep the lesbos from making out on the job. Seriously, they could have gotten us killed. They were so busy making out with each other, they didn't even see us getting ready to leave a while back."

Travis lifted an eyebrow. "What are you talking about?"

"Now, I know you're into the blonde and I'm sure you have all sorts of wild fantasies about her, but if that old Jewish hag is going to be running the guards, she better make sure her lesbos don't make out on duty."

"Okay, I'll let Nerit know," Travis said calmly. Shane was obviously ready for a fight, but Travis wasn't going to be the one to give it to him.

"You better, because I'm not going to get my ass eaten because that blond lesbo chick can't keep her hands off her girlfriend," Shane spat, then stormed off.

Beleaguered, Travis walked into the hotel. Some of the older people were gathered in the lobby, playing board games found in the Dollar Store. He smiled and waved at them. Old Man Watson grinned and returned the wave. Travis felt good about the decision to take the hotel. It definitely had created a real home for the survivors.

Behind him, Calhoun and Peggy entered the lobby.

"When did the town take over a privately owned building? This is socialism or communism, I can't remember which. I don't agree with you pushing your Amazonian agenda on the people of this fine town. . . ."

Peggy sighed as she led Calhoun over to the front desk. "Could you shut up already? Are you staying or not? If you are, I'll give you a room.

When the older man saw Travis, he ignored Peggy and said, "That young man came here to build the old theater and now he's breaking and entering into hotels. Why hasn't he been arrested? If what Juan told me is true, he is the dangerous ringleader of this new cult. . . ."

"Peggy, I'll be in my room," Travis said.

"Oh, fine, just go away and leave me with . . ." Peggy gestured at Calhoun with frustration.

Calhoun grinned at her. "I'm on to something, aren't I? Getting close to the truth."

"Oh, dear God!" Peggy said with exasperation.

Travis winked at a longsuffering Peggy, stepped into the elevator, and thankfully watched the doors slide shut. His bed was calling his name and he was going to take a nice long nap before he had to deal with anything else.

• CHAPTER TWELVE •

1.
The Characters Enter

The ballroom was alive with music, people, and the rich smell of food. The seniors had arrived first and were settled happily at a table in one corner, nestled into the plush velvet chairs. Rosie's dinner crew had laid out a fabulous buffet of chicken, Mexican rice, and assorted vegetables, plus big, flaky biscuits and two different desserts. Music played softly in the background over the hotel's PA system.

Jason and Michelle made their way onto the patio, where the other teenagers and preteens had gathered in the gazebo. Someone had brought a boom box so they could play music they wanted to hear. They had a cooler full of soda, and Ricky, Michelle's younger brother, was hunched down sipping cola and looking at an old magazine. Jason sat down on a pillow and Michelle sat down beside him as they joined the rest of the kids sitting in a circle on the floor.

Altogether, there were a dozen kids in the fort. They tried to stick together as much as possible. The adults were always so worried and scared that they forgot the kids were just as anxious. Since their parents and other adults often tried to shield them from what was really going on, the younger survivors had found their own ways to get information.

Melanie, the oldest at eighteen, and Dylan, seventeen, were smoking some of the pot they had found on the body of one of the waiters. That had been big news yesterday among the "shorties," as they called themselves. It was cool that Melanie, Dylan, Michelle, and Jason had been allowed to work with the adults, but the discovery of contraband had been extra exciting.

"What's up?" Dylan asked as Jason reached out for the joint.

"Just a bunch of old people listening to country music so far. The food looked good," Jason answered.

"We grabbed munchies," Melanie said, sweeping her red hair out of her face. Handing a bag of chips to Michelle, she added, "We were thinking about setting off fireworks later. Dylan bought some off that asshole Shane yesterday."

"Sounds like fun." Jason felt older than his years, smoking dope and swilling cola. He could feel Michelle's hand lying on his leg. It made him nervous. Nerit's talk about taking advantage of the good moments of life had really affected him. He was thinking about a lot of things in a different way. He had even made himself scarce earlier in the evening when it was obvious that Juan and Jenni needed time alone. Now it was time for him to chill out and try to enjoy life.

"Has your mom remembered it's your birthday yet?" Melanie asked.

Jason shook his head. "Not yet. I keep waiting, but I'm not sure she even knows what month it is. She's kinda an airhead at times."

Michelle took the joint and inhaled deeply and swatted her brother's hand away when he reached for it. "You're too young."

Ricky frowned. "I'll tell Dad."

"Go ahead," Michelle dared, and thunked him on the head.

"Bitch," Ricky said sullenly.

The other kids joined them one by one. Soon, they were all joking and laughing, high on sugary soda and candy, buzzed from the caffeine in the cola, or just plain old stoned.

Jason was feeling pretty good when Michelle gave him a kiss—the first real kiss of his life. He hadn't expected that, so he blew it a little when she moved in by trying to ask her what she was doing. Her lips pretty much hit his teeth and tongue. She drew back, startled.

"Sorry," she muttered.

"No, no, try it again," Jason said quickly, and flung his arms around her.

This sent Melanie and Dylan into guffaws of laughter, but Michelle smiled sweetly and kissed Jason firmly on the lips for about two seconds. It was enough to make him blush and grin.

"Ugh, no making out in front of me," Jenni said from above.

Jason looked up to see her standing over him wearing a bright red tank top, a knee-length cotton skirt with black abstract designs on it, and sandals. Her long hair flowed loose around her face. Juan was at her side, a new cowboy hat looking far too neat on his tousled curls. Earlier, Jason had seen Juan trying to break in the hat, throwing it around and smacking it against things.

"Busted," Jason said quickly.

"Yeah, you are," said his mom.

"Oh, gawd," Jason moaned.

"I'm sorry," Michelle said quickly. "It's his birthday, so . . ."

Jenni laughed. "Yeah, yeah, I know." She hugged Jason tightly and kissed his cheek, embarrassing him as only a mother could. She handed him a small brown bag as Juan sat down across from them. "Open it."

Jason smiled and opened the bag to find a copy of *Ender's Game,* his favorite book.

"I grabbed it a few weeks ago when we were scavenging the library," Juan explained.

Hugging his mom, he kissed her cheek. "Thanks, Mom." To Juan's surprise, he hugged his mom's boyfriend, too. "Thanks, dude."

Juan nodded. "No problem. Hope you enjoy it."

Jenni leaned over and snagged the joint from Dylan, who was trying to hide it. "What's this?"

"Look, I . . . uh . . . found it on a waiter. I think it's a cigarette . . . ," Dylan mumbled.

"Sure you do," Jenni answered. She inhaled deeply and handed it to Juan.

"I'll pass," Juan said, and handed it back to Dylan.

"Shit," Dylan whispered in awe, staring at the doorway to the ballroom.

Jason turned to see Katie walking onto the patio. She was wearing a very slinky purple halter dress and high heels. She was wearing makeup and had let her hair fall free and curly to her shoulders and she looked absolutely hot. He must have been staring, because Michelle smacked his arm. Katie walked over to join them, her heels clicking on the patio. Juan whistled as Dylan just stared at her with his mouth open. With a grin, Katie sat next to Jenni and tucked her legs to one side.

"Katie, you're totally hot," Dylan said.

"Thank you!" Katie beamed.

"Yeah, totally," Jason said. Michelle smacked him again and he looked at her and said, "Well, you are, too. Seriously, you are." He kissed her cheek. Her smile was a relief.

"Yeah, I did her makeup and fixed her hair. She has a hot date tonight," Jenni said.

"With who?" Melanie looked very curious. "I didn't think there were other gay girls in the fort."

"With Travis, actually. I'm—" Katie faltered. "—open-minded."

Jason knew this wasn't the case at all, but figured Katie didn't feel like going into details. He was glad Katie was happy, because for a long time, she had been sad.

"Cool," Dylan said with a wide grin that had Melanie glaring at him. "Wanna smoke?"

Katie took the joint and arched an eyebrow. "You do realize I was a prosecutor before the zombies?"

Dylan blinked. "Oh."

Katie shrugged. "Oh, well. I haven't done any since college."

She took a drag and handed it back. Jason couldn't help but stare as the smoke unfurled from her lips. She was really, really hot tonight. Ricky again reached for the joint. Michelle smacked his hand again. There was a brief tussle and lots of giggling between the siblings. The world on top of the hotel was full of laughter. Jason found himself smiling more than he had for a long time.

When his mom and Juan helped Katie to her feet so they could go join the other adults inside, he stood up and hugged them all again.

"Travis is pretty lucky," he said to Katie.

"So is Michelle," Katie replied.

Jason blushed and sat back down as the adults left.

"Super damn hot," Dylan said, watching Katie walk away.

Jason smirked as Melanie smacked Dylan. He turned to Michelle and kissed her very firmly on the lips.

It was an okay birthday after all.

2.
Hell Erupts

Katie felt a little embarrassed as she entered the ballroom. Nerit's amazing work on the Halloween costume had resulted in a slinky dress that made her slim, athletic build look very womanly. The dress tied behind her neck and revealed her strong shoulders before gliding down over her hips and ending in a slanted hemline that accentuated the curve of her legs. Despite all her bruises, she looked amazing.

She felt very much like a girl and that made her a little nervous. She was most comfortable in her running clothes or a pair of jeans and a tank top. Lydia had been good at dressing up while Katie had just tried her best to look presentable when they went out. But tonight, she had achieved a level of femininity that was new territory for her. She felt like a bombshell.

Feeling a bit light-headed and giddy from the pot, she moved to the bar where Felix was playing bartender.

"A glass of wine," she said, and blushed under his awed stare.

Sipping the chilled white wine, she made her way around the ballroom, greeting people and trying not to look too anxiously for Travis.

Juan and Jenni were out on the dance floor, laughing and hoofing it up to some country music. Their moves were fluid and graceful. A few older people were on the floor as well, moving slower but obviously enjoying themselves.

Peggy was trying hard to get away from a tall, older man who smelled so bad that Katie winced. She recognized him as the guy who had arrived on the scooter. He was talking rapidly and waving a video camera around.

". . . so you can tell the mayor that I don't believe he's not feeling well. I think he is avoiding me as he always does, because I alone know the real truth of what he is planning to do. I plan to write to the media and report how he has blocked their transmissions to this town so he can—"

"I swear to God, Otis Calhoun, if you do not leave me alone, I will have your ass dragged out of here," Peggy snapped.

"That's harassment!" he protested before stomping away.

As the two of them passed Katie, Peggy whispered, "Nice dress."

Finishing her glass of wine, she went back for another and found Bill at the bar, drinking a beer.

"Nice dress, Katie," he said with an appreciative smile.

"Thanks, Bill. I'm trying to impress someone tonight."

"Well, I'm impressed, if that counts."

She grinned. "Yes, it does. How are you doing?"

"Still trying to figure out this vigilante business."

"If anyone can sort it out, it's you, Bill." She was feeling very light-headed and a bit tipsy.

One of her fondest memories was of the moment when Lydia saw her for the first time in her wedding dress. The look of awe and love in her beloved's eyes would stay with Katie forever. Now she had a new memory to match it: the look on Travis's face when he entered the ballroom and saw her. Katie finally knew what it looked like to see someone struck speechless.

Walking across the room toward him—he was so handsome in a dark blue shirt, jeans, and a leather jacket, with his freshly washed hair curling slightly over his brow—Katie enjoyed his look of absolute adoration and awe. She set her wineglass down on a table and held out her hand to him. He took it, blinking slowly. His hand was slightly trembling and sweaty in hers.

"Damn," was all he managed to say.

"You like?"

"Damn," he said again.

"Nerit sewed it for me," she said.

"I'll thank Nerit later," Travis stated.

"Want to dance?" she asked.

Travis got the goofiest look on his face. "I have other things in mind, but dancing is good for now."

Taking her hand, he led her out onto the dance floor and drew her close. They danced slowly to a ballad sung by Patsy Cline, slipping across the highly polished floor gracefully. Staring into each other's eyes, they were oblivious of all the looks of approval they were receiving. Old Man Watson applauded as they danced past his table. When the song finished and Travis kissed Katie, the room erupted into applause.

Giggling, stoned, and deliriously happy, Katie clung to Travis, embarrassed. Travis, looking dazed, gave a little bow. The laughter that followed was heartfelt and warming.

A few glasses of wine later, Katie found it even harder to stand in her shoes. Plus, she was having issues keeping her hands off Travis. She was sure they were making a spectacle of themselves, especially since she had sat on his lap during dinner.

"I always knew those rumors about you liking women were bullshit," Peggy said with a wink.

Katie opened her mouth to correct her, but Travis lightly pinched her leg. She thought better of it.

Finally, she knew the wine and the pot had gotten the best of her and excused herself to the restroom. The foyer was empty when she paused to fix her shoe strap. The elevator doors opened and Philip and Shane stepped onto the marble floor of the ballroom's entryway. Both were dressed for the party and holding open beers.

"Fuck," Philip said, staring at her.

When Katie looked up and saw their sneers, her blood turned to ice. She moved quickly to the restroom. The last thing she needed was a confrontation with Shane and his sidekick when she was drunk and a little stoned.

Splashing cold water on her face, she felt a little better. A glance at the mirror revealed that she had smudged her makeup, so she picked up a hand towel and started to dab at her eyeliner. When she looked into the mirror again, she saw Shane staring at her.

Twisting around, she braced herself against the counter. "Get out."

"It's a damn shame that a fine piece of ass like you is a carpet muncher," he said in a low, dangerous voice before taking a long swig from his beer can.

"Get out!"

"Look at those titties," he said, and grabbed one of her breasts.

She thrust his hand away and repeated, "Get out now."

"And that ass," he said. His gaze was dangerous and feral.

Katie felt horrifyingly sober suddenly. This wasn't another stupid confrontation where they threw insults back and forth. This was serious. He had already touched her, so whatever came next would be easier for him.

"Get out now!"

Tossing his beer away, he moved fast and she tried to get away. He gripped the straps of her dress and yanked. The material tore and her breasts were bared. Katie picked up a decorative candleholder from the marble countertop and swung it at Shane's head.

She hit him in the nose and blood sprayed over them both. Enraged, Shane tackled her full force, sending them sprawling across the long marble counter. The candleholder slipped from her grip and rolled into the sink. Gripping her hair, he shoved her hard up against the mirror, trapping her on the counter, and pushed himself between her legs. She beat on him with her fists.

"I'll show you what it's like to be with a man," he hissed. Fumbling with her dress, he tried to grab hold of her panties.

Katie started to scream.

Travis felt too happy for words. After Katie sashayed out in that damn hot dress, many of his friends had come to congratulate and wish him the best.

"You're damn lucky." Bill winked.

"I would say you have the hottest girlfriend in town, but Stacey would kill me," Eric said as he passed by, carrying a couple of drinks. Travis laughed and flushed a little.

Jack, Pepe, and Nerit's old dog, Tucker, scampered around with doggy delight. The party was in full swing now and everyone was having fun. Lenore and Ken were dancing in a corner while Katarina and Peggy were line-dancing to one side. Even Belinda was there, sitting at a table with Rosie and Monica. Belinda's eyes were red from crying. Travis felt terribly for her. If Katie had died yesterday, he didn't think he would even be able to function today. He was so grateful they were both alive and together.

Travis sighed, relieved at his good fortune, and spotted Curtis headed his way through the crowded ballroom, obviously upset about something.

"I found contraband on the kids," Curtis said in a concerned tone as he joined Travis. "They were smoking pot out in the gazebo. I confiscated what they had, but there may be more."

"Pot, huh?" Travis considered this. "Well, they are kids. . . ."

"We're rebuilding society. We do not need drugs to worm their way into it and destroy our youth!"

"Well, Curtis, look around. Half the adults in here are pretty damn drunk. Hell, I'm on my way, too. A little pot isn't going to hurt anyone."

"Pot is a gateway drug!"

"To what? The drug war is over, Curtis. The kids found some pot. Big deal. Once they smoke it, it's gone. It's over. I smoked it myself back in the day. And I'm a fine, upstanding citizen," Travis said in a tone he hoped wasn't too condescending. He was really annoyed with Curtis ruining the kids' party. Yeah, he wasn't fond of the idea of the kids smoking, but it wasn't going to kill them.

"I thought you would be a little more understanding," Curtis said, half-hurt, half-angry. "I really did."

"Well, I am understanding, but I don't think it's such a big deal in the grand scheme of things." Travis sighed. "Sorry, Curtis, but I don't. I'm going to go check on Katie. She was a little blitzed when she left."

Curtis was obviously still upset, but gave a terse nod of his head. "Okay . . . okay. I guess I'll drop it."

Travis squeezed Curtis's shoulder and walked out into the foyer. He noticed Philip standing near the women's bathroom, and for some reason, the sight disturbed him. Rubbing his chin, he moved toward Philip.

"Have you seen Katie?" he asked.

Philip turned, startled. "Oh, um, yeah. She went into the ladies' room with someone."

"What?"

Philip looked flustered and unsure of what to say. "Yeah, she, uh, she, uh . . . you know. She's trying out the other side of the fence."

"What the fuck are you talking about?"

Philip blocked the door, looking vastly uncomfortable. "She came on to Shane, all slutty-like, saying she wanted to know what it felt like to have a man."

Travis pushed Phil out of the way and burst into the bathroom.

Sprawled across the counter, Katie was trapped under Shane as he tried to push his erect penis into her. Katie had one hand planted hard into his throat, but Shane had twisted the other behind her back. Katie was kicking and squirming furiously, but Shane had her pinned. The sight of Katie's ripped dress, exposed breasts, and torn panties sent Travis into a rage.

"Get off her!" Travis shouted. He grabbed Shane by the shoulders, pulled him off Katie, and shoved him across the room. The man crashed into the door of the handicapped stall and slumped to the floor.

"Travis," Katie sobbed, reaching for him.

"Katie, I'm here," Travis said, wiping away her tears and putting his arms around her. His heart was thudding so hard, it hurt; his anger was pulsing in his temples. He was torn between comforting her and beating the shit out of Shane.

Shane resolved that dilemma by punching Travis in the kidney, knocking him into Katie.

Travis twisted around and nailed Shane with a hard left to the jaw. He tackled the would-be rapist to the floor and smashed his fist into Shane's face over and over again. Philip shoved the bathroom door open, saw what was happening, and leaped forward. Grabbing Travis's arm, he yanked him to his feet and propelled him into a wall.

"Run, Katie," Travis grunted as he swung at Philip.

To his relief, she fled, leaving him trapped with Shane and Philip.

3.
Descending into Chaos

The foyer seemed to swirl around her as Katie backed away from the bathroom. She could hear the men fighting inside. Tears streamed down her face as she stumbled to the doorway of the ballroom, pulling the top of her dress back over her breasts.

Already the self-incrimination was starting.

. . . How could she drink so much? . . .

. . . Why had she worn such a sexy dress? . . .

. . . Why didn't she just go back into the ballroom, not the bathroom when she had seen Shane? . . .

Shoving those thoughts away, she concentrated on saving Travis. Her voice felt trapped in her throat, her fear and anger constricting it painfully. Opening her mouth, she tried to scream, but no sound came out. Swallowing hard, she tried again.

Finally, she managed to call out hoarsely, "Help me!" It was as if a dam broke and her voice returned. She screamed, "Help me!"

Though Nerit was halfway across the room, she saw Katie first and immediately started walking toward her, grabbing Jenni on the way. Jenni appeared startled until she saw Katie, then ran to her. Katie threw her arms around Jenni and held on tight.

"Someone needs to help Travis." She was shaking as her adrenaline wore off and her mind was racing.

"What happened? Where is he?" Jenni asked. "Is it zombies? Oh, God, did we miss one?"

Juan was only a step away when Katie pointed toward the women's restroom. "No, no. It's Shane . . . Shane . . . he . . . he . . ." It was a struggle to get the words out. "He tried to rape me! Travis is fighting him!"

"Shit!" Juan cursed. He was almost to the bathroom door when it was flung open. Travis stumbled out backwards with

Shane right after him. Juan dived into the fray immediately, shoving Shane into a planter just before he was sucker-punched by Philip.

"Break it up!" Bill shouted as he ran out of the ballroom with Curtis following.

Shane recovered enough to kick at Travis, trying to trip him. Travis stumbled but did not fall, then whirled around and slammed his fist into Shane's stomach. The men exchanged a flurry of blows as Juan struggled with Philip.

"Break it up!" Bill managed to hook his arm around Shane's neck and haul him away from Travis.

Travis lunged forward for one last punch, but Curtis caught him. "That's enough, Travis."

"He tried to rape Katie!"

Katie clung to Jenni, sobbing. She hated that she was crying and that her emotions had overwhelmed her intellect. Struggling for self-control, she looked at Travis. He was so upset, Curtis had to put extra pressure on his arm to keep him restrained.

Juan and Philip still grappled with each other. Finally, Juan managed to get him down to the ground as Roger and a few other men hurried to help subdue Philip.

"He fuckin' attacked me out of nowhere! I demand you arrest him!" Shane was struggling to get free, his angry gaze on Travis.

"You were hurting Katie!"

"The bitch wanted to try a man. Yer just jealous she didn't pick you!"

Nerit very calmly said, "If you hadn't been late to the party, Shane, you would realize that Katie and Travis made it very clear tonight that they are a couple."

Shane turned his bloodied face toward her and said, "Shut up, Jewbitch. I don't give a fuck what you say."

"It's true, Shane," Bill said. "You better come up with a better story, because that one is an obvious lie."

"The lesbo wanted to try sex with a man," Shane insisted through his bloodied teeth.

"You lying asshole!" Katie shouted angrily. "You tried to rape me!"

"You can't rape the willing," Shane spat back.

"That's it," Jenni said. She let go of Katie and launched herself at Shane. She managed to get in a few good slugs before she was yanked off him by Roger and carried away to a safe distance.

Nerit slid her sweater around Katie's shoulders and drew it closed over her breasts. Katie was still trembling, but she felt like she was more in control of herself. Wiping her tears away, she forced air into her lungs, remembering a meditation trick her Buddhist wife had taught her.

"Let me go," Travis ordered Curtis. "Katie needs me."

Curtis hesitated, then released him. As Travis passed him, Shane yanked free of Bill and landed a solid punch. They went down in a jumble, fists flying once more.

Nerit picked up a candleholder from a nearby table as Bill and Curtis struggled to draw the two fighters apart. It was hard going since both men seemed determined to kill each other. Nerit finally managed to squeeze between the two cops and clock Shane across the back of the head. He collapsed over Travis. Bill and Curtis straightway dragged him off.

Travis struggled to his feet. Katie took his hand and pulled him into her arms. Clinging to him, she glared at the unconscious Shane as Bill put handcuffs on him while Curtis cuffed Philip.

"We didn't do nothing wrong!" Philip shouted.

"I want to know what happened, right now," Bill said in a loud voice.

"That bitch led Shane on, then Travis busted in on them—," Philip began in an almost-shrill voice.

"From Katie, I want to know from Katie," Bill said.

Travis gently rubbed her back as she struggled to regain her compsure.. "I went into the bathroom to splash water on my face and Shane followed me in. Then he . . . he . . . attacked me . . . and . . . I fought him . . . until Travis came. . . ."

"I'm going to kick his ass!" Cursing impressively in Spanish, Jenni started toward the unconscious man, but Juan grabbed her before she could do any damage.

"Jenni, back off," Curtis ordered, standing between the woman and Shane.

Travis was ready to beat the hell out of Shane again, but Katie held on to him and forced him to stay at her side.

"That bitch asked Shane into the bathroom with her," Philip protested. "They asked me to stay outside and not let anyone interrupt. Shane was more than willing to turn the lesbo straight."

"Oh, please," Peggy said, rolling her eyes. "She's with Travis. She's obviously not gay."

"Gay or straight, it don't make no difference, if Shane was trying to rape her," Bill said firmly.

Shane managed to open one swollen eye and slurred, "She fuckin' begged me."

Jenni shouted something about Shane being a *puto* and tried to kick him. Juan dragged her a little farther away.

"Let's get them into the holding cell at city hall," Bill said to Curtis. "We're not going to get anything settled like this."

Curtis obeyed and asked Roger and a few other men to help half carry, half drag Philip and Shane into an elevator.

"What are you going to do with them?" Jenni asked angrily.

"Nothing yet. Need to get the story down and process it. Then we'll decide," Bill answered.

"Throw them over the wall!" someone shouted from the back of the crowd.

There were murmurs of agreement.

"I think the clones would enjoy playing with them," Calhoun said from somewhere in the crowd. "Obviously, those two men have no protection against the alien overlords and are controlled by evil forces."

Bill ambled up to Katie and Travis and said softly, "Katie, want to sit down with me and give a statement?"

She tugged Nerit's sweater tighter around her shoulders,

nodding. "Yeah." She drew on her inner strength and set her jaw with determination.

Bill stood up straight, taking on a commanding stance, and said to the people watching, "Go back to the party. Clear this area. There's been enough drama."

People reluctantly walked away, speaking in hushed voices. Juan was talking to Jenni softly in Spanish, obviously trying to calm her down. When the foyer was mostly clear, Bill pushed the button for the elevator. When it arrived, he gently guided Katie into the cab. Travis was right beside her. Nerit, Juan, and Jenni followed along with Peggy. They rode in silence to the lobby. The cop escorted the somber group into the hotel manager's office, where Bill sat Katie down in one of the comfortable chairs and very gently questioned her about the attack. Peggy settled behind the desk and took notes in shorthand, often cussing under her breath as Katie spoke.

Squeezing her hands into tight fists, Katie tried to quit shivering. She had managed to stop crying and that felt like a small victory even though tears still threatened to fall. The voice inside her head—the one full of self-recrimination—sounded like her mother and she tried to ignore it. How many times had she sat with survivors of sexual assault and assured them that they were truly the victims? It didn't matter how they were dressed, if they knew their attacker or not, or if they had maybe entered into a questionable situation. In the end, being raped was not their fault. Yet, as she sat talking to Bill, she grew increasingly conscious of her dress and heels, her makeup, and the fact that she had gone alone into the bathroom. She searched the faces of those around her, afraid she would see condemnation in their gaze, and was relieved to see only concern and compassion.

"Katie, you didn't do anything wrong," Bill assured her. His huge hand reached out and touched her forearm gently. "Shane is the only one responsible for what went down tonight. Remember that."

A sob escaped her lips as she nodded her head. Fresh tears

spilled, but she smiled as she said, "Thank you for saying that. I know that's the truth, but . . ." She choked on her words, unable to finish.

Jenni slid down to her knees beside Katie's chair and wrapped her arms around her friend. "It's okay, Katie. Every time Lloyd beat me, he told me it was my fault. I kinda believed him even though I knew it was a lie."

Katie kissed the top of Jenni's head and snuggled into her.

"Shane is an asshole," Peggy muttered for the umpteenth time.

"He'll be taken care of," Nerit said firmly.

Glancing at Travis, Katie was comforted by his concerned gaze. Juan stood with his arm around Travis's shoulders, providing support, but also probably keeping him from rushing out the door to find Shane.

Surrounded by people who loved her, Katie forced the accusing voice in her mind to fall silent. "What's going to happen to Shane?"

Bill shrugged. "We'll sort it out, Katie. You just go upstairs and rest, okay?"

"I'll come with you," Jenni said quickly.

"Thank you," Katie said, kissing Jenni's forehead. Secure in her best friend's arms, she realized she had finally stopped trembling.

With Katie's statement over, Jenni and Nerit escorted Katie out of the room. "I'll be up soon," Travis assured Katie, kissing her cheek as she passed. Travis could see Katie struggling with her emotions and was proud of her for not falling apart. He still wanted to beat the hell out of Shane, but he was calming down slowly.

Looking somber, Bill said, "We need to have a meeting about this. We need Mayor Reyes down here."

Travis nodded, his jaw set grimly.

"I need you to be calm," Bill added.

Travis sighed, then said, "I know. But she's . . . she's . . . my everything. . . ."

"I know. But we need to decide what is best for all of us."

Travis rubbed his brow, then nodded again. "Okay. I want to get her settled. I'll be back in an hour."

"I'll get Katie's statement typed up," Peggy said.

"First, I need you to take notes while I question Shane and Philip," Bill informed her. "And try to keep the comments down to a minimum."

"You don't ask for much, huh?" Peggy scowled.

"Travis, meet us down here around midnight, okay?" Bill called after him.

"Okay, Bill." Travis walked toward the door, where Juan was waiting for him. How this was all going to end was beyond him, but it felt as if they were quickly descending into chaos.

4.
The Casting of Lots

Katie could hear Juan and Jenni talking swiftly in Spanish in her bedroom while she, in the bathroom, eased her way out of the tattered remains of her once-sexy purple dress. Jenni was still in full-blown *Shane must die* mode and Juan was trying to calm her down.

"Let me help." Travis sat on the counter, watching her with sad eyes.

She was hurting. She was sure the bruises would be showing up soon to add to all her other bruises. Shane had not actually hit her, but he had wrestled her with brutal intensity.

"My arm hurts where Shane twisted it," she admitted.

Travis drew close and gently helped her out of the rest of her clothes, then turned on the shower and pulled the curtain aside. Stepping in, Katie paused and looked at his battered face. Reaching out, she lightly touched his cheek. "Come in with me?"

"If it won't upset you," he said.

She shook her head. "No. It won't. You make me feel safe."

He smiled and undressed. Climbing into the tub behind her, he tenderly rubbed her back. In silence, they helped each other wash away the blood and grime from their battle. It hurt Katie to see Travis's bruises, but at the same time, it made her feel protected. She knew he would defend her with his life if necessary. Travis helped Katie into her pajamas, then got back into his clothes. Before they stepped into the bedroom, she drew him close and they shared several tender, affectionate kisses.

When they emerged from the bathroom, Juan and Jenni were waiting, sitting on the couch.

"How are you feeling?" Juan asked.

"Okay, I think," Katie answered. She lay down on the bed.

Travis hovered over her, gently stroking her hair. "She's a fighter."

Looking less agitated than before, Jenni sighed and sat beside her friend.

"That *puto* should never have been released after the first time he beat her up."

Travis nodded. "Can't say I don't agree with that." Leaning over, he kissed Katie's cheek.

"What do you think will happen next?" Katie reached out to hold Travis's battered hand.

"Not sure. Something has to be done, but it's not like any of us are elected officials. Bill and Curtis are cops, and people mostly listen to them, but it's out of habit as much as anything else." Travis rubbed his brow. "There is no easy way to deal with this. I better get downstairs and see what's up."

Juan stood up as well. "I'm going with you. Shane's had run-ins with Jenni. It could have been her in there with him, or any woman, really."

"I agree. He's dangerous." Travis leaned over and kissed Katie.

"I trust you to do what's right," she said.

Travis smiled. "I wish I trusted myself."

As the men left the room, Jenni snuggled up next to Katie, spooning her, her body a soothing presence. The men shut the door behind them and left them in the comforting glow of a lamp.

"I punched him pretty hard," Jenni said after a long pause.

Katie couldn't help but laugh. "I noticed. Thank you." She turned and kissed Jenni's cheek. "You're a very good friend."

"The absolute best," Jenni said with a wink.

Snuggling back down, Katie pushed thoughts of Shane out of her mind and slowly relaxed in Jenni's arms until she finally found sleep.

The elevator doors opened onto a lobby full of people. There were thirty or forty people gathered there and none of them was speaking in anything close to calm tones. Voices ricocheted off the marble floor and pink granite columns. As Travis and Juan stepped into the chaos, Rosie grabbed Juan's arm. Her brow was furrowed with worry and her lips were tight with agitation. "Is Katie okay?"

"Yeah, she's resting," Travis answered.

"What's up with all this, Mamá?" Juan looked around in confusion.

"People are very upset," Rosie answered. Her expression was strained. "About what happened . . ."

Juan heard Travis let out a low sigh and understood his agitation. He could feel the tension building around them as people voiced vehement opinions about the events of the night.

Bill stood in the middle of the chaos, looking remarkably calm. Curtis, on the other hand, appeared overwhelmed. Juan couldn't blame him. The rookie cop was the only survivor of the small police department that had once patrolled Ashley Oaks, the small town that was now the wasteland around their fort. It was a good thing Bill was able to keep an unruffled, steady demeanor. Juan didn't feel anything like composed—he wanted to drag Shane and Philip out of the fort and feed them to the zombies.

"This is ridiculous," Travis muttered beside Juan as the two men crossed the room, heading for Bill. "This a mob."

"You cannot allow him to stay in the fort. He's dangerous," Eric said to Bill in a loud voice. He shoved his glasses farther up his nose and gave Bill the sternest look he could muster. Stacey stood at his side, clutching his arm. Their small dog, Pepe, tap-danced around their feet, excited by all the noise.

"You just can't turn him out," Steven Mann declared. He glowered at Bill; Blanche stood at her husband's side, frowning.

"Why not? He's a danger to all the women of this fort." Stacey put her hands on her slim hips and glared at Steven. "You should worry about your wife."

Blanche Mann rolled her eyes. "Please. I wouldn't lead him on like that blond slut did."

Travis took a step forward, but Juan grabbed his arm. "Dude, keep focused."

"What a man and woman do is their own business," Ed said from nearby. His grizzled features were emotionless.

"Ed, you can't believe that Katie allowed Shane to—," Peggy started, but Ed cut her off.

"I wasn't there. Can't say what did or didn't happen. But whatever did go down, it's between them."

"So you won't mind if Katie shoves Shane over the wall?" Juan asked. He folded his arms over his chest to keep from punching someone. He was close to losing his temper, but knew he had to keep it in check. He was already under suspicion for what had happened to Ritchie and Jimmy.

Travis was silent beside Juan, but he was fuming. Juan could see him clenching his hands at his sides.

"Now, I didn't say that," Ed answered. "Just sayin' that it's a personal thing between them."

"She was leading him on," Blanche said. "We all saw it."

"Actually, we all saw her getting cozy with Travis," Peggy drawled. She gave Blanche a look of disgust.

More voices chimed in. Frustration and anger made them harsh with emotion. People argued with one another in small groups.

"All I know is that man is nasty and he shouldn't be allowed to stay!" Lenore stomped her foot and put her hands on her ample hips as she glared at Blanche. "I don't care what the Bitch Barbie says."

"We gotta do something," Curtis said to Bill. "We can't let Shane go around assaulting women."

"What do you we suggest we do? Due process isn't around no more," Bill reminded him.

"Then we find a new way," Juan interjected.

People murmured in agreement.

"A fair and just way to deal with situations like this," Rosie added, supporting her son.

"Because this won't be the last time someone breaks the law," Curtis said in a morose tone.

Travis spoke for the first time. "We are civilized people. We need to remember that." His calmness seemed to cut through the noise that filled the lobby. People fell into silence. Travis rubbed his chin slowly and thoughtfully, scanning the crowd.

"What do you want, Travis?" Juan heard the harshness in his voice but did nothing to soften it. He was pissed off about what had happened, and Katie wasn't his girlfriend. He couldn't imagine how Travis was feeling. The need to protect the women they loved was a trait they shared.

"Yeah, Travis," Peggy said. "What do you want to do about Shane?"

Travis lowered his hand and sighed. "My inclination is to feed Shane and his buddy to the zombies, but that isn't the right thing to do."

"Hey, I'm fine with feeding them to the zombies," Lenore said.

"Me, too," Ken chimed in next to her.

"He is a danger to this fort as a whole," Eric said firmly. "He can't be trusted."

"I think this discussion should be handled in a more discreet setting," Manny, the mayor, said as he moved to the center of the crowd, getting everyone's attention. He had not attended the party, explaining earlier that he wasn't feeling well. Now he stood before them in his robe and pajamas. He was a fading figure in the politics of the fort, but he had the respect of many in the town. He was known for being amiable, good-natured, and a peacemaker—all of which had helped him keep the peace with both a cantankerous city council and the opinionated townsfolk of Ashley Oaks.

Juan thought Manny was right; the discussion needed to be taken elsewhere before the crowd became a mob. He looked at Travis.

"I'm willing to discuss this in a calmer setting," his friend finally said.

"Good. Bill, Curtis, Juan, Peggy, and Travis, please join me in my office in city hall." The crowd murmured, but seemed somewhat satisfied. Smiling like a true politician, Manny shook the hands of a few people as he made his way back through the crowd.

Juan followed, his agitation settling into his shoulders. He felt tense and angry. He glanced at Travis, sure the other man was even more wired. Surprisingly, Travis looked calm, but Juan knew him well, and saw the tension in his neck that gave away his internal turmoil.

"It's going to be okay, man," Juan assured him.

"I keep telling myself that," Travis replied grimly.

A few people patted Travis on the shoulder as he passed them.

"We're behind you on this, Travis," Eric said.

"I say we throw him over the wall!" Lenore said loudly again.

Juan sighed and shoved his hands into the pockets of his jeans as he walked toward the office. Tonight was a bitch and only bound to get worse.

Travis entered the office and looked around the room. The mayor was hunched down behind his desk, his fingers playing with his pen while Peggy slid into a chair near him. Bill and Curtis took their places in deep leather chairs. Juan slid onto a folding chair while Travis leaned against the wall.

"So, are we throwing them over the wall?" Juan asked.

Bill somberly shook his head. "Philip and Shane are both sticking to their story that Katie asked Shane for sex and Travis assaulted them."

"That's bullshit." Travis couldn't believe Bill's words.

"Yeah. But they are corroborating each other's stories," Bill answered.

"And I'm corroborating Katie's. I saw what Shane was trying to do!" Travis felt his temper rising. "She was fighting him!"

Manny hesitated, then said, "Shane and Philip have been invaluable to this community through their salvaging expeditions. We need to take that into consideration."

"They also tried to rape Katie," Travis snapped.

"And Shane beat her up before, that day when she shot his brother because he got chewed up by a zombie," Peggy added. "She was doing us all a favor before he turned."

"He's shit on our heels," Curtis said.

"He deserves some sort of due process," Bill said firmly. "We just need to figure out what due process is here at the fort."

"He deserves to be thrown over the wall!" Juan shouted. "There is no fucking due process anymore. You even said that! The world ended. All that is in the past!"

"C'mon now, Juan. We can't be going off all half-cocked and pissed off and start throwing people over the wall. You know that," Bill said sternly.

Peggy sighed heavily. "And you know that we're the ones everyone looks at when there's trouble. Bill, those people out there expect us to do something. You, especially."

"That doesn't give us the right to choose the fate of these men." Bill shook his head. "I don't want that kind of power. Do you?"

"Toss them over the damn wall," Juan repeated. "I'm willing to take that power."

Bill gave Juan a sharp, thoughtful look. Travis reached out and touched Juan on the shoulder, silently urging him to calm down. The last thing Juan needed to do was draw even more suspicion on himself.

Manny said in a tired voice, "I can't condemn a man just because there is a consensus by a lot of angry people that he did something wrong."

"You have to believe Katie," Travis protested. "You have to believe us. You know those guys are trouble."

"They are entitled to some sort of due process, Travis," Bill said determinedly. "Whatever the hell that is. I'm not even sure anymore, but we gotta come up with something."

Curtis snorted. "They gave that up when they attacked Katie."

"And who makes that choice?" Bill's gaze swept over those in the room. "When did we decide that? And by 'we,' I mean the whole damn fort. I thought we were trying to make a new civilization, not chaos. No one of us should have the power to put a man over the wall because a bunch of people believe he did something wrong or because they don't like him. We leave them to the zombies, and we're all guilty of murder."

Travis winced at the police officer's words and rubbed his hands over his face, trying to focus himself and not let his deep anger overwhelm him.

Peggy fumbled with her collar nervously. "I won't feel comfortable if they stay here."

"But they do contribute to our society as a whole," Manny interjected. "They've brought in many supplies. We have food to eat because they risked their lives to get it. They are not bad men. Maybe stupid, but not ba—"

"Manny, rape is bad! Okay—it's bad. Stop being an idiot," Peggy snapped.

The mayor winced and drew back in his chair. Before he could answer, the door opened unexpectedly.

Calhoun shuffled in with his camera. "I am now filming a top secret city council meeting that was not announced in the public notices. I am filming all conspirators—"

"Gawddammit, Calhoun!" Curtis said. "This is not a city council meeting."

"And it's not top secret," Peggy added. "The mayor announced it in the lobby."

"The city secretary speaks. She is devious and the secret power of this town. She controls the mayors as they come in and out of office. She is the one that sets the true agenda."

"Gawddammit, Calhoun, anyone worth their salt knows the true power in small-town Texas is the city secretary," Peggy responded. "Shit, it's a big joke when I go to Austin with all the city secretaries for election school. Most of us don't even see the mayor except for when we phone 'em up to sign paperwork. Manny wasn't in the office but for a few hours each damn day. So stop jabbering about what everyone knows! No offense, Manny."

Manny sighed as he mopped beads of sweat away from his forehead with a tissue.

Calhoun looked speechless, then turned the camera toward himself. "I now have recorded a full confession of an Amazonian takeover of all the small towns in Texas."

"I so give up on him," Peggy drawled out, and threw out one hand. "Someone else deal with the ol' coot."

"Calhoun, we're just discussing what happened tonight," Travis said. "Why don't you just sit down, film it, and keep quiet?"

Calhoun turned and aimed the camera at his face. "This is the man who beat the asshole into submission. I have yet to determine if he is human or not. . . . As this top secret meeting continues—"

"It's not top secret!" Peggy looked ready to burst a blood vessel.

"Then, if it's not top secret, you won't mind us attending," Steven Mann said from behind Calhoun, dragging his wife, Blanche, into the room with him. "We should have a say in these proceedings."

Blanche drew away from her husband and took a chair far from Calhoun. She smoothed her silk dress and crossed her long, slender tanned legs. "We have always had a say in the town's politics. My sister is a state senator."

"We feel Shane and Philip are valuable resources to our community," Steven added.

"So the rumors that they went out to y'all's place and snagged some of y'all's goodies is true, huh?" Curtis's eyes were very cold and fierce.

"What?" Travis blinked.

"We needed certain essentials." Blanche waved her hand as if to dismiss any argument. "They were kind enough to secure them." She frowned as Calhoun rushed over to her and zoomed in on her face. She shoved him away with one foot.

Manny looked shocked. "But we said that all the runs into town were for supplies, not for personal reasons. We swore that to everyone who wanted to go home and get their things."

"We're not just anyone, Manny," Blanche said with a light laugh, twirling one of her long earrings with a finger.

"I paid them for their time," Steven added.

"A full confession is now on tape . . . ," Calhoun muttered, circling Steven.

Travis turned to Steven and said harshly, "People have died on those supply runs. Going out to your fucking ranch for your personal stuff—"

"It was necessary," Blanche cut him off.

"We can't go around risking people's lives just so you can sit pretty," Juan retorted.

Travis pointed at Steven angrily. "Look, this is tough enough without you coming in here and spouting off about what good guys Phil and Shane are. Lord knows how many lives they put at risk, going into the deadlands to get your fancy shit."

Manny rubbed his face with one hand. "This is not acceptable."

"No, what is not acceptable was that Katie woman acting like a complete tart in the ballroom. It was obvious to everyone that she was intoxicated," Steven said in a tight, controlled voice. "I'm sure she led Shane on."

"What?" Travis was close to losing his temper.

Calhoun whipped around to zoom in on Travis. Travis forced himself not to thrust the old man away.

"I mean that dress . . . that awful dress . . . with such nice shoes," Blanche sniffed.

Juan moved to Travis's side. "Look, bitch, you have no right to say—"

"Excuse me? I have no right? I have every right to express my opinion. And my opinion is that whatever went on tonight is between the two people involved," Blanche snapped.

"Shane is a good man and she is smearing his name in an effort to get him thrown over the wall," Steven said. "We all know she has a beef against him. It has been very obvious. She's been baiting him for weeks now."

Travis took a step forward and Juan, who had moved close to him while the Manns were speaking, grabbed his arm. He had been trying to be rational, but he was not going to be able to keep from punching Steven in the mouth if the man kept it up. He tried to recover his calm.

Manny looked at Bill and said, "There are conflicting stories."

"Yes, there are, but we should consider—," Bill started to answer.

"Just vote," Peggy said simply.

"The Amazonian speaks . . . ," Calhoun narrated, "and all fall silent to listen."

Blanche arched an eyebrow.

"A vote?" Bill blinked.

"Type up their statements and let everyone in the fort read them, then vote." Peggy looked determined, tired, and pissed off. "Let the people of the fort decide what to do. You're saying you don't want us to have all the power, well, fine. Give it back to the people. Let them decide."

"What are the options for punishment?" Juan demanded.

"We could give them a car, weapons, ammo, and food and set them on their way if guilty," Bill offered.

Curtis face flushed crimson. "Why waste our supplies on criminals?"

"Because it's humane," Bill retorted.

"And what's the other option? Letting them go?" Travis practically snarled.

"Of course," Steven and Blanche chorused.

"With a restraining order against him to steer clear of Katie," Bill added.

"So basically Katie's safety is dependent on how people vote," Travis said with frustration. He didn't like that idea. It made him feel helpless.

"I say we dump them over the wall," Juan said firmly.

Travis gave his best friend a warning look. Juan needed to watch his mouth.

"Let our vigilante do it," Peggy said with a sigh. "I'm sure Shane is on his list now."

"I anticipated that, and I plan to have round-the-clock guards on that holding cell," Bill said. "Those two are not going over the wall."

"So we vote," Peggy said again.

Manny nodded. "That sounds fair to me."

"Well, I'm not certain we want everyone voting on this, Manny," Steven said tersely .

"Steven, I think it's a good idea. Get the people involved. We all know that if the people of the fort hadn't raised a ruckus, it would have taken Travis forever to go into the hotel." Blanche offered Travis a syrupy-sweet fake smile.

Steven gave his wife a sharp look, but his expression softened slightly. "Fine."

"I think everyone old enough to understand should vote," Peggy suggested.

"And you will have to hold to the vote," Blanche asserted. "You can't change your minds just because the vote doesn't go your way."

Bill and Manny nodded as Curtis threw up his hands.

"We'll obey the vote," Manny assured Blanche.

"You know what? Do whatever you want. But you'd all better be damn sure you are setting a precedent you can live with," Travis said, and headed out the door.

Calhoun swung his camera around as Travis passed him. "Good point, Travis."

"Thanks, Otis." Travis wasn't sure if it was a good or bad thing that the resident nutcase was agreeing with him.

Juan followed Travis back to the hotel. Travis was silent the whole time, trying hard not to let his temper get the best of him.

"Travis," Eric called out as the two men entered the lobby. Travis sighed—he wasn't really ready to talk to anyone yet—then took several deep breaths to regain his composure.

"What's going to happen?" Eric asked.

"A vote. The fort will decide what to do," Travis answered.

"That seems fair," Eric said.

"I'm not sure if it is or not," Travis confessed.

"Why?" Juan folded his arms over his chest. "This is a good thing."

Travis shook his head. "I hate this feeling. Voting out a person into the deadlands. It doesn't feel right."

"We don't want them here, that's for damn sure," Eric reminded him. "I know you want them gone."

"Yeah, I do want them gone. But I know that's my emotions talking. We have to be civilized. What if we start voting out people for the wrong reasons?" Travis shook his head. He felt compromised by his own beliefs. He wanted Shane and Philip gone, but the thought of the community as a whole forcing someone to leave the safety of the fort was terrifying.

"It's the right thing to do, man. You know it," Juan insisted.

Travis set his hands on his hips as he considered his friend's viewpoint. Finally, he said, "Nothing feels right anymore. Nothing." Without another word, he walked to the elevator. All he wanted was to be with Katie.

When Travis let himself into Katie's room using the key she had given him after their first time, he found her and Jenni curled up together, fast asleep. Travis gently smoothed Katie's hair back from her face. He drew a chair up close to the bed, then sat in silence, deep in thought.

• CHAPTER THIRTEEN •

1.
Justice

The next week was sheer hell.

Voting on what to do with Shane and Philip had seemed like a good idea at first. Printed copies of the depositions were handed out to everyone over the age of seventeen. The most popular reading material in the fort, the papers were also the most talked about and scandalous.

Philip and Shane were tucked away in the city hall holding cell and were always monitored. They had plenty of time to flap their jaws and spread rumors. Roger had become so disgusted by their tales that he had asked Nerit not to assign him to guard them. Nerit had explained to Roger that he needed to keep his spot to limit the number of people Shane and Philip came into contact with.

Katie's sexuality became the focus of a lot of the conversations. Some people staunchly refused to believe she was anything other than straight. Others suspected that she was a lesbian in hiding. That this was even considered part of the decision-making process made Katie feel angry and hurt at the same time.

"Yeah, someone asked me if I was your mustache," Travis said with a wry smile one night.

"Huh? Oh! My beard!" Katie rolled her eyes. "I'm surprised they even knew the term."

"Yeah, I'm the mustache for you and Jenni." Travis teased her with a grin.

"Of course. What else would you be," she said with a laugh. The words hurt more than she cared to admit.

It was a painful reminder of all she and Lydia had gone through. The furtive looks, the guarded questions, the gossip: it had been hell. Somehow, it had been easier with Lydia because they had each other. Travis was trying so hard, but he didn't really know what it was like to know that a good portion of the world hated you simply because you looked at your own sex and saw no issue with loving them.

Explaining all this was too complicated. Even explaining that she loved Travis was complicated. So she didn't say anything except, "Travis and I are together, and I would never cheat on him with Shane or anyone else."

But the rumors continued and Blanche Mann dragged Katie's name through the dirt. The woman's mocking words rang in Katie's ears—and Blanche wasn't alone in the strength of her response. A scary old Southern Baptist named Mary took to saying nasty things around Katie. There were condemning stares from a few. Katie tried to ignore it all.

At the same time, she was embraced by her supporters. Old Man Watson went out of his way to stand up and hug her tight whenever she passed. Nerit, of course, was unwavering. Jenni was almost psychotic in her defense.

Every night, Katie went to bed with Travis's arms around her waist and his chest pressed snugly against her back. He had found a cell phone charger somewhere and plugged in her phone when she wasn't looking, as a surprise. That night she had slipped into bed and looked at the nightstand to see Lydia smiling at her from the phone. She almost cried at the sight. Travis was smiling sheepishly at her from the bathroom. Jumping up and running across the room, Katie had flung her arms around his neck and clung to him, clasping the phone in her hand.

Maybe he understood more than she gave him credit for.

"It scares me sometimes," he whispered in her ear later that night, "to realize that, if not for all this shit going down, I would never have found you. And I know you would be happy without me, since you would be with her, but I don't know what would have happened to me. Would I have found happiness somewhere else?"

Katie had held him close and stroked his hair. "We have to live with what is, not what might have been."

He reached out and snagged the cell phone, studying Lydia's picture. "She was really beautiful, Katie. I like her smile and her eyes. She looks really kind."

"She was amazing. I loved her," Katie said in a soft voice. "And you are amazing and I love you."

Travis smiled. "Oh, I know. I'm not afraid of Lydia's memory. I just want her to know I'm going to take good care of you."

Katie gave him a loving smile and kissed him. "She knows. I know it."

The day of the vote, Travis held Katie tight as the ballots were counted and the result announced. When she closed her eyes and sank back against him, he had kissed her neck and cuddled her close.

At sunset that night, Shane and Philip were given a sedan with a full tank of gas, two rifles with ammo, and a week's supply of MREs. Bill and Curtis escorted them out as a small group of onlookers watched from a distance.

"The bitch will pay," Shane said to Bill as he climbed into the driver's seat.

The gates opened and the two men, who had caused so much pain, were gone.

2.
Vigilante Justice

Five hours later, in the dead of the night, Philip stumbled up to the far corner of the fort where Main Street had been blocked off. "Help me! They're right behind me," he cried out frantically to the guard on watch.

"Where's your friend?" the sentry asked.

"Shane? I don't know. Our car broke down, so we tried to make it back here on foot. We got separated when zombies attacked us. Our guns didn't work. I barely escaped! Let me in, for God's sake," Philip said desperately.

The guard's head tilted. "I don't think so."

Philip looked up in shock. "You can't do this! You have no right. You know I didn't do anything. It was all Shane!"

The guard's head shook from side to side. "Sorry, but it ends here for you."

Slowly, the truth dawned on Philip. "It's you! You set it up! You killed Jimmy and Ritchie! You tampered with our car and rigged our guns so they wouldn't work."

With a slow sigh, the guard nodded. "Yeah, I did. You should have died out there with Shane. Good thing you came to my post." Then the guard's gun barked and Phillip toppled over, screaming and clutching his leg. With satisfaction, the guard watched as the zombies finally caught up with Shane's sidekick and pulled him apart, feasting with ravenous hunger.

3.
The Aftermath of the Verdict

The next morning when Katie came on sentry duty, she found Eric reporting in on his walkie-talkie. "Yeah, I thinned them out a little during the night. Curtis, Katarina, and Juan all said they had to do the same. I don't know where the hell they came from."

"Thank you for your hard work," Yolanda's voice answered. She was on duty at the communication center this morning. "I'll let Nerit know."

"Right," Eric said. "Katie's here now, so I'm about to take off." Yolanda acknowleged and signed off.

Katie looked over the wall at the zombies. They were always a gruesome sight; she doubted she would ever get used to seeing their torn bodies.

"Bad night, I take it?" she said to Eric.

"Yeah. They kept showing up. Gave me the creeps, just appearing out of that mist we had last night. Curtis gave the kill-on-sight order when they became too numerous." Eric waved at the oncoming zombies. "I don't know where they're coming from."

"I'll take care of them," Katie assured him.

"There are a few crawlers down there, but I figure we should leave them for the cleanup crews. No point wasting ammo on them." Eric picked up his small pack and slung it over his shoulder. "I'm off for some breakfast and sleep."

"See you later. Say hi to Stacey for me."

"I will," Eric said, yawned, and left.

Katie set her book bag down near the sentry chair. She'd packed her usual supplies—a bottle of water, a bag of popcorn, and extra ammunition. Curious about the crawlers, she leaned over for a look. Three or four zombies were pulling themselves along with broken limbs, moving slowly toward the wall. One had already reached the barrier and was slamming its hand against the concrete bricks. Slowly, it raised its head to look up at her. Its mangled countenance looked strangely familiar and she studied it with interest. Slowly, she realized it was Philip staring up at her with one eye.

"Shit," she said. "Ah, damnit. Seriously, damnit."

Philip's horribly mutilated form moaned low in its throat as one badly chewed arm lifted toward Katie. He had been torn in half. His torso was propped up by one arm; his legs lay nearby. The Philip zombie let out another anguished cry, and his undead brethren slowly approached from the side streets. As Katie lifted her walkie-talkie to her mouth, a few looked up, saw her, and moaned.

"I've got Philip outside the wall," she said.

"He came back?" Yolanda's voice answered in disbelief.

"Yeah. But he's not alive," Katie responded grimly.

There was a burst of static, then, "Shit."

"Tell Bill and Nerit, please."

"Right."

Jenni bounced up the wooden steps to the platform, carrying two breakfast tacos wrapped in foil. "Hey, girlfriend, what's up?" Her dark hair was in a ponytail and she wore a T-shirt that read ZOMBIE KILLAH in red puff paint. The women of the fort had held a T-shirt-decorating party a few nights back. While most of the T-shirts had been decorated with flowers, animals, or cowboy imagery, Jenni's bore fake bullet holes in addition to her new nickname.

Katie pointed down into the street.

Jenni stared down at the zombie, then shrugged. "That's gross. So what?"

"It's Philip," Katie responded.

Frowning, Jenni looked again. "Oh, wow. I think you're right! Whoa. It's like Ritchie, part two," Jenni said, her eyes widening. "But grosser. It looks like he was a big ol' wishbone."

"Nice way to put it," Katie said, and rubbed her nose. The fragrance of the tacos mixing with the decaying reek of the zombies was not very palatable.

"He is seriously chewed up." Jenni set down the tacos and leaned over the wall, studying Philip's corpse. The zombies howled and beat against the concrete bricks. "Gnawed down to the bone in some places. Wow."

"Let me see, Katie-girl," Bill said as he lumbered up onto the platform.

Katie stepped aside, motioning down below. "I'm sure it's him."

Bill scrutinized the undead man. "Yep. That's Phil."

"I like him better this way," a voice called from a nearby sentry platform. It was Lenore.

Jenni gave her a thumbs-up.

Lenore nodded.

"Zombies definitely had a field day with him," Katie sighed. "Any idea what went wrong?"

"Maybe Shane ditched him to lessen his load," Bill said.

"I wouldn't put that past him. He is such a total shit," Jenni said, eating her taco.

Katie wasn't sure how Jenni could eat with that awful smell wafting up from below, but from her work as a prosecutor, she knew that abused women developed extraordinary coping skills. She'd seen how adept Jenni was at disassociating herself from bad things going on around her. Sometimes Katie wished she could do that, too, just step away from the horrible reality she now lived in.

Nerit joined their small group, her sniper rifle held lightly in the crook of her arm. She glanced over the wall and studied the scene. "I want a closer look at him."

"Me, too," Bill said.

"Why?" Katie arched an eyebrow at them. "He's obviously undead now."

Nerit pointed. "Something is wrong with that leg."

"Well, it is chewed down like a chicken leg," Jenni commented.

"The way the bone is shattered doesn't sit right with me either," Bill said.

"Put him down and let's haul him up," Nerit ordered.

Katie drew her gun. It felt strange to shoot Phil, but somehow right. She fired once and watched his torso flop backwards.

"He so deserved that," Jenni said with satisfaction, licking salsa from her fingers, and shoved the rest of the taco into her mouth.

4.
Ghosts of the Past

Scrambling down the ladder, Jenni landed feet first on the street below Katie's sentry post and raised her pistol quickly. Bill climbed down laboriously behind her, his big belly giving him a little trouble as he went.

Jenni was surrounded by the bodies of the dead zombies eliminated during the night. Jenni knew they were finally, truly dead, but she couldn't help but be afraid. Every time she was outside the walls, she was terribly aware of her vulnerability.

Bill set his booted feet down on the street and heaved his belly upward as he tried to get his belt hoisted up on its girth. His keen eyes surveyed the street from beneath his cowboy hat. Felix and Nerit joined them in the road. Jenni and Felix took up positions to the left and the right, standing guard while Nerit and Bill moved over to the pieces of Philip's body.

"That smell is enough to make me puke," Felix grumbled, and kicked a dead body in irritation.

Jenni looked down at the gray, decaying carcass at her feet. It had been so badly eaten that it was hard to tell what gender it had been. It was naked and most of its hair had been pulled out. Felix might be bothered by the smell, but not Jenni. No, it was seeing their empty eyes, like Mikey's as he snarled and clawed at the window of the white truck on the first day. She blinked hard and shoved the image away.

"Mighty chewed up," Bill said to Nerit. "Can't tell much about what happened before he got ate."

Jenni rubbed her nose and narrowed her eyes as a few shambling figures appeared in the far distance.

"Look at his right leg," Nerit said.

Jenni glanced over to see the older woman squatting down by one of Philip's torn-off limbs. The skin was shredded and muscle and tendons were ripped from the bone.

"Shattered," Bill said after a moment.

"Human teeth couldn't do that," Nerit pointed out.

"What does that mean?" Felix's voice was tight with his fear.

Bill answered, "I think someone shot him in the leg."

"Before or after he was dead?" Felix asked.

"I betcha Shane did it," Jenni offered, and watched as one of the faraway shambling creatures tumbled to the ground. Its struggles to get up resulted in an almost comic series of pratfalls.

"Maybe," was all Bill said. "We better go see if we can find Shane."

Nerit continued to study the shattered bone thoughtfully. She prodded the limb with the barrel of her rifle, then looked around on the ground nearby.

Bill called in to the fort, asking for a vehicle to be brought around. Jenni kept her eyes on the figures in the distance.

"What's going on?" Katie called out from above.

"Heading out to see if we can find out what happened to Shane!" Bill gave her a thumbs-up.

Judging from Katie's expression, Jenni could tell that her friend was probably feeling some sort of misplaced guilt. Jenni didn't mind Philip being in pieces. She kind of wished Shane was lying out here, too. She returned her gaze to the figures a few blocks away wading through the shimmering heat. The one that had fallen had not been able to get up.

Nerit shoved the decaying bodies out of her way, obviously intent on finding something. Bill pulled up on his belt and stared down the road at the zombies moving relentlessly toward them.

"Helluva day," he said at last.

The school bus roared around the corner, Ed behind the wheel.

Felix said, "Thank God."

Jenni understood his relief, though the walking dead were not moving quickly. She liked them slow like this. It was easier to kill them and it was more like the old zombie movies. She hated it when they were fresh and fast.

She was the last one to get on the bus and she paused on the steps to give Katie a thumbs up. The concern in Katie's expression was touching. It was good to know that people actually gave a damn about what happened to her.

"Another day. Another dollar," Felix grumbled as he slung his long body onto a seat.

"We don't get paid," Jenni reminded him.

"Oh, yeah. This job sucks." Felix grinned and winked.

Jenni winked back and grabbed hold of the bar over her head as Ed shifted gears and the minibus roared forward. She watched the approaching zombies with irritation. She didn't feel like dealing with them today.

Nerit sat across from Jenni, her rifle on her knees. One hand gripped the back of Felix's seat as the minibus bounced down the road. She looked eerily calm, as usual. Jenni envied her.

"Nothing is ever simple." Bill let out a weary sigh.

"Never is," Felix agreed.

"We just do our best," Nerit said. "Do our best and hope."

"Do you think we're it? The only ones left other than those little pockets out there that Peggy talks to?" Felix was staring out at the dead town, and his voice sounded weary.

Jenni didn't want to think or talk about other people. She didn't want to think about anything outside their own little world.

"Does it matter?" Nerit finally said. "Does it really matter if we are the last ones or not?"

"Puts a helluvalot of pressure on us if we are," Felix answered.

Bill nodded. "That it does."

Ed plowed over the slow-moving zombies, following the route Shane and Philip would have taken the day before to leave town. "It don't matter if we are or aren't the last. We just gotta not mess up. We gotta do what we have to and hope that anyone out there still alive is doing okay, too. I know my boys are out there somewhere, doing their best to survive. I didn't raise no fools."

"Where are your boys, Ed?" Nerit asked.

Jenni didn't want to think about the families destroyed in the first days, about her own dead children who were now seeking out the flesh of the living. She just wanted to get this job done and get back to Juan and the safety of the fort.

"Got two sons up in College Station, going to Texas A & M."

"Aggies," Felix muttered with the disdain only a Longhorn from the University of Texas could muster.

Ed ignored him. "The youngest is in military school up near Fort Worth."

Jenni gazed out at the abandoned buildings of the town and frowned as several zombies shambled into view to watch the bus pass.

"If they're anything like you, Ed, I'm sure they're fine," Jenni said, hoping that would finish the conversation.

"I raised them good. They're smart boys. I know they're fine."

"They're country boys. They got a better chance than most city folk," Bill agreed.

"Hey!" Felix and Jenni, the only city folk in the bus, both protested the same time.

Nerit chuckled.

"There it is," Ed called out. "There's their car."

The outcasts' sedan was half-on, half-off the road, with its front tire in a drainage ditch. Nearby were a few old buildings and houses. Nothing stirred except the wind in the tall grasses.

"Let's get this done." Nerit slid to her feet.

"Same drill as always," Ed added.

Jenni picked up an ax from the collection of weapons Ed had loaded into the vehicle and double-checked her pistol. The ax felt good in her hands. Her anger against the zombies and the terror they had brought into her life was a hot furnace inside her.

When the bus doors opened, she was the first one out. Her boot heels kicked up dust as she quickly took up her position, covering the others as they disembarked. Felix moved to cover the other side of the road while Nerit, Bill, and Ed went to examine the car.

From where Jenni stood, she could see that one side of the car was smeared with zombie gunk. Nerit picked up a discarded weapon and scrutinized it thoughtfully. Bill squatted down and picked up a box of ammunition.

"All shots fired," Nerit said.

"This box is filled with gravel. I'm not liking how this is looking." Bill stood and adjusted his belt. It was a common gesture for him. He'd been getting thinner since Travis and Katie brought him to the fort from Toombs Hunting Store. He was always hiking up his belt. Jenni found it an endearing and amusing action.

"Got six zombies dead on this side of the car," Ed called out. "And another box of gravel."

"Someone sabotaged them," Felix said. "Who could have done it?"

"A number of people," Nerit answered blandly.

Jenni thought of Juan and briefly wondered if he had done it, then pushed the thought away.

"Why is the car abandoned? Why did Philip head back to the fort?" Bill stood back a few feet from the car and peered in, while Ed hunkered down to look under it.

Jenni saw the zombie lunge for Ed out of the corner of her eye. "Ed!"

The man scrambled backwards quickly as the zombie under the car reached for him. It was terribly mutilated and missing a good chunk of its torso, so it was slow. Its feet scrabbled at the ground, trying to find purchase. Ed got to his feet and kicked it in the face, knocking its head back. Yanking his hatchet off his belt, he motioned to the others that he had it under control.

"Hurry up and kill it," Jenni said, trying not to yell loudly enough to draw more zombies to them.

Ed slammed the hatchet down on the fearsome, growling face thrusting toward him. The zombie shuddered. Its skinless fingers clawed at Ed's boots.

. . . like those tiny fingers pressed under the door on the first day . . . those tiny little fingers . . .

Jenni shook her head to break the memory.

Ed slammed the hatchet down one more time. The thing's fingers finally stilled.

"And here we go," Felix sighed as two badly decomposing zombies appeared from around a nearby building.

"I hate company," Jenni grumbled. Her head was throbbing.

She felt off-kilter. Seeing the zombies' fingers straining to reach Ed had sickened her. She tried hard not to think of Benji.

"Especially the kind of company that wants you for dinner," Felix agreed. "I hate zombies. I hate them. I really, really hate them. I wish they would just go away."

Bill popped the hood behind them while Nerit walked slowly around the car. Ed joined her. They studied the area together.

Jenni frowned as more staggered into view. "At least these don't move too fast."

The shambling dead were a strangely reassuring sight. The zombies were a mess now, often indistinguishable as male or female; white, black, Hispanic, or Asian. Four months of rot, exposure to the elements, and general wear and tear had the walking dead in bad shape. Their skin was dry, cracked, and shredded. Their limbs were mangled and twisted.

Since zombies felt no pain, they had no concern for their bodies. They struggled through brambles, bushes, and low fences, tripped down inclines, fell from heights, and sometimes rammed themselves repeatedly against obstacles. On her trips outside the walls, Jenni had seen the undead do extraordinary damage to themselves while trying to get the living.

"They're getting closer," Felix called out.

"Almost done," Bill answered.

Jenni felt uneasy despite the slow advancement of the zombies. Her rage had dissipated and been replaced by a low pulse of fear. But she couldn't let it get to her. One of the zombies, a female in a truly tacky pink tracksuit, was drawing too close.

"Ax time!" Jenni moved toward the female zombie reaching for her, moaning that terrible sound, and forced back her fear.

The zombie lunged at her. Jenni slammed the flat of the ax head hard into the creature's sternum and knocked her on her back. Jenni quickly pinned it down with one foot placed solidly on the dead thing's chest and heaved the ax over her head. As the zombie grabbed at her boot, Jenni brought down the ax as hard as she could and cleaved its head in two.

"One down!" Jenni yanked her ax out of the zombie's head and took a few steps back.

"I got visitors!" Felix yelled. He successfully took down one zombie with his double-bladed spear, but he'd miscalculated how far away the second zombie was, and it grabbed at him from behind. Felix shoved the spear back hard and impaled the thing. Jenni moved to help him as the zombie pushed its body along the spear, but Felix turned and shot it in the face.

"I got it, Jenni, I got it," Felix said, grinning.

"Good job." She held the ax, her eyes scanning the approaching dead, trying to figure out her next moves.

"I would really like to go now," Felix called out as more dead stepped into view around them.

Bill motioned to Ed. The two men talked in soft tones.

"C'mon, guys! Hurry up!" Jenni called, exasperated.

The limping, gruesome dead were drawing ever closer. They were too clustered together for Jenni to destroy them individually.

Ed got down on the ground and slid under the sedan.

"Guys, seriously! Seriously, this is not good!" Felix wailed.

"I'll thin them out," Nerit said reassuringly. She raised her rifle and fired at the less mutilated, more dangerous zombies.

Jenni watched with fascination as the zombies went down one by one. A plume of blood, brains, and bone erupted out the back of each one's skull before it crumpled to the ground.

Felix also fired at the growing crowd of zombies. A small group of zombies was manageable, but too many swarming together was hard to survive.

Jenni pulled her handgun from its holster and aimed at the remains of a mechanic that was shambling toward her. It didn't have much of a face, but its tongue flicked out between its stained, broken teeth.

Mikey's torn face flashed across her vision. . . .

Jenni shook her head, trying to force the memory away.

"Kill it, Jenni!" Felix shouted.

She had to force her mind to focus as she looked at the zombie again. Now it was Lloyd, her dead, abusive husband. His mouth was open in that terrible zombie moan and his shirt was covered in the blood of her children.

Join us, Jenni, Lloyd's voice whispered.

"Jenni!" Nerit barked.

"Fuck you, Lloyd," Jenni growled. She fired. The bullet sheared off the top of his head.

Lloyd swayed on his feet for a second, then collapsed at her feet. Jenni lifted her foot and slammed it down several times on the zombie's head for good measure.

"Who the hell is Lloyd? Did you know that zombie?" Felix yelled.

Jenni ignored him and looked down at the zombie that was no longer her husband, but some pathetic mechanic. She raised her gaze and lifted her gun to fire into the group of zombies nearing her.

"Let's go! Done here!" Bill called.

Jenni and Felix backed toward the minibus. Nerit disappeared into it, only to reappear at a window, which she slid down so she could provide cover.

Bill jogged around the back of the minibus and headed toward the open door. More zombies were appearing, probably drawn by the gunfire. Jenni reloaded her weapon as Felix backed toward her. Ed fired up the engine.

"You first," Jenni told Felix.

"I'd say ladies first, but—" Felix ducked into the bus.

Jenni slowly backed toward the open door. She was almost to safety. A little boy around Benji's age walked into view, trailing behind the other zombies. When he spotted Jenni, he gave a small cry and lifted his hands. His small fingers reached for her.

Let him bite you. Die and join us. Lloyd's voice again.

An uncomfortable tightness gripped Jenni's throat. She wanted to scream. She stumbled back, gasping. The little boy wasn't just Benji's age—he was Benji! Her baby had found her. He was coming for her. His fingers were reaching for her so he could claim her.

His tiny fingers reached for her . . . strained for her. . . .

Bill grabbed Jenni around the waist and dragged her into the bus. She stared, transfixed, at Benji. The doors snapped shut between her and her son.

"It's Benji," Jenni gasped.

"No, it's not," Nerit said sharply. "It's not him."

"Who's Benji?" Felix asked, sounding completely bewildered.

Bill set Jenni down firmly in a seat. "Jenni, it's not him. It's not Benji."

"But . . ." She couldn't look away from Benji's zombified form and his searching fingers. He was reaching for her, wanting her. "He's coming for me."

Yes, he is. Get off the bus. Embrace him. Join us, Lloyd urged her.

Nerit grabbed Jenni's chin and forced her to look away. "It's not him, Jenni. It's not him. Look away. Close your eyes. Don't look, because it's not him."

Jenni finally tore her gaze away from the small dead boy and squeezed her eyes shut. The terrible fear that had gripped her gradually eased. She took in a shuddering breath. Finally, she looked back out the window.

The zombie wasn't Benji. It wasn't even a little boy. It was a tween girl in a torn nightgown.

Lloyd had tricked her. Anger flashed through her, burning away the last vestiges of her paralysis.

"Sorry," she murmured.

Ed shifted gears, and the minibus lurched forward.

"It's okay," Nerit assured her. She gently rubbed Jenni's back. "It's okay. It was just a bad moment."

"What just happened? 'Cause I'm very confused."

"Felix, it's over. That's all that matters," Bill said calmly.

The bus rumbled on. Ed would take an indirect route back to the fort to avoid leading the zombies to their safe haven.

Jenni felt reality slipping back into place around her. The morning of the first day receded into her memories. Her children were gone. Maybe their bodies sill roamed the earth, but the spark that had made them human was gone.

Jenni looked up at Nerit, who was still gently rubbing her back, trying to soothe her. "I'm sorry I'm crazy."

"Honey, we are all crazy," Nerit assured her.

"That's the truth," Felix agreed.

"I ain't been sane in a long time," Ed said in a grim tone.

"Y'all speak for yourselves." Bill grinned. "I'm as sane as they come in a zombie-infested world."

Nerit smacked him upside the head. "Liar."

Bill laughed. He was obviously trying to break the somber mood.

Jenni lowered her head into her hands and slowly regained her composure. "I'm so embarrassed," she said at last.

"It's all right. We're all fine. That is what teamwork is for. We take care of each other." Nerit touched Jenni's cheek lightly. "Besides, how many times have you saved our lives? We just returned the favor."

"And no need to tell anyone about this," Ed said. His tone implied something the others had not even considered.

"The Vigilante?" Jenni queried.

"Shit," Felix swore. "He killed Jimmy for freaking out."

"She didn't get anyone killed or even nearly killed," Bill pointed out.

"But whoever the Vigilante is has a distorted perception of reality and who deserves to live or die," Nerit reminded him.

"We keep it quiet," Ed said firmly as he drove on.

"Agreed," Bill said.

Felix folded his arms, disgruntled by the situation. "Gotta put up with zombies and crazies."

Jenni sighed heavily. She hated feeling weak.

"It will be okay," Nerit assured her.

Jenni wasn't sure she agreed.

"What did you find out?" Felix asked Nerit.

The older woman directed her gaze at Bill, who shrugged. Nerit sighed, then said, "We learned that the Vigilante is still at work."

Felix slouched down in his chair with a grunt. "Great. Just great."

Jenni rested her head against the cool window and gazed out at the dead town. The world still didn't feel right to her. It wasn't just the Vigilante. It was Lloyd. She felt him, somewhere nearby, watching her.

She was afraid.

· CHAPTER FOURTEEN ·

1.
When Plans Go Awry

By the expressions on the team returning to the fort, it was quickly apparent that something grim had been discovered. Travis was with Katie at her sentry post when the team walked past on their way to report in.

"I better go find out what is going on," Travis said.

"You better tell me everything later." He could tell that Katie was annoyed at having to stay at her post while the fate of Shane and Philip was discussed.

"Do I have a choice?"

"Absolutely not."

Travis kissed her and left, quickly making his way across the old construction site to city hall. He met Juan at the back door.

"It's not going to be good, is it?" Juan pushed his cowboy hat back on his dark curls.

"Nerit had her poker face, but Jenni's expression said it all."

"That's my girl. Destined to lose every game of strip poker we ever play." Juan smirked and wagged an eyebrow.

Travis headed for the mayor's office with Juan only a step behind. Peggy and Manny were already there, along with Curtis and the investigative team. Entering the room, Travis thought Jenni looked pale and a little spacey. He was not surprised when Juan went to her quickly and quietly asked her something in Spanish. What was a surprise was Jenni's response—she shook her head and turned away, leaving Juan looking bewildered as he stood awkwardly at her side.

"So what happened out there?" Travis sat down in an ancient wooden office chair.

Nerit sighed and looked at Bill, obviously deferring to him as the person of authority.

"To put it simply, the Vigilante," the cop said.

"What?" Juan's voice expressed the disbelief Travis felt.

"The ammo boxes we gave them were full of gravel, so once Shane and Philip had used what was in their guns, they were done. To make it worse for them, the fuel line of the car had been cut and patched with cheap tape that gave way pretty quickly. They were dead in the water in no time at all. I actually don't think the Vigilante meant for them to break down so close to the fort—close enough that they might have made it back here." Bill shrugged. "The Vigilante couldn't get them in here, so he or she got them out there."

"Damn," Travis said in a stunned voice.

Manny calmly folded his hands on his desk. "We need to find this person and stop whoever it is. This is not acceptable behavior."

"Manny, don't you think Curtis and Bill are doing everything they can?" Peggy scowled at the mayor.

Sitting back in his chair, Manny fastened his gaze on Peggy. "I'm aware of what they're doing, even if you think I'm oblivious."

Peggy averted her eyes swiftly, surprised at Manny's retort.

"My point is that this situation has become more urgent. This is three people confirmed dead at the hands of an unknown assailant in what should be a safe haven," Manny continued.

"We're doing our best." Curtis sat on the edge of the desk and crossed his arms over his chest. "The Vigilante is not stupid."

Bill laid a reassuring hand on the younger man's shoulder. "We'll find him, son."

"It's not like he's killing innocent people," Juan said. Travis could tell his temper was getting the best of him again and shot his friend a warning look.

"Maybe not, but how he or she is going about this isn't right. No one should hold so much power over the lives of others," Nerit responded.

Curtis looked very tired as he ran his hand over his blond hair. "He's doing what the rest of us don't want to do."

"We're all in this together!" Peggy slammed her hand down on the desk. "One person can't decide who lives and who dies. Or who stays and who leaves."

"Was there any sign of Shane?" Travis asked.

"We looked around a little before some zombies came after us. I'm guessing that when Shane and Philip were attacked, they realized they were in serious trouble. From the footprints around the car and in the nearby field, we think they broke down, encountered zombies, used up their ammunition, tried and failed to reload, and then ran for it. Shane went across the field while Philip stuck to the road and eventually made it back to the fort," Bill explained.

"We didn't find Shane," Ed added. "We took the scenic route around the town to lose the zombies and look for him."

Felix bobbed his head, looking somber. "No sign of him."

"He's probably already a zombie," Jenni declared. "And I can't say I feel sorry about that."

It was the first thing she had said since the meeting started, and Travis heard a rawness in her voice. Jenni seemed unsettled. That bothered him. Juan placed a hand on Jenni's shoulder to comfort her, but she didn't seem to notice.

"Who had the opportunity to do this?" Manny asked, briefly glancing at Juan.

"Pretty much anyone in the whole fort." Bill hooked his thumbs onto his belt and rolled his shoulders. "While everyone was voting, Curtis and I put the survival packs for the guys in the car. That way, if the vote went against Shane and Phil, we could escort them out of the fort immediately. After we did that, we went to help count votes."

"Anyone could have tampered with the car or the ammunition we put in the packs. There are no guards in the garage."

"We have a few suspects, but no proof," Curtis finished.

Juan snorted and Travis gave him a sharp look.

"We need to keep this quiet," Manny decided. "I don't want people panicking."

"We can't keep this quiet," Travis protested.

"C'mon, Manny. People need to know what is going on." Peggy cast an exasperated look toward the mayor.

"People are already figuring it out. People talk more than you realize." Felix leaned forward in his chair, shaking his finger at Manny. "They're not stupid, Mr. Mayor. Philip showed up eaten down to the bone."

"And in pieces," Jenni pointed out.

"We can't have people panicking," Manny repeated. "They're scared enough as it is."

"People need to know so they can be on the alert and report anything suspicious." Bill shifted in his chair and studied his notebook. "The Vigilante isn't going to stop."

"How do you know that?" Curtis asked curiously.

"Because people like the Vigilante don't stop," Nerit answered. "They believe they are right and that they alone can deal with what is wrong."

Travis rubbed his chin, deep in thought. "I think we should have full disclosure. We need to remind people what the real dangers of this world are. Moving into the hotel has already changed things. Rose told me people aren't showing up for kitchen duty like they were when we were still roughing it in the construction site."

Nerit nodded. "The same thing is happening with the guards, though it's not a big problem yet."

Travis continued, "We're safer when it comes to the zombies, but we still have food, water, energy, and sanitation concerns. We don't even have a doctor on hand. People need to understand we are still at risk."

"Don't forget about the men who killed Ralph." Nerit's voice was tinged with pain.

"Fuckin' banditos," Juan muttered.

"We just don't need folks riled up. You know how people get when they feel the city officials or the authorities can't do their job." Manny rubbed his broad forehead, wiping away beads of sweat. He appeared unusually pale today.

"Don't matter," Ed said. "They're gonna be unhappy anyway. Sorry, Mr. Mayor, but the old ways are bullshit now. This ain't about reelection no more, but 'bout keeping alive."

"Everyone who voted to eject those two men deserves to know what happened to them." Travis's tone was firm.

"Why? They shouldn't feel guilty for doing the right thing," Juan said sharply.

"People's actions—and their votes—have consequences. Now more than ever. We all need to be aware of that." Travis stood and swept his gaze over the room. "As far as we know, we are the biggest and best-off group of the survivors in this area. Hell, maybe in the whole state."

"Or country." Jenni met his gaze with great sadness lurking in the depths of her eyes.

"Maybe the world." Nerit's words were chilling, but possibly true.

"So we need to have our shit together. People have got to realize that every choice we make has consequences that affect not only our own lives, but the lives of everyone around us." Travis shoved his hands into his pockets and swallowed hard. The enormity of their situation once more swept over him. He could feel his hands shaking. "We need to let everyone know what happened. We need them to understand what the trouble is with someone like the Vigilante. And they need to understand that just because we are living in the hotel, we are not necessarily safe. Call a fort meeting and lay it out, Manny."

"The political fallout from this—," Manny started to say.

"Fuck politics, Manny." Travis hated how harsh his voice sounded, but he knew he was right.

Manny put his head down, his hand rubbing the back of his neck. "It's what I know, Travis. I'll defer to Bill on this, but I still think this is not going to turn out well."

"This world is messed up," Jenni grumbled.

"Voting those assholes out was the right thing to do," Juan declared firmly. "The Vigilante killed them, not the rest of us."

"We all knew they would probably die out there." Nerit shrugged. "We made the choice."

"God help us do the right thing. From now on, we gotta take this kinda shit deadly serious." Bill flipped his notebook shut. "If this is our new brand of justice, then we all better be damn sure we can live with it."

"Agreed." Travis folded his arms across his chest.

"We're getting close to mob rule," Manny said in a soft voice. "People need leaders. Order. Law."

"If we—the people in this room—try to dictate to everyone out there how things should be, we're going to fail. We can handle the everyday administration, the planning of the fort defenses, things like that, but the big issues need to be in the hands of everyone in the fort." Travis faced the silent group in the room. "We have to do this together or we'll fail."

2.
Turned Upside Down

The first official fort meeting was held in the hotel's dining room, right after dinner. Everyone was there except for the people on guard duty and patrol. Word had spread quickly about the morning's events. There was a mixture of reactions to the news of the Vigilante striking again. Some obviously saw him as a person willing to do what the authorities would not. Others were terrified for their safety. No one wanted to end up on the wrong side of the wall.

Yolanda tucked her hair back behind her ears. She and Peggy were sitting side by side, waiting for Mayor Reyes to arrive and start the meeting.

"Do you know where the mayor is?" Eric asked as he dropped into the seat on Peggy's other side.

"He said he needed to go up to his room to freshen up or something," Peggy answered. "He's been a little under the weather."

Frowning, Eric looked around the crowded dining room, then back at Peggy. "Travis sent me to find him and there was no answer at his room."

"Are you serious? What the hell is he up to?" Peggy sounded peeved and her brows knotted together. "I swear, that man . . ."

Yolanda felt a cold chill rush down her back. "Did you go into the room?"

Eric shook his head. "No. He didn't answer so I came down here. I thought maybe I had missed him."

Biting her bottom lip, Yolanda pondered breaking a promise she had made to her deceased husband. Finally she said, "Manny told Tobias he has coronary artery disease. He takes nitroglycerin pills. He was keeping it secret because of the upcoming election."

"Damnit," Peggy cursed. "Manny and his stupid politics. He never told me!"

"I'm going to go check on him." Yolanda pushed out her chair and stood.

Peggy did the same. "Eric, go tell Travis what is going on. I'm going with Yolanda."

The two women quickly made their way out of the dining room and down the hall to the elevators.

"I can't believe that man! How could he not tell me?" Peggy exclaimed.

Yolanda had an opinion, but wasn't sure she should say anything. She suspected, from things Tobias had told her, that Peggy's paranoia about possibly losing her job had pushed a big wedge between her and Manny.

Peggy swept her brown hair back from her face and paced while they waited for the elevator. "I can't believe he didn't tell me. What if he's lying up there dead?"

"We need to be calm, Peggy."

The elevator doors dinged open, revealing Lenore and Ken, who were supporting Manny between them. Manny's skin was a terrible shade of gray and sweat was running down his face.

"Oh, God!" Peggy was clearly dismayed by his appearance.

"We found him wandering around on our floor. He was real out of it and then he fell down," Ken explained quickly.

Leaning heavily against Lenore, the mayor gasped for breath. "Peggy, don't yell at me."

"You stupid man, I'll yell at you all I want!" Peggy motioned for Ken and Lenore to bring the mayor over to a sofa in the lobby. "Where are your pills?"

"His color looks bad. Like my grandma's did when she had her episodes," Lenore said in a worried voice as she lifted his feet onto the sofa.

Yolanda patted Manny's pockets, looking for a bottle of pills.

Leaning over the sick man, Peggy demanded in a scared voice, "Where are your pills, Manny?"

Forcing his eyes open, Manny whispered, "I don't have any more."

"That's why he's having an episode," Yolanda said. Feeling helpless, she took a deep breath, trying to steady her thoughts.

"Manny, you stupid man! Why didn't you tell me?" Peggy looked close to crying and Lenore laid a comforting hand on her shoulder.

"You'd yell at me. I was going to look in storage for more, but . . ." He faded out, eyes closing.

"The stock from the pharmacy! Go see if we got any nitroglycerin!" Peggy ordered.

"Okay! I'll be right back!" Yolanda rushed out of the hotel, her heart pounding. Lenore followed and together they hurried to Peggy's old office in city hall.

"Is he going to die?" Lenore asked as Yolanda flipped on the lamp on Peggy's desk.

"I hope not, Lenore. I hope not," she answered the frightened young woman. "You did real good getting him downstairs as fast as you did." Pulling open a drawer, Yolanda pulled out the inventory list and scanned through the pharmaceutical section.

"I just don't like seeing people sick. My grandma had real bad blood pressure problems. She died three days before we got rescued. She almost made it here. I just don't want to see someone else die," Lenore said. "Too much death around here as it is."

"I am so sorry for your loss, hon," Yolanda said, reaching out to clasp Lenore's hand.

Lenore's somber expression did not change, but she lightly squeezed Yolanda's fingers briefly before letting go.

Yolanda returned her gaze to the inventory, her finger sliding down the list, reading quickly. "We have some! Three bottles! C'mon!"

Kate and Travis sat in the back of the room, listening as the strain and terror of the last four months spilled out of their fellow survivors. It became apparent that people were very aware of the fragility of their new existence and wanted to be assured that life would continue in safety. Making rules about their society was something that most people didn't want to deal with—and they were increasingly unhappy about the mayor's lateness.

Eric scurried across the room and leaned over their table. "Manny is missing."

"What do you mean he's missing?" Katie blinked in surprise.

Beside her, Travis straightened in his seat. "Are you sure?"

"The Vigilante?" Katie queried, but she couldn't see how that could be the case. It didn't make any sense.

"I don't know, Travis. He's not in his room and Yolanda is worried that his heart is acting up. Apparently, he has a heart problem." Eric kept his voice low, but people were already turning in their seats.

Travis got to his feet. "I better go check on this." Without a word, Katie rose and went with him, her fingers entwined with his. What else, she wondered, could possibly go wrong?

One look at the group gathered around Manny told her that things were rapidly going from bad to worse. The Manns stood near the couch while Peggy fussed over the mayor.

"If he dies," Blanche asked, "who's going to be in charge?"

"What's wrong?" Travis asked.

"He has a bad heart," Ken explained.

"And the bastard didn't tell me about it," Peggy griped. Despite her tone, her expression was stricken.

"Lenore and Yolanda went to look for his pills," Ken continued.

Steven took a seat across from Manny, his expression one of genuine concern. "I didn't know. He never said anything."

Blanche sat next to her husband, on his chair's armrest. "Well, a mayor with a bad heart is just not electable."

"Blanche, be quiet," Steven said sternly.

Startled, she clamped her mouth shut.

Katie leaned over to check Manny's pulse. His skin felt clammy and cool. It took her a few seconds to find the right spot. Then she said, "He has an irregular heartbeat."

"He's been without his pills," Peggy explained. "I don't know why he didn't tell me."

Travis rubbed Peggy's shoulders lightly, comforting her. "Men sometimes have problems fessing up about illness, Peggy. I'm sure it wasn't personal."

People were beginning to drift into the lobby to see what was going on. Katie was relieved when Bill showed up and asked people to give the mayor some room. Gently, Katie smoothed Manny's thinning hair back from his face, fear gnawing on her nerves.

"I have it! I have it!" Yolanda pushed her way through the onlookers, brandishing a small bottle in one hand.

"Oh, thank God!" Peggy cried out.

Katie drew back and Travis joined her as Peggy and Yolanda worked together to get the pill under Manny's tongue. Holding on to Travis's hand, Katie prayed silently and hoped for the best. She could tell from his worried expression that Steven felt much the same; it was a side of him she hadn't known existed. In contrast, Blanche's gaze seemed cool.

Lenore stood beside Katie, breathing a little heavily. She looked somber and Katie patted her back lightly. "He's a good man," Lenore declared. "Don't want to see a good man die."

"He won't die," Peggy said crossly. "You hear that, Manny?"

3.
Haunted

After Manny, feeling better, was returned to his room under Yolanda's watchful eye, the meeting in the dining room reconvened. Though the Vigilante and the fates of Philip and Shane were discussed, the true concern was for the mayor and the leadership of the fort.

Juan was not surprised when people called for an election. He was also not surprised by the first nomination: Blanche swiftly nominated her husband. As Calhoun circled the room, filming every moment, Juan nominated Travis. The expression on his buddy's face was priceless, but Juan believed Travis was the right man for the job. There were no other nominations and it didn't take long for an election date to be set.

Once that was over, Juan and the others took some pains to

get out of the room and away from Calhoun and his camera. At last, they made it into the elevator with Jenni and Katie.

"You're gonna get elected," Juan repeated for the umpteenth time.

"You say that again and I'm going to deck you." Travis scowled. "And thanks for nominating me. That's just great."

"Play nice, boys." Katie ran a hand over Travis's curls to soothe him.

"You're the right man for the job," Juan reiterated.

Travis scowled some more.

"I'm just telling the truth," Juan said, shrugging.

"Which he obviously doesn't want to hear," Katie answered.

Juan thought his buddy was being a big baby about the whole thing. He was amused as hell about the idea of Travis becoming mayor. Besides, giving Travis shit was alleviating the tension he felt from Jenni's silence. Juan watched the numbers over the door light up. Just a few more floors and he could find out what was wrong with Jenni. She had been putting him off all night.

The elevator arrived at the next floor and chimed. Travis slid his arm around Katie's waist as the doors opened.

Juan took hold of his shoulder. "You'll win because you're the best man for the job, Travis."

Travis opted not to punch Juan's lights out. "We'll see."

With that, the couple walked away and the elevator doors shut.

Juan smiled at Jenni, but either she didn't see him or she was ignoring him. She stared into nothingness, her arms folded over her breasts. He loved her, but at times like this, when he could feel her emotions churning just beneath the surface of her eerily detached expression, he felt powerless and incompetent.

Tentatively, Juan reached out and touched her arm. She glanced at him. Her focus appeared to return to the here and now. She stepped closer and he slung an arm over her shoulders and tried to pull her close, but she held herself stiffly away from him. He kissed her cheek, trying to soothe her.

It didn't work.

She continued to stare ahead.

At their floor, Jenni briskly walked out of the elevator and out of his grasp. With a sigh, Juan followed, his tired, battered fingers searching in his pocket for the room key. She stood impatiently at the door as he unlocked it. Unlike other times, when she was flirting and anxious to get him alone, she avoided looking at him and was silent. He had a feeling her lack of patience had nothing to do with sex, but something unpleasant.

When they entered the small suite, Juan glanced around for Jason. A closed door with music loudly thumping behind it let him know where the teenager was. The dog was probably in there, too. The kid and the dog were pretty much inseparable.

"I'm going to bed," Jenni stated.

"You don't want to talk about whatever it is that is making you like this?" He already knew the answer, but he had to ask.

"No."

"Why not?" He couldn't help himself. He wanted to know what was wrong.

"It's not important."

"If it wasn't important, you wouldn't be flipping out."

"I'm just tired."

"You're lying."

"Fuck you!"

"Whoa! Where did that come from?"

"I told you it's not important!" Jenni's dark eyes were full of indignation.

"Then why are you acting *loca,* Loca?" Juan felt his temper rising. He loved her madly, but she was getting on his last nerve.

"Maybe because I am! You knew that when we got together!" Hands on her hips, her jaw set in a defiant line, she seemed to dare him to push the topic further.

He wanted answers and wasn't about to back down. "Something happened out there. I have a right to know what is going on in that *loca* head of yours. I love you."

She stared at him for a few beats of his worried heart, then simply walked out the door.

"Hey! Hey! Hey!" He rushed after her. Their room was close enough to the elevator that by the time he got into the hall, she was already getting into a car. His anger told him to follow her, confront her, make her tell him what was going on, but his love told him not to be a selfish bastard. Struggling to rein in his emotions, he stepped back into their suite.

Taking off his cowboy hat, he ran his hand over his long curls. Loca was nuts, but she wasn't stupid. She wouldn't rush off and do anything stupid. Suddenly he knew exactly where she was going. Snatching up the phone, he dialed Katie's room.

"Hello?" Katie's voice said when she picked up.

"Katie, Loca just blew out of here."

"What do you mean?"

"She was acting all weird—"

"I noticed."

"—and was not telling me what was up—"

"She tends to do that."

"—and I basically ordered her to tell me—"

"A very stupid move on your part."

"—and out the door she went. I think she's headed your way. You're not naked and doing anything sweaty with Travis right now, are you? 'Cause Loca will need you to calm her ass down."

"I'm not naked or doing anything sweaty with Travis. He's actually about to head out and check on Manny."

"Will you take care of my girl?"

"Absolutely," Katie answered.

Hanging up, Juan closed his eyes and rubbed his eyelids. His eyes felt like salt had been poured into them. Jenni not being with him was disconcerting. He felt lost without her. The pounding music from Jason's room did nothing to calm his nerves.

Juan sighed. Loca would be okay. He knew it. She was too

tough to let anything drag her down. He just had to wait for her to come back.

It would be okay.

Katie hung up the phone and stared at it, deep in thought.

"What's wrong?" Travis emerged from the bathroom, his face and hair a little damp. He was feeling tired, but splashing cold water on his face had him looking more alert.

"Jenni is probably on her way here. Juan says she walked out in the middle of an argument." Katie folded her arms over her breasts. "I noticed she was quiet tonight, but I thought she was just tired."

Travis walked over and kissed her cheek. "If anyone can help her, it's you. It'll be fine."

"If she talks to me," Katie grumbled. "She's been evasive on a lot of stuff lately."

"She's haunted. You know better than most of us why—you were with her practically from the very beginning." Travis rubbed Katie's shoulders. "I better go before she lands on our doorstep."

Katie's fingers brushed over his hand and she gave him an apprehensive smile. She was naturally worried about Jenni. She remembered the near-catatonic woman in her truck on that first day. No one in the fort had ever seen Jenni that way; Katie alone knew just how fragile Jenni had been.

Travis pressed a kiss to her lips, then moved toward the door. "See you at breakfast."

"I'll miss you," Katie said with a slight smile.

As Travis touched the doorknob, there was a sharp rap on the door.

"I think she's here," Travis said. He opened the door. Jenni stood in the hall, hands on her hips, head down, her face obscured by her hair.

"Hey, Jenni," Travis said, and brushed past her quickly.

Katie could tell he did not want to upset Jenni any more than she already was. Another reason why she adored him so. He always was considerate of others.

Jenni stepped into the room and slammed the door behind her.

"Jenni?"

Her friend looked up, her face streaked with tears. With a small cry of despair, Jenni launched herself into Katie's arms.

"Oh, Jenni! What is it? What's wrong?"

"He can't see me like this! He can't! He doesn't know how I used to be!"

Holding her, Katie could feel her friend trembling violently. "Jenni, what is it? What is it?" Jenni's tears were soaking her neck and shoulder. Katie stroked Jenni's dark hair soothingly with one hand.

For a minute or two, Jenni wept. Then she raised her head and wiped at her wet cheeks. Struggling to regain her composure, she said, "I think Lloyd is haunting me."

About to reach for the tissues, Katie stopped in midmotion, blinked, and ran Jenni's words through her mind a second time. They still didn't make sense. "Huh?"

"I think Lloyd is haunting me and trying to kill me." Jenni's dark lashes glittered with tears and she stared at Katie defiantly. "And I'm not joking!"

Katie could see the anger, desperation, and fear in Jenni's face. She was not about to argue with her. She had suffered her own struggles with the past and couldn't judge her. "Why do you think that? What happened?"

In a voice that trembled with emotion, Jenni explained the events of the day. Katie listened in silence. It was obvious that the seal that Jenni kept clamped over her past had been ripped off. She was trembling and afraid. Instead of looking like her usual rough and tough self, she appeared emotionally shattered. She resembled the woman Katie had first seen standing on the front porch of her home in her pink bathrobe, watching tiny dead fingers pressed under the door.

"Juan cannot see me like this! He can't! He loves the new Jenni, not the old one. I hate being the old Jenni! I hate it! I don't like feeling this way! I don't like being weak! I thought I was past this!" Jenni flung herself onto Katie's bed in a dramatic finish.

Katie slid onto the bed and soothingly rubbed Jenni's back. "It's okay, Jenni. It's okay to have a bad day. We all have them. It doesn't mean you're the old Jenni. It just means that something happened today that really upset you. We all struggle with reminders of what happened in those first days. When I see in the zombies the people they used to be, I struggle with the knowledge that I did not kill the thing Lydia became. Hell, I struggle with the guilt that I did not put your children and Lloyd out of their misery."

Jenni threw a fierce look over her shoulder. "I don't give a shit if Lloyd wanders out there forever. I hope he rots slowly and that his soul is still in his body! I hope he's aware of every single moment of his decay. Fuck him!"

Katie smiled slightly at this tirade, which sounded more like "new" Jenni. "Okay. So if you feel that way, why let his memory—"

"His ghost," Jenni corrected.

"Okay, his ghost. Why let his ghost upset you like this? Why let him make you weak and scared? You know that. . . ." Katie hesitated, then plunged on. "You know that Benji couldn't get out of the house. It wasn't possible for him to be there today. Lloyd and Mikey are hundreds of miles away. Even if Lloyd's ghost is here, he can't hurt you."

Jenni sat up, her dark eyes burning with raw emotion as she stared into Katie's eyes. "He wants me to die so I will be in his power again."

Taking Jenni's hand gently in hers, Katie said gently, "You don't have to let him. You have a new life here with Juan. You have Jason and Jack. You have friends. You have so much."

"He wants to take it all away," Jenni whispered, and fresh tears fell.

"You can't let him, Jenni. You can't let him have power over you from beyond death. He never valued you for who and what you really are. He never deserved you. You know that, right?"

"He said I should die and be with the boys," Jenni finally said.

Katie heard the awful pain and guilt in Jenni's voice. "It's not your fault that they died."

Jenni looked away. Katie could almost see the invisible walls sliding back up around her. Jenni couldn't deal with her children's deaths right now, Katie could tell. It would have to wait for another time.

"Fuck Lloyd," Jenni said at last, straightening and turning back to face Katie. "Fuck him. I'm not going down without a fight."

Katie kissed her cheek. "That's my girl."

Jenni's lips quirked slightly upward and she raised a trembling hand to wipe away her tears. "I don't want Juan to see me like this."

"He doesn't have to. Stay here tonight." Katie hesitated a moment before saying, "He called me before. He knew you would come here."

"I'm that predictable, huh?" Jenni giggled, her fingers playing with the tips of her hair.

"He knows we're tight. He knows that if you're not with him, you're gonna be here with me. We're kinda like Thelma and Louise."

"Meets the zombies," Jenni added with a soggy grin.

Katie laughed. "Yeah."

"I'm not driving off a cliff with you," Jenni said firmly.

Katie embraced the morbid humor that kept them from falling into the darkest of emotions. "But we can run over zombies together."

"Totally!" Jenni lay down and tucked a pillow under her head. She stared at Katie thoughtfully, her tears finally abating. "I'm not crazy," she said seriously. "It really is Lloyd's ghost trying to kill me."

Katie tucked one hand under the pillow Travis usually slept on. His scent comforted her. "As long as you don't give in to him, you'll be fine."

Jenni rubbed her reddened nose. "Sometimes that first day feels like a hundred years ago. Today, it feels like . . . today."

Katie lovingly smoothed Jenni's hair back from her face. "I know."

Rolling over, Jenni hid her swollen eyes and tearstained face. Katie draped one arm over her friend's waist. They lay in comfortable silence for a few minutes as Jenni regained her composure and her shoulders relaxed.

Katie reached over her and switched off the lamp. Jenni sighed and Katie could feel her friend sinking into the drained weakness that came after an emotional storm. She snuggled down behind Jenni, holding her close.

"You're the best friend in the world. The best I've ever had," Jenni whispered.

"I love you, Jenni. You're my best friend. I'll always be here for you."

Closing their eyes, the two friends held each other until sleep carried them away.

· CHAPTER FIFTEEN ·

1.
The Dead in the Night

"We have a problem. Let's go!"

Travis and Eric looked up as Curtis rushed toward them. Neither one of them could sleep after the events of the day, so they were back at work. They were in the hotel's lobby, studying an antique map of the town that was displayed under glass. Despite its age, it was surprisingly accurate. The town had not changed much in seventy years.

"The Hackleburg survivors are under attack! We have to go! We have to go!" Curtis's young face was flushed under his blond hair. He was agitated and motioning with both hands.

"Shit! Get Nerit!" Travis headed toward the communication center at a run.

"What does Curtis mean? 'Under attack'?" Eric was flustered as he rushed after Travis. He shoved his glasses up on his nose and seemed as alarmed as Travis felt.

"In this crazy world, who knows?"

They burst into the communication center, where Bill was perched over an array of radios.

"Repeat! Repeat! I can't make out what you're saying!" Bill was speaking loudly into a mic.

". . . got through . . . we are fight- . . . please hur . . ." The sounds of gunshots peppered the woman's voice. Her terror could be heard clearly despite the static that ate her words. ". . . hurry! Please hurry . . . Repeat . . . got in!"

"Zombies?" Travis asked, his body tensing at the thought of losing another survivor group.

"I don't know. I can't make it all out," Bill said in a surprisingly composed voice. As always, Travis was impressed by Bill's ability to handle stressful situations in a calm manner.

Eric cocked his head, listening to the frantic woman's garbled message. He frowned. "Are we really going out there?"

Bill looked at Travis, who said, "Hey, I'm not the mayor."

"Not yet," Bill answered.

Nerit entered the room, her yellowed silver hair in a braid over one shoulder and her bathrobe tied tightly at her waist. "What is the situation?"

"Hackleburg is under attack. I can't make out if it's zombies or bandits. Sue just keeps screaming into the microphone that someone got in." Bill rubbed his broad forehead. "It doesn't sound good."

Peggy rushed in with Curtis behind her. She was wearing pajamas and her son was clinging to her like a monkey. "Hackleburg? Shit! They have kids in there!" She heaved Cody onto her hip and shoved papers around on a desk until she found a state map.

"They're here, on the outskirts of town," Peggy said, pointing. "Twenty-two people in a church community center. Mostly old folks, women, and kids. The men went to fight the zombies and didn't come back alive. Anyway, they didn't have any vehicles to escape in and they ended up with zombies banging on their doors. They've held off the zombies by barricading the doors and windows. They even managed to thin them out by dropping things onto the zombies from the church's roof. They were saving the ammo just in case the zombies got in."

"There have been gunshots going off," Bill said quietly.

Through the static, they could still hear the woman crying and begging for them to come.

"We gotta go get them! Save them!" Curtis looked desperately at Nerit. "We gotta go."

Travis sighed. Decisions like this were impossible to make. Did they sacrifice resources, and maybe lives, to save other survivors, or did they stay safe within their walls? His humanity told him one thing; his fear for those he cared about told him another.

"How far away, Peggy?" Travis asked.

"Twenty-one miles going southeast." Peggy was trying to sound calm for the sake of her son, but her eyes were wide with fright.

"We have to go," Eric said. "We have to. We have room and food. We can't let them just . . . die." His voice shook with emotion.

Travis rubbed his jaw and watched Nerit, waiting for her to give her opinion. He wanted to rush out and save the people, but he knew Nerit understood the dynamics of the situation better than he did. When Nerit finally turned to Travis, her expression said it all. Travis was glad to have her to lean on in that moment. She was quick to decide and quick to act.

"We take two trucks and the bus. We leave immediately. Bill, we need Katarina, Felix, Ed, Jenni, Katie, Roger, and Juan down here. Have them meet me in the Panama Canal," Nerit said in a firm, authoritative voice.

"Gotcha, Nerit," Bill said, and reached for the phone as Nerit and Travis headed for the door.

"What are the chances we'll find survivors?" Travis asked as he hurried along beside Nerit.

"Slim to none. But we need to know for sure if it's the zombies or something else attacking them," Nerit responded.

Travis blinked. He hadn't thought of that. "Something else?"

"The men who killed Ralph are still out there," Nerit answered with a grim look on her face. "Let's get moving."

As he walked away from the communication center, he heard the woman's screams distorted by the static.

2.
Into the Darkness

Jenni and Katie were asleep when Bill called.

"Will this day ever fuckin' end?" Jenni had groused at him when she picked up the phone.

But once they heard what was up, they had scrambled out the door as fast as they could, strapping on their holsters even as they struggled to wake up and get focused.

"I hate shit like this," Jenni grumbled.

"You and me both." Katie shoved the wrought iron gate into the old construction site. It squealed open and they stepped out into the humid night.

"I'm so ready to stomp some zombie ass. I'm so sick of this shit. So sick of people dying," Jenni bitched. She braided her hair as she walked.

"We're going to need to try to get all those survivors in here soon," Katie observed. "We have enough room and food."

Jenni shoved pins into her braid to keep it on top of her head. "Fuckin' zombies." She wanted them all dead. Chopped up, mashed up, dead.

In the lock, Juan stood near the ladder, talking to a few of his men. The sight of him made Jenni's heart beat a little faster. He glanced at her from under his cowboy hat and winked. She smiled back at him. Just like that, their fight was forgotten.

"Hey, Loca," he said as she walked up to him. They shared a soft kiss. Her arms felt good around his waist and she rested her head against his shoulder.

"I'm heading out."

"Yeah, I heard. My own little zombie-killin' *loca*." Juan ruffled the fine strands of hair at the base of her neck and kissed her forehead. "Come back."

"I will. Katie's driving and she's a psycho bitch behind the wheel."

Katie grinned in response

"Yeah, but you get all *loca,* Loca."

"Only in a good way," Jenni answered flirtatiously.

Juan laughed and kissed her again.

Jenni felt better now. Everything felt more solid. Lloyd's specter seemed like a bad dream.

Ed drove the small bus out of the newspaper building's garage. The vehicle's bright headlights blinded Jenni for a second, until she raised a hand to shield her eyes. Then she could make out Nerit and Felix already seated inside.

Katie looked like a badass as she walked into the garage and climbed into Nerit's red Ram 1500 truck. Her rifle was slung over her shoulder, a bowie knife was tucked into a sheath at her waist, and her pistol was clearly visible in its holster on her hip. Katie picked up a spear from the weapon storage and tossed it into the truck.

"I better get my ass in gear. We got people to save and zombies to kill," Jenni said.

Juan touched her cheek and kissed her one last time. "Hurry back."

Jenni ran her hands down his chest, feeling his heartbeat for a few seconds. Reluctantly, she stepped away, ready to go. "If Jason wakes up before I'm back, tell him I love him." She hurried past Roger and Katarina as they climbed into another truck, then paused to let Katie and Travis have a private good-bye as he joined her best friend in the garage. Jenni knew that Travis would take care of Katie no matter what, and that made her feel secure. Jenni worried about her loved ones. Her own mortality felt fragile. Who would take care of them if she was gone? Katie would be safe with Travis. And she would look after Jason. But Juan . . .

She looked back at the tall Mexican-American with the gorgeous green eyes and knew she would never leave him. Even if she died, she would watch over him. She couldn't imagine their love ending, not even with death. Jenni snatched up her ax from storage and headed toward the truck.

"Let's go, children!" Nerit's voice was a hard bark in the night.

Jenni swung herself up into her old seat and strapped herself in. Slamming the door shut, she gave Juan the thumbs-up.

Katie slid into the driver's seat.

"Take care, you two," Travis said, worry puckering the flesh between his eyebrows.

"We're Wonder Woman and Supergirl," Jenni chided him. "Sheesh!"

"We'll be back for breakfast," Katie assured him.

Travis forced a smile and shut the door.

"Men are such worriers," Jenni grumbled.

Katie chuckled. "Yeah. We're just heading out into the deadlands. No reason to worry." She turned the key and the engine roared to life.

"Piece of freakin' cake!"

"Absolutely!" Katie placed her slightly shaking hands on the steering wheel, guiding the truck out of the garage.

Jenni felt an adrenaline rush. Though it had her trembling, she embraced it. It reminded her that she was alive. Heading out into the dead world was always terrifying, but she trusted the people she was with. It would be okay.

Katarina and Roger, in a big black truck, were first into the lock system. The bus was second, followed by Jenni and Katie. It felt strangely good to be back in the familiar red truck. She missed Jack, who had occupied the backseat during the first days after the zombie outbreak. Anxious to get out there and see whom they could save, Jenni drummed her hands on the dashboard.

"You're so wired," Katie remarked.

"I just want to get going." Jenni pouted.

"Obviously."

The big gates slid open and Katie drove into the first lock. Jenni looked out the window at the tall cement block wall beside her. She craned her head to look up and waved at a sentry standing post.

Nerit's voice cackled over the CB. "Katarina knows the way. She's leading. Watch out for deer and cows. Some cattle have broken out of some of the fields, according to our scavengers. Don't drive too close together, in case anything happens. Hackleburg is heavily infested, so we are keeping to the outskirts and heading straight for the church. We don't stay around any longer than we have to."

"Gotcha," Roger's voice said through the static.

Jenni snatched up the mouthpiece. "We're good."

The final gate opened, revealing the silent, dark street outside the fort. The darkened world seemed bleak and forlorn.

"Here we go," Katie said.

"Yeah. Again."

Once the red truck was clear of the lock, Katarina took off at top speed in the black truck. The rest of the convoy followed.

The quick drive through the countryside was strangely exhilarating. The cold stars in the velvet darkness above were brilliant. The waning moon was a glowing a Cheshire cat smile. In the dark fields, washed with moonlight, cows slumbered and deer wandered. Occasionally, birds took flight from the tall trees, startled awake by the passing vehicles.

Jenni glanced at Katie, studying her friend's features in the glow of the dashboard. "You scared?"

"Yeah. You?"

"Shitless. Not of the zombies, though. I'm scared those people are all dead." Bill's debrief over the phone had been quick, simple, and to the point.

"Me, too." Katie swept her hand over her hair. "There's no

rest from this stuff. Just when we start to feel a little comfortable, something goes down again."

Jenni propped her feet up on the dashboard and glowered at the bus in front of them. "Seriously, zombies should take a vacation from eating us. Let us unwind. Refresh ourselves before we have to shoot their heads off in the next round."

"If only life were that simple," Katie commiserated.

"And if it's the assholes who shot Ralph, I'm shooting their balls off."

Twenty minutes later, the CB crackled to life. "We're getting close. Katarina, you and Roger cover the north end of the parking lot. Katie and Jenni, cover the south. Ed will pull up in the center and we'll see what the situation is. Everyone be alert," Nerit's voice ordered.

Jenni slid her gun out of its holster and rested it on her thigh. She could feel her heart speeding up. She took a deep breath.

Katie drove the red truck around a curve in the road. An old whitewashed church came into view. Behind it was a rectangular building with aluminum siding and a few windows set high in the walls. The gravel parking lot was empty except for a horde of the walking dead, feasting on the freshly dead or dying.

"Damnit!" Jenni slammed her fist into the dashboard.

"This isn't good," Katarina's voice said over the radio.

Katie grabbed the CB mouthpiece. "Nerit, what do we do now?"

Katarina's voice said, "If we start shooting, the zombies in the town will come for us."

"That's too many to kill by hand," Jenni whispered. "We have to shoot them."

Before them, the feast continued. The zombies did not notice the three vehicles idling just a few yards away.

Nerit finally spoke. "We're going to make sure that if anyone is still alive in there, they have a chance. Kill the ones eating. Make it fast." Nerit continued with her grave instructions swiftly, her voice calm and steady. Katie gripped the steering wheel even tighter.

"This really fuckin' sucks," Jenni said under her breath, flicking the safety of her gun on and off.

"We do what we can and let the rest of it go. Otherwise, we'll go batshit crazy," Katie answered.

Jenni nodded.

Nerit's voice gave the word and Katie drove into the parking lot, along with the minibus and Roger's black truck. Using the big metal beasts as weapons, they ran over the zombies and their partially eaten victims. The big bus did a good job of flattening the disgusting creatures that were so greedily consuming the dying.

After four passes through the parking lot, anything left moving was doing so feebly. Jenni shoved her door open and jumped out, carrying her ax. She headed for the nearest twitching zombie and brought the ax down hard on its skull. Katie followed behind, using a spear to perform the same duties. Jenni dispatched the still-moving zombies swiftly. She felt back to her new, normal self. She wasn't going to let Lloyd's ghost fuck with her anymore.

Once their grisly task was done, the group from the fort stood stoically among the dead. Jenni tried not to notice the old people and children among the bodies.

"Ed, Felix, Bill, and I are going in," Nerit said. "Roger, Katarina, Jenni, and Katie, you stay out here and keep watch. If we call for you, come quick."

Jenni started to protest, not wanting to be left out of the mission inside, but she caught Katie's eye and clamped her mouth shut. Jenni could not quite define what she saw in Katie's face, but it let her know that Katie needed her nearby.

Katarina stared toward the town, her red hair coiled on top of her head, as she held her rifle. The grisly remains at her feet were ignored. Jenni didn't know the quiet woman very well, but in that moment, Katarina reminded her of Nerit. There was a calm coldness to her that Jenni admired. She felt hot and emotional inside in contrast.

The smell of the fresh and rotting dead was terrible. Jenni's eyes watered and she stepped away from the nearest cluster of bodies. A group of zombies had been greedily eating one of the larger women when they arrived. Jenni briefly wondered if the woman had been fat or pregnant, but the thought made her feel unbalanced, so she shoved it away.

"I hate this shit," Roger said. "I really, really do."

"Look," Katarina said suddenly, pointing. "I see headlights. I think a vehicle went down in a ditch over there."

"I'll get the binoculars," Roger said, and hurried to retrieve them from the bus.

Katie stood guard nearby, watching the road and their surroundings. "Is anyone alive?"

Katarina shrugged. "Can't tell, but something is moving. I can see a shape moving in front of the lights."

Jenni strained to see down the road. Roger returned and handed the binoculars to Katarina, who immediately raised them and studied the scene.

"Zombies. Trying to get into a truck that is definitely nose down in a ditch."

Jenni took a few steps toward the road.

"Jenni! We can't leave," Katie called out.

Jenni made a face and stomped her foot. "C'mon. Someone is probably alive over there."

"We have to provide backup to Nerit and the others," Katarina reminded her.

"Ugh!" Jenni felt frustrated by her inability to rescue whoever was stranded down the road. She kicked a zombie for good measure.

Gunshots sounded from inside. Everyone froze. There was a long silence; then Nerit and the others emerged, accompanied by a young woman who was carrying a small boy. Seeing the carnage in the parking lot, the woman pressed the boy's face against her neck to block his view.

"They were in a bathroom with the door barricaded. They're the only survivors," Nerit said.

"Nerit, we got a vehicle up the road with zombies around it. I count six," Katarina explained quickly. "Could be survivors in the truck. But we're gonna have to shoot the zombies to clear them out."

"That'll get any zombies in the town moving our way," Nerit said thoughtfully.

"We gotta save them," Jenni protested.

"I'm with Jenni. We have to save anyone we can," Katie agreed.

Bill walked toward them, his expression dark. "I agree. Let's do it."

"The road is narrow. Take one of the trucks. We'll provide as much cover as we can, but make it quick," Nerit said firmly. "The longer we are here, the more dangerous it is."

Katie headed toward the red truck. "C'mon, Jenni. We'll do this."

Bill jogged after Jenni, saying, "I'm coming with you. There weren't no vehicles left with the survivors. We don't know who is in that truck."

Jenni slid into the backseat and Bill took the passenger seat. Katie shifted gears and slowly drove up the road.

"Maybe they'll rush the truck so we can run them over," Katie mused.

"We're never that lucky," Bill answered.

As they drew closer to the stranded truck, they could see that it was lodged nose first in a deep ditch. The hood was smashed up against the cracked windshield on the right side and only the headlights were shining into the night. The zombies were pounding on the windows, trying to get into the cab. Inside, two young girls were screaming in terror.

"I'll take the two on the left," Bill said, gripping his rifle tightly.

"I can get the ones on the other side, but the two on the windshield are not going to be easy. We'll have to get out of the truck for those," Katie pointed out.

"We need to make this fast." Jenni released the safety on her weapon.

Katie stopped the truck and Bill did a silent countdown with his fingers. At three, they both flung open their doors. Jenni scrambled past Bill's seat and dropped into the road. She darted past Bill and aimed at a zombie as it reared back off the windshield to screech at the new flesh. She fired. The zombie jerked back and fell into the tall grass. Bill and Katie picked off two zombies each. The remaining zombie, trying to force its way through the shattered windshield, ignored the newcomers. The two girls inside took cover when they heard gunfire. Jenni aimed and fired again. The zombie tumbled over the hood and disappeared from view.

"Get them fast!" Katie gestured toward the town. "Company's coming!"

Jenni saw zombies materializing out of the darkness of the trees. "Fuck!"

Bill waded into the tall grass, his form illuminated by the red truck's headlights, both his gun and gaze aimed downward, wary of anything lurking there. Jenni kept him covered as Katie stood ready to jump into the truck and hit the gas.

One of the girls shoved the truck door open. Bill reached for her and she jumped into his arms. Another girl, younger than the first, also dived into his arms. He clutched them tightly.

Jenni watched the terrain around him. "Hurry, Bill! Hurry!"

Bill scrambled back onto the road, glancing over his shoulder at the moaning forms as they drew ever closer. Katie ran over to him and grabbed one of the girls. They hustled the youngsters into the truck while Jenni kept her gun trained on the approaching zombies.

Katie slammed the driver's door shut as Jenni and Bill scrambled into the truck. Bill yanked the other door shut as Jenni crawled into the back with the two girls.

"Are either of you bit?" Jenni felt like a bitch for having to ask such a terrible question of the traumatized children.

"No! No!" they chorused. One girl was blond with huge blue

eyes. The other, the one who looked younger, was Hispanic, with the darkest eyes Jenni had ever seen.

The zombies were closer.

"What drew them here so fast?" Bill wondered. "Couldn't be the gunfire or our headlights."

"Don't know. Don't care," Katie answered, and shifted the truck into reverse. Looking over her shoulder, she drove backwards toward the church parking lot. The other two vehicles waited for them.

Suddenly, a man ran into the glare of the headlights. Waving his arms, he was covered in sweat and breathing hard.

"I have a feeling we now know what is drawing them here," Jenni said. "I think they're chasing him!"

As Katie hit the brakes, one of the girls peeked around Bill and shouted, "That's the bad man! He took us away!"

"A bandit!" Katie slammed on the brakes.

"Leave him! Fuck him!" Jenni said.

"We can't leave him," Bill protested.

Katie glared at Bill. "He opened the door. He got those people killed!"

Bill looked torn for a second, then said, "We can't risk it. Leave him."

Katie looked like she wanted to run the man over, but instead hit the accelerator. The man screamed in anguish as the truck roared away, leaving him to the zombies.

Once Katie cleared the other vehicles, she turned the truck around, switched gears, and headed back down the road.

Jenni looked at the two girls huddled beside her. They were both trembling and staring at her with wide eyes.

3.
The Devils in the Darkness

"So then these fuckers show up, saying they're there to rescue the people holed up in the community center, that they were going to evacuate them to a safe place," Jenni explained to the group gathered in the city council room in city hall. All the usual suspects were there: Nerit, Juan, Travis, Peggy, Katie, Bill, and Curtis. It was nearly two hours since they had returned. The few people they had rescued were resting after having a late dinner.

"How many were there?" Travis sat at the end of the table jotting down notes. He felt sick to his stomach at the loss of life and the helplessness he felt.

"Four," Nerit responded. "They cleared out some of the zombies when they arrived, then used a crowbar to get the doors open."

"The girls told us that the men didn't even wait for the people inside to let them in. They just immediately broke in," Katie added. "Said they were on a tight schedule or some horseshit like that."

"When Esmerelda, the woman who was in charge, said she would call Peggy for confirmation, they shot her," Jenni continued. "They grabbed some of the little girls and held them hostage while they ransacked the place. Every time a zombie wandered in, the guys would shoot it. But there wasn't much to steal, so the bandits loaded the young women and girls into their vehicles and drove away. They left the elderly and the boys behind. The truck we found went off the road when one of the remaining survivors opened fire on it and blew out a tire. The bandits took off on foot, leaving the girls for the zombies."

Nerit shook her head and lit another cigarette. "Animals."

"Bastards don't deserve to live," Curtis growled.

Nerit took a drag of her cigarette and finished the story. "Since the survivors had limited ammunition and the doors were wrecked, it was only a matter of time before they were overrun. Lily and her little boy had hidden in the bathroom when the bandits first arrived. She barricaded the door when the screaming started." People listening shook their heads in sympathy. Nerit continued. "They were the only ones to survive inside the facility. We found them because two zombies were still beating on the bathroom door."

"So four people survived out of all the people who had been living there." Travis ran his hand over his hair as he scribbled down these facts. He couldn't fathom the horror the other group suffered tonight. It was unbelievable that other humans would do this to innocents.

Peggy sat nearby, her face drained of blood. Travis felt for her. He knew she considered all the survivors she spoke to, on the radio or the Internet, her friends. Juan looked pissed off. Curtis looked sick and Bill looked weary.

"Yes," Nerit finally said. "But at least six women and girls were kidnapped. Their fates are unknown."

"Bandits." Travis felt the word hang in the air as the people around him slowly embraced the truth.

"Yes. The men who killed Ralph," Nerit agreed.

"They're a real threat. They're really out there still." Peggy dabbed at her eyes and swallowed hard.

"Let's start bringing them in," Travis said. "Any survivors we can reach safely, let's bring them in."

"You're not mayor yet," Curtis said.

"Well, what do you want to do?" Travis arched his brows and stared at the younger man.

"Bring them in," Curtis said with a weak smile. "Bring them all in."

"Peggy and I will figure out which ones to go after first. Some are pretty far away. Others are heavily surrounded by zombies." Nerit's expression was grim.

"We can only do what we can do," Travis said. It was something they'd all said at times like these, but it was also the truth. Katie laid her hand over his and he rubbed her fingers lovingly. "Bring in as many as we can. Plan well. Be careful." He hesitated. "I don't know if the bandits knew about the fort before, but Esmerelda mentioned us. The bandits may come looking for us now."

The somber expressions at the table said it all. Life had just gotten a lot more complicated.

• CHAPTER SIXTEEN •

1.
The Others

Three weeks slid by. Everyone in the fort was kept busy preparing to take in more survivors. Travis found himself consumed with making sure any new expansions would be secure. He, Juan, and Eric pored over every option before them.

Groups headed out to hunt, salvage, and bring back any supplies they could lay their hands on. Construction workers made sure they had enough building supplies as new expansions were planned and repairs were made.

They began by bringing in the small groups closest to the town while Nerit made plans to recover the ones at farther distances. All the survivors were informed about the bandits—and that when the fort people came for them, they would be notified well in advance.

Things seemed calm out on the deadlands except for the wandering zombies, until . . .

One day, Jenni walked briskly across the roof of the old newspaper building with a rifle in her hand. Her red tank top, cowboy hat, and jeans revealed deeply tanned shoulders and arms. She had suffered a nasty sunburn the week before, but some aloe vera had done the trick and now she had a great tan.

Nearby, Jason and his crew of teenagers, along with Roger, practiced with their giant new slingshot. They were firing coffee cans filled with earth at a group of zombies staggering on the street in front of the hotel. Every time someone managed to nail one, all the teens would cheer.

So far the slingshot and concussion grenades had been the young team's best creations. Now they were trying to combine the two. Jenni thought it looked like more fun than she was having, but then again, being on guard duty meant she was able to hang out with her hot man.

Jenni's cheeks were reddened and her dark eyes bright as she walked up to Juan and handed him a thermos of iced tea. He smiled at her and pressed a kiss to her lips, then took several gulps of the cold brew.

"It's so damn hot," he complained, wiping his brow with the back of his hand.

She poked his chest playfully with one finger. "Wussy. We can always strip naked to cool off."

"On duty," he said regretfully. "Later, though . . ." With a smile, he kissed her quickly and settled back into his chair.

She took her place in the chair next to him. They both stared out over the town toward the hills. It was almost like sitting on a porch on a nice lazy Sunday, except for the intense heat, the gusts of wind, and the zombies.

"They are so going to vote in Travis as mayor," Jenni said with a grin.

"He's gonna be so pissed." Juan gulped down more sweet tea, looking pleased.

"Everyone loves his calm demeanor and peacemaking skills. Plus, they know you got his back and won't let him be too soft. Your hard-line stance has everyone cheering."

"The 'do your damn work or take a hike' stance? What can I say? I'm an asshole." Juan shrugged.

"Yeah, but it kinda makes sense. Except for the really old people like Old Man Watson and the disabled and kids."

"I just liked it when people were doing stuff to help out and nobody had to yell at them." Juan flicked up the brim of his hat and grimaced. "We got into this damn hotel and it was like everyone went soft and stupid. Travis complains about it all the damn time. I don't blame him."

"Well, nobody is going to vote for Steven Mann, that's for damn sure. His bitch wife pisses everyone off." Jenni lifted her rifle and surveyed the town through the scope.

"They're both flaming assholes." Juan watched the teenagers lob another coffee can down the street and flatten a zombie. "They want to be able to tell everyone what to do for their 'own good' and make sure that the social classes are restored. Must be hell for them to be forced to work."

"Yeah. Blanche tends to just stand there and pretend to be doing something." Jenni slowly scanned the section of town they were watching over. "It's so damn annoying. She told Katie that she was too delicate for hard work."

Juan shook his head and looked toward the towering hotel. "My ass, she's too delicate. I'm sure it takes some work to teeter around in those high heels all the damn time. I'm sure that takes some work balancing on them. And her helmet-head hair? How long does that take to shellac?"

Catching a glimpse of something suspicious, Jenni gasped, swinging the rifle back along the line of trees she'd been scanning. She focused on a figure standing under the shade of some trees, watching the fort through a pair of binoculars.

"What are the chances of a zombie knowing how to use binoculars?"

"Those shit for brains?" Then Juan realized the question wasn't a joke and leaped to his feet. "Damn! Where?"

"Two blocks down, near the front porch of the blue house. Under the trees."

Juan lifted his binoculars. "Can't see for shit! Yeah . . . that's someone alive."

Jenni tried hard not to blink as she adjusted the scope and make out the person. As she watched, the figure lifted what looked like a walkie-talkie.

"Bandits?"

"Maybe, Loca. Or someone trying to figure out if we're alive in here."

"Well, obviously we are," Jenni said. "I mean, listen to the sound of the machinery working on the new extension."

"True," Juan said. "So bandits it is. Anyone else would come up and knock. Shit."

Jenni snatched up her walkie-talkie. "Nerit, we have a situation. I've spotted what appears to be a man observing us with binoculars."

"I'm on my way."

Within minutes, Nerit was on the roof with Travis right behind her. "Where?"

Jenni pointed.

Nerit grabbed the binoculars and peered through them. "Near the blue house?"

"Yep."

Nerit's lips pressed tightly together. Beside her, Travis squinted, trying to see through Jenni's rifle scope.

"See them, Travis?"

"Them? I only see one."

"I have three, all men. And a van with fresh mud on the tires. We're definitely being studied." Nerit quickly pointed out the other two watchers. "How many teams do we have out, Travis?"

"Just one. They're picking up that reverend and a family out in Summerville," Travis answered.

"Call them. Tell them to waste no time," Nerit said sharply. "That contingency plan we drew up is now activated."

"Shit." Travis pulled out his walkie-talkie and rushed for the stairs.

Nerit handed the binoculars to Jenni. "Keep an eye on them and keep me informed. Juan, we'll need you down below. I'll send someone else up to help Jenni."

Jenni looked at Juan worriedly as Nerit strode away. He kissed her cheek. "It's gonna be okay, Loca. I gotta get down to the gate."

She kissed him firmly on the lips. "Love you."

"Love you, Loca."

As he hurried away, she couldn't help but admire his taut ass. To steady her nerves, she took a deep breath. She turned toward the team working the slingshot.

"Kids, Roger, we have a situation," Jenni called out. "You better get back inside."

Below, she heard Travis on the bullhorn, calling a Code Red. Her palms sweating, she raised the rifle and looked through the scope at the man down the street.

"Who the hell are you?"

2.
Code Red

"How close are they?" Travis asked Curtis as he entered the communication hub.

Yolanda was at the small computer station. Curtis was perched in front of the radio equipment.

"Are we really Code Red?" Yolanda asked worriedly.

"Yeah. Unidentifieds in the neighborhood. Living," Travis responded as he listened to Curtis calling the rescue team.

Yolanda frowned. "Peggy said another survivor group didn't check in today."

Travis rubbed his chin. "Yeah, I heard that."

"When they've lasted this long and then one day, nothing . . ." Yolanda chewed on her bottom lip worriedly.

"Could be zombies," Travis reminded her.

Curtis snorted. "Fuck, we're worse than them half the time. Humans are shits when it comes to survival of the fittest."

"That's a bitter view of humanity, Curtis." Yolanda frowned at the younger man with disapproval.

"They killed Nerit's husband," Curtis snapped.

Katie walked into the room just then. She had been helping build a new wall. Her hair was up in a ponytail and her face was reddened from being outdoors. "I hear there's trouble. Can I help?"

"Yeah. We're calling a Code Red." Travis tried to keep his nervousness out of his tone.

"That doesn't sound good."

"We knew it was a matter of time." Travis lightly rubbed her shoulder as she moved to his side.

"It's been almost a month. A girl can hope they dropped dead or got eaten or something." She forced a smile.

Travis kissed her. "We ain't that lucky."

She sighed. "Yeah. I'll see you up at the post, then."

"Give me a few minutes and I'll be there, Katie." Travis watched her leave, then turned his full attention back to the situation at hand.

Yolanda slid into Curtis's chair as he stood up. Putting on the headphones, she looked down at Curtis's notes.

Travis asked Curtis, "How far out are they?"

"Twenty minutes. Bill's flooring it."

"Okay. Let me know when he gets in, Yolanda. I'll be in position at the gate with Katie and Juan."

Yolanda gave him the thumbs-up. Travis and Curtis hurried out.

3.
Nowhere Is Safe

In the van, Katarina scrambled between the front seats and scooted past the family and the minister in the backseats as she made her way to the rear window. She held her rifle tightly in one hand as she peered at the receding road.

"Anything?" Bill's voice was tense.

"Nothing." Katarina glanced toward him. "Are you sure you saw a truck?"

"Positive. Out of the corner of my eye as we passed that billboard back there." Bill was frowning at the road ahead of them. He glanced warily toward the setting sun. They had maybe thirty minutes before sunset. His palms were sweating and he knew in his gut things were going bad fast. A cop's instincts never faded.

The family, the Gilbreaths, haggard, thin, and smelly, huddled together behind him. They were an intact family: young father and wife with three small children, a rarity in these terrible days.

The Reverend Thomas sat in the very last seat. He was a poised, older black man with sad, dark eyes.

It had taken almost two hours to get the family out of their home. The reverend had helped talk them into leaving. The older man had been holed up alone in the church, living off the donated canned goods. He had kept in contact with the fort via ham radio. A month earlier, the reverend had spotted one of the Gilbreath kids squatting over the edge of the roof of their family home to defecate. He had thought he was the sole survivor in the town until that point. It was the reverend who had directed Katarina and Bill to the family's boarded-up home.

The rescue had not been easy. It had taken nearly two hours to lure the zombies away from the church and down a back road by driving the van very slowly. Finally, Bill had floored it and doubled back to rescue the survivors.

"Are you sure this is safe?" the father, Harry, asked for the millionth time. "This fort you are taking us to, is it safe? Yer looking mighty scared right now."

"The fort is safe. Getting there is another story," Katarina answered.

"Nothing is truly safe in this world, but it's safer than where you were," Bill added truthfully.

The family clung to one another. The father's sheer determination had kept them alive. A longtime survivalist, his house had withstood the attacks of the zombies in the first days. They had lived in the basement until the plumbing failed. Then they had carried everything up into the attic. Bill had to respect their tenacity.

Katarina stared out the back window, her long red braid curling over one shoulder. "Shit! We have company!"

Reverend Thomas twisted around in his chair and saw a truck racing toward them from behind. "Why are you afraid of them? Aren't they also survivors?"

"Not everyone in this world is a good guy, Reverend." Bill's hands tightened on the steering wheel.

The truck sped after them. Katarina could see two men in the cab. The men looked scraggly and rough. There was a camper attached to the bed of the truck. It looked ominous to her.

"I see only two guys," she said, "but there's a camper in the bed and there might be more people in there."

Bill kept the van moving at a quick pace and dared a peek in his rearview mirror.

Katarina scrambled back to the passenger seat and let out a deep breath. "This feels bad."

"I agree." Bill kept his focus on the road ahead as he accelerated the vehicle. He was determined to get the family safely to the fort.

"Who are those men?" Harry asked.

"We think they're bandits," Bill answered. "I want all of you to get down on the floor right now. Keep your heads down and keep as close to the floor as possible."

"I thought you said my family would be safe!" The young man looked both frightened and angry.

"They will be. Just get down!"

The pursuing truck was closing fast.

Katarina looked back to see that their passengers were nervously obeying. She usually loved rescue missions. The expressions on people's faces when they saw other humans, their relief at being safe, and the exclamations of thanks made it worth the risk. Usually on rescue missions, they had to fight zombies, but this felt worse. Fighting other human beings in a dead world was just wrong.

The truck pulled alongside them. Katarina could clearly see the mud and gore spatters and what appeared to be bullet holes on its roughened side. She flicked off the safety on her rifle.

Katarina glanced over into the cab of the truck as it paced them. A scruffy man with lots of wild blond hair rolled down the window and shouted at them. It didn't take a lip-reader to see he was yelling at them to pull over.

Bill shook his head and pressed his foot down on the accelerator. The van edged ahead of the truck, but only for a moment. The scruffy guy leaned out the window and literally knocked on Bill's window. His voice was barely heard above the whine of the road and the wind.

"We want to be friends with you!" he was yelling. "We want to be friends!" But his expression was too wild and he looked at Katarina in a way that made her want to bash his teeth out with her rifle butt.

Barely glancing at the unkempt man as he kept the van on the road, Bill said, "Sorry. Gotta keep moving." He floored the gas pedal.

The children cried as their parents tried to shush them. The reverend prayed under his breath. Katarina made sure her seat belt was on tight and watched the truck anxiously. The guy who had banged on the window had crawled back into the cab and was talking with the driver.

"We're almost to the bridge," Bill said. "We have to beat them there." He had pulled ahead and swerved in front of the truck.

Katarina wasn't sure when the minivan had been souped up or who had done it, but right then she felt like hugging whoever it was. The van's engine was roaring and it was handling fine.

The truck sped past, then swerved sharply in front of them.

"Shit." Katarina felt her adrenaline rushing through her body.

"They plan to trap us at the bridge," Bill said grimly.

The children were crying louder now. Katarina didn't even want to think about what those men might do to the kids, their mother, or to her.

Katarina took a deep breath as she made up her mind. "We need to do something now."

"Can you pull a Nerit and shoot out the tire?"

Katarina furrowed her brow, then said, "I'll try." She rolled down her window.

Bill concentrated on the road and kept the van steady. The truck was speeding ahead of them, kicking up dirt, heading straight into the sunset.

Katarina perched in the window. The reverend scrambled forward and grabbed hold of her legs to keep her steady. Trying to balance herself, Katarina took aim at a tire.

"Don't swerve!" she yelled at Bill.

Katarina fired. The shot hit the camper and shattered the back window.

"Shit!"

She aimed again, trying to adjust for the speed, and the bumpiness of the road. A face appeared in the shattered window. It was a young girl, maybe thirteen. Her face was badly bruised and caked with blood. Her hands were tied in front of her and her mouth was gagged. She tried to wave at them.

"Sweet Jesus," the reverend whispered.

Katarina felt her gut coil as she stared at the captive in the back of the truck. She couldn't let any of those in her care share her fate. Sadly, she realized what she had to do. Katarina hesitated, but the cries of the children behind her were a reminder of what they had to lose. She had never fought a human being before, but she was certain she could kill the living just as easily as she killed the dead to protect the people in their charge.

"Do it," Bill called out in a ragged voice.

She fired.

The truck tire unrolled like a ribbon and the vehicle careened wildly. The girl fell out of sight. The truck tipped. The camper went flying into the gorge that bordered the road. The truck slammed onto its side and slid off the road in a shower of sparks, revealing the bridge just ahead.

Katarina struggled back into her seat and thanked the reverend for his help. She felt sick to her stomach.

"You had to," Bill said.

"I know," Katarina whispered, trying not to think of the girl's face. "I know."

The minivan roared over the bridge, then sped around a hill. The hotel, in all its lighted glory, came into view. She sighed with relief.

"Almost home," Bill assured the people clustered behind him.

Katarina picked up the CB. "We're almost home. We had some issues, so please keep us covered."

"Copy that," Yolanda's voice answered, then said more softly, "What kind of issues?"

"Bandits," Katarina answered. "It's the bandits."

4.
Watching the Board

The gates closed behind the minivan. After being checked for bites, the newcomers were quickly ushered into the hotel. Just like that, the excitement was over.

Jenni watched through the binoculars as the man who had been watching the fort turned and vanished into the darkness. She never saw the stranger's vehicle leave town.

She dutifully reported what she'd seen to Nerit, then settled in to wait.

They all waited.

The minutes, full of tension, full of fear, ticked by until they turned into hours.

* * *

"What do you think is going on?" Travis asked Nerit at around four in the morning. They were standing on a sentry platform near the gate. Travis's eyes were bloodshot. He was gulping coffee.

Nerit took a slow, luxurious drag off her cigarette. "I have been thinking about it and I have a theory."

"What is it?" Bill asked.

"Their plans went awry," Nerit said simply.

"And?" Travis arched an eyebrow.

"That is all for now," Nerit answered. "They're done for now."

Morning came.

The shifts rotated. People fell asleep in their clothes, guns nearby. Still, there was nothing.

One day slipped away without incident.

Then another.

And another. And another.

"Time to see if my theory is right," Nerit said after the fifth day of peace, and gathered her team of Jenni, Bill, and Travis.

The gates slid open and Nerit's new pride and joy, the Manns' black H2, roared out of the fort, heading for the bridge. The Manns had been furious when they were ordered, in no uncertain terms, to relinquish the vehicle. When they'd protested, Nerit had fastened her steely gaze on them and said, "Do you really think you can just jump into it and go shopping? Because you can't. Not anymore." Finally, they had handed over the keys.

The H2 was far too luxurious for Nerit's taste, but it drove well. If they ran into the bandits, Nerit could take the vehicle off-road with relative ease.

"I could get used to riding around in something like this." Nerit could tell from the sound of her voice that Jenni was happy to be out of the fort and doing something instead of sitting around, waiting.

"Up ahead is where they went off the road, Nerit," Bill said solemnly from the backseat.

Travis sat in the front passenger seat, rubbing his brow. He looked haggard; Nerit could see the stress eating away at him.

"Keep a lookout," Nerit said. "We don't need them sneaking up on us."

"Who? Zombies or bandits?" Jenni asked.

"Both," Nerit answered.

As the Hummer glided over the bridge, Travis looked down into the river. "Heh, there is a zombie down there in fishing gear, wading through the water still clutching its fishing pole."

"Wonder if he's catching zombie fish?" Jenni joked, then frowned. "God, I hope there's not zombie fish!"

Skid marks on the asphalt showed them where the bandits' truck had lost control. Nerit pulled over and everyone cautiously disembarked. It appeared the truck had slid into the gorge that bordered one side of the road. As the group from the fort neared the edge of the road, they saw the camper and truck below, firmly lodged in the trees that grew in the crevasse.

"It fuckin' stinks of the dead here," Jenni moaned.

"Let's check it out. Travis, watch the road," Nerit said, and started downward. The others followed.

Travis stayed on the road, looking far more at ease with a gun in his hands than Nerit had ever seen before. He looked alert and ready. Nerit glanced back at him, feeling pride in how far he had come.

Nerit reached the camper, each step carefully measured. Bill slowly rotated as he walked behind her, taking in all that was around him. Jenni held her gun firmly, alert to the slightest sound.

Gazing into the back of the camper, Nerit said, "One dead. Young female. Broken neck."

Bill sighed sadly. "Probably the best thing for the poor kid."

Nerit descended toward the truck, using the roots of the trees as a natural staircase. She stopped a few yards before reaching the toppled, battered vehicle.

"Two male bodies at the bottom of the gorge. Both bound and gagged. They appear to have been raped, then shot execution-style in the back of the head," she said with no emotion. She'd seen such things before, and worse.

Bill frowned. "Sounds like *Deliverance*. Every man's nightmare."

"These men are a nightmare." Nerit felt no remorse for the fate of the men.

Bill said to Jenni, "Follow me down. I want to get a closer look."

Nerit held her position as they made their way to the bodies. Looking up through the trees, she saw Travis keeping a watch on the road with a troubled expression on his face.

Bill took his time examining the bodies and moving around the crime scene. Nerit observed his expressions and realized that he was coming to some terrible conclusions. With a sigh, he motioned to Jenni and they both struggled up the slope.

"What do you think?" Nerit asked as they reached her.

"Honestly, Nerit, I think they were punished for failing. It's very methodical. Very intense. It feels . . . angry. It's both the guys that I saw the other day. No forgiveness for either of them."

Nerit nodded. "The young girl, the loss of an asset; the loss of the truck, another asset. But what was worse, I think, is that they probably weren't supposed to attack anyone from the fort. We know the bandits have been watching us, probably trying to determine our strengths and weaknesses. Maybe even deciding their approach. Either they would have attempted to deceive us into letting them in or would have just launched a surprise attack. But now the element of surprise is gone. We know they're out here and that they'll be coming for us at some point."

"This is what you've been thinking since that first night," Bill said after a beat.

Nerit slightly rolled her shoulders. "I just needed the proof."

"So now what?" Jenni followed the others toward the truck.

"We stay alert. They will wait now, until they feel we are vulnerable. We are at stalemate." Nerit opened up the door to the Hummer and slid in.

Jenni got into the car, saying, "Great. One more thing to worry about."

Bill slammed his door shut as Travis climbed into the front seat. "Nothing is easy now, is it?"

"No, not at all," Travis answered grimly. "Not at all."

· CHAPTER SEVENTEEN ·

1.
A Move Is Made

A wave of zombies hit the fort two days later. After it was over, Stacey, the guard who first sounded the alarm, explained that she had been leaning over to pick up her thermos when she heard a growl. Standing up and looking over the wall, she had seen a zombie beating on one of the trucks that made up the first perimeter. Stacey had raised her gun to pick him off when suddenly thirty zombies shambled into view and rabidly attacked the boundary.

"Good for sniper practice," Nerit said when she was informed. She lit a cigarette and walked out to view the newcomers, joining Travis, Katie, and Curtis on a guard platform.

"Not from this town," Curtis told Nerit. "I don't recognize any of them."

"Think they're migrating?" Travis asked.

"Maybe following food," Nerit said thoughtfully.

"How do they even sense us?" Katie folded her arms over her breasts, frowning at the thought of zombies migrating toward the living.

Bill yawned as he joined them. "Well . . . shit," he said, looking at the horde of walking dead.

"Understatement." Travis watched the zombies assault the perimeter with tired eyes. Katie slid her arm around his waist to give him comfort. Turning, he kissed her forehead.

"Gawd, the reek of them," Katie murmured.

"Looks mostly like farmworkers," Bill observed. "Clothes are pretty screwed up, but looks like farmworkers."

"Could be from anywhere." Curtis leaned his elbows on the wall and studied the faces of the dead. "Nobody familiar down there at all."

Nerit pointed to one of the male zombies. "That one's wearing a Walmart uniform. Where is the nearest Walmart?"

"Lemme think. About an hour south of here." Curtis glanced over his shoulder at Nerit. "Think they're migrating like Travis said?"

"Maybe someone corralled them, pushed them toward us." Nerit puffed on her cigarette as she scrutinized the situation.

"When Jenni and I were coming here the first time, a crowd of zombies chased us and just kept following the road after we turned off," Katie said. "Someone would just have to give them a little shove in the right direction."

"In our direction," Curtis snorted. "Great."

"Think the bandits are that smart?" Travis tuned his attention to Nerit. She looked coldly detached from the growing tension around them.

Bill hooked his thumbs over his belt and frowned. "Who knows? There are different breeds out in this area. It's remote. Country mentality is strong outside the towns. A lot of hardheaded, old-time mind-sets around here."

"Women as property?" Katie was thinking of the girls who had been taken from the community center in Hackleburg. She was glad Lily was taking care of the two little girls they had rescued, along with her own son.

"You can beat your wife as long as it's on the county courthouse steps with a stick no thicker than her thumb." Curtis shrugged his shoulders. "Old county law that never got erased from the books."

Bill nodded. "Assholes live everywhere. Just in the country, they got more privacy and more leeway. Makes a lot of stuff easier."

"We still have some pockets of survivors to pick up, right?"

Katie put her hands on her hips and tilted her head toward Travis.

"We've been picking them up in order of proximity or if their supplies are low. And now we're sending double teams as much as possible. One group does the rescue, the other gets supplies from any reachable stores. Winter is months away, but we have to be ready." Travis stared down at the rabid crowd below. "We've been putting off some groups because they got bad infestations around them."

"I think we need to bring everyone in as soon as we can." Nerit extinguished her cigarette, grinding it into the top of the wall. "And each time out, we should change tactics. They're watching us, so let's keep them confused."

"I hate to be the devil's advocate, but maybe we should sit tight," Curtis said sullenly. "We got our own to take care of."

Nerit gave him a long look. "Those survivors out there are 'our own.'"

Curtis shrugged. "I just feel like we should be trying to stay safe inside and not going out there."

Travis shook his head. "Part of staying safe is having good, solid people to help build the new world. Some of those people have skills we need. One is an RN; another is an electrician. We definitely need an electrician, since so many of the construction guys left back on the first day."

"We have to get them." Katie couldn't even fathom leaving anyone out in the deadlands.

Curtis was staring at Travis intently. "What if people die going out there?"

"We are all taking risks," Bill answered for Travis. "Got to do what is right."

There was an uncomfortable silence.

Nerit waved to the zombies rabidly growling and jostling each other below. "Target practice for Jason and his crew," she said. "Don't they have some new weapons to try out?"

Katie said, with a brief laugh, "It was nice of the bandits to send us cannon fodder."

Nerit gave Katie a sly smile. "Oh, yes. It gives me a little more insight into their leader's mind." She headed for the stairs, summoning Jason on her walkie-talkie as she went.

"Okay, is it just me, or is she one scary old woman?" Bill blinked his eyes rapidly, his hands on his hips.

"The scariest," Curtis said somberly.

"Glad she's on our side," Katie added.

Travis looked at the zombies thoughtfully. "Yeah, me, too."

2.
It Begins Again

Peggy studied her little map with all its highlighted spots she had spread out on the front desk in the lobby. With Nerit and Travis watching, the city secretary sighed and drew an X through one of the bright yellow circles. After three days of no contact, she had finally given up hope that the survivors there were still alive. It could be the zombies, or it could be the bandits. There was no way of truly knowing.

Looking up, she saw the newest refugees, three little kids running around with her son, playing what looked like a superhero game. When they'd first arrived, the Gilbreaths had been absolutely terrified, half-starved, and reeking to high heaven. When Mrs. Gilbreath had seen their suite in the hotel, she burst into tears. At their first meal, the children stuffed themselves until the youngest had thrown up. It had broken Peggy's heart to think what they had witnessed, what they had survived.

Nerit glanced over at the children, then back down at the map. "Four locations. Which is the most desperate?"

Travis was staring at the map. He was certain to be the new mayor, despite Steven Mann's dirty politicking. Manny was a fading leader as he struggled with health problems. Most people deferred to Travis now. The looming vote was the last step in making him the official fort leader.

"Sadler Farm. The Sadlers and a few workers have been hiding in the main house since the second day of the outbreak. They felt safe in the old stone house with its storm windows and heavy shutters and doors. Originally, they declined joining us. They felt they had it under control. They told me that they'd been going from the house to the garden and chicken coops with no problems. Considering how far out they are, you would think they would be safe, but a wave of the dead arrived on their doorstep about ten days ago. During the initial onslaught, they lost two men. Now they're just about out of ammo and food."

Nerit tapped the map with one finger. "And where is the nurse?"

"Bowie Elementary School in Raymond," Peggy answered. "There are two teachers and four kids with her. Two of the kids are hers. They are almost out of food and have no weapons. She was giving flu shots at the school on the first day. When the school was evacuated to the National Guard base, they chose to remain behind."

"Why?" Nerit's voice revealed her curiosity.

Peggy chuckled. "The nurse loves horror movies and when she saw one of the walking dead, she was pretty sure it was a zombie. Then she noticed bites on some of the people being evacuated. So she and the others hid and waited until everyone else had been shipped off to a rescue center, then barricaded themselves inside the school. It's a very small school, so it wasn't too hard."

Nerit smiled wryly. "Horror movies . . . odd how they became a guideline for survival."

Katie joined them, dressed in hunting gear. She leaned into Travis and he slung an arm around her shoulders. A tender kiss followed.

Peggy grinned. She loved seeing Travis and Katie together. Her own marriage, to a long-haul trucker, had been rocky and never very romantic. She felt bad that she couldn't mourn Zack, though Cody often cried for him late at night. She had fallen out of love with him long ago and knew that he had countless affairs while on the road. Maybe they would have gotten divorced if he'd been around more. Zack had died the first day of the zombie rising and Cody had seen him, undead, just before he was rescued by Curtis. Peggy hadn't even cried when she heard that Zack was dead. She probably never would.

Yet she was still a sucker for country love songs and soap operas. She knew love when she saw it, and she saw it in Travis and Katie. She was happy for them even though she sometimes felt a little jealous. She wished that one day it would happen to her. Of course, in this dead world, what were the chances of that?

"So these are the last two groups?" Travis indicated the circled locations on the map.

"Actually, one more." Peggy sighed as she crossed out a group. "I forgot. They've gone silent, too. That leaves this one right here. It's a family trapped in a trailer up in the hills above Emorton, which is badly infested. They were also holdouts, but they have not been doing so well. They're just bullheaded country folk. They refused all offers of help. Now they need us to rescue them."

Nerit was deep in thought, her finger tracing the roads on the map.

"Who is out there right now?" Looking at Peggy, Travis leaned against the counter.

Peggy really appreciated that he always gave her his full attention and valued her opinion. It wasn't like that with Manny; they'd butted heads constantly.

"Ed is out with a group, harvesting the peach groves on his farm," Peggy answered. "He took Lenore with him."

"Lenore?" Travis blinked.

"I felt she was ready," Nerit muttered as she studied the map.

"Jenni is out on a scavenging run with Curtis, Katarina, Felix, and Dylan," Katie added. "They're due back soon."

"Dylan? We sent Dylan out? Isn't he a bit young?" Travis looked incredulous.

"He just turned eighteen. He could have joined the military at that age," Nerit pointed out.

"And no one out in the field is reporting anything odd? No bandits?" Travis lifted his eyebrows.

"No, just those waves of zombies showing up. Kinda like they do here. I think the bandits are sending them somehow," Peggy answered.

"I agree." Nerit made notes on a pad of paper.

"You don't think they've decided we're too big to take on?" Katie asked.

"I think they're trying to figure out what to do with us." Travis wished he could believe the bandits would leave them alone, but he knew in his gut the bandits were not about to give up yet.

"Agreed." Nerit nodded, then leaned over the map and studied it. "Waiting for a time to strike."

Ken rushed down the hall from the communication center, ran behind the counter, and hugged Peggy, startling her. "Oh, my god! You will not believe my news!"

The corners of Travis's mouth quirked up. "Oh, yeah?"

"Yeah! Ed called in from where they are getting all those delicious peaches!"

"So the good news is we're having peach cobbler?" Katie said teasingly.

Ken gave her a dark look. "I'm building this up. You're cramping my style! Shush, you!"

"Spill it, Ken." Peggy was about to smack him upside the head.

"My girl, Lenore, my bestest girl, is safe and on her way back with mission numero uno under her belt. That's the first part. Second part, Ed's boys were there!"

"No shit?" Peggy was stunned. Ed rarely spoke of his three sons out somewhere in the deadlands. The boys were all the family Ed had after the death of his wife. All three had been away at school on the first day. Peggy knew Ed had hopes they were still alive, but this was amazing news. "Seriously. The boys were all alive?"

"Yep! They fought their way back to Ed's farm! They thought their daddy was dead until they saw him in the peach orchard!" Ken danced around, then added with a grin. "Lenore is trying to find out if any of them are gay."

"I swear to God, all you think about is finding a boyfriend," Peggy groused.

"Like you don't?"

"Hey, my sex life, or lack thereof, ain't your business." Peggy shook her pen in his face.

"Hard up, aren't you?"

"I'm gonna kick your ass, Ken."

Katie smirked. "My money is on Peggy if they throw down."

Travis grinned at the sudden lightheartedness around him. "I dunno. Ken looks kinda vicious."

Ken playfully snarled at him. "Okay, good news time is over! Back to the communication center!" He bounced back down the hall.

"I'm gonna choke him. I swear to God, I will," Peggy muttered. After talking about all the people out there in horrible situations, it was a relief to hear some good news. "Back to business . . ."

Nerit looked up from her map, seemingly impervious to Ken's exploits. "I think they're after resources: food, guns, drugs, and women. We need to lure them out and I think I know how." She tapped the map with one finger. "We need to start here."

Peggy looked at where she was pointing. "Your gun store?"

Travis shifted uncomfortably on his feet. "You said the weapons are in the safe. The bandits can't get to them."

"No, they can't. But we need those weapons and the ammunition. We've put off going back there long enough." Nerit looked very pale, but calm. "We should have gone before." She pulled out her keys and handed them to Travis. "You need the round gold key and silver square one to get into the store. I will give you the safe combination."

An excursion to the gun store to reclaim the last of the gun stock and ammunition had long been on the list of things to do, but they had found other stockpiles to keep them well armed.

Peggy shifted on her feet, feeling uncomfortable with where this was going.

Travis slid the keys into his pocket. "We didn't really need to go until now, you know."

"We didn't go because of Ralph," Nerit said simply. "And we have no time for such sentimentality anymore."

Travis reached out and rubbed her shoulder gently. "We'll be respectful."

"I know," Nerit answered.

Katie slipped an arm around the older woman's waist. Peggy was surprised when Nerit leaned against the younger woman, obviously drawing comfort from her embrace.

"If we make a production of going to the store, that will draw the bandits' attention. It will be a good diversion while we get the last of the survivors in," Nerit said in a slightly quavering voice. "We need to pull them out. Get them to confront us."

"So we're going to get into a fight with the bandits?" Peggy looked at her incredulously.

"No, so we're going to show them they can't beat us." Nerit's face was grim and frightening.

Travis eyed Nerit long and hard. "I get where you are going with this."

"I don't have a clue what you're talking about. Care to enlighten me?" Peggy asked.

Jenni burst through archway into the lobby. Fury was vivid in her eyes, and her skin was flushed. "Where the hell is Bill?"

"Communication center," Peggy said, and pointed down the hall. "He's training Ken."

"What's going on?" Katie stepped toward Jenni.

"This fucktard got Dylan killed," she said, pointing behind her and trembling with rage.

Curtis came into view, his head down, looking pale. "Jenni, I didn't mean to—"

"Oh, shut up!"

Katarina and Felix appeared behind Curtis. Katarina laid a gentle hand on the younger man's shoulder.

"Let it go, Jenni," she said in a soft, firm voice.

"No! I won't! He told Dylan to go into that storeroom, and there was a fuckin' zombie inside! He did it on purpose 'cause he was mad at Dylan for smoking weed!"

Curtis was trembling with emotion and tears streamed down his face. "I thought it was clear!"

"You liar!"

"Get Bill and Juan," Travis told Katie.

Katie hurried down the hall.

Travis moved around the counter and walked slowly toward Jenni. "Jenni, things go wrong out there. You know it."

Jenni whirled around, toward Travis. "Dylan was a boy! Just a boy! Curtis got him killed."

"I thought it was clear!" Curtis's face was red, his hands clenched at his side.

Katarina held on to Curtis's shoulder, partially to comfort him, partially to keep him back from Jenni.

"It was not an easy ride back with these two going at it," Felix grumbled.

"I want him locked up!" Jenni stomped her foot.

"Jenni, calm down. We need to take care of this in a calm manner."

Peggy slowly walked up behind Travis, glad for his gentle demeanor. At that moment, she wanted to slap Jenni and shake Curtis, but she also felt sick at the thought of someone so young dying so horribly. Poor Dylan.

Bill appeared with Katie, hoisting up his belt and looking slightly annoyed. "What's going on?"

Jenni and Curtis started talking at the same time. Katarina

and Felix kept trying to interject, and Peggy felt like screaming at them to shut up as the lobby filled with noise. Mrs. Gilbreath quickly ushered the children out of the lobby and out of sight.

Bill raised a hand. Everyone fell silent.

"Curtis, talk to me. What happened?" Bill looked at the younger man with the fatherly compassion that Peggy so admired.

"We were in the Walgreens. We made a sweep through. I checked the storeroom and didn't see nothing. Told Dylan to go in and start organizing what we needed to take. I went to get a dolly. I heard him screaming and ran in. I guess the zombie came off a shelf or something. I don't know. I shot both of them." Tears were still streaming down Curtis's face. He rubbed at his flushed cheeks furiously.

Bill looked at Katarina and Felix. "Is that what you saw?"

"I didn't see anything, but I heard Curtis telling Dylan to take care of things in the storeroom," Katarina answered.

"I didn't check the storeroom myself, but I heard Curtis call it as clear." Felix shrugged.

"He sent him in there to die!" Jenni couldn't hold her tongue anymore. "He did it on purpose!"

Juan came running into view and skidded to a stop near Jenni. "Babe?"

"Curtis did it on purpose!" Jenni shouted again, tears streaming down her face. "He did it on purpose. He's the fuckin' Vigilante! It could have been Jason! He could have killed my son!"

The minute the words left Jenni's lips, the atmosphere in the room changed significantly. Peggy could feel much of the tension drain away. The accusation against Curtis suddenly felt impotent. Juan put his arms around Jenni. She spun around and clung to him, crying violently.

"Curtis, go to your room. Clean up. Rest up. We'll talk later," Bill ordered. Katarina and Felix both sighed as Bill shooed them off as well. He looked at Katie as she went up to Jenni and Juan.

Katie smoothed Jenni's hair back from her face as Juan whispered in her ear.

"Can you two take care of her?"

Juan nodded, and he and Katie led Jenni away.

"What do you think?" Travis asked Bill.

"Shit happens out there. People die. And it ain't easy," Bill answered.

"Can't disagree with ya there." Slowly, Travis turned back to Nerit, who had returned to studying the map. "C'mon, Peggy. We got work to do."

Peggy looked back at Curtis one more time before the elevator doors shut. She felt bad for the poor kid. He was such a sweetheart, it hurt her to see him so devastated. Her stomach clutched tightly. Her nerves were getting the best of her. It was a fucked-up world and she hated it. But at least Bill and Travis were there to make it better. Trying to hide the trembling of her hands, she followed after Travis back to the front desk.

"What's the plan?" Travis asked Nerit, leaning on his elbows on the counter.

"I heard there was a disturbance! I fully intend to reveal the truth behind the matter to all who will listen! I will not allow the truth of the conspiracies of this illegal fort to go unreported to the—" Calhoun burst into the lobby with his video camera.

"I'll get rid of him," Peggy said with a sigh.

"Actually," Nerit said with a wicked little smile, "we're going to need him for our plan."

Peggy looked at the smelly old man who refused to bathe and then at Nerit. "Him?" She was incredulous.

Travis said, "You sure?"

"Oh, yes," Nerit said. "I'm sure."

Calhoun headed toward them, his foil hat looking like it was about to fly off his head.

"Just the man I am looking for," Nerit said as he neared the front desk.

Calhoun looked shocked, then a little afraid. "I will not assist you in your nefarious plans, Amazonian Queen!"

"Yes, you will" Nerit smiled at him confidently. "Because it will help defeat the marauding aliens attempting land grabs and abductions."

Calhoun looked at her suspiciously from beneath his scraggly eyebrows, then slowly tilted his head. "Okay. I'm listening."

As Peggy listened to Nerit's plan slowly unfurl, she felt her fear subside. Perhaps it would all work out okay after all.

3.
When Nothing Is Clear

Travis handed Katie a beer and slid into the chair next to her. She was sitting with her feet hooked up on the balcony rail, her lean legs looking tan and fit in the waning sunlight. Dinner was sitting, nice and filling, in their bellies. Sitting out on the balcony seemed like the right way to end an evening.

Travis stretched his legs in front of him and stared at his bare feet. They ached, just like the rest of him.

Katie tapped her beer against his and took a swig. "Jenni's okay now. I called Juan while you were in the shower."

He looked toward her. "She took it hard, huh?"

Katie pulled on her shorts a little, still trying to get comfortable. "Yeah. Once she saw Jason, it was better."

"She's still not talking about her other sons, huh?"

"Sometimes I wonder if she ever will. I feel so bad for her. She says she sees Lloyd every day now, out of the corner of her eye, or standing in the shadows. She's ignoring the visions, which is kinda good, but she's not dealing with what happened to her kids."

"We're all fucked in the head right now," Travis said. "I've been hearing a few things around the fort."

"Like what?"

"People seeing ghosts, for one. Or hearing their voices."

Katie nodded. "I guess I have my own ghost."

"You dream of Lydia."

"I miss Lydia," Katie reminded him, then shrugged. "But I do have to admit that, sometimes, in my dreams, I feel her presence. Or at least I think I do. Most of my dreams about her are like flashes of memory, but sometimes, when I dream about her, she feels . . . real."

Travis's brow puckered. "I can't say I believe in ghosts, exactly. But considering that we've got the living dead running around, I can't really discount this stuff entirely. Maybe Jenni's asshole husband really is haunting her, trying to finish what he started. I don't know. But I do know that until she deals with what happened to Mikey and Benji, he's gonna be able to get to her, ghost or not."

Katie ran a hand over her blond curls and sighed. "I agree. Do you see ghosts? Dream them?"

Travis shook his head. "No, but I haven't been that close to anyone in a long time. I'm an only child and my parents died in a car crash a few years back. My fiancée and I had ended things. Coming to Ashley Oaks to help with the restoration was my new beginning in life. Juan was the one who got me out here. He was the one person in my life giving me any sort of grounding, I guess you could say."

"You're kinda like Jenni that way. The zombies gave you a new lease on life, too."

"They gave me you," Travis answered, taking her hand and gazing into her eyes. Life was never easy at the fort. There was always hard work to be done and problems to sort out. His days were spent planning the fort expansion with Eric and Juan, working with Nerit on defenses, and establishing the internal workings of the fort with Peggy and Bill. Travis wasn't officially mayor yet, but everyone was acting like he was. Some nights he was so exhausted, all he wanted to do was lie in Katie's arms and listen to her breathe.

"Travis, did you know that today is the first day of August?"

"No. No, I didn't. Hell, we missed the Fourth of July, didn't we?"

"Uh-huh." Katie looked toward the Texas flag waving in the

wind, most likely over the library. There was a huge one that flew over city hall. "Texas is still here. That's a good feeling. I guess we could celebrate Texas Independence Day next March."

"We can't skip holidays. That's not right," Travis decided. He held her hand as he lifted his beer with his other.

"Halloween, Thanksgiving, Christmas, New Year's. Once we handle the bandits, maybe we can start looking forward to those."

"We should have enough food to get through the winter and beyond. The hunters are bringing in plenty of venison and beef right now. We got that garden planted. Things should be okay. The well is good, we got generators ready for backup, firewood in case of power outages—"

"Travis?" Katie interrupted softly.

"Huh?"

"Stop."

He blinked. "What?"

"Stop. It's okay. It's just us here. Let go. Relax." She motioned at the hills and the approaching night. "Enjoy the view, enjoy the moment. You've done all you can for today."

Travis closed his eyes and tried to shove the day's tensions away. It took about a minute for his pulse rate to drop and his body to relax. When he opened his eyes, he saw the first stars appearing. The sky was beautiful.

"What would I do without you?"

"Let's not find out."

Katie slid out of her chair and snuggled onto his lap. He wrapped his arms around her and relaxed even more as she stretched her legs over his and got comfortable. Travis kissed her brow and relished the feel of her in his arms. All he wanted to do was protect her and their home, but he had to remember that he needed to just relax and enjoy the fact that she was safe.

I'm going to marry you, he thought. And he knew that would be the happiest moment of his life.

All they had to do was get through the next few days, defeat the bandits, and buckle down for the coming fall and winter.

"Stop thinking about work," she chided.

"What?"

"You got all tense again."

"Damnit," Travis muttered.

"Okay. There is only one thing that will get your mind off work. I'm going to have to get naked," Katie said, and slid off his lap and went into their bedroom.

Travis scrambled after her, grinning.

CHAPTER EIGHTEEN

1.
The Countdown Begins

The next morning, Nerit and Peggy were waiting for Travis and Katie in the hotel lobby. Holding hands, the couple looked pensive.

"We're ready, Nerit," Travis said.

The older woman nodded. "You have the vault combination?"

"Yeah. I have it," he assured her, patting his back pocket. He started to say something, then thought better of it.

Peggy marveled at Nerit's matter-of-fact way of dealing with things. After Ralph was murdered by the bandits, Nerit had hidden most of the hunting store's guns and ammunition in a safe that dated back to when the building had been a bank. Once the vault was sealed, Nerit had gathered a few possessions and her dog and set out for the fort. In her shoes, Peggy knew she would have just run, terrified. Nerit's straight thinking in the midst of her personal tragedy had made things a little safer for them all.

Nerit looked down for a long moment, then finally said, "Please don't disturb him."

"We won't," Katie promised, and kissed Nerit's cheek.

Nerit gave her a small smile that quickly slipped away. "Thank you," she said.

"We'll see you when we get back," Travis said before he and Katie walked off, once again hand in hand.

Peggy sighed wistfully and Nerit raised an eyebrow.

"I can't help it. Young love!" Peggy blushed and pretended to scrutinize her map.

"And soon a baby."

"She's pregnant?" Peggy blinked rapidly with surprise.

"I don't think she knows yet." Nerit leaned over the map and studied it.

"Really?" Peggy thought about how long it took her to realize her own pregnancy. Cody had sneaked up on her. "She has the glow, huh?"

Nerit gave a curt nod.

"But she shouldn't be going out if—"

"We all take risks. All of us," Nerit answered coolly. "Even living here is a risk. We never know what tomorrow may bring, or the next hour or minute."

Peggy started to protest, then looked at the bricked-up windows and doors. Nerit was right. Nothing was really safe. In the beginning, Peggy had really thought that the army would come and save everyone, that big trucks would drive up and everyone would be taken to some top secret underground fortress. But that had never happened. She remembered how silly she had believed their truck perimeter was in the beginning and how she had rolled her eyes at the thought of building the wall. *The army will come soon,* she had thought over and over again in those first days. Now she realized the wisdom of them defending themselves and making it safe for everyone taking refuge in the construction site.

"Contact the survivor groups and let them know we are coming today," Nerit ordered.

Peggy chewed on her bottom lip, her nervousness growing. It was always hard for her when their people traveled out into the deadlands. It was horrible to have to wait and see if they all made it back and, if not, to learn who hadn't made it. Dylan wasn't their only loss in the last few months. Nerit slid a paper across the counter to Peggy. "Here are the details."

Looking over it, Peggy scratched behind one ear. "Okay, I'm on it."

Nerit gave her a nod, then walked off slowly, slightly favoring one leg. If she knew Peggy noticed, she'd probably be annoyed.

Peggy hurried to the communication center.

2.
The Countdown Continues

Katie watched the outer gates glide open, her stomach knotting. The inner gates were already closed behind the Hummer and the souped-up minivan. As the gates parted, Katie saw two zombies lurch in their direction, but the fort's snipers took them down with eerie, near-simultaneous efficiency. Nerit had meticulously trained the most gifted of the fort's sharpshooters in her art, and Katie heard that Katarina had risen to be her star pupil.

Katie pushed down on the Hummer's accelerator and started down the road. Glancing into the review mirror, she saw the minivan following closely. Felix was driving and a new guy, Bob, was sitting beside him. She hoped the new people would be able to handle the stress of entering the deadlands.

"This is pretty nice," Katie stated. "Drives real nice."

"Should be for how much it costs," Travis answered. "Blanche used it to go shopping."

"Amazing. And to think I felt guilt over the convertible Lydia gave me."

"You would look cute in a convertible," Travis decided.

"Yeah, but I think I have a fetish for big four-by-four trucks now." Katie winked. "They smash zombies better."

"Oh, you better watch yourself. You're starting to sound like a redneck, not a big, bad, prosecuting attorney," Travis teased.

"Oh, I am still a big, bad, prosecuting attorney," Katie assured him. She gave him her coldest courtroom glare.

"Damn," he laughed. "I hope I never get that look for real."

"Just watch yourself and you'll be okay. Otherwise, you're screwed."

"Ruthless, huh?"

"And I still am."

A zombie staggered out into the road. Katie didn't flinch and drove straight into it, flinging the creature off the road. The van behind them didn't even have to swerve to avoid its flying body.

"See? Ruthless." Katie grinned.

"Ummmm . . . I noticed." Travis gave her a wry smile, settling into his seat.

The zombie threat in town had been greatly reduced over time by the fort's snipers and the scavenging teams. Most of the time, the streets were refreshingly zombie free. The fort's leaders had discussed systematically clearing the whole town, but decided that without a way to keep more zombies from invading the streets, it would be a waste of time and firepower.

What would happen to the town outside the fort that they would no longer use was still up for debate, but Katie knew that Travis had plans for their little fortress.

"Do you think Nerit is right?" Travis asked after a stretch of silence.

Katie was so wrapped up in watching the road and her own thoughts that his voice startled her. "Probably."

"She does have a lot more experience with this type of thing, I guess," Travis said thoughtfully.

"And she has trained and briefed all of us." Katie's gaze swept over the road in front of them.

No zombies.

No bandits.

So far, so good.

"She's done a very good job since we lost Mike." Travis sighed, remembering his lost friend. He looked back at the minivan, then returned his gaze to the scenery quickly flying by the windows. The scorching heat of the late summer had crisped the trees leaves, and the grass was dry and brown. "Having to deal with bandits on top of zombies is such bullshit. Why didn't they try to help people instead of . . . you know . . . killing, raping, stealing?"

Katie slightly shrugged. "Trust me, I've pondered that many times during my career. The only thing I can think of is that it's human nature to try to survive. And some people have a twisted nature and a twisted way of surviving."

They rounded a bend and saw three zombies standing in the road. Katie hit them straight on. One managed to cling to the deer guard on the front of the Hummer for a few seconds, then slid off and bounced down the road. Like most of the zombies they'd seen recently, these didn't look like people anymore. Their shrunken features and mottled bodies didn't seem quite so terrifyingly human as they had been in the first days. It was easier to see them just as monsters, not as the people they once had been.

Travis reached out and rested his hand on her thigh. "You be careful, okay?"

Katie ran her hand over his. "And you be careful, too."

Jenni sat in the front seat of the short bus behind Ed, who was driving. Bill sat across from her, looking grim and anxious. There were four more people in the bus and almost no conversation. Behind them, a large moving truck carried another team. Jenni's team would pick up any survivors; the other team would look for supplies.

The bus was even more tricked out than before. Now it had heavy mesh over all the windows and a heavy deer guard in the front. Jenni thought it was almost like being in a prison bus. They were bringing the last of the survivors in their area today. It was a big moment for the fort.

Running her hand over her rifle, she sighed. She was very hot and the air conditioner was barely working. The world was brown and dead. Occasionally, they would see a zombie wobbling down the road or through a field. It didn't take much imagination to believe that the cities were crammed with the creatures, but out here, they seemed increasingly sparse. Jenni recognized she shouldn't get too comfortable with that thought.

She had come a long way since that first day. It was as if her life before that morning was just a dim memory of another world. In contrast, her days on the road with Katie seemed stark and vivid in her mind. The crazed sense of liberation, the fear, the adrenaline, the passionate desire to live; she had felt stripped of all her boundaries and free to be herself—whatever that was—at last.

Despite all that she had lost, she was happy: happy to have Katie and Jason as her family, to love and be loved by Juan, to be the psycho zombie killer. She still had nightmares about her children. She missed Benji and Mikey horribly. Sometimes she wept uncontrollably when no one else was around. It hurt to think of them out there, decaying slowly as they prowled for flesh.

Benji's tiny fingers still reached for her in her nightmares. Lloyd's damn ghost lingered in the corners of her life. She ignored his taunts and tried not to listen to him. His words only stirred her guilt at surviving. He reminded her of that other time, that other life, that other home.

The fort was far away from her old house and old life. She loved it, but she was terribly afraid that they could lose it all.

If Nerit was right, this would be a decisive day for all of them. It would be a day none of them would forget one way or the other.

Jenni lowered her head and sighed. Her baby's tiny fingers seemed oddly closer today. . . .

3.

Ten, Nine, Eight

When the Hummer drew up to the old hunting store, it was immediately obvious the bandits had not only returned, but had also broken into the store. Decaying bodies littered the street. A van with its tires blown out and all the windows shattered listed to one side of the street.

"Nerit's handiwork," Travis decided, remembering the old woman's story of the death of her husband and the revenge she'd taken. "Move with extreme caution," he said into the CB.

"Understood," came the answer over a crackle of static.

Katie stopped in front of the store and Travis scanned their surroundings. The bandits had gone nuts in the town. All the windows of the buildings on the main street were shattered. Merchandise from the grocery store littered the street. The bars on one of the windows of Toombs Hunting Store were twisted and bent out of their frame. Travis imagined that the damage had been done by the bandits, who perhaps had used a chain and a truck to yank on the strong barricade.

The body of a woman was tied to a lamppost in front of the grocery.

No.

A zombie woman was tied to the lamppost. She had been mostly eaten, but her eyes were moving, watching them; her mouth opened and closed on slender sinews.

"I really hate these guys." Katie shuddered with disgust.

"Yeah," Travis agreed grimly.

Turning off the engine, Katie drew her rifle onto her lap. "Ready?"

Travis gave her a quick nod. He took Nerit's keys from his pocket, climbed out of the H2, and moved toward the store's front door. The people from the minivan followed, guns drawn, looking alert. As Travis moved past the gaping hole that had once been the window of the hunting store, a face appeared, snarling and growling. Travis jerked away and aimed his gun.

"Wait! Don't kill it yet!" Katie stared intently at the zombie's face with its long, scraggly hair and beard. "One of their own, I think. He fits the description of the bandits." She drew her revolver and shot it point-blank in the face.

"You're scary sometimes," Travis said with surprise and admiration. He peered into the store, his gun raised to cover the interior. "Hello! Hey, zombies! Hey, come here!"

Katie stood behind him, giving him cover. Nothing stirred inside.

"Let's go in." Travis went to the front door and unlocked it. Bob and Lenore stood guard. Lenore held her hunting bow and stared somberly at the zombie woman tied to the lamppost. She drew back the string, then let the arrow fly. The shaft punched the zombie woman's eye and deep into her brain, silencing her growls.

Lenore shrugged. "No point in leaving her like that."

Pushing the door open, Travis waited to see if any more of the dead lurked inside. Katie walked past him and into the store. Travis entered after her. Bob was behind Travis. He was sweating profusely and his face was glistening. Travis was worried about him. Bob had been rescued in the last few weeks and had yet to prove himself to the other survivors. This trip was his first big chance. Travis hoped that Nerit's training would pay off.

They made a sweep of the first floor, checking behind every counter, table, and display rack. Most of the merchandise had been scattered across the floor by the bandits. As Katie passed one pile of canvas bags, she pointed out how someone had urinated and defecated on the pile.

"They're animals," she grunted.

"Let's find the vault." Travis tried to ignore the stench and kept moving.

To his relief, the big old bank vault was still locked. Fresh, shiny scratches and dents on the massive door showed that the bandits had tried to get into it, but it had remained impervious.

"Okay, this is a good sign." Travis took the combination out of his pocket and twirled the knob, his brow burrowed with concentration.

Katie glanced toward the stairwell that led up to Nerit and Ralph's apartment. "This place had felt so safe in those first horrible days. Now it's been desecrated. I wish I could walk up those stairs and find Nerit and Ralph in the kitchen, sipping coffee and eating cheesecake."

"I'm sorry, Katie."

"It's what it is," she answered with a shrug.

Travis yanked open the vault. Inside were weapons and boxes of ammo. "We're in business," Travis declared. "Let's get this stuff loaded up."

Katie's hand suddenly gripped his arm. "Travis, I heard a noise upstairs."

"Okay, let's check it out. Bob, you and Felix get the stuff into the van. Lenore and Ken can cover the road."

Bob hustled forward. "Gotcha."

Moving slowly, cautiously, and as quietly as possible, Katie and Travis climbed the stairs into Nerit and Ralph's old apartment. The stench of death filled his nostrils when they reached the landing, and he paused in shock.

The apartment had been destroyed. The furniture had been smashed and the pieces tossed into corners. Mementos, photos, and personal possessions were strewn about. Some of the photos were deliberately defaced. Porn magazines were mixed in with the debris.

"They're animals," Katie gasped.

Travis felt a chill sweep over him. If those monsters ever got hold of Katie . . .

He couldn't bear the thought.

The dining room held the source of the noise Katie had heard.

A woman lay spread-eagled on the floor, naked. Her wrists and ankles were shackled to huge spikes that had been driven into the floor. Her mouth was duct-taped shut. The silver tape went around her head so many times, only her eyes were visible.

There was a nasty zombie bite on her shoulder. Her undead state explained her condition. She was trying to growl and was thrashing about. What looked like a tongue lay on the floor nearby. Travis had a feeling it was hers.

She had been brutally raped more than once. That much was clear. Travis backed out, found a sheet on the floor in the hall, came back, and threw it over the zombie's body. It was too much to bear to see her like that. Then he raised his gun and put her out of her misery.

"Why do I have a feeling the rapes took place before and after her death?" Katie's expression was grim.

Travis sadly shook his head. He used the walkie-talkie to explain the shot and tell the others to keep working.

Katie stepped cautiously into the kitchen, which was also a mess. "They built a meth lab in here."

"Damn. These guys are fucked up."

"Running around, strung out on meth, while zombies eat the living . . . What a nightmare."

Together, Travis and Katie swept the rest of the apartment, finding it in utter shambles. The bandits had used photographs as toilet paper before throwing them against the bathroom wall. It looked like they had squatted in the hunting store for some time.

"The bedroom," Katie said in a pained voice, pointing to a door that was ajar. "We should look in there."

Hesitantly, Travis reached out and pushed open the door. Ralph's remains lay in a jumble in a corner, looking as if someone had ripped the quilt off the bed with the body still in it. Cigarettes, drug paraphernalia, and beer bottles littered the bed. The only relief was seeing that Ralph was still very truly dead. Travis moved to the corpse's side and drew the blanket over its decomposing features.

"I hate these guys, maybe even more than the zombies," Katie gasped. Tears filled her eyes.

"Let's go," Travis said in a tortured voice. "Let's get these bastards."

They hurried downstairs and helped load the rest of the boxes into the van.

"We're being watched," Lenore said around twenty minutes later. "I've seen the glint of glass three times through those trees over there. I'm sure it's binoculars."

"Nerit was right." Travis continued to work as if nothing were wrong. "Call it in, Ken."

The younger man nodded, then casually climbed into the van and pretended to do something other than use the radio to call the fort.

Lenore raised her hunting bow and dropped a zombie just coming around a far corner. "So I guess this is it."

"Can't be sure yet, but my money is on yes." Travis wiped his brow before lifting another box.

Katie shoved more ammunition boxes into the back of the Hummer. "I say we go now."

Felix heaved in a huge box. "I'm with her. Let's roll."

Ken slid back out of the van. Walking calmly to pick up a box, he said, "The scary old woman says we keep to the plan. No deviations."

"How many do you think there are?" Travis looked toward Lenore.

"I've seen at least one set of binoculars. I'm guessing one vehicle; otherwise, more guys would be staring at us."

"Good point." Katie slammed the door to the Hummer shut. "Is the van ready?"

"Last box here," Bob answered.

"Then we go," Travis said, and moved to the passenger door of the Hummer. "Felix, keep to the plan and don't panic."

"Dude, I have more experience out here than you do," Felix griped.

Travis shrugged. "Yeah, but I gotta sound like the condescending leader. It's my job."

Felix slightly laughed and climbed into the van. This time Lenore and Ken climbed into the backseat of the Hummer.

Katie turned on the Hummer and began to U-turn slowly. For a second, Travis, too, saw the glint of glass up in the tree line. Silently, he prayed that they would survive whatever came next.

· CHAPTER NINETEEN ·

1.
Seven, Six, Five

Jenni rubbed her trembling hands together and glanced out the window toward the dead town of Emorton. She could see zombies milling around in the street, aimless without human prey to chase. They were far enough away that the zombies did not see or hear them, but the miniature outlines of their forms still made her stomach clench. It was in Emorton that Katie and Jenni had almost been overrun by zombies while on their way to rescue Jason.

"We're getting close." Bill looked tired and a little anxious. She knew he had been up many nights, talking and planning with Nerit and Travis. "We'll deal with this and keep to the initial plan unless things change."

She pulled her long dark hair up into a knot on top of her head. "I'm really sick and tired of these fuckers scaring us shitless."

"Truer words were never spoken." Bill chortled, but there was something off in the sound.

Jenni finished with her hair and studied him curiously. "You got a bad feeling?"

"Woke up with it in my gut," Bill admitted. "You, too, huh?"

"Yeah. Things feel off." She thought of the long, sweet kisses she had shared with Juan before she left. It was as if they were sharing their last kisses. The thought of him made her stomach twist a little more. She missed him and wanted to crawl into bed with him and feel his warm, strong arms around her.

"We're coming up on it," Ed announced.

Jenni steadied herself, holding on to the back of her seat. Her rifle held tightly in one hand, she looked ahead intently.

They were rescuing what remained of a family—a woman and her three teenagers: one boy and two girls. The grandmother had died of a bite and the kids had had to put her zombified remains down. Until recently, they had been living off their grandmother's preserves, but were now out of food.

The family's truck was broken down. They had tried to walk to the neighbors' in search of supplies, but were chased back by zombies. The rescue team expected to find at least half a dozen zombies in the area.

The narrow dirt road unwound to reveal the trailer tucked in a clearing back from the road. The manufactured home had had at least two additions built onto it. All the windows appeared to be boarded up, but the front door was hanging from its hinges. The muddied driveway revealed tire tracks. A group of zombies was gathered beneath a tree, growling and clawing at the trunk.

"This isn't good," Bill said.

"Damn," Jenni said.

Behind Jenni, her teammates had gotten to their feet and were releasing the safeties on their weapons.

"Jenni, go up top," Bill said just as a half dozen zombies turned and rushed the bus.

Climbing onto the back of the seat, Jenni shoved open the hatch in the top of the bus. Bill helped her get onto the roof. Hot, grainy wind greeted her as she took a seat on the scorching metal roof. Bill handed up her rifle as the bus slowed.

The zombies were closing fast, screeching, growling, clawed hands outstretched. They were more inhuman looking than ever. The elements definitely were having an impact on them. Their skin was dark gray, their hair matted and wild, their faces shrunken. The ones that were nearly whole were still startlingly fast.

Jenni took down the one at the front of the pack. Its momentum carried it into the side of the bus, which it hit with a wet sound. She fired at another zombie. It tumbled to the ground in a jumble of filthy skirts and lace.

Ah, damn, Jenni thought as the image registered. *It was a bride.*

Jenni wiped the thought away. She took aim at another zombie, this one a male. It reached the bus and banged on the driver's window. Startled, Ed jerked the wheel, and the bus swerved sharply. Jenni pitched to one side, losing her shot. Her long braid unfurled as she gripped the edge of the roof. Her rifle tumbled away, but the strap over her shoulder kept it from falling off. Staring down, she saw a zombie gazing back up at her. Horrified, she knew what was about to happen.

The zombie grabbed her hair and pulled.

She managed to hook her feet on the edge of the hatch and clung desperately to the edge of the roof.

"Goddammit, Ed!" Bill shouted inside the bus.

Jenni pushed herself back from the side of the bus; the pain from her hair made her gasp. Gripping the braid, she tried hard to wrestle free, but the zombie was holding tight. She heard a window slide open beneath her, then a shout, followed by two gunshots. The pull on her hair vanished. Grabbing her rifle, she steadied herself as the bus came to a stop. She took aim at the other zombies heading toward them.

Gunfire from within the bus chorused with her shots. One by one, the zombies fell. Nearby, a few persistent ones kept jumping up and down, reaching toward the branches of the tree. Now that the bus was close enough, Jenni could see an emaciated young woman and a boy hardly older than Jason clinging to the trunk and branches.

Jenni efficiently took out the zombies at the base of the tree. "We need to move fast," she said, leaning over to speak to Bill. With a start, she noticed blood splattered all over the interior. Then she saw the body of a woman—a newcomer whose name Jenni kept forgetting—slumped over a seat. She had been shot in the head. It took Jenni another moment to realize that the woman's hand was freshly bitten.

"She was trying to shoot the one that had your hair. She had pulled the window down to get a clear shot and it bit her." Bill met Jenni's eyes as he answered her unspoken question.

Jenni blinked back tears. "We need to get the kids out of the tree."

Ed pulled the bus close to the tree, trying not to get cornered up against the trailer or the forest. The boy scrambled out onto a branch.

"Jump down!" Jenni ordered, waving to him.

"They got my sister and mom!"

"The zombies?"

"No, some guys! They came and kicked in our door and grabbed my mom and sister. I was in the back room with Annie and we went out through the window."

"Jump!"

The boy motioned to his sister, who shook her head, clinging desperately to the trunk of the tree.

"Annie, c'mon," the boy said.

She violently shook her head again. "Daniel, I'm scared!"

"Jump, now," Jenni ordered.

"Annie, please come with me," Daniel insisted.

The girl once more shook her head, terror in her eyes.

Jenni fastened her gaze on the girl and felt sick to her stomach. Was this the way she looked when Katie had first seen her, shell-shocked and dazed? If so, too damn bad. "Annie, get your fuckin' ass down here now! Otherwise, you're gonna have to sit in that damn tree until the zombies figure out how to climb or you pass out and fall. Now, if you want to die that way, be my guest, but I am taking your brother and we're getting the hell outta here."

Trembling, Annie sluggishly crawled out onto the thick limb until she reached her brother. With infinite care, Daniel helped lower her to the top of the bus, then dropped down beside her.

Jenni nearly retched at the utter reek of them. "Daniel, the men who came here . . . Why did they leave you in the tree?"

The girl disappeared through the hatch into the bus as Bill gently helped her down.

The boy rubbed his nose with a shaking hand. "I don't know. They kept trying to get us down, saying all sorts of sick shit. But we kept climbing higher. I knew we couldn't make a run for it with the zombies around. Anyway, they were even telling me stuff . . . about . . . you know . . . doing me in the . . ." The boy took a breath. "Anyway, one of the guys—one of the ones in the truck—started yelling about a gun store and they all just went crazy. They told me and Annie that they would come back for us later if the zombies didn't get us first."

"Bill, did you hear?"

"I heard, Jenni. It's working," Bill answered, gazing at them through the hatch.

Jenni and Daniel scooted down into the bus just as Ed slammed the back door shut. The woman who had tried to save her now lay with the zombies on the cold, muddy ground.

"Son, how many trucks?" Bill asked.

"Three," Daniel answered. "Those guys were really fucking scary."

His sister sat in a seat nearby, wrapped in a light blanket and shaking uncontrollably. "Daniel, we have to get our mom and sister."

"Ed, call it in," Bill ordered. "Nerit was right. It's going down today."

They had deliberately used back roads that morning. In all likelihood, they had just missed the bandits on the main roads.

"How long ago did they leave?" Bill asked.

"Thirty minutes, maybe." Daniel was shaking violently from nerves.

"Let them know, Ed," Bill said.

"Taking care of it." Ed turned the bus around and headed back down the road.

Jenni held tight to the pole near the front door.
It was time.

2.
Four, Three

In the communication center, Nerit's eyes narrowed when the first report came in from Ken at her old hunting store. The sound of his voice made her go cold inside. She tucked away her emotions as Katarina let out a swear word.

Peggy, who was manning the center, looked up at Nerit worriedly.

"Everything going as planned here. But, you know, you can't help but feel the ghosts," Ken's voice said.

Katarina lifted an eyebrow.

"You know what to do, Katarina" Nerit said.

"On my way." Katarina strode out of the communication hub.

Peggy chewed on her bottom lip, her hands trembling.

"What is the status on the Sadler farm?" Nerit asked.

"Curtis's team has them and they are almost back. That one was easy. There were no zombies around when they arrived," Peggy answered. "I wonder if they just ran out of food and lied about the zombies."

Nerit slightly shrugged. "It doesn't matter. A successful rescue is good enough for me. Now for everything else to go just as well."

Thirty minutes later . . .

"We've reached our target and all is quiet except for the undead. We have two missing, maybe carried off by the baddies. We saw three zombies running on down the road. I swear one of them had a shopping bag," Ed's voice said over the radio.

Curtis looked up from his seat in the corner. He had joined them once his team was safely back from their mission. "Nerit?"

"The bandits got two of the people we were rescuing, but we

saved two others. Three of the bandits' vehicles are heading toward Katie and Travis," Nerit translated.

"Are you sure we can do this?"

"Of course," Nerit answered.

There was a coldness in her voice that terrified Curtis. She could see it in his eyes. Sometimes she wondered if he understood what it meant to protect the fort. Certain things had to be done that not everyone might agree with, but opinions did not matter. Safety did—the protection of the all. The individual be damned.

"Peggy, make sure everyone is in position," Nerit said firmly.

Peggy turned her attention to the communication center, her brow furrowed as she listened to the incoming responses. "Nerit? Old Man Watson wants a gun. He says, and I quote, that he fought in WW Two and that if he took out the Japs, he can take out some punks." She sounded annoyed and amused at the same time.

"Give him one. Put him on the third floor," Nerit answered.

"Nerit, he's an old guy," Curtis said in protest. "You can't expect him—"

"Why not?" Nerit regarded him coolly. "I'm no spring chicken."

Curtis gave a weary laugh. "Yeah, true, but—"

"Give him a gun and plenty of ammunition, Curtis. Make sure he understands he has to stay behind the curtains." Nerit gave him a look that silenced his protests and only reinforced his fear of her.

Good.

He needed to be afraid.

She walked briskly out of the room, ignoring the dull ache in her hip. It was bothersome, but she wouldn't let it slow her down. She could be extraordinarily strong when she had to be. It wasn't uncommon for her to ignore discomfort and push her body to get things done. Later she would allow herself to feel pain, once they had won and she was behind closed doors.

Calhoun emerged from the shadows, flipping on his video camera and aiming it at her face. The red light blinked at her.

"The queen of the Amazons is in full battle mode. There is a look of death in her eyes and she is—" He faltered as she stared into the camera. "—kinda hot."

Nerit burst out laughing and patted Calhoun's shoulder as she passed him.

"She walks confidently, preparing to amass the defenders of this illegally built fort. The mayor has yet to explain himself and release an accurate accounting of how much taxpayer money was used in its construction. Meanwhile . . ."

Nerit turned and gave Calhoun a look. He stared, suddenly silent.

"Yes, Your Majesty?"

"It's time for you to turn off the camera and do what you're supposed to," Nerit said.

Calhoun dramatically sighed, then tucked it away in his backpack. "You're a mean old bitch."

"I haven't pitched you over the wall yet."

"Are you the one pitching people over the wall?"

"Would you be surprised if I was?"

Calhoun considered this, rubbing his grizzled chin. "Nope."

Nerit shrugged. "Just get to your position."

"Wanna go out?'

"No."

"Have sex?"

"Definitely not." Nerit smirked and walked away.

"Damn Amazons."

Jenni hit the ground running. Already the growing humidity was filling her lungs, making her feel slow and sluggish. The day was definitely going to be hot and muggy. Behind her the bus was idling, and about half a mile beyond the bus, a large crowd of zombies was coming.

The high school they had pulled up in front of was very small, very modern, and locked up tight as a drum. There was no response when they tried to contact the school by CB, but they had seen someone standing on the roof, watching their approach. Jenni was taking a chance it was one of the people they were looking for. Bill, Ed, and the others were covering her.

Racing up the steep slope at the back of the school, she ran to a set of double doors and banged on them.

"Open up! It's the rescue team from the fort!"

A woman's voice said from the other side, "We're not opening up unless we know you're not with the assholes who were here before."

"Look, I'm from the goddamn fort and there is a crowd of very dead townspeople on its way here right now, so get the fuck out of there or we're leaving you!"

The door opened slightly; through the gap Jenni could see the thick chain that kept it partially locked. A large woman with mousy brown hair looked at her for a long second.

"There were these guys—"

"No freaking time. We've gotta leave now," Jenni said urgently. "I am not going to wait out here and get eaten by zombies while you make up your damn mind!"

Jenni turned and ran down the hill, her lungs burning, her eyes on the swiftly approaching undead. To her relief, she heard the clattering of the chain and then footsteps behind her.

"But we need to get our—," someone started to protest.

"No time!" Jenni pointed at the zombies.

There were no more protests.

She clambered onto the bus. The nurse, her kids, and the rest of the surviving students and teachers piled in after her. They were amazingly clean and looked well fed. For a moment, they stared in shock at the two scraggly, skinny survivors the team had rescued earlier.

"Sit down," Jenni ordered.

They obeyed.

Ed shifted gears. The bus lurched forward.

"So, on the third day?" Jenni asked, picking up the thread of their earlier conversation.

"Oh, yeah. So on the third day, the lady walks by the parrot in the doorway of the pet shop and it says again, 'Hey, lady!' And she says, 'What?' all angry, because she knows what's coming." Ed drove swiftly down the drive as the zombies rounded the corner behind them. "And the bird says, 'You're damn ugly.' The woman marches into the shop and says to the owner, 'I'm going to kill your bird and sue your pants off. Your parrot tells me that I'm damn ugly every day.' And the owner says, 'Lady, I'll take care of the parrot. You don't have to do anything crazy.' So she leaves and the bird just laughs." Ed swung the bus around the front of the building and creamed a zombie loitering in the road. "Fourth day comes along. The lady passes the parrot and it says, 'Hey, lady!' And she is righteously pissed off and says, 'What?' And it says, 'You know.' " Ed grinned at Jenni.

"You're so lame, Ed." Jenni rolled her eyes.

Ed shrugged and the minibus lurched back onto the country road, the zombies in hot pursuit.

Travis pressed the button on the mouthpiece. "Is it just me or are the shadows longer in the summer?"

Peggy's voice crackled back. "I hate this damn hot weather."

"It's putting us in a bad mood, too," Travis sighed as he understood her code.

More trouble was coming.

"Still pacing us," Lenore said from the backseat. "I keep seeing flashes of light off the windshield."

"Fort's in sight," Katie said as they crested a hill. The towering hotel loomed in the distance.

"If they're gonna make a move, it should be now," Ken said, looking as strained as they all felt.

The minivan passed the Hummer as planned. Katie watched the vehicle take the lead with a mixture of relief and fear. Now their job was to protect the ammunition and guns.

"They're making their move!" Lenore shouted, and Katie glanced into the rearview mirror to see the vehicle that had been tailing them suddenly come roaring into view.

The CB radio crackled again. "About those shadows." Peggy's voice was trembling. "Four more are heading in from the north."

Katie's hands gripped the steering wheel even more tightly as the minivan and Hummer accelerated to top speed.

Behind her, a mud-covered truck came barreling down the road.

3.
Two

From her bird's-eye view on top of city hall, Nerit watched it all happen with a strange sense of pride.

The minivan and Hummer split up the second they reached the town. The minivan took a predetermined course that would eventually lead it straight to the fort gates. As expected, the bandits in the beat-up green truck followed. The three trucks racing into Ashley Oaks from the north also changed course, trying to cut off the minivan.

"They're talking to each other," Nerit said into her headset. "Find their frequency." She adored Calhoun for rigging up a hands-free system for her. He might be insane, but he was a wizard with electronics.

"On it," Peggy answered.

Next to Nerit, Juan was crouched down, alternately fidgeting with his gun and with the microphone Calhoun had set him up with. He looked nervous and worried.

The Hummer whipped around a corner. It was now heading directly toward the bandits' trucks on the north end of town to intercept.

The minivan took another turn, keeping just ahead of the truck pursuing it. Below Nerit, the gate was already slowly yawning open. The minivan slowed as it neared the lock and the battered, mud-covered truck accelerated. The distance between the two vehicles closed rapidly.

"Nerit?" Juan asked uncertainly.

"Katarina's on it," Nerit assured him.

Then through her binoculars, she saw the windshield of the bandit truck explode into shards of glass. The vehicle veered off the street, crashing through a storefront and plowing into the building, disappearing out of sight.

"Shit."

Nerit smiled proudly. "I trained Katarina well."

Juan was clearly impressed.

The minivan slid safely into the first lock of the entrance. The gate slid closed behind it.

"Objective one accomplished," Nerit said with satisfaction.

She watched as the Hummer continued on its mission.

Katie listened to Peggy's voice, her stomach tightening. "Turn on Madison." Travis was gripping the dashboard with both hands, watching the road anxiously. Behind him, Lenore and Ken were armed and ready. Katie twirled the steering wheel and the Hummer ripped around the corner, nearly cutting off a bandit truck as it headed down Madison. There was a great crash as the truck swerved to avoid the collision and barreled into a lamppost, crumpling the front like an accordion. Glancing into the rearview mirror, Katie watched the last two bandit trucks—a big white 4x4 and a smaller blue one—veer around the accident and keep coming.

"Just like Dallas traffic," Travis observed with a lopsided grin.

Katie turned sharply down another side street. A lot of the downtown streets were narrow red-bricked affairs that ran in weird directions—some were diagonal and others made big loops. Nerit and Katie had spent hours studying a map of the town. It had been hard, boring work, but it was paying off in a big way now. Katie knew where she was going. The bandits did not.

Lenore sat silently, watching out the back window. Her jaw

was set and her dark eyes were blazing. "All ugly, crazy white men."

Ken glanced back, into the truck that was right on their tail. "I may be hard up for a man, but not *that* hard up."

Lenore high-fived Ken. "Amen."

Katie didn't have time to study the men behind them. She was busy trying to make sure they didn't die as they drew the bandits away from the minivan. She whipped the Hummer around another corner. The minivan needed to get into the second lock before the Hummer could make its run for safety.

Peggy's voice came through the static. "Hate to say this, but shadow number five has arrived. It's a huge-ass 4x4 black truck."

"Where is it?" Travis asked.

"Heading straight up Main Street," Peggy answered.

"Let's go play chicken," Katie said with an evil grin.

"Damn," Ken sighed. "I'm going to die without ever getting laid again."

Katarina lay perfectly still on top of the newspaper building. Covered in a bedsheet spray-painted to look like the roof, she blended in perfectly. Her sniper rifle was poised, ready, and warm in her grip. Her eye was just as cold and just as deadly. Her long hair was braided down her back. The wind whistled in her ears.

"We have a change in plans. Another truck has arrived," Nerit's voice said in her earpiece.

"Same dance as before?" Katarina asked.

"No. Let Katie play with them, and then we're going to drop our surprise on them. Then we continue as planned."

"My dance card has empty slots," Katarina answered into her headset.

"I have a feeling they'll be filled."

Katarina smiled and watched the spread of road before the gates.

* * *

Katie led her pursuers down Main Street, toward the new arrival. The big black 4x4 didn't see the Hummer coming straight for it until it crested the hill.

"Shit," Travis muttered.

The oncoming black truck swerved sharply to the left and clipped a streetlamp. It shimmied, then came to a stop. The two bandit vehicles behind Katie slammed on their brakes and nearly piled up.

Taking advantage of losing the three trucks, Katie wrenched the H2's wheel to the left and turned down a side street. "Fuck the gate. It's getting too crowded out here and I'm low on fuel. Let's ditch the Hummer."

"I am all for that," Lenore agreed.

"We're switching to Plan B. We're taking the side door," Travis said into the mouthpiece as the Hummer roared up to the hotel.

"Understood," Peggy answered. "I'll let them know you have a delivery."

The Hummer drew up to the service entrance of the hotel. As the car stopped, the loading dock's heavy iron door slid open and two guards stepped out. Jumping out of the car, Katie, Travis, Lenore, and Ken made a run for safety. The guards watched the road, weapons poised.

"Hurry up!" Bill was just inside, waving at them.

Travis scrambled onto the dock, then turned to pull Katie up. She quickly got to her feet and spun around to make sure Ken and Lenore were following. Ken was right behind her; he easily climbed onto the dock.

"Lenore, hurry!" Ken screamed.

"I'm coming. I'm coming. Hold on!" Lenore, being a bigger girl, huffed behind the rest. She was almost to the loading dock when the white truck came squealing into view.

"Lenore!" Ken sounded frantic and almost jumped back into the street. Travis barely caught him in time.

With seamless grace, Lenore stopped running, turned, and

loosed an arrow from her bow. The shaft drilled into the front tire. The tire blew and the truck slammed into the back of the fort's Hummer. The screech of metal and the smell of burnt rubber filled the air, accompanied by a metallic groan as the H2 was shoved a few feet toward the loading dock. Lenore jumped out of the way.

A huge, disgustingly dirty man staggered out of the truck, bleeding fiercely from a wound on his forehead. Lenore seemed to use this as a target. The man fell back, the end of the arrow protruding from between his eyes. The two men still in the truck ducked down. Lenore started to run again. The guards on the loading dock moved into a better position to fire at the bandits, covering Lenore.

Katie shouted, "Hurry, Lenore!"

Lenore hauled herself up onto the loading dock.

"White people," she muttered, slipping past Katie. "Always screaming about something."

Ken threw his arms around her. "Girlfriend, you scared me shitless!"

"Get off me!" Lenore growled.

"Get inside!" Travis ordered. "Let's not wait for them to find their guns."

As soon as everyone was inside, the doors were sealed shut.

Nerit watched as the last two bandit trucks—a black one and small blue one—finally found their way down the road. They were moving a little more cautiously than they had been. Their leader was wising up. Peggy hadn't been able to find the frequency they were using to communicate. It didn't matter anymore—Nerit was sure her opponent had ordered radio silence. She could see someone in the black truck motioning to the others.

The trucks were about ten feet from the gate when Juan gave the signal. The crane, which had been stationed overhead early that morning, dropped a small storage unit onto the bandits' vehicles. Nerit smiled with satisfaction as it crashed down, clipping the front end of the blue truck and sending the hood flying. The big black truck jackknifed across the road.

All went silent below.

Juan clutched his binoculars tight. "We're winning, right, Nerit?

"We're not planning to win."

Juan frowned. "I don't understand."

"We're going to make them fear us," Nerit answered with a cold smile. "And that is far more effective."

4.
One

"It's the Boyds," Curtis said to Nerit and Juan. He was watching the video feed from the cameras Calhoun had rigged up on the walls. Four small black-and-white TVs were serving as monitors. "Drug-smuggling, raping, murdering assholes. The whole family has been the bane of this county for more than a century. Half of them are in jail. Or at least they were."

The three of them were hidden by a false front Juan had built on top of city hall that was dubbed "the eagle's nest." They could see quite well, but it was hard to see them from below. Nerit watched the street through the scope of her sniper rifle.

"I bet they went and busted Martin out," Curtis went on. "He was up for murdering his ex-girlfriend and her husband. He didn't take to her dumping him and marrying someone else while he was in jail."

Juan took a deep breath. "Nerit, I don't know if I can—"

"You're a strong man, Juan De La Torre. You just have never faced this sort of situation before. I have faced similar situations, so I will guide you. They will not respond to an old woman with an Israeli accent, but they will listen to a strong male voice with a good West Texas accent." She smiled, trying to encourage him.

Juan rubbed his face. "Okay, you have a point."

"What are they doing?" Travis asked as he joined them, breathless from running. Katie was right behind him.

"Sitting there." Nerit continued to watch, her mind flipping through all the scenarios and outcomes that could occur. "They came this far. They will not want to leave empty-handed. Juan, say what I say." She spoke swiftly, never letting her gaze leave the view below. So far, they had the situation under control. She hoped they could maintain the upper hand, but she was not about to underestimate her enemy.

Juan pressed down on the button Calhoun had told him would make the microphone work. "Attention, trespassers. You are to leave immediately."

On the small monitors set up in the eagle's nest, Curtis watched a man in the black truck flip off the fort. "Nice answer. I hate these guys."

Nerit gave Juan his next speech. He listened, then spoke into the mic. "We know of your acts of violence against others and will not tolerate your presence. You must leave immediately." He hesitated, then ad-libbed, "Because your shit doesn't fly around here."

Katie chuckled and Nerit nodded. She appreciated his improvisation. It made him sound more in control.

Curtis frowned as the men inside the trucks talked to one another. A few flipped off the fort again.

Calhoun slid into the now cramped eagle's nest and fiddled with the equipment he had set up. "If I had more time, I could have gotten the sound perfect. The equipment I had to work with was ridiculous. Do you realize how hard it was to—?"

Nerit put her hand over his mouth.

Faintly, the microphones hidden along the wall picked up the bandits' voices shouting out insults.

Finally, a large bald man stepped out of the black truck. Clad in jeans and a black shirt, he didn't look quite as ratty as the other men they had seen. Cupping his hands to his mouth, he shouted, "We're here for food and supplies! You attacked us."

"Tell him you want to speak to their leader," Nerit said to

Juan. The man's voice sounded hesitant and not like a man in control.

"That's bullshit," Juan replied. "I want to talk to your leader."

"I am the leader," the bald man answered.

"Katarina," Nerit said softly into her mouthpiece.

The man went down, screaming, gripping his shattered knee.

Juan blinked.

"He's not the leader," Nerit explained.

"Oh." Juan hesitated, pushed the button, and then said, "I said your leader, not his girlfriend."

Curtis laughed.

Calhoun snorted and said, "Yeah, damn aliens. They have ugly-ass women."

After a few minutes, the doors opened on the opposite side of the truck and a few men got out. The bandits from the smaller blue truck also stepped out onto the street. All were armed. The last to appear was a tall, almost handsome man clad in jeans and a Dallas Cowboys jersey. He was dragging a girl with him, holding a gun firmly pressed to her temple. The girl looked to be around sixteen. Her face was battered and swollen, and her arms and legs were covered in bruises and cuts.

"Enough bullshit. We want guns, ammo, and enough food to get us through the winter, or I'm going to kill this little girl!" the man shouted.

"That's Martin Boyd, goddammit. They busted him out of prison. He'll do it. He'll kill her," Curtis said.

"No, he won't," Nerit answered, then said into her mouthpiece. "Katarina."

"High or low," Katarina's voice said, small and tinny.

"Low," Nerit said regretfully after a pause. "It will be merciful. We can't save her anyway."

On the monitor, Martin Boyd was jerking the girl about by her hair, making a good show. Suddenly her head jerked back and blood splattered his face. Startled, Martin froze for a moment, staring at the now very dead young woman while her blood dripped from his startled features. Then, with a wordless exclamation, he dropped her and stepped back. The men around him immediately took cover, but Martin remained in the open.

Katie covered her face with her hands and turned away.

Curtis jerked his head toward Nerit. "What the fuck?"

"It's a better fate than the one they would have dished out," Travis said in an agonized voice.

"We don't kill innocent people," Juan protested, then hesitated, before adding, "do we?"

Martin called out, "Oh, so you'll kill someone who doesn't mean shit to you, huh? Then what about one of your own?"

Nerit arched her eyebrow at this unexpected announcement, then realized what was about to happen.

Travis later thought he shouldn't have been surprised when a large burly man dragged Shane out of the back of the camper. He should have known that the bastard was too mean to die at the hands of the zombies. He wondered if Shane had sought out the bandits, intending to join them. Obviously things hadn't worked out that way. The once-arrogant asshole was wearing a ragged dress. Makeup had been smeared all over his face. He was gagged and his hands were tied with rope. It bothered Travis to no end to see tear marks streaking Shane's face. It was too terrible to bear seeing him treated this way even if he was a bastard.

Beside him, Katie put her head down and whispered, "Oh, God."

"I got one of your boys right here! He's a pretty thing, don't you think?" Martin grinned and patted Shane's cheek.

Jerking his head away, Shane strained against his captor's hold.

"What did they do to him? What the fuck? That ain't right!" Curtis was horrified.

"Katarina," Nerit said into her headpiece, "take care of it."

Shane struggled to get away, screaming behind his gag. The big guy cuffed him and Shane staggered. He fell to his knees. As he straightened up, his head snapped back as Katarina put him down.

Running his hand over his hair, Travis studied the monitors with the rest of the group. Martin Boyd was gazing up at the fort with a stunned expression on his face.

"This is what you need to say now," Nerit said to Juan. "Tell him that we have much more to lose than he does, that we have no problem fighting to the death. That we will sacrifice our own to protect the fort. That we have no problem with killing him or his people. Tell him that we cannot be intimidated. Tell him that we have contingencies on contingencies. Tell him that right now, my sniper can blow his fucking head off without blinking and that right now she's not aiming at his head, but his dick."

Juan laughed. "I'm gonna love saying that." And he did, adding his own flair.

On the black-and-white monitors, Travis watched Martin take a step back, his bravado gone. Beneath all the grime, the arrogance, and the wild eyes was a man strung out on drugs and booze and living at the edge of the abyss. For once, he was not in control and he shifted uneasily on his feet.

"Now, let's put the cherry on top," Nerit said. "Signal Jason."

On top of city hall, a camouflage sheet was thrown off, revealing the huge slingshot. The teenagers and Roger quickly loaded it with a homemade Molotov cocktail. The kids had been practicing for weeks, so when their first shot hit the truck pinned by the storage container and it burst into flames, Travis wasn't really surprised.

The bandits panicked. Through the smoke, they could be seen scrambling into their trucks.

It was then that the minibus flew down Main Street with zombies flowing behind it like a river. Ed was leading the zombie horde like the pied piper. The smoke from the burning truck concealed the minibus and the zombies from the bandits until it was too late.

The minibus turned in through the quickly opening gate. Behind it, the zombies, encountering the living bandits, fell on them with gusto. They ripped at Shane's body, the guy Katarina had shot in the knee, and the body of the dead girl. They lay siege to the remaining truck, beating on it, desperate to feast on those within. The gates closed quickly and quietly behind the minibus. Not one zombie slipped in with it. They were too intent on the bandits.

When the black truck sped away, the fresher, stronger zombies raced behind it.

Left in the street outside the fort's main gate was one burning truck, a few staggering zombies, and the dead.

Silence filled the eagle's nest. They had won. But to do that, they had gone to a place that was not quite pleasant. No one seemed to be able to look at Nerit. She understood their discomfort and did not take it personally.

Finally she stood and shouldered her sniper rifle.

"That'll teach them to mess with the Amazons," Calhoun said approvingly.

"They're afraid now." Nerit looked at Katie and Travis, then at Juan and Curtis. Calhoun jigged away to the music in his head as Curtis sat in sad silence, his hands over his face, weeping. Katie rested her hand on Travis's shoulder and he kissed her forehead soothingly.

She almost envied Calhoun's joy. She only felt cold inside, remote, and strong.

Katie raised her eyes to regard Nerit with respect. "We did the right thing."

Nerit shrugged, then said, "I need a smoke," and walked away.

She could hear people cheering throughout the fort as she made her way to a quiet corner where she often sat to enjoy a nice leisurely smoke. The cigarette was lit and dangling from her fingers when Katarina sat down across from her a few minutes later. In silence, Nerit offered her a cigarette. The younger woman took it. Katarina lit up and took a drag.

They looked at each other and said nothing, but something powerful was exchanged in their gaze. They would always be the ones to do what was right, no matter how hard that was.

After two cigarettes, Katarina finally spoke. "I should have shot his dick off."

Both women laughed.

5.
Aftermath

Bill was weary, bone weary. Every muscle in his back was cramping. If it was possible, even his eyes were cramped. Rubbing his grainy eyes, he sat on top of city hall. These days, most people hung out on the hotel's roof, with its gazebo, pool, and nice patio furniture. Personally, he still preferred city hall, where he now sat in a plastic chair, staring out over the fort.

He could hear sounds of the party in full swing up on the top of the hotel. The music and laughter were loud. People were ecstatic at their victory. He wished he was.

Popping open another beer, he took a swig. Nearby, Katarina was on patrol. She was so silent, he barely noticed her. Well, that wasn't true—when they were not working, he definitely noticed her. She was pretty in a sort of rough way. Her face was lean, her cheek bones high. Her eyes were very keen and had fine lines around them. What was truly beautiful about her was her long, thick red hair that she always kept braided. He had considered asking her out, but because he wasn't sure what that meant in this dead world, he just gave up.

Bill sighed.

Right now, he hated his job.

A lot of people had thought it was all over when the bandits hightailed it out of town. While they celebrated, Bill, Curtis, and a small group of armed guards had gone out through the loading dock door and grabbed one of the surviving bandits. It had been easy to grab him since he had been banging on the door, crying hysterically. The two survivors from the vehicle that had chased Travis's team tried to shoot their way out of town. Out of ammo and his partner being eaten by the zombies, the last man standing had run back to the fort.

It had been Clyde Pipkin. Bill knew him. At twenty-two, Clyde was the youngest of a family of crooks that hung out with the Boyds. The Pipkin Auto Repair Shop was nefarious for underhanded dealings and for scamming unlucky travelers who broke down in the county. Though the Boyds were the main crime family in a three-county spread, the Pipkins were tied to the Boyds by marriage and association.

Clyde smelled—of sweat, dirt, and alcohol. His red-rimmed eyes and haggard expression spoke of hard-core drug use. He was unshaven and pale. His pupils were dilated and his nose raw.

He cried for nearly an hour, all through his capture, through being tied to a chair and left to come down from his most recent high.

Once he was calm, his story came out in angry, then desperate answers to their questions.

When the zombie plague hit, the Boyds rounded up their buddies and went on a crime spree. The first few days were full of looting, raping, revenge murders, and zombie hunting. The Boyds took full advantage of the situation. Clyde wept again when he said his mama and girlfriend had been eaten, but admitted that the gang had not attempted to protect their womenfolk, just gathered up all male children and headed off in a caravan of death.

They picked up women survivors along the way, used them until they were lost to the zombies or died. Sometimes they played games with the women, dangling them off a rooftop over crazed zombies. Sometimes the women were bitten and they tied them down until they died. Clyde swore up and down that he had nothing to do with it, but Bill had seen all the classic symptoms of a man who was lying.

The bandits lived in a blur of violence, drugs, and alcohol.

The new, violent, deadly world was to their liking at first. They used the fort's own contact with survivors to figure out where the survivors were located, then swoop in if there was any indication of women or food. Through his tears, Clyde described the ruse that had often worked: The men would hold a woman or young girl at gunpoint and threaten to kill her if the bandits were not given supplies. It got the survivors to open up their safe havens.

Despite their bloodthirsty nature, the bandits had slowly dwindled in numbers, thanks to infighting, zombies, and confrontations with armed survivors. From the sound of it, most of them had been inebriated or high through most of the first months.

For a long time, the bandits had avoided the fort out of fear of a military presence. It was only later that they realized the fort was just civilians. Once the hot weather blew in, they began scavenging for food. Then they realized that the fort they had been ignoring had claimed the food before they arrived. They had done some drunken hunting to sustain themselves, but eventually, their desire for guns and food had pushed them toward the fort.

Bill took a long drink and stared out toward the hills.

How long the bandits had watched, Clyde wasn't sure. But their leader, Martin Boyd, had been smart and sober enough to herd some zombies down to the fort to see what happened. He had put the gun store under constant watch. Martin had been sure that the people in the fort would return to the hunting store when they felt threatened enough by the bandits and zombies. He had monitored enough of the conversations between the fort and Ralph to know of its importance.

Bill rubbed his brow and sighed.

The survivors in the fort had been so terrified of the bandits. The precautions taken had been extraordinary. Every inch of the fort had been scrutinized. Extra spears had been made. They had attached barbwire along the tops of the walls. Contingency plans were made for every possibility they could think of. Everyone had been gripped with paranoia. Even the children had been instructed in protecting themselves. One of the worst images in his mind was of Peggy's son wielding one of their makeshift spears. Peggy had to take it away from him before he stabbed someone.

Taking a long swig of his beer, Bill sat back in the plastic chair and let the warm breeze flow over him.

The bandits had been routed, but they were nothing more than drug-addled hoodlums. What if there were more dangerous and clever people out there? That thought terrified him. Could they make the fort safe enough to withstand anything? He looked over the street, wondering. There were no lights to be seen anywhere but the fort. The world was so black and empty, the stars shone with unequaled brilliance above.

How long the fort's lights would stay on was anyone's guess. So far it was good, but there were plenty of generators on standby. Hopefully things would remain as they were for the fall and winter.

He was glad that his wife, Doreen, had not lived to see this day. She had fought the cancer diligently, but now he was glad she had lost that battle. It would have been sheer hell to see her endure this.

When they finished interrogating Clyde, they'd pushed him out the loading dock. The young man had been sobbing again, begging to be allowed to stay. Curtis had handed him a spear and sent him on his way. Clyde had taken only a few steps before Katarina ended his life. Even though Bill had seen it coming, he flinched.

He lifted the beer to his lips and took another long drink. He was thinner now, but his beer belly persisted. Rosie was planning on brewing her own beer, so chances were it was not going away once the local supply was used up.

Katarina walked up to him, her sniper rifle cradled in her arms. "Shouldn't you go to your room to sleep? Or maybe go up to the party?"

"Ever think we missed something important?"

She lifted an eyebrow, then shrugged. "No."

Bill frowned. "How can you be so sure?"

"Well," Katarina said, kneeling down. "We have all worked pretty damn hard to do everything we can do. At this point, we have covered everything possible. But—" She shrugged again. "—something impossible may happen. We just deal with it as it comes. So I don't worry about it."

With a slow sigh, Bill reached down to his side for another beer. "The bandits sure weren't the enemies we anticipated, eh?"

"Always go with the worst-case scenario," Katarina answered.

"Nerit's advice?"

Katarina nodded.

Bill popped open a fresh can, then said, "Well, then, I guess we're doing okay, considering what has gone down."

"We're alive," she agreed. "That's saying a lot."

With a laugh, Bill could only agree. "Yeah. Yeah, it is." He stood up, his knees creaking. "I'm going to take this and go to bed now."

"Good night, Bill." Katarina moved on, her gaze returning to the perimeter.

He trudged down the stairs, all at once eager to sleep and not deal with reality. Maybe . . . if he was lucky . . . he would dream of Doreen and their wonderful day in Venice. . . .

And maybe, just this once time, he wouldn't dream of everyone around him turning into zombies chasing him and Doreen into the ocean.

That would be nice, he thought. Very nice.

6.
Time of the Dead

Katarina watched the zombies beating against the wall. She knew that in the morning, they would be destroyed and the area around the fort cleared. She would be asleep by then, and that was fine with her. She had done enough killing to last her for a while.

The deadlands beyond the fort were dark and full of mystery. She had no idea what lurked out there and she wasn't sure she wanted to know. There was enough weirdness in her world as it was. She wasn't sure when she'd first become aware of the ghost. At first, she'd thought she was dreaming. But recently she had overhead other people talking about dreaming of dead ones or thinking they saw them in darkened corners.

Her mother appeared more and more often now. The ghost didn't speak to her, just stood there and glared at her with disapproval. That stern, angry face, so familiar from life, was unchanged in death.

Katarina rubbed her eyes and looked over her shoulder. Her mother stood in the shadows near the doorway.

"You're not really here," Katarina said.

The ghost remained, watching her. Shaking her head, Katarina looked back toward the street and the zombies.

"So, if hell is full and the dead are walking the earth, Mr. Romero, where are their souls?" Maybe she should ask Reverend Thomas. No—or at any rate, not now. She had too much work to do.

"Fuck the dead," she whispered. "This is our world."

· CHAPTER TWENTY ·

1.
The Election

Travis was exhausted, but in good spirits. At first, he had been deeply bothered by the violence the fort had used to defeat their enemy. Yet he could not think of another way they could have won and ensured their continuing safety. It was difficult to accept the brutality of the zombie-infested world he now lived in, but he was acclimating.

Manny was recovering, slowly, but had decided not to run for reelection. With Steven Mann the only other candidate, Travis had had to embrace the inevitable. He might not have wanted to be the fort's leader, but he had already taken on many of the responsibilities of the job. Today, he'd learn if he was going to get the title to go along with those responsibilities.

Heading to the dining room for the debate Steven Mann had insisted on, Travis glanced at the election posters a few people had taped to the walls. "Travis is the MAN! You don't need a Mann!" one read. "Steven Mann—On YOUR Side" read another. A smile flitted across his lips. As he walked, he tucked in his shirt and smoothed back his hair. The lobby was fairly empty. Most of the fort's inhabitants were already in the dining room.

Yolanda stood near the archway with the Reverend Thomas. A radiant smile graced her face and she exuded a quiet peace that Travis found refreshing. Working with Peggy had obviously given her a new purpose and he was glad to see her doing so well.

"Travis, come here!" she ordered.

He obliged her, wondering what she wanted. "Reverend Thomas, good to see you again. Sorry we haven't had much of a chance to talk."

"We'll find time later on, I'm sure," the reverend assured him.

Yolanda scowled as she fussed with the collar of Travis's blue button-down shirt. "Why aren't you wearing a tie?"

"Zombies are roaming the earth. Can't a man do without a tie at times like these?" Reverend Thomas said teasingly.

Yolanda smiled slightly. "A mayor should always look respectable."

"I'm not the mayor," Travis reminded her.

"Yet."

Travis laughed and shook his head. "I swear . . ."

"And in front of the reverend. What would your mama say?" Yolanda chided him.

"Are you going to help me out here?" Travis appealed to Reverend Thomas.

The reverend chuckled and patted his shoulder. "You're doing fine."

Ken and Lenore strolled up. As usual, Ken was smiling brilliantly while Lenore scowled. "I'm voting for you because you're not as stupid as most people," Lenore informed Travis in her usual monotone.

"Uh, thanks," Travis replied, not certain if he had been complimented or not.

With a nod of her head, Lenore walked on, Ken trailing behind her.

"Well, there are two votes." Travis rubbed his jaw. "Let's see how the rest of this goes."

"Good luck, Travis," Yolanda said with a smile.

"I'll be praying for you," Reverend Thomas assured him.

"Thanks. I'm going to need all the help I can get."

Every table in the dining room was packed with people ready to hear the two candidates speak. The buzz of conversation filled

Travis's ears as he wove through the maze of tables and chairs to the front of the room, where a podium and two chairs had been set up. A Texas flag had been hung on the wall behind the chairs.

Katie, Jenni, Nerit, and Juan were sitting at the table in the front. Blanche sat at a nearby table with a few of her husband's supporters while Steven chatted with Manny and Peggy, who were seated at a third table. The soon-to-be-former mayor appeared to be in much better condition than he had been a few days earlier, and Travis was glad to see him.

Leaning over, Travis kissed Katie's cheek. "Wish me luck?"

"Is that so you become mayor or so you don't?" she asked.

"I've decided that I should be mayor," Travis admitted.

"About damn time, dumb-ass," Jenni chided him, grinning.

"You're the man, man," Juan declared.

"You made that poster, huh?" Travis laughed. "Nice play on his name."

Juan shrugged but smiled proudly.

"I think we should start, don't you?" Steven said, walking over with Peggy at his side.

Travis felt a little afraid, but his resolve was firm. He straightened up. Peggy said, "We're flipping a coin to see who gives the first opening statement. Heads or tails?" She pulled a quarter from her pocket and showed it to the two men.

"Heads," Steven said firmly.

Peggy flipped the coin, caught it, and slapped it down on the back of her hand. "Steven, you're up."

Smugly, Steven stepped behind the podium and Travis sat in one of the candidates' chairs. He rubbed his sweaty palms on his jeans, then caught Yolanda's disapproving look and stopped. Turning his attention to Katie, he focused on her serene green eyes and her tender smile of encouragement.

"What I have to say is very important to the future of this so-called fort." Steven Mann was an imposing figure behind the podium. His height, rugged face, and startling blue eyes, matched with his cowboy attire, gave him a definite Texas charm. "As you know, my family was one of the first to settle in this area. This town was named for one of my great-great-grandmothers. We made our money from farming, ranching, and oil. We're Texan through and through."

There was a smattering of applause, and Blanche beamed with pride.

"With my support, this fine hotel was renovated. My money helped finance the reinvigoration of Ashley Oaks. In other words, I have been a force to be reckoned with around these parts." His wide grin and Texas twang gave just the right spark to his words. A few people laughed and clapped.

Travis felt more than a little jealousy as Steven spoke. Travis was beginning to wonder how he could compete with Steven's polished presentation.

"So, when I tell y'all that I believe in Ashley Oaks and its good people and that I am thinking about what is best for all of you, you know I'm telling the truth," Steven said in a firm tone. "In the last few weeks, we have seen the violence that exists outside our walls. We understand that our enemies are not just the dead, but also the living. These are dire times. Which is why I want to tell you that this man—" He turned and pointed to Travis. "—is the right man to be your mayor."

"What?" Blanche gasped.

Startled, Travis turned toward Steven, not sure he was hearing right.

"Travis Buchanan has proven himself to be a strong leader. From the initial construction of the fort to our fight with the bandits, he has proven without a shadow of a doubt that he is the one we should be following. Do I agree with everything he says and does? Not always. But he is building a better future for all of us, and right now, right here, he's your man."

"Steven!" Blanche sprang to her feet.

"I withdraw my candidacy." Steven stepped away from the podium and offered Travis his hand.

"I don't know what to say," Travis said, shaking Steven's hand.

The room erupted into noise as people turned to each other in astonishment.

"Don't fuck up," Steven said simply. "And don't think this means we're friends or that we won't find ourselves on opposite sides in the future. But I didn't build a successful business by being a fool, and I can see that right now, you're the man who needs to be in charge."

Peggy hurried to the podium and raised her hands to quiet the din. "Okay, does anyone else want to run? Anyone?"

Silence filled the room. People turned in their chairs, craning their necks to see if anyone was going to step up.

"Are we still going to vote?" Ed called out.

"We should," Travis said quickly. "And allow write-ins."

Nodding, Peggy loudly explained how to cast the votes while Yolanda and Reverend Thomas took up positions by the ballot boxes.

A little shaken by the turn of events, Travis joined Katie at her table. She took his hand and kissed him.

"That was surprising," Travis said, chuckling.

"He just woke up to the truth," Juan decided.

"His wife is pissed, though," Jenni said, gesturing at the side of the room, where Blanche was speaking forcefully to her husband.

"You're the right man for the job, Travis," Katie said. "Everyone knows that."

Travis nodded, watching the lines forming in front of the ballot boxes. "We'll see."

Manny Reyes cast his vote, then crossed to Travis's side and reached out his hand. Travis quickly stood and shook the former mayor's hand.

"Manny, I want you to know—"

Manny waved his hand, dismissing Travis's concerns. "My time is done. I voted for you because I believe in what Steven said tonight. In fact, we spoke about you earlier today and I had a feeling he would do the right thing." Manny smiled. "I'm out of my depth now. Peggy is right. I'm a politician. You're a leader."

Travis felt a lump forming in his throat, and his voice was thick with emotion when he spoke. "Manny, you're a good man and I will still ask you for advice."

"And I'll give it to you. Whether you want it or not," Manny joked. He hugged Travis, patting his back.

As Manny walked on, Travis slumped down in his chair, and said, "This is one helluva night."

Two hours later, Travis listened as Yolanda revealed the final tally to the waiting crowd. Both relieved and overwhelmed when he heard his name, he stood up and faced the people who believed in him.

"I'll do my best," was all he managed to say before the applause and cheers began.

· CHAPTER TWENTY-ONE ·

1.
The Good Things in Life

Jack, the German shepherd, wanted a cookie.

Lying on the floor, watching Jason on the phone, he wondered if the boy could see his hunger for a cookie.

Jason was talking and talking and talking. . . .

Jack yawned, his sharp teeth flashing in the early morning light. He couldn't understand why his boy was always talking on that stupid phone with Michelle. She lived just a few doors down. Jack could hear her voice without the phone. Girls were loud.

The dog whimpered a little and was rewarded, not with a cookie, but a pat on the head.

Jason finally hung up and walked out of their very untidy bedroom into the small living room. Jack followed, head down and tail limp, trying to show Jason how desperately he needed a cookie. He could hear Jenni and Juan snoring in the other bedroom. He had heard them wrestling a lot last night, but despite his scratching on the door, they had not let him in to play.

Jason leaned down and hugged the dog tight, kissing his head and nuzzling him. Jack forgot his cookie for a moment. He loved his boy very much.

They left their rooms and went to the strange little room Jack wasn't too sure about. There were never cookies in it, and the doors always opened to a different room. He didn't like the way the little room seemed to move. It made his head swim. Still, his boy went in there a lot, and where his boy went, Jack went. With a doggy sigh, he walked into the small room, head down, and endured the strange noises and feelings.

Happily, after they left the nasty little room, they went to the dining room. Jack inhaled the rich fragrance of food and felt much better. As he walked through the room, many people gave him pats on the head and nibbles of bacon. He gave them his biggest grin and wagged his tail extra hard. Surely someone had a cookie.

But no one did.

With a certain amount of grumpiness, he wandered over to his dish and was happy to see a few pieces of bacon and some of that good yellow stuff on top of his kibble. Tucker was already at his bowl. Jack knew that Tucker was very old and that he liked to sleep a lot, but when Tucker was awake, he enjoyed Jack's occasional companionship. The two dogs touched noses briefly in greeting, then went back to eating.

Jack gulped down his food and drank a bit of water. Tucker ambled away, rubbing against the young shepherd as he passed, and they sniffed each other, mostly as a courtesy. Licking his muzzle, Jack trotted away, searching for someone who might give him a cookie.

Glancing back at Jason, he noticed that the boy was holding Michelle's hand under the table. Ah, his human puppy wanted to mate. Well, that was okay, but he really needed to be better about cookies.

Jack strolled down the hallway, looking for one of his many human friends.

"They took my Hummer, and now I have to scrub floors and toilets! My nails are broken and there is not a decent manicurist to be found!" a woman shrieked from the stairwell. "And now Travis is mayor and you're nothing!"

"You need to keep your whoring mouth shut," her mate answered in a terse voice.

"Don't you dare bring up Shane again!"

"So you admit it?"

Jack kept walking. He didn't like that woman. She smelled too clean and kicked him when no one was looking. He wanted a cookie, not a kick.

Around the corner, Jack found the smelly man, who was holding up what he called a camera and talking to himself. Jack thought the man smelled great, like chickens, dogs, and other good stuff. Jack wondered, if he rolled around with Calhoun, would he get that great scent on him? But if he did, Jenni would probably give him a bath, like she had when he had managed to play with a dead squirrel before she caught him.

Jack pushed past Calhoun and into a room where Travis was talking to Pepe's man. Pepe's man had nice leather shoes that Jack wanted to chew on. Peggy was there, too, and Jack looked around for her puppy, who usually had cookies or candies. But to his disappointment, he didn't see the human puppy with goodies in his pockets.

". . . had just received a grant for community development. We were trying very hard to improve the city," Peggy was saying.

"So," Pepe's man said thoughtfully, "most of the city is on septic tanks or rudimentary sewer systems."

"Exactly. We didn't start actually zoning the city until a year ago. It pissed off a lot of people, that's for sure."

Jack stared at Peggy. Surely she would realize he needed a cookie.

Travis sighed. "We're dealing with an archaic system for the hotel and city hall. We'll have to come up with something else soon. This isn't a big city with a network of underground systems. Sewers will become an issue sooner or later."

Pepe's man frowned as he studied something on the desk. "It's better to start planning now. We need to think long term."

Jack walked over to Travis, leaned on his leg, and looked up. *I need a cookie*, he thought intently.

Travis patted his head and scratched him under the chin. No cookie. Jack sighed and left the room.

Entering the lobby, he saw the human puppies playing. They

were running around and screaming, but none of them even smelled like cookies.

Jack sat down and yawned. Katie walked up to him and leaned down to give him kisses. She wasn't nicely smelly like the old man, but she smelled like a mother. He kinda liked it. She hugged him tight, then wandered off.

No cookie.

Jack flopped down and chewed on one paw, studying his surroundings. The human puppies might not smell like cookies, but maybe one of them would get some before too long. Yes, waiting here was his best bet.

Tucker's human mother walked up to him, knelt down carefully, and patted his head. "You're a good boy, Jack." She smiled and rubbed his ears.

As she reached into her pocket, his ears perked up and he thumped his tail, catching a whiff of cookie. With a smile, she slipped him an Oreo, then rose and walked away.

Jack chewed the cookie, grinning to himself.

Now he could enjoy the day.

He stood up, stretched, and headed into the construction site. Maybe if he was lucky, they'd let him sit next to the guard and bark at the loud, stinky, dead things.

Too bad he couldn't roll around on them. . . .

2.
Banishing the Ghosts

Jenni sat up in bed, the covers pooled around her waist, her long hair falling over her bare breasts. Beside her, Juan was sleeping soundly, one arm thrown over his head. She had woken up after a particularly bad nightmare.

She could feel its terrible tendrils still infecting her mind. Staring out the window at the stars, she tried to reclaim her mind and her life from the ghost of her nightmares.

Rubbing her nose, she took a deep breath.

The bandits were beaten. The zombies were held at bay by the walls of the fort. Juan was her lover. Jason was alive and safe. Katie and Travis were happy together. Life as a whole was good . . . until she slept.

Sliding out of the bed, she walked naked to the window and laid her hands on the warm glass. She looked down and saw, in the street, Lloyd staring up at her. His torn face was twisted into a deadly smile. Jenni took a deep breath. She reached deep inside herself and pulled on her strength and love. Her anger was useless against Lloyd.

"Lloyd," she whispered.

Come die with us.

"You are not the beginning or the end of me."

His smile faded.

"I'll die when I choose. And I know one thing for sure—when that happens, I'm not going where you are."

His smile disappeared.

"Fuck you, Lloyd. I don't need you to be afraid of anymore. You're not the biggest or the baddest monster in my world." Jenni flipped him off and turned away from the window.

There were worse things in this world to fear than the stupid ghost of her dead, asshole husband. There were wonderful things to enjoy and love. Jenni didn't have the patience to be afraid anymore, to ruin her new life.

Sliding into the bed, she ran her hand over Juan's chest. He stirred and drew her into his arms. She settled down against the solid realness of his body.

"What's wrong?" he asked, more than half-asleep.

Jenni slung her arm over his waist and draped one leg over his. "Nothing," she answered truthfully. "It just took me a while to figure that out."

Already fading into slumber, Juan kissed her on the forehead.

Jenni soon fell asleep. For the first time in a long time, she wasn't afraid to dream. Lloyd's time was done.

3.
The Time of Beginnings

Katie stared at the little stick, squinting in disbelief. She checked the box again, then sat back on the edge of the bathtub.

Despite all the insanity of their life, despite the dead world and the terror, she and Travis had decided to fully embrace life.

"Travis!" She pulled the rayon robe tighter around her body and held the stick in one hand as she crossed her legs.

The door opened and he peered in at her. Judging by his bleary eyes and mussy hair, he had fallen asleep while she showered. He was clad only in pajama bottoms.

She held up her announcement and he padded into the bathroom to squint at it. It took a few seconds for it to register.

"For real?"

Katie lifted her eyebrows and nodded. "Oh, yeah."

Travis let out a wild laugh and dragged her to her feet. "Amazing!"

Katie laughed and tossed the stick into the trash. "Yeah! We are! We've just made our lives a hell of a lot more complicated."

"Fine with me!"

Happiness and fear were jumbled up inside her, but Katie embraced those feelings. In a world full of death, life was something to embrace.

Joyously, Travis held her in his arms and kissed her.

· CHAPTER TWENTY-TWO ·

1.
The Seasons

Fall lived up to its reputation as a time of harvest as the occupants of the fort loaded up on as many supplies as possible. With the area around the fort pretty much clear of zombies, they worked as hard as they could, preparing their winter stores. The hunters brought back venison, fowl, and beef to fill the hotel freezer. Every bit of food was carefully cataloged by Yolanda and Peggy, and menus were planned to take full advantage of their stores by Rosie.

Halloween came and went. Despite the obvious reality of monsters, the children in the fort had fun dressing up and trick-or-treating through the hotel. Ed knew where there was a pumpkin patch and jack-o'-lanterns were carved and placed on the fort's walls. To everyone's surprise, the distorted faces seemed to disturb the few zombies that were hanging around. After the holiday, the teenagers had fun pelting the dead with the rotting gourds.

Thanksgiving was surprisingly joyful. The menu included wild turkey and pumpkin pie, a wonderful delicacy that everyone enjoyed. As December approached, the world seemed remarkably peaceful, despite the occasional zombie.

It felt like the fort was truly secure, that a true victory had been won over the dead.

2.
Silent Night

What had once been dubbed the "zombie corral" was now a nice, walled-in courtyard. It was coated in a thin film of fresh snow that glimmered with the reflections of the Christmas lights strung all over the fort.

Katie leaned against the rail of the guard post, looking down over the wall where children were being hustled back into the hotel after an impromptu snow fight. The snowflakes were still falling, but she knew that by morning the snow would melt away. Snow never lasted long in these parts.

After the bandits had been routed, construction had gone into overdrive in the fort. It had felt like it had been nonstop until December 16. Throughout November and the first two weeks of December, they had worked hard, reclaiming Main Street and the former zombie corral, and moving the trucks out to form a new perimeter with new sentry posts. Their only break had been for Thanksgiving as bit by bit they spread out and made the fort more secure.

Travis had not taken over the mayor's office in city hall, preferring the manager's office in the hotel. He and Eric and the others met there frequently and for long hours, but even when he was alone, he always seemed to be deep in thought. Sometimes, when she peeked in on him, Travis looked overwhelmed, and she didn't blame him—Ashley Oaks was a lot to worry about. But every night, when he held her, she could see that he was happy and at peace.

Katie looked up. More flakes touched her lips and cheeks. The sky was clear and beautiful. She sighed at the wonder of it.

Down in the street, Bill and Katarina were trying to build a snowman with Peggy and her son, Cody. The peaceful scene made Katie smile. In a few years, Katie and Travis would have a little one to build a snowman with. If things didn't go to hell . . .

No, she couldn't think like that.

Calhoun was running around in the snow, arms outstretched and mouth open to catch the snow. Nearby, Eric and Stacey were playing with their little dog, Pepe. Lenore and Ken slipped out of city hall to join the others. The best friends immediately began pelting each other with snowballs.

Beside Katie, a sniper took aim and fired. Katie didn't look, knowing that beyond the wall a zombie lay in the snow, truly dead at last.

Travis joined her, wrapping her tight in his embrace. She snuggled into his warmth and smiled.

"Love you," he whispered, and kissed the top of her head.

"Love you," she answered.

Behind her, the hotel was illuminated. People were still celebrating the turning of the year. Christmas lights were strung in many of the hotel's windows and along many balconies. A huge fake Christmas tree, dragged up from the city hall basement, twinkled on the municipal building's roof.

The all-volunteer Santa Patrol had successfully brought back all the gifts the younger kids had asked for. Calhoun had explained that Santa had to rendezvous with the crew away from the fort due to the messed-up clones and aliens. The kids had bought this hook, line, and sinker. It had been nerve racking to watch the volunteers leaving, knowing that they were going into danger so that the fort's children could have a good Christmas. The Reverend Earl Thomas had prayed over the group before they left. When all had returned safely, there had been many tears.

Christmas Eve had been lovely, with caroling and a midnight service in the makeshift church set up in one of the old conference halls. Katie and Travis had squeezed in along with everyone else and sung their hearts out. During the service, the reverend announced that Katie and Travis were with child. Then Travis had shown Katie what the Santa Patrol had brought back for her.

The ring was silver with a cubic zircon, but she didn't care. She had sobbed like it was a diamond. Clad in jeans and sweaters, they had said their vows right then and there, in front of everyone, including Baby Jesus and the Holy Family tucked into a manger scene in the corner.

"Couldn't show it for years in city hall 'cause of the Supreme Court," Peggy had said as it had been set up in the makeshift church. "I guess all that is done with now."

Now, snuggled into her husband's arms, Katie watched the scene in the street with a small smile on her face.

"A new year," Travis sighed.

"A new year," Katie echoed.

"Couldn't be much weirder than last year," Travis said.

"No, probably not."

Had it been only nine months since the first day? It felt like a lifetime ago. At times, her serene life with Lydia felt like a dream. She still missed Lydia terribly, but that time was long gone, lost like the rest of the old world.

She tilted her head to look up at Travis's face. The stress was showing between his eyes. She reached up with her cold red fingers to brush away the wrinkles. He relaxed and smiled at her.

"It'll be the best year we can make it," Katie decided, then pulled him down for a kiss.

The snowball caught them smack-dab in the middle of their kiss. Sputtering, they both looked over the wall to see Jenni and Juan wrestling in the snow, shoving the white stuff down each other's clothes. Then they spotted the guilty party. Nerit was fashioning another snowball with a grin on her face. With unequaled accuracy, she nailed Jenni.

Calhoun ran past, whirling around as he went, laughing hysterically.

Jenni snagged a handful of snow and tossed it at Nerit, who couldn't duck fast enough. Jack ran around barking as Jason hurled snowballs at his girlfriend, Michelle.

Scooping snow off the rail next to her, Katie tossed it at Travis, then ducked around him, shouting, "Beat you down there!"

Beyond the walls, a lone zombie stood staring at the twinkling Christmas tree in the distance, fixated and confused, just staring . . . and staring . . . as the snow fell all around.

· EPILOGUE ·

Lieutenant Kevin Reynolds used binoculars to watch the snow fight from beneath a tree. Clad in army fatigues, he shivered in the cold and wiped snow from his face. Behind him, a woman soldier was sitting behind the steering wheel in the jeep that would carry them back to the waiting helicopter.

"What do you think?" the driver asked.

The lieutenant lowered the binoculars and turned toward his companion. "It's perfect. Exactly what we need," he answered.

He slid into the passenger seat and settled in as the private drove the jeep toward the edge of town.

From the darkened sky above, the snow continued to fall.

AUTHOR'S NOTE

Since the original inception of the story online, the section that became *Fighting to Survive* has always been the most difficult part to write. I wrote about the bandits and their brutality, Shane and his attempted rape, and the haunting of Jenni by her abusive husband's ghost while the murderer of my cousin was standing trial. Frustrated and angry with real life, it was hard to write about terrible things happening to my favorite characters.

Yet, strangely, some of the scenes and character development in *Fighting to Survive* are some of my favorites. The friendships, love, and dark humor threaded throughout the story reminded me during a very difficult time that life does go on after a loved one dies. As Katie and Jenni faced some of their worst moments and overcame their difficulties, they taught me that I, too, could move on from deepest despair. My cousin's murderer was convicted as I finished writing the scenes with the bandits. It was a relief to find justice not only in the pages of my story, but in real life as well.

Revisiting *Fighting to Survive* for this new edition was extremely cathartic. With the help of my amazing editor, Melissa Singer, I was able to see the story with fresh eyes and polish up all the rough edges from the original.

Without a doubt, this version of *Fighting to Survive* is the story I originally envisioned, but enriched.

I hope you enjoy it as much as I love it.

Sincerely,
Rhiannon Frater